THERE SHE GOES

Lynne Shelby

ISBN 9781786156556
eISBN 9781786156563

Printed and bound in Great Britain by Clays Ltd, Elcograf S.p.A

CHAPTER 1

On shaking legs, I took one step and then another, until I was standing directly in front of the guy. His mouth lifted in a smile, and he put his arms around me, holding me close against his hard chest. My heart started beating so furiously that I felt sure he must be able to hear it. Telling myself firmly that I could do this, that it wasn't as if it were the first time, I tilted up my face and looked directly into his eyes. He bent his head and kissed me on the mouth, softly at first, just a brush of his lips, but then more firmly, his hands moving smoothly down my back to settle on my hips.

When we came up for air, he led me to the bed and drew me down beside him. We lay facing each other on the bare mattress, our bodies pressed together, and kissed for a long time. I tried, unsuccessfully, to remember his name.

I thought, there can be few professions apart from the obvious that require you to simulate desire for a stranger on a regular basis.

The director said, 'Cut.'

The guy stopped kissing me, and we both sat up. While the director conferred with his assistant, who'd videoed our audition, I stole a glance at my fellow actor's profile. He was a few years older than me, I thought, in his mid- to late-twenties, and extraordinarily good-looking, with his dark hair falling over his forehead and just the right amount of stubble on his tanned face. I wondered if he might be Italian, or maybe Spanish.

'We've got all we need for today,' the director said. 'Thank you.'

The guy (what *was* his name?) got off the bed and said, 'Thank you. Good to have met you.'

I swung my legs over the side of the mattress and stood up. I tried to think of something, anything, to say that might persuade the director to cast me, but decided that throwing myself at his feet and begging (please, please, *please*, give me the job. I'm an out of work actress, and my rent's due next week) would be unprofessional. The dark-haired actor was already heading towards the door of the studio, so I echoed his 'thank you', snatched up my bag and coat, and hurried after him.

We'd just stepped out into the corridor when the director's voice drifted after us quite clearly: 'Like watching paint dry. Absolutely no sexual chemistry between those two.' *Seriously?* At nine a.m. in a cold studio, it hadn't been easy to act like a girl and boy madly in love – or in lust, as the director had put it – but until that moment, I'd thought the dark-haired guy and I had done pretty well. Apparently, I was mistaken.

The guy shut the door and rolled his eyes. I followed him across the reception area, where a crowd of actors were still waiting to audition, and out into the car park.

'No chemistry?' he said. 'The man's an idiot. You and I were on fire in there. We nearly set the bed alight.'

I couldn't help laughing. 'I'm so glad you said that. I thought we did a good job too.'

'Directors. What do they know?' He grinned, a flash of white teeth. I smiled up at him, noticing that his eyes were so dark they were almost black, and that he had a small white scar on the underside of his jaw. In the studio, the only thing on my mind had been to turn in a convincing performance that would get me cast, but now I found myself wondering what it would be like to kiss him again, and not in front of a camera. I became aware of a delectable warmth low in my stomach.

He said, 'See you around, Julie.'

'Ye-es,' I said. 'See you.'

I watched him as he strode over to a large silver car and drove off, leaving me alone and feeling strangely empty. He'd put his arms around me and kissed me and lain next to me on a bed – and I'd most likely never see him again.

Shivering at a sudden gust of wind, I told myself to get a grip, and started walking towards the tube station. Yes, I'd shared a kiss with an attractive man, something I'd not done in too long a while, but it was a stage kiss and nothing more. I didn't even know his name.

***

Zac edged the car slowly through the mid-morning traffic, turning the heater to high. That was one thing he'd miss about California – the constant sunshine. He'd forgotten how cold and dismal London could be at this time of year, the trees still bare of leaves, the sky permanently grey. He reminded himself why he'd returned. However hard it was to start again, he was sure he'd made the right decision. Even if it meant he had to grovel in front of idiots like that pretentious fool of a director. Not that this morning's audition was the worst he'd ever been to. He smiled ruefully – at least no one had asked him to take off his shirt.

Although the lights at the next junction were green, the traffic ground to a halt. Zac drummed his fingers on the steering wheel. His mind wandered back to the audition. It certainly hadn't been a hardship to improvise a scene with Julie Farrell. Like so many of the young actresses he'd encountered in LA, she was stunning: her body slender and her hair long and dark. It occurred to him that only a few weeks ago he wouldn't have walked away from her before he'd invited her for a coffee, or they'd at least swapped cell numbers. He congratulated himself on his restraint. He was, he told himself, back in London to focus solely on his work. He couldn't afford any distractions.

CHAPTER 2

I stood outside the staff entrance to Club Zone, in an alleyway not far from Leicester Square, and willed myself to go inside. I could, I supposed, just walk away and never go back, but there was that matter of my rent, and my need to eat – and pay the fees for the occasional acting workshop or singing lesson or dance class so that I didn't forget everything I'd learnt at drama school. Squaring my shoulders, I went into the club.

In the staffroom, amongst the waiters and bartenders who'd yet to start their evening shift, I spotted three of my colleagues on the six-strong promotions team, sitting in a circle of armchairs around a low table, on which were six untidy piles of advertising flyers and a number of Styrofoam coffee cups. I went and sat down next to my partner on the team, Laurie Fryer, whose head was bent over a dog-eared paperback copy of *Othello*. Opposite us, Nadia Pincher, was flicking through a glossy magazine. Her partner, Ben Locke, was lounging next to her, eyes shut, his foot tapping out the beat of whatever music he was listening to on his phone.

'Hey, Julie.' Laurie's amiable face broke into a smile, and he slipped the play into his jacket pocket. Ben opened his eyes, nodded at me, and shut them again. Nadia didn't bother to acknowledge my arrival.

They all left drama school several years before I did, I thought. They've acted professionally in theatre or on TV, but they can't afford to give up the day job. In two or three years' time, I still could be here, still working as a promo girl, still waiting for my proverbial big break. With a mental shudder, I pushed the thought away.

Laurie said, 'How did your audition go today?'

'You went to an audition?' Nadia's head jerked up from her magazine. 'What was it for?'

'A TV advert. For toothpaste, I think,' I said, reliving the moment the dark-haired actor's eyes had locked on mine, and the way he'd smiled as he'd leaned in to kiss me. Again, I reminded myself that he'd been acting.

Nadia leant forward in her chair. 'Did you get the job?'

'No, I didn't get the job,' I said. 'I thought the audition went well. The director disagreed.'

'Never mind, lovely.' Laurie's hand rested briefly on my arm. 'It's not like your life's ambition is to act in TV commercials.'

'I don't know why someone who wants to perform in musicals would even bother to go to that sort of casting,' Nadia said, tossing her blonde curls over her shoulder.

'I'll take whatever acting work I can get,' I said. 'I need to get a professional credit on my CV.'

'Well, I think it's very brave of you to put yourself out there,' Nadia said. 'It's not as though you stand much chance of landing an acting role when you're competing against straight actors like me – or even Laurie. All that singing and dancing you musical theatre people do – it doesn't really leave you much time to learn how to act, does it?'

Not for the first time in the six weeks I'd been working at Zone, I tried to decide whether Nadia actually meant to be so obnoxious, or if she merely lacked any social skills.

6

'It's called the triple threat, Nadia,' Laurie said. 'I'd have thought you'd have known that.'

Nadia ignored him, her attention caught by another girl, very tall and thin, who was standing by the coffee machine. I'd not seen the girl in the staffroom before, but apparently Nadia knew her, as she leapt out of her seat and ran across the room. Drawing the tall girl into a far corner, she began an intense, whispered conversation, accompanied by a great deal of affected laughter.

'It's extraordinary.' Laurie shook his head as though to clear it. 'I've known that woman since drama school, but she still manages to astound me.'

Ben took his earphones out of his ears and looked from me to Laurie and back again. 'What's wrong?'

'Nadia,' I said.

'Ah,' Ben said.

'I don't know how you stand partnering her night after night,' I said, 'I really don't.' Realising that my hands were clenched into fists, I made myself relax.

Ben shrugged. 'Oh, I never listen to a word she says. I just let her witter on and grunt occasionally in reply.'

'Don't let her get to you, Julie,' Laurie said. He raised his arm to wave at Cora Woodville and Harry Vincent, the other two members of the promotions team, who'd just entered the staffroom. They joined us, both of them looking at me enquiringly.

'So how did it go today?' Harry said. I decided that next time I had an audition, I'd keep it to myself.

'I didn't get the job,' I said.

'Oh, I'm so sorry, hun,' Cora said.

'It was only a toothpaste commercial,' I said. 'Although the way the director went on about the characters' motivation, you'd think it was an audition for *Hamlet* at the National.'

Cora laughed. 'I've been to auditions like that,' she said, 'and then when you see the advert on TV, the actors are just doing their hoovering or cooking fish fingers.'

Harry said, 'Who's that gorgeous girl Nadia's talking to?'

'Her name's Esse,' Laurie said. 'She's just started working in the restaurant, but she also does a bit of modelling. Her boyfriend is a casting agent. Obviously that has nothing to do with why Nadia has decided to be her new best friend.'

'And you know all this how?' Cora said.

'If you want to be a successful actor,' Laurie said. 'You have to be good at networking.'

At that moment, Austin Fleming, Head of Promotions and Events at Club Zone – at my job interview, he'd informed me of his title in a tone that made it very clear he was extremely proud of it – put his head round the staffroom door. When he saw me and the others relaxing in easy chairs, his pale eyebrows drew together in a frown. He held out a skinny wrist and tapped his watch. Everyone on the promotions team hastily drained their coffee, collected up coats and bunches of flyers, and trooped out into the cold and dark.

While Nadia and Ben stayed in Leicester Square, Harry and Cora headed off to the Covent Garden piazza, and Laurie and I made our way to our favourite hunting ground: Piccadilly Circus. Even on a week night in February, the place was swarming with the tourists and sundry revellers who were our prey, some posing for selfies on the steps that surround the statue of Eros, others watching the street performers who vied for their attention and their spare change against a backdrop of illuminated advertising signs and double-decker buses.

Laurie stepped into the path of two girls, one tall, one petite, both wearing biker jackets, very high platform shoes and very short skirts. They must be so cold dressed like that, I thought. I was freezing, and I was wearing a parka, a hat, gloves – fingerless so I could hold my flyers – two jumpers, jeans and fur-lined boots.

'Your shoes – I adore them,' Laurie said. 'Totally to die for. Here, let me give you a couple of flyers for Club Zone. Hand them in to any of the bar staff and your first drink is free.'

'Do you get footballers coming in your club?' the taller girl said.

'All the time,' Laurie said.

The girls happily relieved him of two of his flyers, and tottered away.

'Your turn, Julie,' Laurie said. 'I'll count you in. From the top – five, six, seven eight.' Fixing a smile on my face, I held out a flyer to a besuited, twenty-something man who looked as though he might be in need of a beer after a hard day in front of a computer screen.

'Hi, there,' I said, brightly. 'Would you like a Club Zone flyer?'

Twenty-something Man leered at me. 'I'll take a flyer if you write your phone number on it'

'Seriously?' I said. 'Do you really expect me to give out my phone number to a total stranger?'

'You can't blame a guy for trying.' Twenty-something Man took the flyer anyway, and walked off in the direction of the club.

Laurie roared with laughter. 'Your face, Julie.'

I shot him a look. 'Have I ever told you how much I love this job?'

Three years training in acting, singing and dancing, I thought, and I'm earning my living by handing out flyers and being hit on in the street.

CHAPTER 3

I arrived home from work after midnight, cold and tired, and wanting nothing more than to crawl into bed. Then, as I trudged up the stairs that led from the front door to the landing, I heard voices coming from the other end of the flat: the cut-glass accent of my best friend and flatmate, Alexa Hamilton-Jones, and a deeper, male voice. For a moment, I thought Alexa's ex-boyfriend was back on the scene, but on second thoughts, given the decisive way she'd ended the relationship – 'It was all getting too much, Julie, he wanted me to *meet his parents*...' – this seemed unlikely.

Curiosity overcoming exhaustion, I tossed my bag, coat and one of my jumpers into my bedroom, and went into the living room, where I discovered that Alexa's mystery guest was Michael McCabe, who'd been in our year at drama school. He was sprawled on the sagging sofa, and she was sitting in an armchair, her long legs drawn up under her. As always, even without make-up, her blonde hair caught up in a messy pony-tail, and wearing an over-sized shirt and skinny jeans, she looked terrific.

'Hey, Julie,' Alexa said. 'Would you like some wine?' She reached down beside her chair and picked up a dark green bottle. 'Oh – it's empty.'

'I can't think how that happened,' I said, noticing a second empty bottle on the dining table. 'Hello, Michael. Long time no see. Not since the summer.' I sat down next to him on the sofa. There was a twang as another of the springs broke.

'How was your audition?' Alexa said to me.

'Can we not talk about it?' I said. 'Let's just say that I'm still a resting actor.'

'The last time I auditioned was for panto,' Michael said. 'I was right down to the last two for *Aladdin*, but the other guy got the part. I spent most of December in a shopping mall, working as one of Santa's elves. Not even Santa, just a frickin' elf.'

'So when do we give up on this awful profession?' Alexa said.

'Never!' Michael said.

'Never,' I said, but with less conviction.

Michael glanced at his watch. 'Do you know it's nearly one o'clock in the morning? I must get going. I have to be at work by half past eight.'

'Santa having made his elves redundant after Christmas,' Alexa said to me, 'Michael is now building houses for his dad.' I vaguely remembered that Michael's father owned a construction company.

'I'm not physically laying bricks,' Michael said. 'I'm in my dad's head office. Playing the role of the Boss's Son.'

'How's that working out?' I said.

'Oh it's just fantastic.' Michael got to his feet. 'Obviously my dad's employees treat me just like one of the gang. It's not like they stop talking when I come into the room or anything. Alexa, I think I left my coat in the hall –'

'Bye, Michael,' I said.

Alexa followed him out onto the landing. For a few minutes, I heard them talking, although I couldn't make out what they were saying. Then I heard Michael's footsteps receding down the stairs, and the front door open and close again. It occurred to me that Alexa's plans for the evening may not have included his going home.

'Sorry for barging in on you,' I said, when she came back into the room. 'I didn't mean to interrupt anything – with Michael.'

'Nothing to interrupt,' Alexa said. 'He just called in for a chat.'

'You and he do have a history…'

'I hooked up with him once, two years ago,' Alexa said. 'Been there, done that, moved on. Besides, he's still living with Suzanne.'

'Is he?' I said. 'I'd heard they broke up a couple of months ago.'

Alexa shook her head. 'No, they went through a bad patch, but they're OK now.'

'What's she up to these days?'

'She was actually doing some acting,' Alexa said. 'She had a small part in no less than five episodes of *Law of the Land*. There was apparently some talk of her being in the next series, but nothing came of it, and now she's working nights as a waitress. Michael was complaining that they hardly get to spend any time together.'

'So you two really are just good friends?' I said.

'I do have rules, Julie,' Alexa said, 'and my most important rule is that I don't do the dirty with other girls' boyfriends.'

'I'm extremely impressed by your moral compass,' I said.

'I was tempted to shag him, though,' Alexa said, 'just to cheer him up. The Boss's Son. That has to be fairly ghastly.'

'I would think so,' I said. 'I wonder if he has to wear a suit and a tie to the office.'

'An office job,' Alexa said. 'But that's a great idea. I'll apply for a job in the office at Joe Garcia's production company.'

I stared at her. 'I'm sorry, did you say you want to work in Joe Garcia's *office*?'

'Think about it, Julie,' Alexa said. 'How many times have you sent your CV and headshot to Garcia Productions?'

'A few,' I said. 'Well, more than a few. I've lost count. They could probably wallpaper their entire building with the number of CVs and headshots I've sent them.'

'Exactly,' Alexa said. 'I'm guessing hundreds of actors send their CVs to the great Joe Garcia every day. He's never going to see everyone who wants to audition for him. So I get a job in his production office, and burst into song…'

'… he's totally overwhelmed by your amazing voice…'

'… and he gives me the lead in his next West End musical,' Alexa said. 'I'll persuade him to let you into the back row of the chorus.'

'You are such a good friend to me,' I said.

'Of course, if the office staff at Garcia Productions discover that I can't touch type,' Alexa said, 'they may fire me before I get the chance to sing for Joe Garcia.'

'There is that.' I sighed theatrically. 'We'll just have to keep sending him our CVs.'

'Seriously,' Alexa said, 'can you imagine what it would be like to be in a musical directed by Joe Garcia?'

'I can,' I said. 'I do. Every single day.'

I can imagine it, I thought, but I'm finding it increasingly hard to believe it's ever going to happen.

CHAPTER 4

I sat on the sofa, my laptop on my knees, and checked through my emails. Over the last couple of weeks, I'd sent my CV and headshot to five casting agencies, two production companies, and an independent film-maker, but I hadn't been called in to audition by any of them. I sighed. Closing my email, I brought up the recruitment section of the online showbiz newspaper, *In the Wings*, and found myself looking at an advert for an open audition for a musical.

I leapt off the sofa, almost knocking over the mug of tea I'd put down by my feet, ran into the hall, and rapped loudly on Alexa's bedroom door.

'Alexa, wake up!' I shouted. 'You have to see this!' After a minute or so, I knocked again. The door creaked opened. Alexa shuffled past me and into the living room, wrapped in her duvet.

'Less noise,' she said, lowering herself carefully onto the sofa. 'I feel rough.' She closed her eyes. 'Need to phone in sick to day job.'

'Poor you,' I said.

'More sympathy required,' Alexa said.

'Sending you sympathetic vibes,' I said.

'Went clubbing with old school friends,' Alexa said. 'Danced all night. Drank all night. Didn't leave club till five. Didn't get home till six.'

'Sympathy officially withdrawn,' I said. 'But I do have the perfect medicine for a hangover. An audition. For a musical.'

16

Alexa's eyes flew open. 'Give me your laptop.' Hangover apparently cured, she snatched my laptop out of my hands. "'*Pride and Prejudice: The Jane Austen Musical*,"' she read aloud. "'A six-month regional tour, with a possible West End transfer."'

'We *have* to get this job,' I said.

'I wonder how many girls they're looking for,' Alexa said.

'Well, there are the five Bennett sisters to start with,' I said. 'I would so love to play a character like Elizabeth Bennett.'

'What about the ensemble?' Alexa said. 'Isn't there a ball in *Pride and Prejudice*?'

'More than one,' I said. 'They'll need loads of girls.'

Alexa read the rest of the advert: "'Strong singing and jazz dance required. Register nine a.m. Be prepared to stay all day."'

I said, 'How do you make yourself look like an actress who could play a Jane Austen character when you're dressed for dancing in a leotard and tights?'

Alexa thought for a moment. 'I'm going to wear my pink leotard with the puff sleeves. That would suggest those dresses they wore back then.'

'I've got that leotard in pale blue. Do you mind if I wear it as well?'

'Of course not, seeing as it's you.' Alexa smiled. 'You know, I feel so much better now I've an audition to go to.'

'I thought you would.' I glanced at my watch. 'And you've still got time to get to your shift at the call centre.'

'I don't feel *that* much better,' Alexa said.

***

On the day of the *Pride and Prejudice* audition, we left our flat at seven a.m., which meant that even if every train and bus in London were cancelled, and we had to walk, we would still have time to get to Hoofers – the dance studio where the audition was being held – well before the doors opened at nine. The underground was heaving with commuters, some bleary-eyed and yawning, others absorbed in their newspapers and Kindles, but we didn't have to wait long for a train. We even managed to find seats next to each other.

'We're really early,' Alexa said, as we came out of the station just after seven-thirty. 'I doubt many people will arrive for at least another hour. We'll probably be in the first group to dance.'

'Or maybe not,' I said.

In front of us, blocking half the pavement and stretching around the corner, was a queue of girls and guys of around our age. Many of them were clutching sheet music.

'There must be over a hundred people here already,' I said. 'We may not even get seen.'

'Don't be defeatist,' Alexa said. 'You stay here and keep us a place in the queue. I'll go and see if there's anyone we know further along who we can go and join.'

I went and stood at the back of the queue. Soon more people came out of the station and stood behind me.

'See anyone?' I asked, when Alexa returned.

'Only Polly,' Alexa said. 'She's right near the front.' Neither of us said it aloud, but I knew we were both thinking that Polly – who, when we were students, rarely made it through a dance class without tripping over her feet – was one rival for a part in *Pride and Prejudice* that we didn't have to worry about.

'Why don't we go and join her?' I said.

'In all honesty,' Alexa said, 'I think if anyone jumps this queue they're going to get lynched. Polly said there were people already here when she arrived at half past six.'

The boy directly in front of us in the queue turned around to face us. 'I'm thinking we'll have to kneecap the competition,' he said.

The boy standing next to him said, 'I'm going with a quick blow to the back of the neck while they're warming up – they'll never know what hit them. I'm Jonas, by the way. He's Toby.'

Toby was tall and in his late twenties, while Jonas was of medium height and maybe a couple of years younger. They both had dark blond hair, and the athletic physique of musical theatre actors who regularly attend dance class.

Alexa gave Jonas a dazzling smile. 'I'm Alexa, and this is Julie.'

Jonas smiled back at her. 'So now we all know each other,' he said. We were still chatting with the guys when the queue, which by now trailed back past the station, began to move.

'Here we go, here we go, here we go,' Toby said.

'At last,' I said.

Alexa said. 'Did you feel rain?' Even as she spoke, I felt rain on my face. Neither of us had an umbrella.

'It's OK,' I said. 'We'll be inside in a few minutes.'

Half an hour passed before we finally got inside Hoofers, and by then it was raining hard. In the foyer, a

19

boy who looked young enough to be in school still, was seated behind a folding table. He wrote down our names and handed us numbered cards to pin to our leotards.

'Are there many more outside?' he said, running a hand through his hair.

'Oh, yes,' Alexa said, 'there's still a long queue.'

'Really?' the boy said. 'We were only expecting about a hundred people at most.'

Alexa and I looked at each other. She was number 151; I was 152.

'You need to go upstairs to Studio 2,' the boy continued. 'We're using it as a holding area. Wait in there until your number is called.'

'An open audition for a new musical advertised online, and they were only expecting a hundred auditionees?' Alexa said to me, as we made our way up the stairs. 'Are they insane?'

Studio 2 was already packed, and unbearably hot. There were a few chairs against the wall, but most people just dumped their bags on the floor and sat down beside them. At least half of the girls were wearing the same puff-sleeve leotard as me and Alexa. As always at musical theatre auditions, there were far fewer men than women. Most of the guys were wearing trackies and vest tops, but I saw a couple of billowing white shirts that would have made perfect costumes for the male ballet dancers in *Swan Lake*. On this occasion, I suspected they were meant to suggest the wearer would make the ideal Mr Darcy. I spotted Polly on the far side of the room and waved.

'Let's sit with Jonas and Toby,' Alexa said. We joined the boys who'd managed to find some floor space under the windows.

'Quick, put your bags down,' Jonas said. 'Stake a claim before our hard-won territory is invaded.'

As one, Alexa and I stripped off the jeans and sweatshirts we had on over our dance gear, and dropped to the floor. I fished a mirror out of my bag and repaired the damage the rain had inflicted on my make-up. I'd have liked to do some warm-up exercises before I had to dance, but there simply wasn't room.

'We thought it would be cooler over here,' Jonas said, 'but it doesn't seem to make much difference.'

'I tried to open a window,' Toby said, 'but they're all locked. We're attending the Audition from Hell. Abandon hope all ye who enter.'

'And still they come,' Jonas said. I glanced towards the studio door. A group of girls who'd just come in, were looking round desperately for a place to sit. They were followed by a guy who, with a lurch of my stomach, I recognised as the dark-haired actor from my commercial casting. His gaze travelled round the room and came to rest on me. I smiled at him and, after a moment during which – from the blank look on his face – he appeared to have no idea who I was, he smiled back. I felt quite irrationally disappointed when instead of joining me by the window, he turned away and found himself a space on the opposite side of the studio. I watched as he peeled off a sweatshirt to reveal broad shoulders, muscular arms and a toned body that a tight black vest top and cut-off trackies worn low on his hips did nothing to hide. It was strange to think that I'd lain on a bed with those strong arms around me…

Jonas said, 'Something's happening.'

Focus, Julie, I thought. I tore my gaze away from the dark-haired actor. Three men and a woman, all of them carrying clipboards, had come into the studio. I recognised the woman as Irene O'Connor, a well-known theatre director. Gradually the room fell silent.

'Good morning,' Irene O'Connor said. 'First of all, I'd like to thank you all for coming. Whenever I hold an open audition, I always have this dread that no one will turn up.'

There was a ripple of polite laughter.

'No, I mean it,' Irene said. 'Anyway, we'd like to make this whole process as painless as possible for everyone concerned.'

More laughter.

Irene smiled. 'What we're going to do is ask you to come next door into Studio 3 in groups of twenty. You'll be taught a short dance routine, and then we'll be making a cut. Those of you we want to see again will be asked to come back this afternoon. Those of you we don't keep – please don't go out, change into a different coloured leotard, go to the back of the queue and come in again, because we *will* recognise you and you'll only annoy us. Good luck, everybody.' She turned to the youngest of the men. 'Give us five minutes, then send the first group in.' Then she and the other two men went out of the room. At once, every performer in the room began talking.

'I've heard that Irene O'Connor is a really good director to work for,' Jonas said.

'Does anyone know who the others on the audition panel are?'

'I think the man in the red T-shirt is the choreographer,' Toby said. 'I don't know who the other guy is. Probably the musical director.'

A voice rose above the clamour. 'Numbers 1 through 20 to Studio 3, please.'

Nineteen girls, including Polly, and one boy stood up and filed out of the room.

Fifteen minutes later they came back into Studio 2. A few were smiling, one girl was in tears. Polly rushed over to us.

'I've got a recall,' she said. 'I'm so excited. It's the first time I've ever got through a dance round at anything.'

'Well done you,' I said. 'That's terrific.'

'I'm so pleased for you,' Alexa said. 'How many did they keep?'

'Two other girls,' Polly said, 'and the boy.'

I said, 'What was the routine like?'

'It was easier than I thought it was going to be,' Polly said. 'Just a few kicks and turns. You need to watch out on the turns though – the floor's really sticky. Listen, I'm going to have to dash. I was too nervous to eat breakfast this morning and I need to find somewhere to buy lunch before the next round. Good luck and all that.' She bustled off.

'Good for her,' Alexa said.

'Absolutely,' I said.

'You know those girls we met in the queue for the *Pride and Prejudice* audition,' Toby said.

'The blonde and the brunette?' Jonas said.

23

'Yep,' Toby said, with a wry grin. 'Those two. They are *so* thrilled that their friend got a recall.'

Jonas laughed. 'That is *so* sweet of them,' he said.

We lost track of the exact numbers getting through to the next round of the audition after that, but as far as we could tell, most of the boys were getting recalls, and just a few of the girls in each group.

'It's so much easier for us lads,' Jonas said.

'I'm not arguing with you on that one,' Alexa said, just as our numbers were called.

'This is it, chaps,' Jonas said. 'Over the top.'

Along with the other performers in our group, the four of us trooped out of Studio 2 and into Studio 3. At the far end of the studio, the audition panel were sitting behind a long, wooden table. Director Irene O'Connor was in the middle, between the man in the red T-shirt who was probably the choreographer, and the other man who might have been the musical director. A middle-aged woman sat at a piano. A tall girl in dance gear stood to one side.

'Thank you, Jade,' Irene said.

The tall girl, evidently named Jade, stepped forward and taught us a short routine. It was a simple jazz dance, but there were a couple of difficult turns that were clearly in there to weed out the less able dancers. In between trying to memorise the choreography, keep a smile on my face, and turn a perfect triple *pirouette* on the decidedly sticky floor, I managed to snatch a few looks at Irene O'Connor. At one point, I was sure that she was watching me, but after that she didn't so much as glance in my direction. I tried to avoid reaching the depressing conclusion that she'd already decided to cut me.

24

After we'd all danced the routine twice through with the piano, we were told to move to the sides of the studio and were then called forward in groups of five to dance one more time. When my number was called, I just had time to mouth a quick 'good luck' to Alexa before running to my place. I heard the first few notes of the music and began to dance. Before I knew it, the music had ended and I was back at the side of the studio, trying to get my breathing under control. It all felt a bit of a blur but I was fairly confident I'd danced well. Alexa gave me a thumbs up. Toby smiled in our direction, which I hoped meant neither of us had disgraced ourselves.

Once everyone had danced, we returned to our original lines in front of the audition panel and waited for their verdict. My heart yammering in my chest, I forced myself to smile.

Irene O'Connor looked along the row of hopeful faces in front of her. She looked down at her notes. Then she conferred with her colleagues. Eventually she handed a piece of paper to Jade.

'Numbers 142, 149, 150, 151, and 158, we'd like to see you again this afternoon,' Jade said. 'As it's so crowded in here, I suggest you go out and get yourselves a coffee or whatever, but please make sure you are back in the building and ready to dance by three p.m. The rest of you, we don't need to see you again. Thank you all very much.'

Alexa was through to the next round. Jonas and Toby were through. I was not. A wave of disappointment washed over me.

I said, 'Well done, Alexa.'

'I wish you'd got through as well,' Alexa said.

'So do I, obviously,' I said, gathering up my bag and coat, 'but I'm glad that you did.' I was genuinely pleased for her, I realised, but that didn't mean I wasn't gutted for myself.

Jonas and Toby were waiting for us in back in the holding area.

'We're heading out to the café round the corner,' Jonas said. 'Would you ladies care to join us?'

Deciding that my goodwill towards fellow performers who'd done better than myself in an audition did not extend to drinking coffee with them while they discussed the recalls, I said, 'Thanks, but I'd better go straight home. I've loads I need to do, and I've got work tonight.' I retrieved my street clothes from my bag, and put them on.

'I'll come with you,' Alexa said to Jonas.

We waded through the still crowded holding area. There were auditionees waiting out in the corridor as well by now, and we had to clamber over people sitting on the stairs. Right at the back of the queue, we came across Michael, his girlfriend, Suzanne, and a couple more people we knew from drama school, but the line began to move before we had a chance to talk to them, other than to wish them all good luck.

'How many people turned up in the end?' I asked the boy on the door.

'Two hundred and seventy-eight,' he said. 'I ran out of numbers. I had to improvise with bits of torn up paper. I've been told not to let anyone else in.'

At least I danced for the audition panel, I thought. I've had my chance at the big time, even if I've blown it.

Outside the rain had stopped, the sun had come out, and the wet pavements were shining – inappropriately brightly it seemed to me. Alexa and Jonas headed off towards the café.

'For what it's worth,' Toby said to me. 'You danced really well in there.'

'Irene O'Connor didn't think much of my dancing,' I said.

'A lot of talented dancers were cut,' Toby said. 'But this audition was always going to be brutal – they're only looking for a couple of swings. The main roles were cast months ago.'

'The leads are already cast?' I said.

Toby raised his eyebrows. 'I'm guessing you've not been to many auditions?'

'No, I haven't,' I said. 'I graduated from drama school last summer, but I haven't managed to get an agent yet, so I can only audition when it's an open call.'

'Well, at most auditions they're only looking for one or two people,' Toby said. 'The last West End show I was in, they auditioned a hundred and fifty girls to replace one girl who was leaving.'

I blurted out, 'You've actually been in the West End?' Inwardly, I cringed at how starstruck this made me sound.

'Several times, but only ensemble.' He glanced up the road. 'I'd better get along after the others. Jonas will think I'm trying to avoid paying for my coffee.'

'Good luck in the recall,' I said.

'Best of luck to you in your next audition.' Toby said, as he walked off towards the café.

27

I turned on my heel – and almost fell over as I collided with a guy who'd just come out of the dance studios. He reached out a hand to steady me, and I found myself looking into the eyes of the dark-haired actor from the commercial casting. What with dancing for the panel and the disappointment of not getting a recall, I'd forgotten that he was there.

'Oh, hello again,' I said. 'Sorry, I –'

'You OK?' he said.

'Yes, I'm fine,' I said, although standing so tantalisingly close to this ridiculously attractive man was making my knees feel distinctly weak. 'Well, apart from being cut.'

'Yeah,' he said. 'I know just how you feel.' Removing his steadying hand from my arm, he side-stepped around me and continued on his way, his long stride taking him swiftly around the corner and out of sight.

If this was a scene in a musical, I thought, he'd have swept me into his arms and we'd have tap-danced along the pavement. Instead, he can't get away from me quickly enough. I sighed. If only real life was more like musical theatre.

***

'It's not the first time I've been cut first round,' I said to Laurie that night, while we were handing out flyers along Shaftesbury Avenue, stopping now and then to read the cast lists on the billboards outside the theatres that lined the street. 'But it doesn't get any easier.'

'If they were looking for a particular casting type, and you weren't it, there's not a lot you can do about it,' Laurie said. 'I remember getting cut at an audition for being too small.'

I looked sceptically at his six-foot frame. 'What was the role?'

'The giant in *Jack the Giant Slayer*.'

'Ha, ha. Very funny.'

'No, it's true,' Laurie said. 'I thought the audition was for the role of Jack, but when I got there I found out I was mistaken. I assured the casting director that I could *act* taller, but he didn't believe me.' He turned away to offer a flyer to two lads, who from the leers they were giving a hen party on the other side of the road, were very probably out on the pull, and definitely part of our target demographic. It occurred to me that I'd been complaining about the iniquities of the *Pride and Prejudice* audition all evening. I need to stop whining, I thought. It's not fair on Laurie, and it's not making me feel any better. I couldn't remember a time when getting cut at an audition had made me feel quite so low.

My phone announced the arrival of a text. It was one word, and it was from Alexa: *No*.

***

As usual, it was gone midnight before I got home. The flat was silent, but I could see a light still on in Alexa's room. I knocked, before putting my head round the door. She was sitting on her bed, texting on her phone.

'Want some company?' I said. Alexa nodded, and tossed her phone onto her duvet. I sat down next to her.

'Am I allowed to cry?' she said. 'I know we think it's unprofessional to burst into tears if you get cut at an audition, but I really could do with a cry right now.'

'I think just this once it would be OK to cry,' I said. 'I may join you.'

'Actually, I don't think I'll bother,' Alexa said. 'I'm too tired. And I'm getting a headache.'

I fetched her an aspirin and a glass of water.

'I was *sure* I was going to get the job this time,' she said, when I was once again sitting next to her. 'It all seemed to be going so well.'

'What happened?' I said.

'Everyone who'd got a recall danced the routine again, and then there was another cut. Michael and Suzanne were cut at that point. Those of us who were left, were asked to hand in our CVs and wait in the holding area, as the audition panel wanted to hear us sing.'

'Did Jonas and Toby get through to the singing round?' I said.

'Jonas, Toby and Polly,' Alexa said. 'The audition panel called us in one at a time. I got to sing my song right through – which is usually a good sign – so I was feeling reasonably confident.'

'And then?' I prompted.

'And then we all hung around for ages, until Jade came in and announced who they wanted to see at the final round next week. Six boys. Eight girls. Not me. Jonas and Toby got through again. So did Polly, incredible as it may seem.'

'She really can sing, you know,' I said.

'You and I can sing,' Alexa said. '*And* we can dance. Polly can hold a tune, but she has two left feet. She

30

completely messed up the routine this afternoon, but still she gets a final recall. It's so frickin' unfair.' She lapsed into a morose silence.

After a while, I said, 'Toby reckoned most of the parts in *Pride and Prejudice* are already cast.'

Alexa nodded. 'Michael told me he'd heard a rumour that Elizabeth Bennet is going to be played by the winner of last year's *Karaoke Challenge.*'

'Please don't tell me that the only way I'm going to get into a West End musical is to win a reality TV show,' I said.

'But that's an excellent idea,' Alexa said, in an abrupt change of mood. 'I think we should enter *Dance With Me.*'

'Is that the show where the girls all dance round their handbags while the boys prop up the bar?' I said.

'That's the one,' Alexa said. 'The boys ask the girls to dance, and the girls have to decide if they'll accept or wait for a better offer. Then they dance in couples, and one couple gets voted off.'

'But they're supposed to be members of the public, not professional performers,' I said. 'We'd be disqualified.'

'Good point,' Alexa laughed. 'I guess I'd better forget reality TV as a passport to West End success, and keep practising my acting, singing, and dancing.' She paused, and then she said, 'At least today wasn't a total washout.'

'If you're about to give me your every-failed-audition-is-still-good-experience speech,' I said, 'I may have to start looking for a new BFF.'

'No, it's not that,' Alexa said.

'What then?'

Alexa's eyes were shining now. 'Jonas asked me out. He's taking me to *South Pacific* on Saturday.'

***

Zac sat on the balcony, cradling a glass of Rioja, oblivious to the magnificent view of the city at night, its bright lights reflected in the river Thames. He thought, I was the best male dancer in my group today. How the hell did I get cut first round? He drained his glass, and poured himself another. Not that he'd expected to come back to London and walk straight into a starring role in the West End – he was no longer arrogant enough to believe that would happen to him twice – but he'd assumed that he'd have a good chance of being cast in an ensemble. Not even getting a recall was a salutary reminder that he might have as hard a time finding work here as he had in LA. He made himself remember his agent's warning that it would take a while for him to re-establish himself. At least she took me back on the agency's books, he thought, even if only on probation.

His mind went back to the auditions he'd attended since he'd arrived home. Apart from *Pride and Prejudice,* they'd all been for what his agent described as bread and butter work: voice-overs and commercials that would bring in money until he got a role he really wanted. It had been at one of those commercial castings, he remembered, that he'd met the stunning dark-haired girl who'd crashed into him outside Hoofers. Anger at the audition panel, at his own failure to impress them, had made him curt with her, he realised, and now he felt bad about that. He wondered if she'd already got over being cut from the audition, or if she still felt as gutted as he did.

The ringing of his cell phone broke in on his thoughts. He picked it up and checked the caller ID: Rosalind. Deciding that he wasn't in the right frame of mind to talk to her, he let the call go through to voicemail. It would be afternoon now in LA, he thought. She would most likely be stretched out by her pool, reading through the script of her next film. Memories surfaced of the many afternoons the two of them had spent lazing by that pool, the turquoise water sparkling in the sunlight, purple bougainvillea tumbling from terracotta pots, Rosalind in one of her barely-there bikinis, the scent of the suntan lotion as he smoothed it over her skin…

I should call her back, he thought. Then he thought of another phone call he needed to make. One that he'd put off for far too long. Tomorrow, he decided. I'll call both of them tomorrow.

It had grown cold out on the balcony. Picking up his wine glass, he went inside. His gaze alighted on his piano. Putting the unsuccessful audition, the phone calls he needed to make, and the stunning Julie Farrell, out of his mind, he sat down and began to play, losing himself in the music.

CHAPTER 5

The following Saturday, I was trying to decide whether I would need to wear two jumpers for work that night or if it was warm enough that one would suffice, when Alexa appeared in the doorway of my room.

'What do you think of my choice of outfit for my first date with Jonas?' she said.

She was wearing a dress that the fashion magazines would have referred to as a classic LBD. Somehow, a little black dress that would have been demure, frumpy even, on anyone else had become a knockout on her, merely because she'd undone a couple of buttons, and added a bit of bling.

'You look amazing,' I said. 'I feel quite sorry for Jonas. He won't be able to keep his mind on the show.'

'Then my work here is done,' Alexa said.

I narrowed my eyes and regarded her critically. 'There is just one thing…'

'What?' Alexa hurriedly scrutinised her appearance in my full-length mirror.

'Would you like to borrow – cue drum roll – my gold shoes?' I reached under my bed and located the box containing the fabulous shoes that I'd treated myself to with my first wages from Zone – I'd never had occasion to wear them – and handed it to Alexa. She opened it with due reverence and ran her fingers over the satin and diamante within.

'Ooh. They're *lush,*' she said. 'I'd love to borrow them. If you're sure you want to lend them to me.'

'Well, I was planning to wear them tonight while I'm pounding the pavements handing out flyers...' I said. 'No, you go ahead, your need is greater than mine.'

'Killer heels,' Alexa said. 'Jonas won't stand a chance.'

'So go slay him,' I said.

Alexa was meeting Jonas for pre-show drinks at around the same time I had to get to Zone, so we travelled together on the tube to Leicester Square, jostling our way up the escalators and out of the station amongst the crowds heading into Theatreland. It was still light, but standing at the edge of the square, I could already sense the heady atmosphere of London on a Saturday night.

'I just adore first dates,' Alexa said.

'I expect I do too,' I said. 'Remind me, what are they exactly?'

Alexa laughed. 'Don't wait up for me,' she said, before heading off across the pedestrianised square. I saw her edge her way through a group of tourists taking photos of the white stone statue of Shakespeare, and then she was lost to view behind the ragged line of people queueing at the booth that sold discount theatre tickets. I noticed that most of the people in the queue, and in the square, were couples. Everywhere I looked I saw men and women bending their heads together over maps and tourist guides, arms around each other as they studied the menus outside the restaurants. I watched as one of the square's resident cartoonists drew a sketch of a man and a girl of about my age and presented it to them with a flourish. For the first time in months, I found myself thinking of Matt, my only serious boyfriend, and now my ex. It was almost a year, I realised, since we'd broken up, and I no longer missed his presence in my life. But if I was honest with myself, there were moments – like right now – that I did miss being part of a couple. Turning away from the square, I started walking to Club Zone, quickening my pace when I realised that I was already late for my shift.

When I got to the staffroom, the first person I saw was Austin. I took a deep breath and started to frame an apology for my tardy arrival. To my surprise, instead of chastising me for my bad time-keeping, my boss seemed only interested in discovering my taste in music.

'I take it you've heard of Obsidian?' he said. 'The rock band?'

I nodded. 'I listen to them all the time.' Obsidian's *Vampyre Lover* was one of my favourite albums.

Austin beamed. 'Then you'll be delighted to hear that Club Zone has been chosen as the venue for the launch party for their new album, *The Howling*.'

'Ye-es,' I said. Realising that my response probably lacked the required level of enthusiasm, I added, 'How exciting.' It's not like I'm going to be on the guest list, I thought.

'Obviously, you won't be required to hand out flyers on the night of the party,' Austin went on, 'but I do hope that you will agree to join us in the club. Can I put your name down on my list?'

I gaped at him. Will I agree to attend a celebrity party? Let me think about that.

'Yes,' I said. 'Yes, of course. Thank you, Austin.' I knew I was grinning idiotically, but I couldn't help myself. A night off from handing out flyers is exactly what I need, I thought.

36

'Your own clothes will be fine, but they must be appropriate.' Austin said. 'And we'll provide you with a discreet name badge.'

My grin started to fade.

'We're going to hire extra hosts and hostesses,' Austin continued, 'but our permanent promotions staff are ideally placed to ensure that the event runs smoothly, and that every single one of Obsidian's guests has a fabulous night.'

I'm going to an A-List party, I thought. As a steward.

'With you on board, that makes everyone on the promotions team,' Austin said. 'Now, let's get tonight's show on the road.' I stared after him as he practically skipped out of the staffroom. Laurie appeared at my side and handed me a bunch of flyers.

'You thought Austin was putting your name on the guest list, didn't you?' he said.

'No I didn't,' I said.

'Never mind, Cinderella,' Laurie said. 'We may be the hired help, but at least we get to go to the ball.' He started walking towards the staffroom door.

I looked down at the flyers in my hand. I call myself an actress, I thought, but I'm not. I'm a promo girl.

My life was not supposed to be like this.

***

'You're very quiet,' Laurie said to me a couple of hours later, as we flyered along the Strand. 'You've hardly uttered a word since we left the club. Are you OK?'

'I'm fine, Laurie,' I said, 'I – I –' A tight knot of misery formed in my chest. To my mortification, tears welled up in my eyes.

'What's wrong?' Laurie said.

'Everything.' I said. 'I – I d-don't know if I can do this any more.'

Laurie's brows drew together in concern. 'You're not just talking about tonight's shift, are you, lovely?'

I shook my head. 'I – I can't go on pretending to myself that I'm an actress when I can't get through one round at an audition. Maybe I should just give up and do something else.' A tear ran down my face. I wiped it away with my hand. 'I'm s-sorry. I'm not usually like this, really I'm not.'

Laurie handed me a tissue and gave me a moment to get myself together. 'Do you want to skip the feast at the communal board tonight?' he said.

I hesitated. One of the reasons I kept working for Club Zone was because I got a free meal each shift, but I really wasn't in the mood to sit in the staffroom and be sociable.

'I'll treat you to a burger,' Laurie said.

'Oh, I can't let you do that –' I began.

'You can.' Laurie said. 'I'll just let our beloved leader know what we're doing, or he'll assume we've skived off early and dock our pay.' He fished his mobile out of his jacket. 'Austin, it's Laurie... No, there's nothing wrong... I'm calling to tell you that Julie and I still have a whole load of flyers left, so rather than come back to Zone to eat, we're going to grab a burger, and then go straight to Embankment station... Yes, Austin... No, we won't take more than an hour's break.' He rang off. 'You'd better make the most of this, Julie. It's not that often I take a girl out to dinner. Or a guy for that matter.'

We went to the nearest fast food restaurant. I found us somewhere to sit, while Laurie fetched our meals.

'Burger, chips and cola,' he said, setting down two trays on the plastic table and taking the seat opposite mine. 'Do I know how to give a date a good time or what?'

'I'm sorry about the meltdown,' I said. 'I'm such a loser.'

'Forget it,' Laurie said. 'You're bound to be upset. I'm upset.'

'You are?' I said, bemused.

'You should have told me you were pregnant,' Laurie said. 'I'll stand by you, you know I will.'

Two middle-aged women seated at the next table looked towards us and then at each other.

'You will?' I said.

'We'll get through this,' Laurie said. He clasped both my hands in his. 'You, me and the baby together.'

Keeping my face deadpan, I said, 'But what about your wife?'

'I'll leave her,' Laurie said.

'And your other six children?'

'I'll leave them too.'

'Darling,' I said, 'there's something I have to tell you. The baby – it isn't yours.'

'Oh, well, in that case, I won't leave my wife,' Laurie said, withdrawing his hands from mine. 'Pass me the ketchup.'

The women at the next table nearly choked on their cappuccinos. I turned my head away so they couldn't see me trying not to laugh.

'Nothing like a bit of improvised street theatre to make a girl smile.' Laurie said. 'Seriously, I know you took it hard when you didn't get into *Pride and Prejudice,* but you can't give up on the stage because of one unsuccessful audition.'

'But it isn't *one* audition,' I said. 'It's *every* audition.' I drank some cola and took a bite of cheeseburger. 'I don't remember a time when I didn't want to be an actress, but what if it never happens? I can't spend the rest of my life handing out flyers.'

'Keep telling yourself it *will* happen,' Laurie said. 'You *will* get cast in a West End musical, Cinderella.'

'And some day my prince will come,' I said. 'Or not.'

'We can all hope for that,' Laurie said.

An uncharacteristic wistfulness in his voice, made me ask, 'Are you seeing anyone at the moment, Laurie?'

'You mean long-term rather than for a quick shag?'

'I wouldn't have put it quite like that,' I said, 'but yes.'

'I'm not in a relationship right now,' Laurie said, 'but I was with a guy for most of last year. We split up on Christmas Eve.'

'Ouch,' I said.

Laurie shrugged. 'The relationship had run its course, and it had to end. But there were breakages.'

'Breakages?' I said.

'Plates,' Laurie said. 'A bottle of rather good wine. Other sundry household items. Someone's heart.'

'Yours?'

'No, not mine,' Laurie said. 'I was the one who walked out. My choice, but I wasn't proud of myself. What about you? Are you dating anyone?'

'No,' I said. 'My long-term boyfriend and I split up a year ago. Since then, my love life has been as exciting and fulfilling as my stage career.'

Laurie leant forward. 'Are you telling me you've not had sex in a year? No wonder you're feeling so down.'

'That's *not* what – OK, I haven't, but – I've been on a couple of dates, but not with anyone I've liked enough to – Oh, I don't know why I'm telling you this.' I threw a chip at him. He caught it and ate it.

'I'm a good listener,' he said. 'I invite confidences.'

'You,' I said, 'have an insatiable appetite for gossip.'

Laurie grinned. 'So, tell me, Julie, is there anyone you've got your eye on? Some guy you do like enough to…?'

'No,' I said. The image of the dark-haired actor's handsome face floated into my mind. 'Actually, there was a man I sort of met.'

'What does *sort of met* mean?' Laurie said.

'At one of my many unsuccessful auditions I had to play a love-scene with this ridiculously good-looking actor. I saw him again, very briefly, at the *Pride and Prejudice* audition as well. I wouldn't mind kissing him for real. Not that it's ever going to happen.'

'Why not?' Laurie said.

'It's not like he asked for my phone number,' I said. 'I don't even know his name.'

'If you're in the same casting bracket,' Laurie said, 'you'll most likely run into him again. I meet the same

41

bunch of actors at practically every audition I go to. They're all the same playing age as me – twenty-four to thirty – and like me, they get called in for parts like Student Doctor or Rookie Detective. I've become really good mates with some of them.' He broke off to answer his mobile. 'Hi Austin... Yes, Austin... We're heading down to Embankment station even as we speak... Oh, right... OK... See you later, Austin.' He ended the call and stood up.

'Are we going out again already?' I said.

'We'd better,' Laurie said. 'Austin's heard that Embankment station is closed. He wants us to go to Charing Cross. He's probably on his way right now, sprinting along the Strand, to check up on us.'

I pictured Austin running on his spindly legs, his arms flapping like the wings of an elongated flightless bird. I ate my last few chips and reached for my coat.

Laurie put his hand on my arm. 'It's tough when you're just starting out as an actor, but you need to hang on in there, Julie. Don't give up the dream.'

'Maybe I'll keep on auditioning a while longer,' I said. 'Thanks, Laurie. For the meal and for listening to my ranting. Talking to you has made me realise I'm not ready to give up my dream quite yet.'

'You're welcome,' Laurie said. 'That's what friends are for.' His face creased into a smile. 'I know we haven't known each other that long, but I think we can call ourselves friends.'

He is such a lovely guy, I thought. 'Straight back at you,' I said.

CHAPTER 6

My new dress was fabulous. And it made me look pretty fabulous too, I thought, as I surveyed myself in my mirror, ten minutes or so before I was due to leave for Zone on the night of *The Howling's* launch party. The dress was red, with shoe-string straps, a deeply plunging neck-line, and a flared skirt that skimmed over my hips and fell to just above the knee. I wore it with the thin gold necklace that my parents had bought me for my eighteenth birthday, dangling earrings, and my gold shoes. Smiling to myself, I raised my arms above my head and swayed in time to the strains of 'I Feel Pretty' coming from my phone. That was when I discovered a slight problem.

I hurried along the hallway to Alexa's bedroom, and almost barged in without knocking – which would have broken one of our very few house rules – before I remembered that she wasn't alone. I rapped on her door, tentatively at first, and then with more force. There was a muffled reply from within.

'This is an emergency, Alexa,' I said. 'I have a costume malfunction. Do you have any tit-tape?'

My flatmate's first date with Jonas had gone extremely well. So well, that she'd spent that night, and the next night, at his place. I suspected she'd have stayed even longer if he hadn't had his final recall for *Pride and Prejudice* the following morning. After the audition, he'd come round to our flat, and we'd all passed an anxious couple of hours waiting for his phone to ring, before a call from his agent telling him that he had a place in the ensemble meant that we were able to open a celebratory bottle of sparkling wine – texts from Toby and Polly had told us that neither of them had been so fortunate. It occurred to me that since then, for the last couple of weeks, Alexa and Jonas had spent almost every night together. She's going to miss him when he's off on tour, I thought. I knocked again on Alexa's door.

'Here you go.' Alexa, wearing a man's shirt that presumably belonged to Jonas, came out of her bedroom, and handed me a roll of lingerie tape and a pair of scissors.

'Thanks,' I said, cutting off a short length of tape, and sticking the red silk in place. 'I knew I wouldn't be able to wear a bra with this dress, but I thought it was tight enough that I wouldn't fall out of it.'

'Let me look at you,' Alexa said.

I twirled around.

'Breathtaking,' Alexa said. 'That colour really suits you.'

'I adore this dress,' I said. 'I just had to buy it as soon as I saw it.' I was *not* going to think about the damage the purchase of the dress had inflicted on my bank balance. 'I'd have worn it tonight even if I'd had to stick it to my skin with double-sided Sellotape.'

'Ow,' Alexa said. 'Mind you, with all the paparazzi that'll be there tonight, perhaps you should have left off the tape and staged a costume malfunction for the cameras. It could have made you famous.'

'But would providing a strip show for the lads help me in any way to get into a West End musical?'

'Possibly not,' Alexa said.

'In that case, I may as well keep my kit on,' I said. I checked my watch. 'I need to get going. I'll see you later – or more likely tomorrow.'

'Wait a minute,' Alexa said, and dived back into her bedroom. After a moment she came out again, holding a leather jacket. 'You can't possibly wear your hideous old parka over that dress. Borrow my jacket.'

I took the jacket and put it on.

'Have fun,' Alexa said.

'As I'm working at Zone tonight,' I said, 'I doubt very much that fun is going feature very highly in my immediate future, but I'll do my best.'

***

Coming out of the underground, into the bright lights of Leicester Square at night, I heard Laurie call my name.

'Nice ballgown, Cinderella,' he said, emerging into view from the throng of people milling around the square. 'I like the leather jacket, too. Not your usual style.'

'Not my jacket,' I said. 'I borrowed it from my flatmate. I like your suit.'

'Not my suit,' Laurie said, brushing a speck of dust from the sleeve of the charcoal-grey suit that had replaced his habitual jeans and jumper. 'Borrowed from my brother. Although, as it looks a lot better on me than him, I may not give it back.' He offered me his arm, and gestured in the general direction of Zone. 'Shall we?' Together, we left the square and strolled down the side-street that led to the club. Catching sight of our reflection in a restaurant window, I decided that even in borrowed finery, we looked every inch a couple of A-Listers heading for a showbiz party.

Arriving at Zone, we found that it had already been cordoned off from the public. The very large man who was Head of Security, his top bouncers, and extra muscle hired just for this night, were jealously guarding the way onto the newly-laid red carpet that led to the club's main entrance. Thanks to the publicity the event had received in the media, a crowd had gathered by the security barriers to await the arrival of the famous, and a fair number of photographers were already in position on the recently-constructed press stand. This was where my fantasy of being a celebrity came to an end.

'I know what you're thinking,' Laurie said, as we both stood looking at the red carpet. 'But we can't.'

'We could just step on it for a moment to see what it feels like,' I said.

'We're the hired help, remember,' Laurie said. 'It's the tradesman's entrance for us.'

Our instructions for the night had been specific. Hosts and hostesses were not permitted to walk along the red carpet. No exceptions. Reluctantly, I allowed Laurie to lead me to the staff entrance in the alleyway at the back of the club.

'Never mind, Cinders,' Laurie said. 'When I'm up for an Oscar you can be my escort at the awards ceremony.'

'Straight back at you,' I said. 'Anyway, that carpet clashes with my dress.'

***

46

Club Zone's sleek, modern interior had been transformed. Gossamer cobwebs now hung from the ceiling, ivy wound itself around the stair rails and the balustrade on the first floor, and the main dance area was obscured at regular intervals by white mist. The overall effect was Goth with a touch of decadence, reflecting the stylistic intentions of *The Howling*. Although the band was not expected to show much before midnight, the doors to the event had officially opened at ten p.m. Now, at eleven p.m., the club was packed, and pulsating with dance anthems and flashing lights.

Laurie and I were stationed at the top of the central staircase that led from the foyer to the dance area on the first floor of the club, ideally placed to see the A to Z-Listers entering Zone on the floor below, and to gaze at the uber-celebs being escorted to the VIP area. The other members of the promotions team were scattered around the club, along with the permanent hosts and hostesses, and those hired just for the night.

'Laurie, look,' I said, 'The Thorne Sisters have just come in.' Laurie grabbed my arm before I could wave at my favourite girl band. The three Thorne Sisters, accompanied by three athletic-looking guys who could have been their backing-dancers or their boyfriends – or both – were ushered straight past Laurie and me to join their fellow VIPs.

'Repeat after me,' Laurie said. 'Hired help.'

'Hired help,' I said, 'Hired help. It's no good. I just don't feel it.'

'Did you not study the Method at drama school?'

'I skipped that class,' I said. 'I took a singing class instead.'

Nearly an hour later, Obsidian, flanked by their considerable entourage, made their entrance in a blaze of camera flashes and to thunderous applause from their assembled guests. Club Zone's manager, with Austin hovering at his shoulder, greeted them at the door, and personally escorted them across the foyer and up the stairs to the first floor. The dance hits that the DJs had been playing up until then were taken off the turntables and the strange and haunting sound of Obsidian's new album filled the club. The several hundred people who had been awaiting the band's arrival clustered as near to them as their various minders and publicists would allow. The band did appear to know most of them – or the PR guy at their side was keeping them well briefed. Raven, the lead singer, with his kohl-lined eyes, his hair falling past his shoulders, and dressed as he was tonight in midnight-blue velvet, was as androgynously beautiful in real life as in his photos and videos. Just as beautiful were the musicians, Lilith, Charis and Melisande, floating ethereally behind Raven in diaphanous white and silver.

After some air-kissing and some posing for their official photographer, the band and their attendants went through the door to the inner sanctum that was the VIP area and vanished from our sight.

'I'm throwing a party next week,' Laurie said. 'A small intimate affair. Just five hundred of my closest friends and their plus ones.'

'Am I invited?' I said.

'You're not nearly famous enough to be on the guest list,' Laurie said, 'but you can come and hand round the canapés. As long as you wear that red dress.'

Two giggling girls in their early twenties, who I recognised as contestants from a reality TV show, approached us at that point, and asked us the whereabouts of the chill-out room. I showed them the way and saw them safely ensconced on cushions in the designated quiet area. Here, in semi-darkness, soft-footed waiters and calm first-aiders attended those guests for whom the excitement of the launch party had all got a bit too much.

When I got back to Laurie, he said, 'I've just spotted a friend of mine.'

'You have celebrity friends?' I said.

'Oh, he's not a celeb,' Laurie said. 'He's probably gate-crashing.' He pointed to the foyer. 'Do you see the tall guy dressed all in black?'

I leant over the ivy-covered balustrade. The foyer was not quite as crowded now as it had been earlier in the evening, when there had been a steady stream of celebrities following one another along the red carpet, but late-comers were still arriving. A group of young men were standing just inside the entrance to the club. One was taller than the others, dark haired, and broad-shouldered, and dressed in a black suit and shirt. From where I stood, I couldn't see his face clearly at first, but for some reason – maybe he sensed my staring at him – he looked straight up at me. And I saw that Laurie's friend was my dark-haired actor.

The last time I'd seen him he'd barely acknowledged my existence, but now his face broke into a smile of recognition. My heart leapt, and I smiled back. For a fleeting instant, the sounds of the club, the music, the laughter and chatter, the clink of glasses all faded, and it felt as if we were alone on a dark stage, just me and him in a single spotlight...

'Julie?' Laurie's voice brought me back to myself.

'Sorry, did you say something?' I said. 'I didn't hear you.'

'Are you OK?' Laurie said.

'Of course I am,' I said. 'Why shouldn't I be?'

'You seemed like you were completely out of it for a moment,' Laurie said.

Another male voice said, 'Look at me.'

I turned my head to see a frowning Austin. I hadn't noticed him standing next to me until he spoke.

'Your eyes look odd,' Austin said, studying me suspiciously. 'What's the matter with you?'

'Nothing,' I said. 'I'm totally fine.'

'Have you taken something?' Austin said. 'What have you taken?'

'What?' I said. '*Oh*. No, Austin, I haven't taken anything. Illegal or otherwise.'

'I can insist you take a drugs test at any time, you know,' Austin said. 'It's in your contract.'

Without thinking, I said, 'Don't be ridiculous.' It occurred to me almost immediately that telling my boss he was ridiculous was probably not one of my brighter ideas. Fortunately, Austin hadn't heard me, being distracted by a disembodied voice coming from his two-way radio mentioning a shortage of glasses. Without another word, he scurried off in the direction of the bar. I looked back down at the foyer, and saw that the dark-haired actor and his companions were gone.

I clutched Laurie's arm. 'Your friend,' I said. 'What's his name?'

'His name's Zac,' Laurie said. 'Zac Diaz. Why?'

'He's the guy I told you about,' I said. 'The actor I met at the commercial audition.' *Zac Diaz.* I wondered if it was his real name or his stage name. 'I can't believe that you know him.'

'Oh, I know everybody,' Laurie said, unfazed by what seemed to me an extraordinary coincidence, 'but Zac is one of my oldest friends. Not that I've seen him lately. He's been living in the States for the past three years, but now he's back in London and –' He smiled. 'And here he is.'

I followed Laurie's glance, and saw the dark-haired actor – Zac Diaz – walking up the stairs towards us. My heart started beating very fast.

'Hey, Laurie,' he said. 'Good to see you.' He put his hand on Laurie's shoulder.

'You too, mate. It's been too long.' Laurie pulled him into a full-on man-hug. When they broke apart, he said, 'I gather you've already met my friend and co-worker, Julie Farrell.'

'Yes, we've met,' Zac said, his gaze settling on my face. 'Hello again, Julie.'

I'd forgotten how dark his eyes were, so dark they were almost black.

'Zac,' I said, trying out his name, and liking the sound of it in my mouth.

He said, 'Will you dance with me, Julie?'

'Don't mind me, Zac,' Laurie said. 'I'm just your best mate who you haven't seen in *three years*.'

'I would dance with you, Zac,' I said, ignoring both Laurie and the fluttering in my stomach, 'but I'm working.' I indicated the name badge pinned to my red dress.

'I can remedy that.' Zac reached out, unpinned the badge, and put it in the inside pocket of his jacket. 'Now will you dance with me?'

'Yes, I'll dance with you.' I said. I was vaguely aware that if Austin saw me dancing, it could – would – cost me my job at Zone, but at that moment, with Zac Diaz's dark eyes fastened on mine, I really didn't care. 'Cover for me if Austin turns up,' I said to Laurie, as Zac led me towards the crowded dance floor. I didn't hear Laurie's reply.

Zac was a good dancer, moving easily in time to the music amongst the other dancers and the lights, sometimes resting his hands lightly on my waist, sometimes watching me with an appreciative smile as I raised my hands above my head and rolled my hips. When the music slowed, he reached for me and drew me close. I put my arms around his neck, and matched the swaying of my body to his. I could feel his strong hands on my back through the thin silk of my dress, and his hard body pressed against mine, and for the first time in a long while I felt the unmistakeable stirring of desire. How I'd managed to lie next to this man on a bed and stay focused on my acting, I'd no idea. He murmured my name and a shiver ran down my spine. I tilted up my face towards his.

I thought, he's going to kiss me.

'Shall we go and get a drink?' he said.

52

Or maybe he isn't going to kiss me. 'Sure,' I said. Zac put his hand lightly on my arm and steered me off the dance floor. Then he headed towards the VIP area.

'Zac,' I said, 'we can't go in there.'

He laughed. 'We can.'

At the entrance to the VIP area, our way was barred by no less than six large security men. None of them were Zone's regular bouncers, so they didn't know that I was staff, but I still couldn't see us getting past them into the room where, just a few feet away, the four members of Obsidian were holding court from a long, low, cushioned divan.

A security man holding a clip board said, 'May I have your names?'

Zac didn't answer. Instead he raised his hand and said, 'Hey, Raven.' To my surprise, Raven interrupted his discussion with the girl sitting next to him and waved back.

'Hey, man,' he said. The security men moved aside, and Zac and I went into the VIP area. Zac went straight up to Raven and, as he still had his arm round my shoulders, I had to go with him.

'Love the new album, Raven,' Zac said. 'Your best yet.'

'Thanks, man,' Raven said, from the depths of the divan.

'Catch you later,' Zac said. He nodded at the other members of the band, and the chosen few sitting with them, and then guided me swiftly away through the throng of celebrity courtiers in orbit around Obsidian's throne to the far side of the room where there was a bar.

'Do you actually know Raven?' I said, sliding on to a bar stool.

'Never met him in my life,' Zac said, 'but I figure that he meets so many people, he's not going to remember all of them.' He smiled at me, and I smiled back. I looked around the room for the Thorne Sisters, but it appeared they'd already left. Two rock legends, whose numerous hits my parents had danced to in their youth, were propping up the other end of the bar. In one corner of the room, a mega-famous DJ was chatting up a super-model. In another corner, the young actress who starred in *Trashed*, a TV series extremely popular with teenage girls – my fifteen-year-old sister, Daisy, never missed an episode – was talking to a celebrity chef.

'Julie, what the hell are you doing in here?' Alan, one of Zone's permanent bar staff, was regarding me anxiously from behind the bar. 'You're not expecting me to get you a drink, are you?'

'It's OK, mate,' Zac said. 'She's with me.'

Alan still looked dubious, but he put two glasses of champagne in front of us all the same. 'Just so you know,' he said to me, 'Austin's been in and out of the VIP area all evening.' He went off to serve an alternative comedian and a TV talent show judge.

'Are you even on the guest list for tonight?' I said to Zac.

'In a way,' Zac said. 'The brother of one of the guys I came with works for Obsidian's record company. He gave us the names of some employees who couldn't make it that we could use to get us in the door.' His eyes on mine, he smiled. 'I'm not much into clubbing these days, but I think I made the right decision when I let my friends drag me here tonight.'

Before I could frame a suitably flirtatious response, a man in his mid-thirties sat down on the bar stool next to Zac, and was handed a glass of champagne without having to ask. I recognised the newcomer as the editor of *Goss,* and almost as much a celebrity as the A-Listers whose photos appeared on the pages of his glossy magazine. Unexpectedly, he turned towards Zac and me and held out his hand.

'Hi, there,' he said. 'I'm Aidan Heywood.'

'Zac Diaz,' Zac took Aidan's hand and shook it.

'Hi,' I said, rather more hesitantly. 'I'm Julie Farrell.' I've just introduced myself to Aidan Heywood, I thought. Check me out.

'You here with the band?' Aidan said.

'No,' Zac looked the editor of *Goss* straight in the eye. 'We're not part of Obsidian's entourage. We just blagged our way into the VIP area.' There was a moment's silence when I fully expected Aidan Heywood to call for security, but instead he laughed out loud.

'I like it,' he said. 'Let me guess – you're an actor, right?'

'That I am,' Zac said.

'I'm sure I've seen you in something,' Aidan said. 'Have you done much TV?'

'No, the last time I worked in London, it was in the theatre,' Zac said, 'but I've been in the States for the last three years.'

Aidan studied Zac's face. 'Have we met before?'

'I don't believe we have,' Zac said.

'Strange,' Aidan said. 'I'd have sworn I knew you from somewhere.' He smiled disarmingly. 'Sorry about the

55

interrogation – force of habit for a journalist, even when I'm not working, like tonight. Although in a way I am working, because going to showbiz parties is part of my job. Lord, I do love my job.'

'Here's to showbusiness,' Zac said. He and the editor of *Goss* clinked glasses, just as a rotund middle-aged man wearing far too much gold jewellery came and tapped Aidan on the shoulder.

'Evening, Aidan,' he said, 'Come and meet my boys.'

'Be right with you,' Aidan said. With a flash of a gold signet ring, the man wandered off into the crowd.

'Duty calls,' Aidan said. 'The boy band that guy has just signed is going to be stellar – you heard it here first.' He downed his champagne in one gulp and stood up. 'What about you, Julie Farrell?' he said to me, suddenly, 'Are you an actress?'

'Yes,' I said. 'That is, I'm trying to be. I'm auditioning.'

'As a showbiz journalist,' Aidan said, 'I know how tough it is out there, but I wish you every success.' He smiled at me, nodded at Zac, and headed after the jewellery-bedecked boy-band manager.

'Have we really just had a conversation with Aidan Heywood?' I said. 'That's surreal.'

'Yeah, it can be strange when you meet someone famous,' Zac said. 'I guess it's because you feel that you know them already.'

'You sound like you've met a lot of famous people,' I said.

'I've met a few,' Zac said. He added, 'Your barman's trying to get your attention.'

I looked along the bar. Alan was pouring drinks for a brace of chat show hosts, but as soon as he had finished, he came over to me and Zac.

'You've got to get out of here, Julie,' he said. 'We've just had word that Obsidian are about to leave, which means Austin's going to be here any minute now.'

'Thanks, Alan,' I said. 'I owe you. Zac, if I want to keep my job, I really do have to get out of here. I should get back to Laurie in any case.'

'Then I guess I'll have to let you go for now,' Zac said, 'but I don't want to wait until we're both called into another audition to see you again. What time do you finish work?'

My heart thumping, I said, 'four a.m.'

'We could have breakfast together,' Zac said.

'I – I'd like that,' I said. Zac stood up and moved closer towards me. Once again I thought that he was going to kiss me. I longed for him to kiss me. Instead, he merely held out a hand to steady me as I got off the bar stool. Which was just as well, because I was feeling distinctly lightheaded.

'Where shall I meet you?' he said.

'The staff entrance is in the alley at the back of the club,' I said.

'I'll see you there.' Zac reached into his jacket and brought out my name badge. Then he smiled, and returned it to his pocket. 'Later,' he said.

CHAPTER 7

'Austin was asking after you,' Laurie said, when I rejoined him at our post by the main staircase. 'I told him you were snorting cocaine in the VIP area.'

'Oh, that's all right then.' I said. 'Actually, I was in the VIP area. I was talking to Aidan Heywood.'

'You're joking me.'

'No, it's true,' I said. 'We didn't speak for very long. He had to go and see a man about a boy band.'

'As you do,' Laurie said. 'So how did you get a VIP pass? Was it fluttering your eyelashes that did it?'

'No. Your friend Zac blagged our way in.'

Laurie raised one eyebrow. 'I suspect he was trying to impress you. Did he make an impression?'

'Absolutely,' I said. 'I'm meeting him after work.'

'Bless you, my children,' Laurie said. 'Try not to forget his name.'

I shot him a look. Then a thought struck me. 'You said Zac isn't a celebrity, but is he – how can I put this – is he a successful actor?'

'Define successful,' Laurie said.

'An actor Aidan Heywood thought he recognised.'

Laurie regarded me silently for a moment, and then he said, 'Zac was in the same year at the Royal College of Drama as me and Nadia. Unlike us, when he graduated he went straight into the West End. It was a small role, but it got him noticed. He was the lead in the second play he did, the Detective in *Film Noir* – and he was still the lead when the play transferred to Broadway.'

I gasped. 'Zac's been in the West End and on Broadway?'

'Yeah,' Laurie said. 'So I guess you could say he's had some success as an actor in the past, but not recently.' He gestured towards the VIP area. 'Looks like the band are heading home.'

Obsidian and their entourage, with Austin trailing in their wake, made their stately way past Laurie and me, down the stairs and out of the club. Once they'd left, the launch party very quickly began to wind down. For me, four a.m. couldn't come quickly enough. That last hour, while I smiled at the celebs as they were leaving and pointed the more ditsy amongst them in the right direction, all I was thinking about was Zac, and the way I'd felt when he held me. I looked for him amongst the people streaming out of the club, but didn't spot him. Finally, Austin informed the hosts and hostesses that they were free to go. I practically ran to the staffroom, grabbed my jacket and bag from my locker, said a hurried goodbye to Laurie, and was out the door.

It was still fairly dark outside, but I immediately caught sight of Zac standing in the pool of light from a street-lamp directly opposite the club's entrance. Surprisingly, given the hour, he was talking animatedly on his phone, but when he saw me, he ended the call, and his mouth lifted in a smile.

'So,' he said. 'Breakfast. Shall we go to my place?'

And what *exactly*, I thought, is going to happen if we do? I reminded myself that until a couple of hours ago, I hadn't even known this undeniably attractive man's name.

Somehow, looking into Zac Diaz's dark eyes, it didn't seem to matter.

'Sure,' I said. 'Where do you live?'

'I have a flat in Docklands,' Zac said. 'I'll call a cab – we shouldn't have to wait more than a few minutes.' I nodded in agreement, although my usual mode of transport in the early hours was the inexpensive night bus.

A short while later, I was sitting next to Zac in the back of a cab, driving through the empty, early-morning streets of London, discussing Obsidian's music while thoughts about what might happen at his flat skittered around my head. I didn't realise we were nearing our destination until we drew up outside a high-rise apartment building. Zac got out, holding the door so I could follow, and paid the driver while I stood gaping at the place he'd brought me to. He'd said he lived in Docklands, so I'd guessed his home might be a little more salubrious than mine and Alexa's, but I hadn't been expecting this luxury development overlooking the river. I wondered how someone only a few years older than myself could afford to live here.

'This way, Julie,' Zac said. I followed him into a brightly-lit foyer, where a concierge in a dark blue suit was sitting behind a large wooden desk. To one side of the desk was a bank of lifts.

'Good morning, Mr Diaz,' the concierge said.

'Good morning, George.' Zac walked over to the lifts and pressed a call button. The doors opened immediately. He said, 'I'm on the top floor.'

That would be the penthouse then, I thought. Still speculating as to how an out-of-work actor had acquired such a desirable postcode (Was he a lottery winner? Was he the son of extremely affluent parents?), I followed Zac into the lift, and we sped smoothly and noiselessly up twenty stories. The lift doors opened on to a small landing, and directly in front of us was the door to his flat, which he unlocked, before standing aside so that I could precede him into the long, narrow hallway that lay beyond. He flicked on a light, and ushered me along the hall and through a door at the far end. I found myself in a white-painted room that was spacious enough to accommodate an L-shaped sofa, two easy chairs, a dining table, six high-backed leather dining chairs – and a grand piano. I marvelled at the size and airiness of the room, but what really took my breath away were the floor-to-ceiling glass doors and windows that made up the far wall, and the wide balcony beyond that ran the entire length of the flat.

Seeing the direction of my gaze, Zac slid open the glass doors, and we went out onto the balcony. The city of London lay before us in the pale dawn light, with the Thames a ribbon of silver winding through it.

'This is an amazing view,' I said, picking out the familiar landmarks of the Gherkin and the Shard.

'It is,' Zac said. 'I probably should take more time to notice it.' He switched on a heater and indicated a wicker table and chairs. 'Have a seat. I'll get us a drink. We may as well stick to champagne, if that's OK with you.'

'That'd be lovely,' I said. He has *champagne* in his fridge to offer unexpected guests?

Zac vanished into the flat and came back with a bottle and two flute glasses. He freed the cork from the bottle and poured the champagne – actual champagne, not sparkling wine – quickly and competently, before taking a seat in the chair next to mine. We clinked glasses and drank, and looked out over the city skyline as London woke up for another day.

'So you're an actress,' Zac said. 'Have you done mainly theatre or film?'

'What I *want* to do is musical theatre,' I said. 'Unfortunately the West End has so far proved remarkably uninterested in my undoubted talent.'

'Musical theatre is what I want to do,' Zac said, 'although it's taken me a while to realise it.'

'But didn't you train at the Royal College of Drama with Laurie?' I said. 'I thought they only taught straight acting.'

'Has Laurie been talking to you about me?' Zac said. 'Not that I mind, as long as he only said good things.'

'He said you were a very talented actor who'd been in plays in the West End and on Broadway. That sounds good to me.'

'Yes, those were good times,' Zac said. 'Then, after the Broadway play ended, I went out to California with the idea of working in Hollywood. That didn't go so well. So three years after I went to the States, here I am back in London, older and wiser.' He refilled our empty glasses. 'I'm guessing Laurie's told you most of this already?'

'He did mention some of it,' I said.

'I'll bet.' Zac sounded amused.

'Are you glad to be back in London?' I said.

'Right now I am.' Zac gave me a look that made my heart miss a beat. 'I'm certainly glad to be away from the hell on earth of LA auditions. The only roles I ever got seen for were Pool Boy, Surfer Dude and High School

Jock. Casting agents never asked me to read a script, they just wanted me to take my shirt off. It was soul-destroying.'

I pictured Zac without his shirt. I had to gulp my champagne to cool myself down.

'At least it got me back into musical theatre,' Zac continued. 'I was taking an acting class – every actor in LA takes class – and there was a musical theatre class in the same building. I signed up for that as well. It made me realise I should have trained professionally in all the performing arts and rather than just acting.'

'Why didn't you?'

He hesitated, and then he said, 'It's complicated. When I was eighteen and auditioning for drama school, I thought I wanted to act in straight plays. Now, I'm going to have to make up for lost time.' He poured out the last of the champagne. 'Let's take this inside. I'll cook you that breakfast I promised.'

Inside, I took off my jacket, and followed Zac through the main room and back along the hallway to the kitchen. It was fitted out with sleek grey cupboards, dark granite worktops, a central granite-topped kitchen island with a bar stool on either side, and what to my – admittedly unknowledgeable – eyes was a state-of-the-art stainless steel oven. I sat on a stool, drank the last of my champagne, and watched Zac admiringly as he chopped onions and mushrooms, and did remarkable things with eggs and milk in a frying pan, while the kitchen filled with the mouth-watering aroma of omelette and fresh coffee. While we ate, he told me about some of the places he'd visited while he was living in California. I sat across from him, eating the delicious food he'd cooked for me, listening to his sonorous actor's voice conjure up images of LA and San Francisco, palm trees and sun-soaked beaches, and became conscious of an intensely pleasurable warmth deep inside me that made it increasingly difficult for me to concentrate on either the food or the conversation.

After we'd eaten, Zac made more coffee and, at his suggestion, we went back into the main room. I took a seat on the sofa, my stomach tightening when he sat down next to me, leaving just a few inches of space between us. I thought, if his plans for his immediate future include sleeping with me, what am I going to say? Am I really going to have sex with a man I barely know?

Zac said, 'There's a lot to like about California, but now I'm back in London, I can't imagine living anywhere else.' He lifted his arm in a sweeping gesture that took in the whole room. 'I feel that this is my home.'

'Well, this is certainly a fabulous flat,' I said. A sudden thought occurred to me. 'Do you live here alone?'

'Yes, it's just me living here right now,' Zac said.

I couldn't resist asking, 'Whose flat is it?'

'It's mine,' Zac said. 'I own it.'

'It's *yours*?' I gasped. 'But how can you possibly afford it? Sorry, I shouldn't have said that. It's just that everyone else I know is either living with their parents or living like me in rented squalor.'

'Most of my friends are the same,' Zac said, 'but I have a very rich and very generous uncle who gave me this flat as a twenty-first birthday present. He also set up a trust fund that pays for its upkeep and gives me a small income.'

My mind reeled. 'So you don't have to take a day job while you're resting?'

'No, I don't,' Zac said. 'But I'm doing casual bar work to tide me over until I get my acting career back on track. I'm twenty-six years old, and if I lived solely on my uncle's money I'd feel like a total waste of space. Does that make sense?'

I nodded. If I was in his situation, I wondered, would I feel the same?

'I'm not planning on being a bartender for ever,' Zac went on, 'but it'll bring in some filthy lucre while I sort my life out.'

I glanced round the room. 'Your life seems pretty well sorted to me.'

'I'm getting there.' Zac fell silent for a moment, and then, in an abrupt change of subject, he said, 'When I was in California, Laurie and I used to Skype each other all the time. Just before I came back to England, I remember his telling me that he had a new partner at work – that must have been you.'

I nodded. 'Yes, we've been working together since the beginning of the year.'

'What Laurie didn't tell me,' Zac said, 'was how beautiful you are.'

'Oh – I…' Suddenly, my pulse was racing.

His dark eyes gazing into mine, Zac reached out a hand and trailed a finger down the side of my face and throat. Desire, a searing heat, shot through me. Zac bent his head towards me and I melted into his arms, shutting my eyes as finally he kissed me. He was gentle at first, almost tentative, and then as the kiss went on, he became more fervent, his tongue in my mouth, his arms holding me tighter. Together, still kissing, we sank back on the sofa, so that I was lying beneath him. I felt the electrifying touch of his hand on my leg, as he pushed aside my skirt and stroked my thigh.

A mobile rang. It wasn't my ringtone, so it must have been Zac's. The mobile fell silent. Then another phone rang. Almost immediately, it went through to an answer machine and a woman's voice could be heard from the speaker:

'Zac? Pick up if you're there. It's Felicity Sanders.'

Zac's head jerked away from mine. I opened my eyes. No, I thought, don't answer it.

The woman's voice continued, clipped and precise. 'I need to speak to you urgently. Call me as soon as you get this.' She rang off.

'My agent,' Zac said. 'I doubt it's anything that important, but I should call her.' He lifted his hand from my leg and in one lithe movement sprang off me and onto his feet. I raised myself up onto my elbows and then into a sitting position, in time to see him lift a house phone off a table by the door, and key in a number. The pleasurable sensations that had been flooding through my body rapidly began to fade.

'Felicity,' he said. 'Zac Diaz, returning your call… Yes… Yes, I know the studios… Not a problem. I'll be there. Thank you.' He replaced the phone, stared at it for a moment and then he looked at me. 'I've been called in last minute for a casting. At eleven o'clock today.'

I glanced at my watch. To my surprise it was already nine-fifteen.

Zac said, 'I feel really bad about this, but I'm going to have to call you a cab. I need to change and shave.' His chin, I noticed, was dark with morning stubble.

'Oh – yes…' I said, belatedly understanding that he wanted me to leave. 'Of course. I should get going.' I didn't have anything like enough cash on me to pay for a minicab to ferry me from Docklands to Alexa's and my flat in Archway. 'Don't call a cab. I'll get the tube. At this time of day, it'll be quicker.'

'If you're sure,' Zac said. 'I'll walk you to the station.'

'There's no need,' I said. 'I'll be fine.' I made myself smile at him, but inwardly I felt as deflated as if I'd just been cut at an audition. Is this it? I thought. A dance, a glass of champagne and a kiss? I willed him to ask to see me again. He gave me directions to the station. I picked up my bag and jacket, and followed him out of the room and along the hall. He opened the front door.

'Best of luck in the casting,' I said. 'Break a leg and all that.'

'Thanks, Julie,' he said. He bent and lightly kissed the side of my face – the sort of kiss actors give everyone all the time. I walked across the landing and pressed the button for the lift. The doors opened and I stepped inside.

He said, 'I'll call you.'

Before the lift doors closed, I just had time to give him another smile – unforced this time. I was still smiling as I walked to the station and rode the tube across London.

***

The production company's reception was packed with dark-haired young men, all of them around six feet tall, all of them broad-shouldered and with athletic physiques. It was like being in a room full of mirrors: wherever Zac looked, he saw what could have been multiple reflections of himself. One at a time, the auditionees were being called in to see the casting director, only for them to come out just a few minutes later. Zac asked one of the other actors if he'd seen a script.

'There isn't a script,' the boy said.

'So it's improv,' Zac said. That was fine. He was good at improvisation.

'Sorry to disappoint you, if you've come here to do some *acting*,' the boy said, 'but from what I've heard, this casting's only about image.'

That figures, Zac thought, glancing round at the other auditionees. He found a chair to sit in, and settled down for what he suspected would be a long wait, letting his mind drift back to the moment he'd kissed Julie Farrell. His mouth curved in a smile as he remembered the smoothness of her skin, the warmth of her body against his, the taste of her mouth... I could be in bed with that girl right now, he thought, if I hadn't sent her away so I could come to this over-crowded casting for a job I don't even want. He reminded himself that there were plenty of out-of-work actors who would walk barefoot over hot coals to try out for a TV advert, and that he was no longer a West End leading man who could pick and choose which auditions he'd deign to attend.

Almost an hour after his appointed time, he heard his name called. Fixing a smile on his face, he strode confidently into the casting director's office, where he was confronted by two women, one young and one middle-aged. They didn't introduce themselves.

'Good morning,' Zac said, turning his head so that he was addressing both of them.

The middle-aged woman, presumably the casting director, said, 'We just need you to say your name and which agency you're from.'

Zac obliged. The younger woman, he noticed, was holding an iPad on which she was filming him.

'And your profiles, please,' the younger woman said. Zac swivelled left and then right.

The older woman said, 'Would you mind taking your shirt off?' It took all his acting skill to hide his irritation, but Zac unbuttoned his shirt. He took it off, and held it slung over one shoulder, hooking his other hand in his jeans. The women's gaze went straight to his abs.

The woman who had first spoken said, 'Have you ever done any modelling?'

'No,' Zac said. 'Not as yet.' He resisted the urge to remind them that he was an actor, not a model.

'OK,' the middle-aged woman said. 'Thank you. We'll let you know.'

'Thank *you*,' Zac said, managing to sound as if he meant it. 'It was good to meet you.'

For this, he thought, I spent three years at drama school, studying Ibsen, Chekov, and the complete works of Shakespeare. He put his shirt back on, smiled at the women, and left the room. He'd barely got outside the building, when his phone, necessarily on silent while he'd been in the casting, began to vibrate. He fished it out of the back pocket of his jeans, and checked the caller ID, before answering.

'Hello, Rosalind,' he said. 'Yes… Yes, I'm in London for the foreseeable future… You are? When do you arrive?'

CHAPTER 8

My mind still on the events of the previous night, I walked slowly up the stairs to the first floor landing and let myself into the flat. Taking off my gold shoes – by now my feet were protesting at the height of the heels – I went into the living room, where I found Alexa curled up in a chair, watching *Crazy For You* on her laptop.

'And what time do you call this, young lady?' she said, pausing the film. 'It's way past your curfew.'

I laughed, and sat on the sofa. For once the springs remained intact. 'I had the most amazing night... and morning.'

Alexa raised her eyebrows. 'Weren't you working at Zone?'

'Yes, I was,' I said, 'but I met this guy. After I finished work, he took me to his flat.'

'You met a man in a bar and you went back to his place?' Alexa said. 'Julie Farrell, you little slut!'

'It wasn't like *that*,' I said. 'His name's Zac, and he's a friend of Laurie's; they were at drama school together. I – I really liked him.'

'You mean you slept with him?' Alexa said. 'You go straight to your room, young lady, and think about what you've done.'

'I didn't sleep with him,' I said.

'You didn't?' Alexa said. 'You're not going to tell me *nothing happened*?'

'Oh, no, plenty happened,' I said. 'We sat on his balcony drinking champagne and watching the sun come up. Then he cooked me breakfast.'

'And then?'

'And then I would have slept with him,' I said, 'but he had to go to an audition – Oh, no! I've just realised something.' My hands flew to my face.

'What's wrong?' Alexa said.

'He said he'd call me, but he doesn't have my number.' My heart sank. 'How could I not have given him my phone number?'

Alexa rolled her eyes. 'He knows where you work. He's a friend of Laurie's. He can probably figure out a way to get in touch with you.'

'I guess he can,' I said. 'I suppose it's not likely he'll call me today.'

'Not *very* likely,' Alexa said.

I yawned, which reminded me that I'd been up all night. 'I need to get some sleep.' I stood up and took off Alexa's jacket. 'Thanks for the loan.'

'Any time, hun,' Alexa said, turning her attention back to her laptop screen, now filled with tap-dancing chorus girls.

Leaving Alexa singing along to 'I Got Rhythm', and after a brief detour to the bathroom to rid myself of yesterday's make-up and clean my teeth, I went into my bedroom. I unzipped my dress, and then winced as I tried to take it off before remembering that it was firmly stuck to me with tit-tape – something that had completely slipped my mind when Zac had been kissing me on his sofa. Carefully peeling the tape away, I saw that it'd had left marks on my skin. Not a good look, I thought, making a mental note not to wear the red dress in future if there was the slightest chance I might be taking it off in front of a handsome, dark-haired actor. Pulling on a T-shirt, and placing my phone within easy reach on my nightstand, I climbed into bed. And instantly fell asleep.

I was startled awake by the ringing of my phone. I sat bolt upright and snatched it up.

'Hey, Julie,' a man's voice said. I recognised it as Laurie's

'Oh, hello, Laurie,' I said.

'You sound like you were expecting someone else,' he said. 'Or hoping I might be someone else…'

'No, not at all,' I lied.

'I've just been talking about you.'

'Have you?' I said.

'Yeah, I had a call from my friend Zac Diaz,' Laurie said. 'He asked me for your mobile number.'

My heart fluttered. 'Did you give it to him?'

'No, I told him I'd have to check with you first,' Laurie said.

'Oh. Right. Well, it's fine,' I said. 'Do give it to him.'

There was a silence at the other end of the line, and then Laurie said, 'OK. If you're sure.'

'Yes, I'm sure,' I said.

'I rather thought you might be,' Laurie said. 'And now I expect you'd like me to end this call and phone Zac.'

'I would, actually.'

'Just tell me one thing, Julie.'

'What's that?' I said.

'Did you *like* him? Enough to –?' Laurie laughed, and rang off before I could answer.

The alarm clock on my dressing table showed me that I'd only slept for four hours, but I was no longer tired. I replaced my mobile on my nightstand. It rang again almost immediately – a call from an unknown number. Taking a deep breath, I put the phone on speaker.

'Julie. It's Zac.'

'Zac. Hi.' I drew my legs up to my chest and hugged my knees. 'How was your audition?'

'I got the job,' he said.

'Ooh, that's wonderful, I said. 'Congratulations. You must be thrilled.'

'It's not that great,' he said, 'it's an advert for sunblock, but it's reassured Felicity Sanders that I'm serious about pursuing work in London, and not about to go running back to LA. I'm just sorry that you and I didn't get to spend more time together this morning.'

'So am I,' I said.

After a moment, he said, 'This advert will be my first job since I came back to England, and I feel like going out and celebrating. Will you have dinner with me tonight?'

'Dinner would be lovely,' I said.

'I'll try and book us a table at Rafe's,' he said. 'Can you meet me outside Sloane Square station at eight o'clock?'

'Yes, I can do that,' I said.

'I'll see you later then,' he said, and ended the call. For a while I just sat on my bed, with my arms wrapped round myself, savouring the fact that he'd phoned me. Then I went in search of Alexa, finding her in her bedroom.

'He called me,' I said to her.

'Who called you, hun?' she said.

'Not funny, Alexa.'

She laughed. 'Sorry.'

'He asked me out,' I said.

'I expect you played hard to get,' Alexa said.

'Oh, I did,' I said. 'I really made him beg.'

'So where's he taking you?' Alexa said.

'He said he'd try and get us a table at Rafe's. Dinner was mentioned so presumably that's a restaurant.'

'Are you serious?' Alexa said. 'You must have heard of Rafe's.'

I looked at her blankly.

'It's that fabulous place on the King's Road,' Alexa said. 'My brother Charles took Hillary there to celebrate their tenth wedding anniversary. It's *the* place to go to right now.'

'If it's that flash, what on earth am I going to wear?' I said.

'Oh, it's flash, but trendy,' Alexa said. 'Your black skinny jeans would be fine.'

'Jeans and my black lace shirt?'

'Perfect,' Alexa said. 'And you must borrow my leather jacket again. I insist.'

'Thanks, Alexa,' I said, 'I love your jacket. Should I curl my hair do you think?'

'No. Keep it straight the way it was last night.' Suddenly, Alexa grinned. 'Putting out on a first date. Julie Farrell, what are you like?'

'Strictly speaking, yesterday was our first date,' I said. 'And I didn't sleep with him.'

'But you're going to tonight,' Alexa said.

The memory of Zac's kiss and where it might have led if his phone hadn't rung, made my stomach clench. I hadn't felt like this about a guy in a very long time. In fact, I couldn't remember ever feeling like this.

'Maybe,' I said. 'If he asks me. If – tonight – it feels right.'

I rang Austin to tell him I wouldn't be coming into work that night, and rang off before he could ask me why. I texted Laurie to say I wouldn't be in as I was seeing his friend Zac, and he texted back a smiley face. I showered, did my make-up, and blow-dried and straightened my hair. I put on my newest and tightest black jeans and tried on several tops, before settling for the black lace shirt that I'd tried on first of all. After one final check in my mirror – I decided I'd managed to achieve a look that was hot, but not slutty – I went to fetch Alexa's leather jacket from the living room. She was seeing Jonas that night, and had already gone out, but I found her jacket still lying on the chair where I'd left it. On top of it was an envelope with my name written on it, in Alexa's handwriting. Bemused, I tore it open. Inside were a toothbrush and a condom. Glad that there was no one there to see me blush, I put them both in my bag.

Arriving at Sloan Square just before eight p.m., I glanced around for Zac, spotting him studying one of the posters outside the theatre next to the station, dressed in a white shirt, black jacket and tight jeans. Despite having left his flat only a few hours ago, I was taken aback by how handsome he was – and how strongly I was attracted to him. For a long moment, I just stood there on the pavement gazing at him, drinking him in, and then I walked up to him and touched his arm. He turned towards me, and his face broke into a smile.

'Have you been waiting long?' I said.

'Not that long.' He bent down and air-kissed me on each side of my face as actors do. 'I did manage to get us in at Rafe's,' he said. 'Have you been there before?'

'No, I haven't,' I said. 'Have you?'

'Once or twice,' he said. 'We'll walk – it's not far.' I fell into step beside him and, as it grew dark and the streetlights came on, we strolled along the Kings Road with its art gallery and pubs, its cafés and designer shops. The noise of the traffic made it impossible to hold a conversation, but there was nothing awkward in our silence. I felt as though I was floating on air.

Rafe's was indeed a fabulous restaurant, with low lighting that subtly changed the colour of the walls from blue through purple to red, and dark wooden tables separated from each other by carved, filigree wooden screens, giving diners a semblance of privacy. Although it was still early to be dining out in London, every table was taken, and people were being turned away at the door. The waiter, who showed Zac and me to our reserved, candle-lit table for two, had a strong Spanish accent, and introduced himself as Juan. Zac spoke to him in Spanish, and they talked for several minutes in that language, before he left us to peruse the menu. My menu had no prices on it – Rafe's was that sort of place.

'Do you speak Spanish fluently?' I said to Zac.

'It's my first language,' he said. 'My mother is of Spanish heritage, although her family have lived in England for three generations. My father is

American, Hispanic-American, but he's lived in England since he was a student.'

'Are your parents actors like you?' I said.

'My mother works as a translator,' Zac said, 'but she was a dancer back in the day. My father is a session musician. What do your parents do for a living? Are they in showbusiness?'

I shook my head. 'They both work in retail. I'm the only one in my family who's ever wanted to perform on stage. My parents have always tried to be supportive, but when I decided I wanted to become an actress none of us had any idea how to go about applying for drama school. Fortunately, my drama teacher was better informed.'

'I guess coming from a theatrical background can have its advantages,' Zac said.

'I don't see it having any disadvantages,' I said.

'Well, my mother, having danced professionally, was sometimes less convinced than she might have been that her only child was the greatest dancer since Nureyev.'

I laughed. 'Did she teach you to dance?'

'Not exactly,' Zac said. 'In my parents' house there were always people singing and dancing. My father's musician friends would call round with some wine, and someone would start playing the piano or a guitar, and the dancing just used to happen. Adults, children, it was just what you did. Very often, the party went on for days.'

'It sounds wonderful,' I said. 'Bohemian.'

'To me, as a child, it was just normal,' Zac said. 'It was only when I started going to sleepovers with my school friends, that I realised not everyone gets woken up in the night by somebody playing a saxophone or singing the drinking song from *La Traviata*. I did go to dance classes eventually, and singing and acting classes, but it was my father and his friends who taught me to read music and play.'

The waiter came to take our order. Zac chose steak and I had lamb, and Zac asked him to bring a bottle of Rioja which, he said, was his favourite wine. He told me that he'd first met Laurie at a youth theatre summer school when they were ten years old, and when they'd both ended up training at RoCoDa, they'd shared a rented house for a while. I told him how I'd met Alexa on my first day as a student at the London Academy of Performing Arts, and that we'd been friends ever since. He talked about the auditions he'd been to since he'd been back in England, making me laugh at the sheer awfulness of some of them. I sat opposite him while we ate and drank wine, the candle flickering between us, and thought how easy he was to talk to, how good it felt to be with him. How much I wanted him. When we got to the coffee stage, we drank it in silence, without the need to talk.

Zac reached across the table and covered my hand with his. His touch made my body sing. His eyes, coal-black in the candlelight, fastened on mine.

'Shall we go?' he said.

I nodded. He didn't tell me where we were going. I didn't ask. We both knew.

***

Zac shut his front door and locked it. Then he folded me in his arms and kissed me, a long, demanding kiss that left me breathless and aching for him to kiss me again.

'*Te deseo*' he said. 'I want you.' He picked me up and carried me into his bedroom. One of my shoes fell off, and I kicked off the other. He set me down so that we were both kneeling, facing each other on the bed. The bedroom curtains were open, and there was just enough light for us to see each other.

He put his arms round me and kissed my forehead, my mouth and my throat. Slowly, he unfastened all the buttons on my shirt, and slid it over my shoulders. I tried to do the same for him, but my hands were shaking too much. With a smile, he reached up and unbuttoned his shirt himself, and shrugged it off. He reached behind me, unfastened my bra and took it off, and drew me close against the smooth planes of his chest, so that I could feel his heart beating as fast as mine, his toned body firm and unyielding, before he gently lowered me down onto the bed. He undid my jeans, and I raised my hips so that he could tug them off, and the thong I was wearing underneath. He bent over me and kissed me again, his hand cupping my breast.

'*Eres hermosa,*' he said. 'You are very beautiful.' He stripped off the rest of his clothes and lay down next to me on the bed, his erection pressing hot and demanding against my thigh. Sensual pleasure surged through me as he kissed and caressed my body, trailing his fingers slowly down my spine, taking my breasts in his mouth, his hand straying between my legs, setting my body aflame.

'A moment, *cariño,*' he said. 'I need to –'

He half-sat up and twisted away from me. I heard the drawer of his nightstand open, and then the sound of tearing foil. He turned back to me, positioning himself between my thighs, covering my body with his. And then he was inside me, his body arching and falling above me, and my legs were around his hips, desire a crescendo of sensation within me, and it felt... it felt so right.

CHAPTER 9

I was woken by bright sunlight shining in my eyes, as I lay close to Zac in a tangle of white cotton sheets. He was asleep, his face shadowed with morning stubble, his hair very dark against the white pillow, and one of his arms thrown over my waist. I kept very still, breathing in the scent of his skin, watching him as he slept, until he stirred and opened his eyes.

'Julie,' he said, his face creasing into a smile. '*Hola*, Julie.'

'Hi,' I said, smiling back at him.

He raised himself up on one elbow, resting his head on his hand. 'Any idea what time it is?'

'No, I've only just woken up myself,' I said. I thought, what do I do now? Should I get up and go home? I was in no hurry to leave Zac's bed, but I didn't want to outstay my welcome, as it were.

Zac sat up and stretched, and picked up a small alarm clock that was on his nightstand. 'It's gone twelve,' he said. 'Do you have somewhere you need to be? Or can you stay and have something to eat?'

I also sat up, instinctively clutching the sheets to cover my breasts, which was somewhat superfluous given the circumstances. 'I don't have to be at work until five-thirty.'

'Then we can have an early lunch together.' Zac got out of bed, giving me an intensely pleasurable view of his rear, and the rippling muscles in his back, as he pulled on his jeans. 'There's an ensuite bathroom through there,' he said, gesturing towards a door in the wall opposite the bed. 'Clean towels are in the cupboard. I'll leave you to it.'

'Thanks, Zac.' He certainly knows how to alleviate any morning-after-the-night-before awkwardness, I thought. It occurred to me that he was probably rather more used to waking up next to an overnight guest than I was.

'I'm going to take a shower in the bathroom down the hall,' he said, 'and then you'll find me in the kitchen.' He left the bedroom, closing the door behind him.

I took a moment to look round properly at the room in which I'd slept – its style was very masculine, with dark wooden fitted wardrobes, dove-grey walls, charcoal duvet and curtains, and a complete lack of any visible clutter – before getting out of bed, and showering in Zac's black and white marble, ensuite bathroom. Wrapped in a thick bath towel, I made a sortie into the hall to retrieve my bag and the toothbrush (thank you, Alexa) from the console table where I'd left it, found my last-night's clothes which were scattered around the floor, dressed, and put on a little make-up. Inspecting my appearance in the full-length mirror on one of the wardrobe doors, I decided that I looked as presentable as I possibly could, given that I didn't have access to clean clothes or hair straighteners, and went in search of Zac.

If I hadn't remembered the whereabouts of the kitchen, I'd have found it anyway by following the scent of cooking. Zac, now fully dressed in jeans and T-shirt, was standing by the hob, frying peppers, onions, courgettes and tomatoes.

'Good timing, Julie,' he said, giving me a smile that melted my insides. 'Our lunch is just about ready.'

'It smells wonderful,' I said. He dished up the vegetables, and added sliced chorizo and hunks of bread, and we carried our plates along the hallway and into the main room. We sat at the dining table and ate, the conversation flowing as easily as it had the previous night in the restaurant. We'd finished eating but were still lingering at the table, when he mentioned that, as a student, he'd had a part-time job in a piano bar.

'Would you play something now?' I said to him, tilting my head towards the piano at the other end of the room.

'Sure.' He stood up, pushed back his chair, and went and sat at the piano. He thought for a moment, flexed his fingers, and then played 'A Better Thing I Do' from *Two Cities*.

'*Two Cities* is my favourite Joe Garcia musical,' I said, when the last notes of the tune had faded. 'Actually, it's my favourite musical.'

'Mine too,' Zac said.

'The musical on which the curtain never comes down,' I said. 'Do you think it's true, that somewhere in the world that show is always playing?'

'I think it's possible,' Zac said. 'Only Joe Garcia would know for sure.'

'I was in a school production of *Two Cities*,' I said. 'I was the Girl in the Tumbrel. Except my school drama club couldn't afford a tumbrel, so the Girl and Sydney Carton had to walk rather than ride to the scaffold while he sang 'A Better Thing I Do,' and my drama teacher didn't know how Joe Garcia had worked the whole Sydney Carton and Charles Darnay looking identical and being played by the same actor thing. Our schoolboy Carton and Darnay looked nothing like each other, which made the show rather hard to follow, if you didn't already know the plot.'

Zac laughed. 'I was in a production of *Two Cities*. I was the Youngest Urchin.'

'Did your production have one actor playing Carton and Darnay?' I said.

'It did,' Zac said. 'But as I was only six at the time, I've no idea how they worked it either.'

'This production you were in,' I said, 'was it the West End one?'

'Yes, it was,' Zac said.

I gasped. 'So you've actually worked with Joe Garcia?'

'No, I've never worked with him,' Zac said. 'The show had been running for five years by the time I auditioned, and had another resident director. I was only in it for a few months – the licensing laws for child actors were very strict back then.' He returned his attention to the piano, and began to play another song from *Two Cities*, Lucie Manette's solo. I'd known all the female parts from the show since I was twelve years old – although I hoped my singing had matured since then – and, as the familiar music filled the room, I couldn't resist joining in with the vocals. Zac had been facing the piano, but now he turned his head and looked at me intently while I sang, playing the song through to the final verse.

'You have a lovely voice, Julie,' he said, when the song had ended.

I flushed with pleasure. 'Thank you,' I said.

He said, 'Do you know Lucie and Darnay's duet from Act I well enough to sing it with me?'

'I do,' I said.

'Come over here.'

'OK.' I walked across the room, and Zac shifted along the piano stool so that I could sit next to him. He played a couple of bars of intro, and then sang Darnay's opening verse in a rich, powerful tenor. I sang Lucie's verse, and we sang the rest of the song together, gazing into each other's eyes, just as the actors playing Lucie and Darnay perform the song on stage. As the last notes of the piano died away, Zac leant towards me and kissed me on the mouth. By the time we broke apart, I was breathless and incapable of singing another note.

Seemingly unaware of the effect his kiss had on me, Zac turned back to the piano. 'We sounded good together,' he said, picking out a melody with one hand.

'We did, didn't we?' I watched his fingers move lightly over the piano keys, warmth spreading through me at the memory of his touch on my body. Then I noticed the time on his watch.

'Zac,' I said, reluctantly, 'I'll have to make a move pretty soon.'

Zac looked down at me with hooded eyes. 'Are you sure?' he said. 'Can't I persuade you to stay?'

I recognised the tune he was now playing on the piano as the background music to the love scene between Lucie and Darnay in Act II, the scene which ends with him taking her to his bed. Every fibre of my body yearned to stay and re-enact that scene for real, but if I didn't turn up for work at the club, I didn't get paid, and I'd already taken last night off.

'Unfortunately, I really do have to go,' I said. 'I need to call in at home to change, and I'm cutting it fine if I'm going to get back to central London in time for my shift.'

'Pity.' Zac stopped playing. I stood up and located my bag, and together we went out into the hall. He handed me my jacket and opened the front door. For the first time since I'd woken up next to him, I thought to ask myself if the night we'd spent together was going to lead to something more. I knew I wanted it to. I just hoped he felt the same.

Zac said, 'I'm filming the sunblock advert tomorrow, and then I'm tied up for the next few days. I'm going to visit my uncle at his country pile.'

'The uncle who bought you this flat?' I said.

Zac nodded. 'The prodigal nephew returns.'

I looked at him quizzically.

He said, 'My uncle and I fell out around the time I went to California, and this visit is my chance to make things right with him. I'm not sure how long I'm going to be away. I'll call you when I get back to London.'

My heart plummeted. Would he call me? Or was last night nothing more than a casual encounter for him?

I forced myself to smile. 'OK.'

Zac reached out and brushed a strand of hair off my face. Then he bent his head and kissed me, and any doubts that he would call faded away.

CHAPTER 10

I only just managed to get to Zone by five-thirty, and was relieved to have made it on time, as Austin was again skulking in the staffroom.

'So where were you last night?' he said to me.

For a moment, I thought he was asking me where I'd slept. Laurie, standing nearby but out of Austin's sight line, didn't help by grinning at me. Then I realised that my boss simply wanted to know why I hadn't made it into work.

'There was an audition,' I said. 'It was going on really late.'

'I do know these things come up at the last minute,' Austin said, 'but if you need time off, it would be helpful if you could phone before midday.'

'Right,' I said. 'Will do.'

'If we are very short-staffed, I have to arrange casual cover,' Austin said.

'I appreciate that,' I said.

'Anyway, you will be pleased to hear that Obsidian's management have conveyed the band's thanks to everyone at Club Zone for making their launch party such a huge success,' Austin said.

'It was a wonderful night,' I said with a sidelong glance at Laurie. 'In fact, I can truthfully say that it was one of the best nights of my life.'

'I'm sure you're not the only one who would say that,' Laurie said.

'I'll never forget it,' I said.

'And who knows what may come of it?' Laurie said. 'I mean, look what's come of it already.'

'Well, er, keep up the good work,' Austin said, taken aback by our enthusiasm. He scuttled off to speak to Ben, who had just come into the staffroom.

'So,' Laurie said. 'You and Zac. Did you and he–?'

'As if I'd tell you.' I couldn't help smiling.

'That'd be a "yes" then,' Laurie said.

'Are you trying to make me blush?' I said.

'I've already succeeded,' Laurie said.

From the other side of the room, Austin caught my eye and tapped at his watch. Still smiling, I picked up a handful of flyers and passed half of them to Laurie, and we headed out of the club.

***

Alexa had already left for work when I'd called in at the flat that afternoon, and she was still out, presumably now with Jonas, when I arrived home that night. Unusually, after six hours of flyering, I didn't feel like going straight to bed. I made myself a cup of coffee, checked my emails, and was curled up with a book on the living room sofa, when I heard my flatmate's key in the front door.

'Julie?' she called. 'Anyone home?'

'I'm in here,' I called back.

Alexa came into the living room and sat down next to me. Tonight, she was wearing a short, tight, sleeveless denim dress and suede ankle boots, and as usual, she looked effortlessly stunning.

'Jonas not with you?' I said.

'I didn't see him tonight,' Alexa said. 'I just went out for a quick drink with Michael McCabe.'

'Did you?' I reminded myself that there was absolutely no reason at all why a girl couldn't have drink with a male friend. 'How is he?'

'Still fed up,' Alexa said. 'Suzanne's working such long hours... And how are you, Julie? You're looking very well. In fact, I'd say you're positively radiant. Anything you want to tell me?'

'Like what?' I said, my eyes wide.

'Like how was your date with the man who picked you up in a bar?' Alexa said. 'Did it lead to a night of torrid passion?'

'Oh, it was... It was *definitely* passionate,' I said. I pictured Zac's face, his smile when he woke up and saw me lying next to him, the look in his eyes as we sang together, the music fading as he leaned in for a kiss. 'Last night was wonderful, but waking up in Zac's bed this morning, just being with him, that felt *so* good.'

'So the show's opening night was a huge success,' Alexa said. 'Is there going to be a repeat performance?'

'There is,' I said. 'Zac has to leave London for a few days to visit a relative, but he's going to call me when he gets back.' I smiled. 'I really like him, Alexa.'

'I can see that.' Alexa said. Then she yawned. 'Sorry, much as I'd like to stay up and talk about your love life, I'm going to have to say goodnight. I'm on the early shift tomorrow.' She stood up and walked across the room. In the doorway, she looked back over her shoulder and said,

'Even if it turns out that the show closes after only one performance, it's good that you're back on stage.'

'It is,' I said. 'I've been standing in the wings far too long. But I'm centre stage right now. I'm in the spotlight.'

Alexa laughed and went off to her bedroom.

I thought, I don't want a walk-on role for one night only. I want to star in a show that runs for a very long time.

CHAPTER 11

I'd just opened my laptop, when my phone rang. I snatched it up off my nightstand and tried not to be disappointed when I saw that it was Laurie who was calling me, and not Zac, who'd been out of town for over a week now and hadn't even sent me a text.

Laurie said, 'I went to an audition this morning. It was for the lead in a new play entitled *Iago,* a reworking of Shakespeare's *Othello* from the villain's point of view.'

'How did it go?' I said. I closed my laptop, which I'd been balancing on my knees as I sat cross-legged on my bed, and moved it to a less precarious position on the floor.

'I've got a recall,' Laurie said. 'A final recall.'

'Oh, Laurie!' I said. 'Well done you! A lead in a new play. Are we talking big break here?'

'We could be,' Laurie said, 'which is why I couldn't wait until tonight to tell you about it. *Iago* opens in the West End this summer.'

'But that's fantastic,' I said. 'The West End!'

'Hey, don't get too excited,' Laurie said, 'I've not got the part yet. And please keep all this to yourself. My agent told me that the producers don't want anything about the play appearing on social media before they do a press release.'

'You have to get this show,' I said. 'I want comp tickets for your opening night.'

Laurie laughed. 'See you at Zone, Julie.' He ended the call.

Over the last few months, as we'd strolled through Theatreland handing out flyers, I'd discovered a lot about Laurie's career as a jobbing actor. He'd had walk-on roles in most of the soaps. He'd performed in pub theatre and he'd done a TIE tour. He'd spent the five years since he graduated from drama school getting as much performing experience as he could and perfecting his craft. And, in between his acting work, he'd earned his living working in shops or bars. He's worked hard to get this far, I thought, I so hope he gets the part.

The front door slammed shut, reminding me that Laurie was not the only one of my acquaintances who'd been at an audition that morning. After a moment, Alexa made her entrance through my bedroom doorway.

'How did it go?' I said, and thought, am I the only unemployed actor in London who has *not* been auditioning today?

'It was fine,' Alexa said. 'All I had to do was say a few lines of dialogue in front of a camera. I was in and out of the room in less than ten minutes.' She sighed. 'It would be such a fabulous job. While I was waiting to go in, I got talking to some of the other actors trying out for parts in the show. Apparently, it's a huge Anglo-American production – much bigger than I thought – an urban, twenty-first century version of the Robin Hood legend, working title *Sherwood*. The casting director told me they're looking at me for the hero's sister.'

'That sounds like a main role,' I said.

Alexa nodded. 'I'd be appearing in every episode of a thirteen-week TV series. Not that there's much chance of my getting it. They're much more likely to go with a household name.'

'You've every chance,' I said. 'You're a terrific actress, and if they weren't prepared to consider casting a newcomer, they wouldn't have bothered to audition you.' It wasn't as if they were seeing everyone who'd sent them a CV, I thought. I'd emailed my CV and headshot to the show's production company on the same day as Alexa had sent hers, but I hadn't had a reply. 'So what happens now? When will you know if you convinced them to cast you?'

Alexa shrugged. 'I'll have to wait and see.'

'I don't know what's worse,' I said, 'waiting for "The Call", or waiting for *a* call…'

'Zac still hasn't been in touch?' Alexa said.

'No, he hasn't,' I said. 'The only explanation is that he's lost his phone. It's not as though a guy would ever have sex with a girl and then never contact her again.'

'Yeah, when did that ever happen?' Alexa said. 'Oh, there's the doorbell. It'll be Jonas. He texted me that his rehearsal finished early today. He's bringing wine and we're going to order a pizza.'

'Sounds like a perfect night in,' I said.

'I'm sure it will be,' Alexa said, getting to her feet. 'That boy of mine is insatiable. And I'm not talking about food and alcohol.'

'Too much information, Alexa,' I said. She smiled, and went off to answer the door.

I picked up my laptop and opened it with every intention of hitting the online casting sites, but without enthusiasm for what was beginning to seem like a pointless task. I heard Jonas laughing, Alexa's bedroom door shutting, more laughter, and then the strange, eerie first track of Obsidian's *The Howling*. Much as I liked the band's sound, it wouldn't have been my choice of background music for a night in with a boyfriend – the ambience it created could hardly be described as romantic. Not that it seemed I was likely to be in need of a romantic soundtrack any time soon. Why hasn't Zac called me? I thought. Is he back in London or not?

Telling myself that I wouldn't be the first girl who'd tried to track down a guy she liked on social media, I logged in to Facebook and attempted to find Zac's page, but without success. As he wasn't among Laurie's Facebook friends, I could only conclude that, uniquely among the actors I knew, he didn't have a Facebook account. Nor could I locate him on any other social networking site. I typed *Zac Diaz actor* into Google. His name came up on a number of theatrical websites, along with details of the parts he'd played, the sort of information that would be on any actor's CV. I also found several reviews of *Film Noir,* all of which lavished praise on his performance, heralding him as an up-and-coming talent. I shut my laptop.

I knew little about Zac Diaz other than that he was a talented actor. I didn't want to believe that the way he'd looked at me when we'd sung together, the way he'd kissed me, was nothing more than an act.

***

'Have you heard anything from Zac lately?' I said to Laurie that evening, as we handed out flyers along Charing Cross Road. 'Do you know if he's in London right now?'

'I've no idea,' Laurie said. 'Why do you ask?'

'He told me he was visiting a country-dwelling uncle for a few days, and he'd call me when he got back.' I realised that I sounded far more petulant than I'd intended.

'Then I'd imagine he's still out of town.' Laurie's amiable face grew serious. 'Zac is one of my closest and oldest friends, and I love him dearly, but he hasn't always made good choices and his life is complicated. Give him time to sort it out.'

Suddenly, my pulse was racing and my mouth felt very dry. 'When you say complicated, do you mean that he's sleeping with someone else apart from me? Does he have a girlfriend?'

'No,' Laurie said. 'No he does *not*. Why would you think that? If Zac had a girlfriend, I'd have told you before I let you go running off to meet him after Obsidian's launch party.'

I felt light-headed with relief. 'Then what's so *complicated* about Zac Diaz's life?'

Laurie hesitated, and then he said, 'Has he told you much about his family?'

'He did say something about falling out with this uncle he's visiting, and needing to make things right.'

'That's what I was talking about,' Laurie said. Before I could ask him to elaborate, he turned away to hand out flyers to a raucous hen party wearing pink sashes emblazoned with the word 'Bridesmaid'. The 'Bride' had a white sash and was carrying a giant inflatable penis, brandishing it aloft in the manner of a tour guide holding an umbrella.

96

When Laurie turned back to me, he said 'Did I ever tell you about the time I played a juror in *Twelve Good Men and True*?'

'I'm sure you haven't,' I said. 'I wouldn't forget that credit on your CV, it's my father's favourite radio show.' I thought, is he trying to distract me from talking about Zac? I remembered that they'd been friends for a long time, far longer than either of them had known me. Much as I wanted to interrogate him about Zac's complicated life, I decided that it wouldn't be fair, and allowed him to change the subject.

We spent the rest of the night planning our Oscar, BAFTA and London Theatre Awards acceptance speeches.

***

It was ten days – not that I was counting – after I'd slept with Zac, when I found Alexa in the kitchen, unpacking a shopping bag which appeared to hold only cans of lager and packets of crisps.

'Are we having a party?' I asked her.

'No,' Alexa said. 'Michael rang and asked if he could come over and watch the game tonight. He and Suzanne don't have a TV, and his laptop's broken.'

'Is Jonas coming over too?' I said.

Alexa shook her head. 'Jonas and I broke up.'

'Oh, Alexa! I'm sorry.' I gave her a hug. 'Are you OK, hun?'

'I'm fine,' Alexa said. 'I've only known him a few weeks.'

'But I thought you liked him,' I said.

'I do like him,' Alexa said. 'He's easy to like. But from tomorrow he's going to be off on tour with *Pride and Prejudice* until the end of the year. Neither of us is exactly the faithful type. We both decided it was better to call it a day. I'm once again a single girl.'

I thought, Alexa is single and Michael is coming over to watch TV. 'Will Suzanne be watching the football with you and Michael?' I said.

'No. She's waitressing tonight,' Alexa said.

'Suzanne is working, and Michael is spending the evening with you? Alexa!'

'Would you stop that,' Alexa said. 'I have rules, don't forget. Anyway, Luke Harvey's coming over as well, so no more insinuations about me and Michael, OK?'

'OK.' I remembered that Luke had been the first one in our year at LAPA to make his professional debut – in a BBC historical drama – but he'd had no acting work since, as far as I knew.

Alexa surveyed her shopping with a critical eye. 'I hope I've bought enough,' she said. 'Apparently it's compulsory for men to drink lager when they watch a football match.'

I took myself off to Club Zone, leaving Alexa rearranging our furniture in a semi-circle around the television.

That night, in the staffroom, when the promotions team had assembled for their meal break, Nadia somehow accidently let drop that her agent had managed to get her an audition for one of the main parts in a new reworking of a Shakespearean tragedy. Obviously she couldn't say any more. She really shouldn't have mentioned it at all at this early stage, but she knew that we, her co-workers, would want to know.

'Can you believe it?' Laurie said to me, when we were on our own, flyering along the street that links Leicester Square to St Martin's Lane. 'I get a shot at the lead in a great play, but I could be playing opposite Nadia. She might even be cast as my wife.' He shuddered. 'I don't think I'm a good enough actor to play a convincing love scene with that woman. If I get the part of Iago and she's in the cast, I'll have to turn it down.'

'Don't joke about turning down the West End,' I said. 'It's not remotely funny.'

'I'm not joking,' Laurie said. 'I remember what Nadia was like in student productions at RoCoDa. Snide remarks to other actors, an uncanny ability to make her mistakes look like someone else's, winding up the techies –' He interrupted his impassioned monologue to accost two women wearing silver-sequinned cowboy hats, and give them each a flyer. They were very keen for him to personally escort them to Zone, but he declined, assuring them he'd be along later.

'You wouldn't really turn down a part in a West End play because of Nadia, would you, Laurie?' I said, once the women had sashayed away from him.

'No, of course not,' Laurie said. 'I was just creating a bit of dramatic tension. After all, I'm an *actor*.' A smile flickered over his face. 'The lead in *Iago*, if I get it, could change my life. And I'm not talking about fame and fortune, although I wouldn't be averse to either. I'm talking about the chance to do what I've always wanted.'

'It could lead to your playing the great iconic roles that all actors dream of,' I said.

'And more than that,' Laurie said. 'If it's the breakout role I think it is, I'll never have to hand out one of these frickin' flyers ever again.'

***

When I arrived home from work, the flat was in darkness. I let myself in, and immediately tripped over an object on the hall floor. I switched on the light. A large pair of trainers had been left just inside the front door. A man's shirt and various articles of clothing I recognised as belonging to Alexa made a trail from the living room to my flatmate's bedroom. I told myself that if she'd chosen to break her own rules, it was nothing to do with me, but it was with a sense of unease that I switched off the light and went to bed.

I didn't bother setting my alarm that night, and when I finally surfaced around midday, Alexa was already up, throwing empty cans into a black bin liner. The living room stank of stale beer and there were crisps ground into the carpet. I opened a window and fetched the vacuum cleaner.

Alexa put her finger to her lips. 'Don't switch that machine on now,' she said. 'I've a guest asleep in my room. I'll do the vacuuming later.'

'Please tell me it's not Michael asleep in your bed,' I said.

Alexa sighed. 'Michael and I are *friends*. I believe I've told you this before –' She broke off suddenly and looked over my shoulder. 'Morning, Luke.'

Luke Harvey, wearing just a pair of jeans, had materialised in the doorway to the living room.

'Morning, Alexa,' he said. 'How're you doing, Julie?'

'I'm good,' I said, relief flooding through me. 'Yourself?'

'Not so bad. Alexa, darlin', do you know what I did with my shirt?'

'In the hall,' Alexa said. 'And your shoes.'

Luke vanished for a few minutes and returned fully dressed. 'I'm going to have to shoot,' he said. 'I'm late for work.'

'Acting work?' I said.

'Sadly, no,' Luke said. 'Burger flipping.' He smiled at Alexa. 'I had fun last night. Watching the football.'

'So did I,' Alexa said.

'Anything you want to know about football, I'm your man,' Luke said.

'I'll remember that,' Alexa said.

'I know a lot about sport.'

'Go to work, Luke,' Alexa said.

Looking very pleased with himself, Luke went.

'I wonder why Luke and I never hooked up back in drama school,' Alexa said. 'He's pretty good in the sack.'

'Is there going to be a return match?' I said.

'Oh, I shouldn't think so,' Alexa said. 'He's not *that* good.' She added, 'In other news, Luke auditioned for job on a cruise ship last week. He didn't get cast – but guess who did.'

I shrugged.

'Polly,' Alexa said.

CHAPTER 12

Flyering along Shaftesbury Avenue, a fortnight after I'd slept with Zac Diaz, five men asked me for my phone number, and two women and two men asked Laurie for his.

'Do you suppose they think they're being amusing and original when they say they'll take a flyer if we write our phone number on it?' I said to Laurie, as we came out of Zone at the end of our shift,

'You mean you've been asked for your phone number before?' Laurie said.

'It's so exhausting being polite to slime balls,' I said. 'All I want to do now is get home, crawl under my duvet and fall asleep.'

'Do you, Julie?' Laurie said. 'Well, I hate to break it to you, but you may be disappointed.'

'What do you mean?' I said. He put his hands on my shoulders and turned me around. A figure detached itself from the shadows on the opposite side of the alleyway and I saw that it was Zac. I'd convinced myself that I was never going to see him again, but here he was walking towards me. I'd never believed that any girl outside a rom com would go weak at the knees when she saw a man, but at that moment my legs actually started to shake.

'Hi,' Zac said, when he reached us. 'I was just passing–'

'Sure you were,' Laurie said. 'You just happened to be passing Club Zone at eleven-thirty at night.'

'OK, I wasn't just passing,' Zac said. 'Julie, do you fancy going for a drink?'

'Am I invited?' Laurie said.

'Not tonight, mate,' Zac said.

Laurie laughed and gave me a gentle push towards Zac. 'Play nicely, children,' he said, before heading off towards the tube.

Zac said, 'So about that drink?'

I thought, I shouldn't be too eager. I should make him suffer – just a little. Because he didn't frickin' call.

'I'll have a drink with you,' I said.

'Where would you like to go? There's a bar in Drury Lane that's pretty good.'

'The Troubadour?' I said. 'Yes, I know it. Laurie and I walk past it almost every night.'

'Or we could go to my place,' Zac said. 'My car's parked right by Waterloo Bridge. I've literally just got back from the country.'

I thought, I should go for a drink with him and then I should go home. Alone. I have to let him know that he can't vanish for weeks at a time and then expect me to jump straight into bed with him. Even if I want this as much as he does.

'Your place,' I said.

***

As soon as the lift doors shut, Zac kissed me, and he kept on kissing me until we reached his floor. We literally ran across the landing, and once we were inside his flat, he kissed me some more, grinding his hips against mine so that I could feel his arousal, even through his jeans. I wanted him inside me very badly.

'Would you like that drink now?' he said hoarsely, reaching for me with one hand and his bedroom door with the other.

Through a haze of lust, I managed to say, 'No, I would *not* like a drink.'

Still kissing, we staggered into his bedroom, shedding our clothes in a frenzy. I heard fabric rip as Zac tore off his shirt; he upturned a drawer to find a condom. Then we were falling onto his bed, bodies and limbs entwined, losing ourselves in desire, in each other, Zac lying on his back, thrusting into me as I straddled him, my head thrown back, his strong hands on my hips, our bodies moving together, waves of passion rising, cresting, Zac gasping, as I collapsed breathlessly on top of him, both of us slick with sweat.

Slowly, my heartbeat returned to its normal pace. I rolled off Zac and lay next to him on the bed. Murmuring in Spanish – I had no idea what he was saying, but I liked the sound of the words – he pulled the duvet over both of us.

I said, 'Did you have a good visit with your uncle?'

'It was intense,' Zac said, 'but we cleared the air. I've managed to put things right between us.'

'That's good to hear,' I said. 'It's sad when relatives fall out. Families are important.'

'I agree. Even if they drive you crazy at times.' He kissed the top of my head. I lay contentedly beside him.

After a while, he said, 'I've not been to the theatre since I got back from the States. I know you work nights – I'm pulling pints every night next week myself – but would you like to come with me to a matinée? How about I meet you after work on Friday, we spend the night here, and head into Theatreland together on Saturday afternoon?'

My heart soared. He was planning to see me again. He wasn't about to vanish out of my life. 'That'd be great,' I said.

'Are there any shows that that you particularly want to see?' he said.

I thought of the musicals that were currently playing in the West End. 'I haven't seen *Warrior Queen*, but it's really hard to get tickets unless you book months in advance. Any musical would be lovely.'

'I'll see what I can do,' Zac said.

***

'After two weeks offline, he just turns up outside the club and expects you to have sex with him?' Alexa said, spooning instant coffee into two mugs. 'I'm sure you gave him a hard time about that.'

'I did think about it,' I said, taking a bottle of milk out of the fridge and passing it to her. 'But I decided that all things considered I'd rather go back to his place and have sex.'

My mind filled with images of the previous night, of earlier that morning when I'd woken up in Zac's arms. For some time, neither of us had been inclined to leave the pleasurable warmth of his bed, but eventually he'd got up and made tea and toast, which he'd brought back into the bedroom. Hunger satisfied, I'd persuaded him to tell me all about the filming of the sunblock advert – 'It was a crowd scene, Julie. I doubt anyone'll be able to spot me when it airs on TV...' – and then he'd declared his intention of taking a shower, suggesting with a wicked smile that I might like to join him. Which is how I discovered that being kissed by a naked man while warm water cascades over both of you can be an extraordinarily erotic experience. I was in no hurry to leave his flat, but at the same time I knew I had to go home at some point – apart from anything else, on this occasion I'd neglected to bring a toothbrush. With reluctance, I told Zac I needed to make a move, and he insisted on walking me to the tube station. In the ticket hall, we kissed long enough for two people to tell us to get a room, before I made myself step away from him and go down onto the platform.

The ringing of my mobile – placed within easy reach on the kitchen counter – broke in on my thoughts. I picked it up and saw Zac's name emblazoned across the screen. I smiled and answered the phone.

'Hi, Julie,' he said. 'I'm calling to let you know that I've got us matinée tickets for *Warrior Queen*.'

'That's amazing, Zac,' I said. 'How on earth did you manage to get tickets at such short notice?'

'Oh, I made a few calls,' Zac said.

'I've wanted to see that show for ages,' I said. 'I'm so looking forward to it. And to seeing you, of course.' Realising that I was gushing, I added, 'Maybe not as much as the show.'

Zac laughed. 'I'll meet you outside Zone on Friday.'

'Yes, see you Friday,' I said. He rang off.

'So where's he taking you?' Alexa said, not even pretending that she hadn't been listening to my half of the conversation. To be fair, it was impossible not to overhear another person's phone conversation if you were both standing in our miniscule galley kitchen.

'He's got us Saturday matinée tickets for *Warrior Queen*' I said.

'Oh my gosh, how did he manage that?' Alexa said. 'It's supposed to be fully booked 'til August.'

'He said he made some calls,' I said.

'First he wines and dines you in one of the most fashionable restaurants in London,' Alexa said, 'now he displays an uncanny ability to get hold of hot theatre tickets. I'm assuming he has a certain amount of talent in the bedroom?'

'I've no complaints,' I said.

'You're blushing, by the way,' Alexa said.

'I am now,' I laughed, as I felt my face flush.

'I'm beginning to see why you like this guy,' Alexa said. 'Especially now he seems to have remembered how to use a mobile phone.'

I smiled. 'Zac is… he's lovely.' In three days, I thought, I'll see him again. A warm glow spread through my body.

'Do you know anything about his family?' Alexa said, unexpectedly.

'A bit,' I said. 'His mother used to be a dancer; his father's a musician. He has a rich uncle.'

'Any siblings?'

'No,' I said. 'He's an only child.'

'Damn,' Alexa said. 'I was hoping he might have a brother.'

***

107

Zac picked up his guitar and went out onto the balcony. He sat down on a wicker chair and played a few chords, letting his mind drift.

It felt good to know that his estrangement from his uncle – the man who'd been like a second father to him – was at an end. It hadn't been easy, but after some ruthlessly honest conversations, he was satisfied they were back on good terms. I should have swallowed my pride and visited him sooner, Zac reflected. Julie's right, families are important.

His thoughts strayed to the long drive back to London from the country: his sudden impulse to meet Julie Farrell outside her workplace; the powerful physical attraction he felt for her that had been impossible to resist; the night in his bed that had followed.

She was so delighted when I told her I'd got tickets for *Warrior Queen*, he thought, touched that something so simple for him to do had seemed to mean so much to her. It would, he realised, be easy to get involved with her, and he was not about to let that happen. I need to take a step back, he thought, keep it casual, and make sure she and I are on the same page.

He glanced at his watch, and realised that while he'd been organising theatre tickets, Rosalind's plane had landed at Heathrow. She'll be in Kensington by now, he thought. He pictured Rosalind climbing elegantly out of a limo, her entourage following her into the Georgian mansion rented for her by her film's production team, the domestic staff hastening to welcome her, holding open doors, carrying in her luggage. He remembered another house in another city, a bedroom, Rosalind stretched out languorously on a circular bed…

Laying aside his guitar, he stood up, rested his hands on the balcony rail and looked out over London.

The view was clear for miles, with just a faint heat haze on the horizon. He wondered who else Rosalind had invited for drinks at her house tomorrow night, or if he was her only guest.

CHAPTER 13

'The fight scene was so well done,' I said to Zac, as we and the other members of *Warrior Queen's* audience emerged from the cool, dim interior of the Langtry Theatre into a sunlit Shaftesbury Avenue. 'Just ten dancers on stage, but I believed I was watching a battle.'

'It was the music that really impressed me,' Zac said.

I strolled with him through Theatreland, my head full of heartrending songs and expressive choreography. *Warrior Queen*, as I said to Zac, was everything you'd expect of a Joe Garcia musical – and then some. I knew I was far too young to play Queen Boudicca, but I now had a burning ambition to play one of her daughters. We entered Leicester Square and cut along one of the diagonal paths that led to the statue of Shakespeare. The fountains that surround the statue were sending jets of water high into the air and two teenage girls were daring each other to stand ever closer, shrieking when they got soaked. A group of American tourists took photographs.

'Thank you for this afternoon,' I said to Zac. 'When I see a show like *Warrior Queen* it reminds me why I'm an actress – or trying to be.'

'Live theatre,' Zac said. 'It's just a group of men and women standing around on wooden boards under artificial light, speaking words written by someone else, and yet they can make an audience of thousands laugh or cry. How does that happen?'

'Didn't they tell you at drama school?' I said. 'It's a kind of magic.'

'It is,' Zac said. For a long moment, he looked at me silently. Then he put his arms around me and kissed me on the mouth. When he lifted his face from mine, both of us were breathless.

He said, 'Julie, are you around next weekend? I thought we might go out for a drink – or maybe lunch?'

'I'd like that.' I smiled up at him. If I'd been on stage at that moment, I'd have leapt into a song-and-dance routine.

'I'll be in touch,' Zac said. Kissing me lightly on the side of my face, he headed off to his bartender job – that night he was working nearby in Soho – and I went to Club Zone.

In the staffroom, I was trying unsuccessfully to turn the key that would open my locker, when Nadia came up behind me, making me jump.

'Was that Zac Diaz I saw you with just now in Leicester Square?' she said. Her voice had an accusatory tone that I found offensive.

'Yes, it was,' I said.

'Are you *with* him?' Nadia said. 'Are you and he a couple?'

Are Zac and I a couple, I thought? Not yet. It's too soon for us to be *in a relationship*. But I'd like us to be.

'I'm seeing him,' I said. Not that it's any business of yours, I thought.

'Have you known him long?' Nadia said.

'Not really,' I said. 'I only met him properly at Obsidian's launch party.'

'I was at the Royal College of Drama with Zac Diaz,' Nadia said.

'I know,' I said. 'Laurie told me you were all in the same year.'

'I've known Zac far longer than you,' Nadia said.

'Well, yes,' I said, 'you would have if you were at drama school with him and I only met him a few weeks ago.'

'I know what he's like,' Nadia said. 'He had quite a reputation at RoCoDa'

'Did he?' I said. 'What for?'

'How can I put this?' Nadia said. 'Well, there's only one way to say it – he slept around. Of course, a lot of girls threw themselves at him, but he didn't exactly fight them off.'

'Really?' I said. 'A young, single, straight, good-looking guy, and he enjoys female company. Who'd have thought it?'

'I'm just saying –'

'What exactly *is* it that you're saying? Could you get to the point?'

'Be careful. That's all,' Nadia said. 'Zac Diaz has always been a player, and he never stays with any girl for very long. I'd hate to see you get hurt.' She smiled, displaying her perfect teeth, and walked away, settling herself on a chair and calmly getting a magazine out of her bag. I resisted the impulse to run after her and give her a slap.

'Bitch,' I muttered under my breath.

A deep voice asked, 'Now what's she done? What did she say to you?' I spun around and saw Harry looking at me enquiringly.

'Oh, nothing worth repeating,' I said. Just her usual spiteful drivel, I thought. I tried to turn my locker key the other way. It wouldn't budge.

'Want a hand with that?' Harry said. 'Not that I'm suggesting for a moment that a strong, independent, twenty-first century woman like yourself is reliant on a mere male for help in any way.'

I laughed. 'Be my guest.'

Harry flexed his biceps and gave my locker door a hefty shove. It swung open immediately.

'Thanks, Harry,' I said.

'I knew my weight training would come in useful for something,' Harry said. He added, 'Was that Zac Diaz I saw you with earlier?'

'Oh my goodness,' I said. 'I thought I was living in impersonal, anonymous London. I'm actually living in a village exactly like the one I was brought up in. But yes, you saw me with Zac.'

'Are you and he dating?' Harry said.

'I've been out with him a couple of times,' I said. I remembered that Harry was another graduate of the Royal College of Drama. 'Did you know him at RoCoDa?'

'I didn't know him well,' Harry said. 'I was two years below him. What's he up to these days? Is he still acting?'

'Auditioning like the rest of us,' I said.

'I saw him in *Film Noir*,' Harry said, 'just before it transferred to Broadway. He's a frickin' fantastic actor –' He broke off as Austin came into the staffroom, effectively putting an end to any further discussion. 'Time to hit the streets. See you later, Julie.'

113

Hastily, I stowed my bag in my locker. Another long night of flyering lay ahead. I thought of the actors I'd seen that afternoon in *Warrior Queen*, who tonight would be embarking on another performance on a West End stage, enthralling their audience with the magical experience that is live theatre. I told myself it had to be my turn soon. I almost believed it.

CHAPTER 14

I was woken by the ringing of Zac's mobile. The mattress shifted as he sat up in bed. I rolled over to face him.

'No, Laurie, it's fine,' Zac said. 'No, I'm not doing anything this morning... Sure... See you in an hour.' He ended the call. '*Buenos días*, Julie.'

'*Buenos días*,' I said. 'That means "good morning", right?'

Zac smiled. '*Sí*. Yes, it does.' He added, 'Laurie's got his final recall for *Iago* tomorrow. He wants me to run through the scenes he's been asked to prepare – we used to rehearse each other when we were in drama school. I told him to come over.'

Which is my cue to go, I thought. Five days had passed between his leaving me in Leicester Square and his calling me to arrange a date for the following weekend – which was plenty of time for me to begin to worry that he'd done another vanishing act – but as soon as I'd heard his voice on the phone all my misgivings had fled. Yesterday, Sunday, he'd driven us to Greenwich, and we'd eaten lunch at a pub on the river that he used to go to before he went to the States. It was unexpectedly warm, so we'd whiled away the afternoon in Greenwich Park, mingling with the tourists to take selfies either side of the Greenwich Meridian. It was still warm when we arrived back at his place, so we went out onto the balcony. Hungry again after a day in the open air, we ate French bread and cheese, and he had a beer while I had a glass of wine. It had been a lovely day, and

I'd certainly no complaints about the night that had followed.

I pushed back the duvet. 'I should be getting home. Casting sites to check out. Emails to send.'

Zac's gaze travelled from my face to my breasts. 'You don't have to rush off just yet,' he said. And then he thought of a way to persuade me to stay a little longer.

It was the sound of the doorbell that finally got us out of bed. Zac hurriedly pulled on a pair of jeans and a T-shirt, and went to open the door. I waited until I heard him and Laurie go through to the main room and then got up myself, and quickly washed and dressed.

Going out into the hallway, I could hear their voices: Laurie was talking in a wheedling tone, quite unlike his usual speaking voice. After a moment's hesitation – they were obviously in the middle of rehearsing, and I was reluctant to interrupt them – I pushed open the door of the main room and went inside.

Laurie, in the title role, was acting out a scene from *Iago*, and Zac, holding a script, was reading the part of Othello. I sat down quietly on the sofa to watch them, except I wasn't watching Zac and Laurie, but Othello, a charismatic, yet arrogant and over-bearing soldier, and Iago, a man eaten up with jealously for his lord and master, who was everything he wanted to be and was not. By the time the scene ended, I was on the edge of my seat.

'Well?' Laurie said to Zac.

'Just a couple of suggestions,' Zac said. He went over the script line by line, offering a different interpretation here, a different emphasis there. Then the two of them ran through the scene again, and I saw that Zac had been right to suggest each change.

'That was much better,' Zac said. 'That was good.'

'Thanks, mate,' Laurie said. 'I feel I've got my head around that scene now.'

'Ready to go on to the next?'

Laurie nodded, and then – the first time either he or Zac had seemed to notice my presence – he turned to me and said. 'What are you like at sight-reading, Julie?'

'I was fine when I was at drama school,' I said. I'd always been good at sight-reading. Not that I regarded it as a particular achievement; it was just something I'd always been able to do.

'How about I play the other scenes with Julie?' Laurie said to Zac.

'That'd work well for me,' Zac said. 'I can be more objective if you do that. Would you mind, Julie?'

'Of course not,' I said.

Zac tossed me the audition script. 'You're Desdemona. Read it through once, and then we'll try it.'

I read the scene. 'She's a bit of a cock-tease,' I said. 'Not like in Shakespeare.'

'In this play, she's a spoilt brat,' Laurie said.

'Go for it,' Zac said.

I stood up and faced Laurie. We played the scene, and then Zac gave Laurie notes. We did the scene again.

'Good,' Zac said. 'Right. Let's move on. Julie, this time you're Emilia.' He passed me another script. I read the scene. Then I read it again. It was very short, but I saw that it could be very powerful.

'Can you do it off the book?' Zac said.

117

'I think so,' I said. 'Give me a prompt if I need it.' We played the scene. I was Emilia, down-trodden wife, forced to realise that I was married to a psychopath, terrified that he was going to kill me, while Laurie as Iago prowled menacingly around me, a predator circling its prey.

'OK,' Zac said. 'There are a couple of things I'd like you to try.'

Laurie and I listened to Zac's notes. We did the scene again, and the threat of violence was palpable and terrifying. When Iago left the stage, Emilia sank to her knees with relief.

Then Iago was just Laurie again, picking me, Julie, up off the laminate floor.

'I've no notes for either of you,' Zac said. 'Laurie, you've nailed it, mate.'

'I so enjoyed that.' I sat down on the sofa next to Zac. 'You're such a good actor, Laurie.'

Zac and Laurie exchanged glances.

'What?' I said.

'She doesn't seem to realise what a talented actress she is,' Zac said to Laurie.

'We won't tell her,' Laurie said. 'She'll only get up herself.'

I smiled delightedly. 'Do you want to go through the scenes again?'

'Not right now,' Laurie said. 'I've taken the night off work, so I've got the whole evening to go over my scenes and read through the rest of the play.'

'You don't want to over-rehearse,' Zac said.

'I'll shoot off, then,' I said. I stood up and gave Laurie a hug. 'I know you're going to get this job. Phone me tomorrow, let me know how you get on.'

'I will, lovely,' Laurie said. He ran his hand through his hair. 'I just want the whole damn thing to be over.'

Zac and I went out into the hall. I collected my bag from his bedroom, smiling to myself when I saw the unmade bed.

'I've never known Laurie so tense before an audition,' Zac said.

'Auditioning is always stressful,' I said. 'Sometimes – especially when I've just been cut – I wonder why I put myself through it. Then I see a show like *Warrior Queen*.'

Zac glanced along the hallway. 'I should get back to Laurie –'

'Yes, do,' I said. He kissed me lightly on my mouth, stepped away from me, and opened the front door. I smiled at him, and went out. By the time I was reaching for the button to call the lift, he'd already closed the door to his flat, and gone back to his friend. I told myself that his attention was understandably focused on Laurie's audition, and tried not to mind that he'd said nothing about the next time we'd see each other or even that he would call me.

***

Zac returned his empty coffee cup to the tray which the housekeeper had left on the low glass table. 'It's time I made a move,' he said.

'Can't you stay a little longer?' Rosalind said.

'I have work tonight,' Zac said.

'Cancel,' Rosalind said. 'Ring in sick.'

'Not going to happen,' Zac said, getting to his feet.

Rosalind pouted, but she stood up also, turning her head as the sound of laughter drifted in from the street. She walked over to the open window, her high-heeled sandals loud on the highly polished wooden floor. Zac joined her, and they both looked out over the communal gardens where a young couple were chasing a toddler around the immaculately mown grass. The sky above the square of white Georgian townhouses was streaked with red and the setting sun suffused the scene with golden light.

Zac studied Rosalind as she watched the young family in the garden, her auburn hair shining in the evening sunlight as though it was aflame. His glance travelled admiringly over her trim figure, which her tight, pale yellow dress did nothing to conceal. She may be thirty-eight, he thought, but she certainly doesn't look it.

'One thing I like about living here,' Rosalind said, 'is that I can sit in those gardens and nobody bothers me for an autograph. My neighbours are so polite. Maybe it's a British thing.'

'Maybe none of them recognise you,' Zac said.

'Unlikely,' Rosalind said.

Zac laughed. 'Ros – I do have to go.'

Rosalind flicked her hair back over her shoulder, and Zac caught the scent of her once-familiar signature perfume.

'It seems wrong for you to be working on such a lovely summer's evening.' she said. 'I have a very difficult scene to shoot tomorrow. I could do with some distraction.'

CHAPTER 15

I was in my bedroom, packing my bag to go to a dance class, when Laurie called my mobile.

'Do you have good news?' I said.

'I don't know,' Laurie said.

'This is not the time for false modesty,' I said.

'I *honestly* don't know,' Laurie said. 'I think the audition went well. The casting team saw all the scenes we rehearsed yesterday, and they seemed pleased. They said they'd call my agent later today.'

'If you were half as fierce as you were yesterday, the part's yours,' I said.

'Julie, you are the sweetest girl,' Laurie said. 'I do have one bit of good news, though. I met the actresses up for the roles of Desdemona, Emilia and Bianca – and none of them were Nadia. Anyway, I'm going to ring off now. I'm going to find a bar, order myself a beer, and wait for my agent to call. If I don't get the part, I'm going to get very, very drunk. And if I do get the part, I shall take great pleasure in coming into Zone and handing in my notice.' He rang off.

I'd just about finished packing my dance bag when Alexa arrived home from the call centre. 'Going somewhere nice, Julie?' she said, coming into my room and indicating my bag.

'Only to class,' I said to her. 'Do you want to come too?'

'I don't have time,' Alexa said. 'I'm going to the theatre with Michael tonight. He's got comp tickets for *Scheherazade* from some guy he knows who's in the ensemble. Suzanne's waitressing, so he asked me to go with him. It was all very last minute.' She spoke with what seemed to me exaggerated casualness, gratuitous detail, and an avoidance of eye contact. Alarm bells went off in my head.

Choosing my words with care, I said, 'Has Michael told Suzanne that you and he are going to see a show together?'

'I have absolutely no idea,' Alexa said.

'Do think she'd be OK with you spending time alone with Michael?'

Alexa groaned. 'Haven't we had this conversation? Several times.'

'You may see Michael as a *friend*,' I said, 'but does he see you the same way?'

Alexa did look a little taken aback, but after a moment she said, 'Don't worry, Julie. If Mike's thinking of taking our friendship to another level, he'll soon realise it's not going to happen.'

***

Having attended a ballet class, I was in the changing rooms at Limelight, my favourite of all the London dance studios, untying the ribbons on my point shoes, when Laurie called me again.

'I've got it,' he said, by way of greeting, causing me to shriek with delight.

'Oh, Laurie, I am *so* pleased for you,' I said. 'Your West End debut. Many, many congratulations.'

'Thank you,' Laurie said.

'I was sure you'd get cast,' I said. 'You're going to be brilliant as Iago.'

'You know what, Julie,' Laurie said, 'I think you may be my greatest fan.'

'Oh, I am,' I said. 'You will autograph one of my flyers tonight, won't you? Now you're a star, I can sell it on the internet.'

Laurie laughed. 'I need to make some more calls. I want my family to hear it from me, before tomorrow's press release. I'll see you at Zone.' He'd not long rung off, when my phone announced the arrival of a text: *Great news from Laurie. I'm meeting him in the Syrinx Bar in Seven Dials after work to celebrate. See you there? Zac.* It wasn't the most romantic message I'd ever had from a guy, and it wasn't arranging another date, but it still made me smile. I texted back a very definite: *Yes*.

Laurie didn't turn up at the club and announce that he'd landed a lead in the West End over the sound system, but he told Cora and one or two other people, and by the meal break everyone on the promotions team and most of the bar and restaurant staff seemed to know as well.

'Just give me a few seconds to envy you with a passion,' Harry said to him, between mouthfuls of the Thai green curry that was our meal that night. 'OK. Done that. Now I can congratulate you. Well done, mate.'

'I'm so happy for you, Laurie,' Cora said. Her eyes brimmed with tears. Bemused, Laurie handed her a tissue.

'Sorry,' Cora said, 'I always cry when I'm happy.'

Ben smiled benignly and clapped Laurie on the back.

Until then Nadia had been listening to the conversation stony-faced, but now she said, 'I, too, have had an extremely gratifying day. You know I've been flat-hunting?'

I thought, why am I not surprised that Nadia can't bring herself to offer Laurie one word of congratulation?

'I simply had to find somewhere new to live,' Nadia went on. 'My flatmate is so irritating. Totally self-centred.'

'That can be such a problem,' I said.

'Then today,' Nadia said, 'I got a phone call from none other than Cassie Clarke. I met her when I had a small, but very significant, role in her show's Christmas Special, and we've kept in touch. She happened to have a spare room in her house, so I'm moving in next week. Isn't that fabulous?'

'Who's Cassie Clarke?' Harry said.

'Honestly, Harry,' Cora said. 'Have you never watched *Princess Snowdrop*? She plays the title role.'

'Oh, *that* Cassie Clarke,' Harry said. 'Of course I watch the show. Every week without fail. Saturday mornings just wouldn't be the same without Snowdrop. Although it's Snowdrop's friend Princess Poppy I like best. Hey, Nadia, if Poppy drops by your place, would you get me her autograph? Or her mobile number?'

'I suppose I might be able to.' Nadia looked at her watch. 'I need to run up to the office and give Austin my new address. Ben – Ben! Take your earphones out! You go and start flyering, and I'll meet up with you in Leicester Square, in front of the statue of the Bard. OK?' Ben smiled and nodded. As he'd already been nodding his head in time to whatever music was on his phone, the chances of his making the rendezvous were not great.

'Eat your heart out, Laurie,' Harry said, when Nadia had gone. 'You may have the lead in a West End play, but Nadia has a new best friend. I wonder if she really will try and get me Poppy's phone number.'

'I'm sure she will,' Laurie said. 'You do realise she believed every word you said? She doesn't understand sarcasm.'

'Did you think I was being sarcastic?' Harry said.

'Harry, please tell me you're not really a fan of *Princess Snowdrop*,' I said.

'You do seem to know an awful lot about the show,' Cora said.

'I know way too much about *Princess Snowdrop*,' Harry said. 'I have a six-year-old niece, and whenever I babysit, putting on a *Snowdrop* DVD is the only way I can get the little demon-child to sit down and be quiet. Without *Snowdrop*, I simply couldn't cope.'

'So what's the show about?' Laurie said, genuinely curious.

'Oh, it's ghastly,' Harry said. 'Unicorns. Mermaids. Talking animals. But that Princess Poppy sure is hot.'

CHAPTER 16

Alexa was singing 'Bright New Dawn' from *Two Cities,* her pure soprano voice carrying from the living room into mine. I opened my eyes. My alarm clock showed me it was not even eight o'clock. The song, reputedly Joe Garcia's favourite, was at least appropriate, if not exactly welcome at that hour. Next to me, in my bed, Zac stirred in his sleep and muttered a few words in Spanish.

After work, Laurie and I had gone straight to the Syrinx Bar in Seven Dials. Once his shift pulling pints had finished, Zac had joined us, and bought a bottle of champagne. When the Syrinx closed, we went to another bar that stayed open later, and then we'd gone on to a club somewhere near Trafalgar Square. I'd managed to drag Laurie out onto the dance floor for one short track, although he'd insisted – repeatedly – it was only happening because he'd had too much to drink. It was after four a.m. when we left the club. My soon-to-be-ex-flyering-partner was still telling us that he'd had the best night ever, and that we were the best friends a guy could have, when our cab had dropped him off at the terraced house in Kentish Town where he rented a room. I wasn't quite sure if it was me or Zac who'd suggested we stay at my place because it was nearer than his, but I did remember that I'd drifted off to sleep in his arms after the most amazing sex.

Alexa started to sing the title track from Obsidian's *The Howling* easily as well as Raven sang it, although, obviously, in a higher key.

126

Zac half-opened his eyes. 'Is that your flatmate singing?'

'Yes, that's Alexa,' I said. 'Whatever else she does or doesn't do, she practises her singing every day without fail. Not usually this early.'

'She's good,' Zac said. 'But not as good as you.'

'Not that you're biased or anything,' I said, 'because I'm lying next to you naked in bed.'

'No, I'm being honest.' Zac said. 'Like I am with Laurie.' We dozed a while longer. Alexa continued to sing. She appeared to be working through her entire repertoire. I realised I was not going to get back to sleep.

'Would you like some breakfast?' I said to Zac. 'There might not be anything edible in the flat, but there's a supermarket on the corner. I can run out and get us something.'

'Just coffee would be fine,' Zac said.

'I'll be back,' I said, getting out of bed and reaching for my dressing gown. 'Unless you want to get up and meet Alexa?'

'I'll come and meet her,' Zac said. I waited while he found his jeans and his shirt, then led him into the living room.

'Julie!' Alexa started when she saw us. 'I didn't know you were home. Or that you had company.'

'Alexa, this is Zac,' I said, 'Zac – Alexa.' They exchanged the usual pleasantries.

'So how come you're up so early?' I said.

'There's no time to lose,' Alexa said. 'I – we – have to choose an audition song.'

'What for?' I said.

127

Alexa was smiling now. 'Oh, it's nothing really. Nothing important. Only a new musical by Joe Garcia opening at the Aphra Behn Theatre in August.'

I gasped.

'There's an advert on the *In the Wings* website.' Alexa gestured towards her laptop, which was on the dining table. 'See for yourself.'

In two strides I was across the room and reading the advert aloud. '"Garcia Productions are holding open auditions for *La Pasionaria,* a new musical, directed by Joe Garcia."' I looked up from the screen. 'What does *La Pasionaria* mean? Do either of you know?'

'It's Spanish,' Zac said. 'It means "The Passionflower". It was the name given to a heroine of the Republican side in the Spanish Civil War.'

'Do you know when that was?' Alexa said.

'1936 to 1939,' Zac said.

'So we're thinking this musical could be set during a war in Spain in the 1930s?' I said.

Alexa shrugged.

Turning back to the casting site, I read, '"Female dancers/singers, 5' 2" to 5' 10". Strong technique in ballet, contemporary, and jazz. Please wear close-fitting dance clothes and bring skirts and heels. Ability to belt up to E. Male dancers/singers 5' 9" to 6' 3". Strong technique etc etc. All voice types required."'

Zac came and stood beside me. 'May I see the advert, Julie?' I positioned the laptop so he could see the screen.

'The auditions are next week at Danspace Studios,' Alexa said. 'Registration nine a.m. Boys on Wednesday, girls on Thursday, recalls on Friday.'

'Do you think Joe Garcia will be there at the first round?' I said. 'It would be so amazing to perform for him.'

'Isn't he is supposed to be very hands on?' Alexa said.

Zac was still studying the advert. 'I knew Joe was working on a new musical – I'd heard the rumours – but I'd no idea he'd be holding auditions so soon.'

'Let's have a look at the Garcia Productions website,' Alexa said. She and I watched over Zac's shoulder as he brought up the official site for Garcia Productions. The first page featured a headshot of Joe Garcia and a brief biog.

'He's hot – for an old guy,' Alexa said. 'If he were twenty years younger, I'd so go there.'

'Focus, Alexa,' I said. 'Is there anything about the auditions?' Zac scrolled down. A slightly expanded version of the advert we'd already seen appeared on screen, informing us that Joe Garcia had written his new musical's lyrics, and naming his collaborators who'd written the music and the book.

'"*La Pasionaria*,"' Alexa read. '"A love story based on real events that took place during the Spanish Civil War."'

'So we were right about the background to this musical,' I said, 'but we still don't know how many boys or girls they're looking for.'

'Or if the auditions are for parts or just the ensemble,' Alexa said. Then she gasped. 'Oh my goodness, is that the time? I'm way behind schedule. I have another audition today, a recall for that TV series I told you about, Julie. Not that I'm desperate to audition for anyone else when Joe Garcia is casting, but I'd feel pretty stupid if I didn't go to this recall, and then got cut first –'

'Don't say it,' I said. 'Don't even think it.'

'I'm just being realistic,' Alexa said. 'Anyway, I need to get going. Lovely to have met you, Zac.'

'Likewise,' Zac said.

'Good luck, Alexa,' I said, as she hurried out of the room, and clattered along the landing.

Zac said, 'Your flatmate seems nice.'

'She's my best friend,' I said. 'Most people who share flats fall out from time to time, but we never have.' I yawned, suddenly very aware that I'd only had a few hours' sleep. 'I could do with that coffee I never made you.'

'I also have an urgent need for coffee,' Zac said. 'Then I'll head off home.'

We went to the kitchen and Zac stood in the doorway, leaning against the frame, while I made the drinks.

He said, 'What are you planning to sing for Joe Garcia?'

'I'm not sure,' I said, passing him a steaming mug. 'I'd like to sing 'You Are Mine' from *Warrior Queen,* but I'd have to work on it. I'll need to buy the sheet music – and book some singing lessons.'

'I've got the sheet music for *Warrior Queen*,' Zac said. 'Why don't you come over to my place tomorrow, and I'll play 'You Are Mine' on the piano? You can't know if it'd be any good as an audition song until you've sung it with an accompanist.'

'Oh, would you?' I said. 'I'd really appreciate it.'

'It's always a pleasure for me to play Joe's music,' Zac said, and silenced my thanks with a kiss.

***

130

The following morning found me standing centre stage in Zac's living room, while he sat at the piano with the sheet music for 'You Are Mine' in front of him, his fingers idling over the keys.

'So how are we going to do this?' he said.

'How do you mean?' I said.

'Well, do you want to sing the song through straight away,' Zac said, 'or shall I play it for you first?'

'Could you play it first?' I said.

'Julie, how well do you read music?'

'I can follow a melody if someone's playing,' I said. 'I can't sight-read a score.'

'Come and stand next to me,' he said. 'Follow the music as I play it.'

I did as he said, and found that I liked the tune even more than when first I'd heard it in the theatre.

'I'll play it again,' Zac said. 'You sing.' He played the song a second time and I sang the lyrics. After I'd sung the final chorus, he turned his head to face me, looking up at me thoughtfully, but making no comment.

'So what do you think?' I said. 'Tell me honestly. Should I sing it for Joe Garcia?'

Zac's dark eyes locked on mine. 'That song suits your voice,' he said. 'You could audition for Joe Garcia tomorrow and have a good chance of being cast.'

'But?' I said.

'You sang the song well,' he said, 'but I can help you sing it better. I'll coach you… if you'd like me to.'

'Oh, Zac, that'd be great,' I said.

He continued to hold my gaze. 'You won't get upset or angry with me if I tell you that you've failed to hit a high note?'

'I want to get cast in Joe Garcia's new musical,' I said. 'I would really appreciate help with my audition song.' I smiled. 'And I'm good at compartmentalising. Even if you tell me I'm singing flat, I'll still sleep with you.'

'In that case,' Zac said, 'you can sing the song again.'

I did sing 'You Are Mine' again, several more times, and each time Zac made a couple of suggestions – I was breathing in the wrong place, I needed to hold a note half a beat longer – that made me think I still had work to do on the song, but also that I was perfectly capable of doing it.

'You are *so* good at this,' I said, when he'd suggested a change of phrasing that really brought out the emotion in the words of the last verse. 'You're seeing and hearing things in the music that I don't. Not until you point them out to me.'

'It's just the way I was brought up,' Zac said. 'I knew how to read a score before I ever read a novel.'

After an hour or so he told me we'd done enough for now.

'We've got a week 'til the auditions,' he said. 'I think the best way for me to help you with this song is if we work on it together for a short time each day. If that's OK with you?'

'Absolutely,' I said, quickly. The thought of seeing Zac Diaz every day made my stomach clench for reasons that had little to do with his musicality. 'What are you going to sing for the audition?'

'I've not decided yet,' Zac said. 'Obviously one of Joe's songs. Playing for you has made me wonder about doing something from *Warrior Queen* too. Maybe 'Brothers In Arms'. Will you hear me sing it and tell me what you think? By the way, I should warn you that if you tell me my singing sucks, I won't have sex with you ever again.'

'I would love to listen to you sing that song,' I said. 'If you sing it badly, I just won't tell you.'

He found the music, and started to play and sing, and although he was just sitting at a piano in his own flat, his voice was so beautiful, and the way he sang so moving, that my eyes filled with tears. I blinked them away.

'What do you reckon?' Zac said, as the final chord faded.

I said, 'You should definitely sing that song for Joe Garcia.'

'Perhaps I will,' he said. 'I'll see how I feel when I've practised it a few more times. I may sing something a little more upbeat.' He closed the piano and got to his feet. 'You did well today, Julie. Same time tomorrow suit you?'

'Absolutely. Thanks, Zac.' I followed him out into the hall. Evidently, now that my singing lesson was over, he wasn't expecting me to linger at his flat. Which was fine, I told myself, because I really should get myself to a dance class. I picked up my bag from the hall table. I said, 'I'm going straight to Trey Gilbert's jazz class at Limelight. There's not much point in our working on my audition song if I can't get through the dance round.'

Zac paused in the act of opening the front door. 'If you wait while I find some clothes I can dance in,' he said, 'I'll

133

come with you. I'd like to see you dance – other than in a nightclub.'

He went off to find his dance gear, leaving me waiting in the hall. The thought floated into my mind that if I joined him in his bedroom, we'd probably come up with a way we could amuse ourselves for the next few hours that didn't involve dancing. But I reminded myself that an afternoon in his bed, however pleasurable, wasn't going to help either of us to get cast in a musical.

***

'I used to come to Limelight all time before I went to New York,' Zac said, as we joined the queue to get into the studios. 'I don't remember it ever being this crowded.'

A girl queuing behind us said, 'It's the Joe Garcia effect. When he's casting, every dance class in London is packed.'

Once inside the studios, Zac went off to the male changing rooms and I went to the girls'. Having changed into a crop-top and leggings, I went upstairs to Studio 5 where Trey Gilbert taught, and paid him his fee for the class. The studio only held forty people, and there were nearly that many dancers there before me. I made a mental note to arrive early at any class I wanted to attend between now and the *La Pasionaria* auditions. Spotting Michael and Suzanne sitting on the floor amongst the throng, I dumped my bag at the side of the room, and went to join them.

'We thought we might see you here,' Michael said. 'Is Alexa not with you?'

'Not today,' I said. 'I came to Limelight with a guy you don't know. His name's Zac. He'll be up here in a bit.'

'Oh, yeah,' Michael said. 'Alexa told me you had a new man in your life.'

Michael's apparent inability to utter a sentence without mentioning Alexa brought my doubts about the nature of their friendship flooding back. Then it struck me that if he did have ambitions to be more than a friend to her, he'd hardly be talking about her in front of his girlfriend. I decided I had a nasty, suspicious mind.

Just then, Zac, now wearing a sleeveless T-shirt and low slung, cut-off trackies, strolled into the studio. Ignoring the flutters in my stomach brought on simply by seeing him, I waved to attract his attention. He waved back, and went to pay Trey for the class.

'Zac? Zac Diaz?' Trey's voice, loud enough to direct dancers on stage from the back of the stalls, echoed round Studio 5. 'Good to see you, man.' Every head in the room turned in Zac and Trey's direction. Zac said something to Trey, too quietly for the rest of us to hear, and shook his hand. Then he walked over to where I was sitting and sat down next to me. I introduced him to Michael and Suzanne.

'Do you know Trey?' Michael asked him.

'Only through coming to his class,' Zac said. 'And the last time I saw him was over three years ago. I'm surprised he remembered me.'

As always, when Trey announced that the class was about to begin, I went and stood in the second row of dancers, the front row being unofficially reserved for West End Wendys – who were so dedicated to their craft that they took jazz before rushing off to the theatre in time for the half – and for a handful of well-known commercial dancers who appeared when they weren't out of town on some fabulous gig. Zac stood on my left, while Michael and Suzanne were on my right.

'Zac,' Trey said, 'would you come forward into the front row, please.' This was not an entirely unknown event – Trey did occasionally move people from one line to another – but it was rare enough that it created a stir of interest throughout the class. Zac stepped forward, the music from Limelight's state of the art sound system swelled through the studio, and Trey took us through a warm up before teaching us several short, but challenging, routines. Seeing Zac dance, it wasn't hard to work out why Trey remembered him. He was good. Exceptionally good.

'Alexa never told me that Zac could dance like that,' Michael whispered to me, while Trey demonstrated the final routine.

'Alexa didn't know,' I said. 'I didn't know.'

'Please tell me he isn't a brilliant singer as well,' Michael said.

I smiled. 'He has an amazing voice.'

'And he's one of my rivals for the male roles in *La Pasionaria*?' Michael said.

'Yep,' I said.

'Oh, great,' Michael said, turning his attention – with renewed focus – back to Trey.

***

Zac strode to his bar job through a crowded Soho, side-stepping a party of tanned American tourists with West Coast accents that vividly reminded him of his time in LA, accepting a copy of a free newspaper from a street vendor, and declining the services of a rickshaw. His thoughts were all of Julie Farrell, her pure soprano as she'd sung to him that morning, the reflection of her toned body in the wall-mirrors in the studio that afternoon as she'd danced. And then there was her acting with Laurie... She had it all – the triple threat. Zac became aware of an unfamiliar excitement within him. This must be what the great Joe Garcia feels, he thought, when an unknown and unemployed musical theatre actor turns up at one of his auditions and their raw talent simply blows him away.

'You're such a fierce dancer,' Julie had said to him after Trey's class, as he'd walked her to Club Zone.

'As are you,' he'd said. 'I was watching you in the mirrors. You were one of the best dancers in the studio today.'

Her eyes had widened. 'Did you really think that?'

'I wouldn't say it if I didn't think it, *cariño*,' he'd said, kissing her before leaving her at the entrance to the club.

She has no idea how talented she is, Zac thought, as he paused at a kerb for a taxi to pass. Not that talent on its own was any guarantee of a successful acting career. That took hard work, honing and refining techniques learned in training – and luck, as well. Zac reminded himself that there would be literally hundreds of talented musical theatre actors looking to get cast in *La Pasionaria*, and many of them would be far more experienced performers

CHAPTER 17

'Cora Woodville, one of the girls on the promo team, has invited me to a house party tomorrow,' I said to Zac, as we were lying spooned together in his bed, his breath warm on the back of my neck. I hesitated – it would, after all be the first time we'd gone to any sort of social gathering together – before adding, 'I was wondering if you'd like to come with me?'

'Sure,' he said, drowsily.

Over the last few days, he and I had fallen into a routine of his coaching me on my audition song before we both went to Limelight, where every dance class we attended was packed, before we went our separate ways for the rest of the day. Tonight, Saturday, we'd met up after we'd finished work, and gone back to his flat. He'd opened a bottle of wine, and I'd sat back on the sofa while he played the piano, and then he'd taken me to his bed and made love to me. It was only now that I was lying in his arms, both of us already half-asleep, that I'd thought to mention Cora's last-minute invitation.

I said, 'Laurie'll be there. And Harry Vincent.'

'Harry?' Zac said. 'Oh, yeah, he was at RoCoDa.'

'Nadia Pincher may also be at the party,' I said.

Zac's body stiffened. 'Do you count Nadia among your friends?' he said, 'Because I have to tell you that she was the only student in my year that I didn't like.'

'Oh, Nadia's no friend of mine,' I said, rolling over in the bed to face him.' None of the promotions team can stand her, but Cora, who is an exceptionally nice girl, would have felt bad leaving her off the guest list. And from the sound of it, there are so many people coming to this party that it'll be easy to avoid anyone we don't want to talk to.'

'Good to know,' Zac said. 'Although, as I'm not in a position to further Nadia's career, I doubt she'll be particularly anxious to renew my acquaintance.' He brushed my forehead with a kiss, and shut his eyes. I turned back onto my side, and he draped an arm over me, pulling me close to him, curling his body around mine.

He's agreed to accompany me to my friend's party, I thought. Surely he is at least beginning to think of us as a couple?

Having pushed myself hard for the last few days, I wanted to give my body a rest, so on Sunday morning I just did a bit of stretching. Zac heard my song once and said I was sounding good, and that I should give my voice a rest as well. After an exchange of texts, Laurie joined us for a leisurely lunch, Zac's cooking all the more delicious for being eaten outside on the balcony. Lunch over, I left the guys talking while I went to get ready to go out. Knowing the previous night that I'd be staying at Zac's, I'd packed an overnight bag, and fortunately it included a top that was suitable to wear to a house-party. Alone in Zac's bedroom, I re-did my make-up and re-straightened my hair, and when I surveyed the result of my handiwork in the full-length mirror, I thought I looked good. I covered myself liberally with perfume, and went back to the men.

I was half-way across the open-plan main room, when Zac and Laurie's voices reached me from the balcony. I heard Zac say my name. Laurie said something in reply that I didn't catch. Although the floor to ceiling glass doors were open, the curtains were partially closed, and I knew that Zac and Laurie couldn't see me. I also knew that I should keep walking, go out onto the balcony and let them know I was there. But I didn't. I stood still and listened.

Laurie said, 'She mentioned that you're coaching her for the *La Pasionaria* auditions.'

Zac said, 'Do you two often discuss me while you're out littering Theatreland with flyers.'

'We've hardly talked about you at all this week,' Laurie said. 'We're far too self-centred.'

Zac laughed.

There was a pause and then Laurie said, 'Have you told her?'

'Told her what?' Zac said.

'That thing we never speak about,' Laurie said.

What thing? I thought.

'Oh, that,' Zac said. 'No. There's no reason for me to tell her.'

'She's going to think it very strange if someone else tells her before you do,' Laurie said.

What hasn't Zac told me? I thought. And do I need to worry about it?

'It's hardly likely that anyone else will mention it,' Zac said. 'So few people know.'

'We've gone over this often enough,' Laurie said, 'and I do realise that you have your reasons for not telling just anybody, but keeping it from Julie seems wrong.'

'I don't see why,' Zac said.

'Apart from anything else,' Laurie said, 'it puts me in a very uncomfortable position.'

'I'm not asking you to lie for me,' Zac said.

'Just as well,' Laurie said, 'because I won't. Not if she asks me directly.'

'OK, let's leave it at that,' Zac said.

Maybe, if I'd known him a while longer, I'd have gone out onto the balcony and simply asked Zac what he and Laurie were talking about. At that moment, I just couldn't. I was disturbed to know that he was keeping something from me, but our relationship – if it could even be called that – was still very new, and I didn't want to cause any awkwardness between us, or appear clingy. Besides which, however irrational, I felt guilty for listening to a conversation that I was obviously not meant to hear. I retraced my footsteps across the main room, opened and slammed shut the door, and walked heavily towards the balcony, so that Zac and Laurie couldn't fail to be aware of my approach.

'Hi, guys,' I said. The smile that lit up Zac's face when he saw me made me think that whatever it was he hadn't told me, it couldn't be anything too terrible. Not when he looked at me the way he was looking at me now. Resolving to put the unnerving conversation out of my mind, at least for the rest of the evening, I smiled back, and we headed out to the party.

Cora lived in a rented house in Tooting with four other actors whose preferred day for socialising was Sunday, as they all worked Saturday nights. They'd only decided to hold a party a couple of day before, but with a flurry of posts on social media, they'd managed to invite almost everyone they knew. Although Zac, Laurie and I arrived unfashionably early, we found the party already spilling out of the house and into the garden where an expanse of lawn, surrounded by greenery, led to a thicket of trees and bushes. Cora's boyfriend, who was training to be a set designer, had decorated the foliage with Chinese lanterns that flickered off and on again according to some schedule of their own devising. There was beer and wine – lots of it – loud music, and dancing in a room that had been cleared of furniture. Nearly everyone seemed to be a performer of one sort or another, or they worked backstage in the theatre, or in TV or film. I had a very interesting talk with an actor who'd taken his own show to the Edinburgh festival, and with a singer who was trying to get a record deal. All of Club Zone's promotions team turned up, including Nadia. She arrived with a thin, geeky-looking boy, who she proceeded to ignore for the rest of the night.

Towards midnight, the party began to quieten down. Zac got into an intense conversation with Harry about a student play they'd both been in when they were at RoCoDa. I left them to it and drifted out into the garden where people were now sprawled on the grass. Seeing Laurie lying on his back gazing up at the night sky, I went and flopped down beside him. He passed me the bottle of wine he was holding, and I took a swig.

'Are you drunk enough to dance with me?' I said.

'I am nowhere near drunk enough to dance with anybody,' Laurie said. He sat up and held out his hand for the wine. I drank some more and passed it back to him. A few feet away Nadia was sitting on the grass, flirting outrageously with an extremely good-looking man of about thirty, who was vaguely familiar to me, although for a moment, I couldn't think why. I'd just recognised him as an actor who'd recently been cast in a soap – his face had been all over the media – when the pair of them stood up and wandered down to the bottom of the garden, where they were hidden from view among the bushes and shadows.

'That girl is a piece of work,' Laurie said. 'I feel really bad for her boyfriend.'

'You mean she's actually dating the guy she came here with?' I said. 'What does he do?'

'He's some sort of financial advisor,' Laurie said to me. 'He's a friend of Nadia's old flatmate, and they hooked up when he offered to do her tax return. It saves her having to do it herself or hire an accountant. His name's Phillip. He's never known anyone like Nadia, and he'd do anything for her.'

'And you know all this how?' I said.

'I met Phillip in the kitchen,' Laurie said. 'Nadia had sent him to fetch her a drink, and we got talking. It's strange, but people I meet at parties are always telling me about their love lives. I seem to invite confidences from total strangers. If I wasn't an actor, I'd be a therapist.'

'I can't help thinking that Phillip doesn't seem like the sort of man that Nadia would date,' I said.

'Oh, I don't know,' Laurie said. 'She probably likes having someone around who worships her even when she treats him like shite.'

A tall figure came out of the house, looked round the garden, and began to walk towards us over the grass.

'Toby!' I said, as he reached us, and I could make out his face in the dim light.

'Hey, Julie,' he said.

144

'This is Laurie,' I said. 'He has wine. Come and talk to us.' Toby sat down, and Laurie passed him the bottle.

'I didn't know you were here,' I said. 'Where've you been hiding all night?'

'I've only just got here,' Toby said. 'I had a singing gig tonight, hence the late arrival, but I promised Cora I'd show up at some point.'

'How do you know her?' I said.

'She and I did panto together a couple of years ago,' Toby said. 'What about you?'

'Laurie and I work with her at Club Zone,' I said. 'Although Laurie's only got a couple more weeks to go before he starts rehearsals for a West End play.'

'I knew you had to be an actor,' Toby said to Laurie. 'We've not met before, but your face is ever so familiar. What might I have seen you in?'

'Well, I've played some extremely important and iconic roles on TV,' Laurie said. 'I'm particularly proud of my performance as Man with Knife in Head in *Law of the Land*. You probably recognise me from my blood-covered close-up.'

Toby laughed. 'That must be it.'

I said, 'I assume you're going to the *La Pasionaria* auditions, Toby?' We talked about the auditions for Joe Garcia's new musical, and then moved on to our mutual acquaintances. *Pride and Prejudice,* Toby told me, was going really well for Jonas. We watched with interest as Nadia and the soap actor reappeared from the bushes and took separate routes back to the house.

'What do you reckon?' Laurie said. 'Did the earth move?'

'Neither of them looked like it did,' Toby said.

Zac came out into the garden and crouched down next to me. 'Is it OK with you if I call us a cab?' he said. 'It looks like a lot of people are planning on crashing here, but I'd rather we went back to my place.'

'Me too,' I said, with feeling. Stay all night at a house party or sleep in Zac's bed? Let me think about that.

'Do you want to come with us, Laurie?' Zac said. 'It'll take you hours to get back to your place at this time of night. You're welcome to stay at mine if you want.'

Laurie shook his head. 'I'll stay here.'

'Are you sure?' Zac said. 'I have a spare bed at my place. You'll be lucky to grab a sofa here. You'll probably end up on the floor.'

'I'll be fine here, mate,' Laurie said. 'You should go now.'

'See you, then,' Zac said.

''Night,' I said. We went back into the house and said goodbye to Cora and her boyfriend, who were with a group of people in the kitchen, drinking the last of the wine, while one of Cora's housemates sat on the kitchen table and played a guitar. By the time we left the house, our cab was already outside.

'Was I very cruel to Laurie?' Zac said to me, when we were in our seats, and the cab was speeding across London.

'What do you mean?' I said.

'Teasing him about his wanting to stay at Cora's,' Zac said.

'Were you teasing him?'

Zac raised his eyebrows. 'Didn't you notice the way he was looking at that other guy you were talking to?'

'You mean Laurie's interested in Toby?' I said. 'Ooh – it'd be so great if they got together. I'm going to call Laurie first thing to find out what happened.'

'Knowing Laurie,' Zac said, 'if *anything happens,* you won't need to phone him to hear about it. He'll most likely phone everyone in his address book.'

CHAPTER 18

On Monday morning, Zac and I were just about to leave his flat to go to Limelight, when his phone rang.

'It's Laurie,' Zac said, 'I told you he'd call… Hey, Laurie… Yes, I did have a good time at Cora's… Yes, Julie's here with me… Hold on, I'm going to put you on speaker.' He winked at me. 'So what time did you leave the party? Did many people stay 'til morning?'

'Did Toby stay 'til morning?' I said.

'He did,' Laurie said.

'And?' I said.

'And what?' Laurie said.

'Come on, Laurie,' Zac said. 'Last night, you couldn't take your eyes off him.'

'Was I that obvious?' Laurie said. 'I'm such a tart.'

'What happened after Zac and I left?' I said.

'Nothing *happened*,' Laurie said. 'Unlike our dear friend Nadia, I don't go in for very public al fresco seductions.'

'But you are seeing him again?' I said.

'Well, it's difficult,' Laurie said. 'I'm going to be tied up in rehearsals very soon, and he's got some audition coming up. I think he said it was for a new musical by Joe… Joe something… I forget the name.'

'Laurie, behave,' Zac said. 'Tell us when you're seeing him.'

'We're meeting up for a lunchtime drink next Thursday.' From the tone of Laurie's voice, I knew he was smiling.

148

'Good for you,' I said.

Zac said, 'Laurie, I'm really pleased your love life's looking up, and I'll talk to you later, but right now I'm going to cut you off. Julie and I have a jazz class to get to'

'I'll see you at Zone,' I said.

'Yeah, I'll see you later,' Laurie said. 'Hey, if Toby's in your class today, perhaps you could just happen to mention how wonderful I am.'

'Enough, Laurie,' Zac said, and ended the call.

Once again, Limelight was very crowded, but I got a lot out of Trey's class, and I felt that I'd danced well, even though he didn't promote me into the front row. Zac danced superbly, and I overheard several people commenting on what a fabulous dancer he was. Toby wasn't in the class, so unfortunately I couldn't put in a good word for Laurie.

'Shall we grab a coffee and a sandwich in the canteen?' Zac said to me, after the class.

'I would if I could,' I said, 'but I've only just got enough time to get home, changed and back into central London in time for my shift.'

'Right.' He looked at me thoughtfully. 'Julie, would you like to stay at my place for the next few days?'

A delicious warmth stole through me. 'Well, you do have a piano,' I said. 'It does make practising my audition song so much easier.'

'Obviously there's no other reason for you stay over,' Zac said, with a grin, 'but with the audition so close, it occurs to me that you can do without trekking backwards and forwards between my place and yours each day for me to play for you.'

'But do you want me with you the night before the boys' audition?' I said. 'I mean, if you'd rather be alone without my distracting you, I understand.'

'That's very considerate of you,' Zac said, 'but I don't think a night of abstinence is going to improve my dancing and singing that much.'

'I'm sure I read somewhere that footballers don't have sex the night before an important match,' I said.

'I'll risk it,' Zac said. 'Do you want to sleep alone at your place the night before the girls' audition?'

'No way,' I said. 'My make-up has to be perfect for Joe Garcia, and your bathroom has great lighting.'

He smiled, but then his face grew serious. 'After today, I'm going to take the rest of the week off work, and I think you should too. Standing around in Leicester Square late at night isn't going to help you kick your legs up past your shoulders the next morning.'

He's right, I thought. 'I'll speak to Austin,' I said. I'd worry about the wages I couldn't afford to lose after the auditions.

***

I'd laid everything I could possibly need for the rest of the week out on my bed, and was wondering if I owned a bag large enough to take it all, when Alexa came into my room.

'I've not heard any more about that TV series,' she said. 'I'm assuming I've not got the part.'

'You don't know that,' I said.

'In any case,' Alexa said, 'all I can think about at the moment is *La Pasionaria*.' She surveyed the dance clothes covering my duvet. 'Having trouble deciding on your audition outfit?'

I shook my head. 'I'm staying at Zac's between now and the auditions. I'll be home at the weekend.'

Alexa arched her eyebrows. 'He must be keen.' Moving aside a neatly folded leotard, she perched on the end of the bed.

'Ye-es,' I said. There had been moments in the last few days when I'd felt that Zac and I were definitely at the start of a *relationship*, and other times when I'd no idea where I stood with him. For all the hours I'd spent singing with him – and in his bed – I didn't know much about his life, what he did or where he went when we weren't together, and I'd not met any of his friends. In many ways I hardly knew him at all. Until then, I'd not given another thought to the strange, disturbing conversation I'd overheard on the day of Cora's party, but now it reared up in my mind. *That thing we never talk about.* I sat down heavily on the bed next to Alexa.

Alexa peered at me closely. 'Is something wrong?'

'I don't know,' I said. 'I need to ask your advice. About Zac'

'Well, I am a whole year older and wiser than you,' Alexa said. 'Ask away.'

'I heard him and Laurie talking…' I outlined what Laurie had said. And what Zac had said in reply.

'So you were eavesdropping,' Alexa said when I had finished. 'I'm shocked!'

'I didn't mean to,' I said. 'I wish I hadn't.'

'This is what happens when a girl hangs around with actors – they're a bad influence.'

'Please take this seriously,' I said. 'There's something that Zac isn't telling me. Do you think I should be worried?'

'That rather depends on what the *something* is,' Alexa said. 'I guess a mad wife in the attic is unlikely?'

'Alexa!' I rolled my eyes.

She struck her hand against her forehead. 'I have it! Zac's a hell of a lot richer than he's letting on – a billionaire – and he needs to be sure that you're not just after his money. Hey, isn't that the plot of a musical? I forget which one.'

'I'm really not finding this funny,' I said, although I was finding it hard not to laugh.

'Sorry, hun,' Alexa said.

'You think I'm being ridiculous, don't you?' I said.

'I think you're obsessing over a half-overheard conversation,' Alexa said, softening her words with a smile. 'You've met a guy you like. He likes you. Enjoy. Stop inventing problems where they don't exist.'

'I expect you're right,' I said. I need to lighten up, I thought. 'Thanks, Alexa. I feel better now I've talked it through with you.'

'You're welcome,' Alexa said. 'I am your best friend, after all.'

***

On Wednesday, the day of the boys' audition, Zac was up and out of bed at six thirty, as soon as his alarm went off.

I sat up, rubbing my eyes. 'Morning,' I said.

'*Buenas diás, cariño,*' Zac said. 'Try to get back to sleep.' He went off to shower and shave. I lay down again, but stayed awake, listening to him moving about the flat. He came back into the bedroom, dressed quickly, and then he lent over me, and kissed me softly.

'I'll see you later,' he said. 'I've left my spare keys on the dining table so you can go in and out of here when you like.'

'Good luck, Zac,' I said. 'Break a leg. And call me as soon as you know if you've got through to the next round.'

He kissed me again. 'However the audition goes, I'll call you before I call anyone else.' After he'd gone out, I rolled over onto his side of the bed, and put my head in the dent in his pillow where his head had been. Then I did go back to sleep.

I surfaced again just after nine. I got up, showered and dressed, and pulled the bed together. Then I went into Zac's kitchen and helped myself to tea and cereal. It was strange being in his flat without him, doing whatever I liked, as though I was his live-in girlfriend and this flat was my home as much as his... I gave myself a firm mental shake. I was *not* going to spend the day fantasising about living in Zac's flat. I finished my breakfast, loaded the dishwasher, and went into the main room to practise my singing.

I'd recorded Zac playing 'You Are Mine' on my phone, but singing to a recording was hardly the same as having him there listening to me, so I only sang the song through once. By then, it was still only half past ten, far too early for Zac to call. The day was really dragging, I thought. I decided to go to Limelight. Not because I felt I needed another dance class to prepare myself for the girls' audition, but just to use up the time.

Dance studio etiquette meant I had to switch my phone off during class, but afterwards, when I switched it back on, there was a text from Zac telling me he'd got through the first dance round. There was also an imaginative suggestion of how we might spend the evening. I texted him back, making it very clear that I was entirely willing to fall in with his plans.

There was no one I knew in class, so I had no excuse to linger at the dance studios. Instead I did some shopping, buying two steaks, some salad and a bottle of Rioja, Zac's favourite wine. The girl on the check-out made a comment about dinner for two, and we exchanged conspiratorial smiles. Then I went back to Zac's and sat out on the balcony. My mother phoned for a chat and when I told her I had an important audition the following day, assured me that she had a really good feeling about this one – 'This is your moment, Julie, I just know it…' – which was more or less what she said every time I told her I was going to an audition, but I appreciated the sentiment. Alexa called and we discussed audition outfits. Then I watched a dire film on Zac's TV. I called Suzanne to ask her if she'd heard anything from Michael. She was waiting for her phone to ring, same as me. Finally, shortly after seven, Zac rang. He'd got a recall, and was on his way home. I'd just enough time to touch up my make-up, smooth my hair, and be sitting elegantly on the sofa, before he let himself in. Jettisoning my elegant pose, I jumped up and kissed him.

'I could get used to being welcomed home like this,' he said, kissing me back.

I could get used to doing the welcoming, I thought. I led him out onto the balcony, made him sit on a wicker chair, and fetched him a glass of Rioja.

'You have to tell me everything about the audition,' I said. 'Absolutely everything.'

'I'll tell you something,' he said. 'Dance calls for musical theatre are a hell of a lot harder than acting auditions.'

'They are?' I said.

'Think about it,' Zac said. 'Acting auditions, you turn up at a set time. You meet the director and you do your monologue, or you read their script, and you have a chat. Then you go home and your agent lets you know if you've got the part or if they want to see you again or whatever. Musical theatre auditions, you queue for hours, you don't even know if you're going to get seen, you dance with a load of other people –'

'But today you got a recall,' I said.

'Yes, I did,' he said.

'So how many boys were there?' I said.

'Over three hundred,' Zac said.

So many, I thought, and there'll probably be even more girls auditioning tomorrow. 'Did you see anyone you know?' I said.

'I saw people *you* know – Michael and Toby. Michael was with a boy called Luke who said he knew you too. They all got recalls.'

'They must be so pleased,' I said. 'Did you get a chance to put in a good word for Laurie with Toby?'

Zac raised his eyebrows. 'I don't know that an audition was the quite the right time or place.'

'Perhaps not,' I said. 'OK. The audition. First round – what did you have to do?'

'It was simple: steps-kicks across the studio, but a harsh cut. You reached the other corner of the room and if you hadn't made the grade, if they didn't call out your number, you had to leave. They kept about a hundred.'

'And then?' I prompted.

'We were taught a jazz routine,' Zac said. 'We danced it in groups of ten. And there was another cut. I reckon about fifty of us got a recall for the next round.'

'Do you remember the routine?' I said. 'Can you show me?'

'Yes, I'll show you,' Zac said, 'but there's no point in your learning it, because there's no guarantee they'll use the same dance for the girls tomorrow.'

I said, 'Was Joe Garcia there?'

Zac laughed. 'I wondered when you'd get around to the most important question of all.'

'Zac! Was he there?'

'Not for the first round,' Zac said. 'But after that, yes, he was there.'

'So what was it like to audition for *Joe Garcia*?' I said. 'Was it weird?'

Zac seemed taken aback. 'How do you mean?

'Well, he's just *so* talented and *so* famous,' I said.

'Oh. Right.' Zac thought for a moment. 'I guess it was a little weird. Mostly, it was like auditioning for anyone else.'

'I can't believe that,' I said.

'He was just sitting there with the rest of the audition panel,' Zac said. 'Oliver Brady was there too.'

'The guy who was his MD for the original production of *Two Cities*?' I said.

'Yes,' Zac said. 'The choreographer is Nathan Nyembe. He's worked on a couple of West End shows, but he's not choreographed for Joe before.' He lifted his glass. 'Aren't you having a drink? One glass of wine won't affect your singing tomorrow.'

'Maybe later,' I said. 'With dinner. I thought I'd make us dinner tonight.'

'I didn't think this day could get any better,' Zac said, 'but it just has. Why don't I show you the dance now, and then we can eat.'

We pushed back the leather sofa so that there was enough room for Zac to dance, and he went through the routine that the boys had been taught at the audition. It was sharp and strong, and very masculine. It did seem unlikely that the girls would be asked to dance the same steps.

'One thing I did notice,' Zac said, 'was that the boys who were getting through all got the style perfectly. Anyone who messed up an arm line got cut.'

'I'll remember that tomorrow,' I said.

While he went off to shower, I went to the kitchen, made a salad, put the meat I'd bought earlier under the grill, and two portions of frozen chips in the oven. I laid the dining table, and even found a candle in one of the kitchen cupboards along with some matches. Zac reappeared, dressed in loose black trousers and a white collarless shirt, his hair still wet from his shower. He looked so hot that my stomach actually lurched, and it was only with a great effort that I managed to keep my distance from him and start dishing up. We carried our plates through to the dining table, he put on some music, and we ate. I restricted myself to half a glass of wine with the meal – after all the work I'd put in, I wasn't about to risk turning up at the *La Pasionaria* auditions with a hangover.

'That was so good,' Zac said to me, when we'd finished.

'The way to a man's heart and all that.' I laughed, but I was delighted that he liked my cooking. I started to gather up the plates and cutlery, but he told me to leave the clearing up for him to do the next day.

'So are you ready for tomorrow?' he said.

I nodded. 'I'd like you to hear my song though.'

Zac got up from the table and sat at the piano. By now neither of us needed the sheet music. I sang 'You Are Mine' once, while he played. Then I waited for his comments. He didn't say anything.

'Zac?' I said. 'Was the song OK?'

He smiled at me. 'Come here.'

I went and sat next to him on the piano stool.

'It was really good,' he said. '*Really* good. I've not got any notes for you. That last verse… I swear you made the hairs on the back of my neck stand on end. I just wish I'd thought to record you the first time you sang that song to me, and then I could record you now, and you'd be able to hear how much your singing has improved in only one week.'

'You're not just saying that?'

'No, I mean it.' He closed the piano. His finger traced the line of my arm. 'You remember that text I sent you this morning?'

'I remember,' I said.

'I meant that as well.' He slid his hand under my skirt and stroked the top of my thigh.

'But Zac,' I said, 'aren't you tired after that stressful audition?'

'Not that tired,' Zac said.

CHAPTER 19

I'd set the alarm for six, but woke up a few minutes before it went off. Today, I thought, I'm auditioning for *La Pasionaria*, a new musical by Joe Garcia. No pressure there. Carefully, trying not to wake him, I lifted Zac's arm from my waist, and slid out of bed. I showered quickly, and was blow-drying my hair, when he came into the bathroom with a cup of tea for me.

'Can I get you anything to eat?' he said.

I wasn't hungry, but I knew I ought to eat something. 'Please. Toast would be good.'

'I'm right on it,' Zac said. 'And I'll make you sandwiches to take with you.' I smiled my thanks.

Having tied back my hair in a ponytail, and done my make-up, I put on a deep red leotard with a low back, and black tights, and went back into the bedroom. Zac was stretched out on the bed flicking through the channels on his wall-mounted TV. He passed me a plate of toast, and foil-wrapped sandwiches.

'What do you think of my audition outfit?' I said, as I ate. 'I've got a matching knee-length skirt that I'll put on when I get there.'

'You look fabulous,' Zac said, sitting up. 'You'd better be out of here pretty soon or I'm not going to be responsible for my actions.'

I laughed, put on a pair of jeans and a zip-up top, and picked up my bag. Zac offered to drive me to the audition and, since he was up anyway and the underground is always a nightmare when you're lugging a bag full of

160

dance shoes, I agreed. He pulled up outside Danspace where, although it was still only seven-fifteen, a queue of about twenty girls turned their heads to watch as I opened the car door. Zac leaned over and kissed the side of my face.

'I'd kiss you properly,' he said, 'but I don't want to mess up the perfect make-up. *Buena suerte,* Julie. Good luck. Break a leg.'

'I'll call you when I have any news,' I said. I got out of the car and went and joined the queue. Zac drove off. About ten minutes later, a crowd of girls appeared from the direction of the station. One of them actually broke into a run so that she would reach the queue first. I wasn't entirely surprised when I saw that it was Alexa.

'Oh my days,' Alexa said, as she joined me. 'The entire underground is jam-packed with musical theatre actresses.' She glanced back at the now-lengthy queue. 'There are so many girls here already.'

'We're near the front though,' I said. 'We'll get seen.'

'Yes, we'll be fine,' Alexa said, chewing her bottom lip.

As always, the waiting was interminable, but Danspace opened at nine o'clock sharp. There was a small table set up just inside the entrance, behind which two girls sat handing out handing out numbers. I was number 24; Alexa was 25. A young guy with a two-way radio, wearing a T-shirt with *Garcia Productions* printed on the front, was waiting to direct the auditionees along a corridor to the spacious studio being used as a holding and warm-up area. A girl in her early twenties, dressed in a T-shirt of the same design and also carrying a radio, was in the studio making sure everyone had enough room to warm up, and telling us to wear jazz shoes for the first round. I was impressed: in my admittedly limited experience, auditionees were very much left to figure it all out for themselves.

'This is all scarily efficient,' Alexa said.

'It is,' I said, shrugging off my jacket. 'I reckon we should warm up straight away. I'm guessing they're going to get started as soon as they can.'

While I was stretching, I looked surreptitiously at the other girls streaming into the holding area. Most of them were in leotard and tights, some in catsuits, and as always, there were a few who didn't understand the meaning of close-fitting dance gear and were in loose, baggy T-shirts. The majority were in their twenties, but there were a few who looked no more than sixteen. There was also one woman who looked to be in her late thirties, although her body was in far better shape than some of the girls who were more than a decade younger. Several girls from our year at LAPA came in and smiled a greeting before beginning their own warm-ups.

The girl with the radio called for our attention. 'Numbers 1 through 40, the audition panel will see you now. Please follow me to Studio 1. Make sure you take all your belongings with you.' Grabbing our bags, Alexa and I got to our feet.

'Are you nervous?' Alexa asked me.

'Not at the moment.' Warmed up now, energised, my body yearned to dance. I felt like a coiled spring. 'You OK?'

'I'm a bit jittery,' Alexa said. 'I just want it to be over.'

'You'll be all right once we start dancing,' I said.

As well as being accessible from a corridor, the studios at Danspace were all linked to each other by double doors. The radio-girl led us through to a light-filled, airy dance studio, larger than the holding area, and directed us to put our bags at the back of the room and line up along one wall. The audition panel of two men – one silver-haired, the other in his mid-thirties, both vaguely familiar from photos in theatre programmes – and one young woman, were already seated behind the long table that seemed to be standard furniture for auditions. To one side, there was a piano where an older woman sat with her hands poised and ready to play. I had just a few seconds to get my bearings and take all this in, before a guy I judged to be in his late twenties, who had been leaning against the piano, walked to the front of the room. He was accompanied by a girl of about the same age. They were both wearing dance gear.

'Good morning, everyone,' the guy said. 'I'm Josh Cavanagh, Assistant Choreographer, and I'm taking the first round of the auditions. All I want you to do is step-kick across the room in time to the music. Kate, our dance captain,' he indicated the girl standing next to him, 'will count you in. If I don't say your number it means you're not right for the show we're casting here today. Please collect your belongings and leave the audition. If I *do* say your number, please wait on the far side of the room. If the audition panel think I've overlooked anyone, they'll let me know. And if I say your number and you don't hear me, I'll send Hannah,' he gestured towards the girl with the radio, 'chasing after you to bring you back.' He nodded at the pianist and music filled the studio. My future career hung on how high I could kick my legs.

and checked the time. 'We were only in there for ten minutes,' I said.

'It seemed a lot longer,' Alexa said.

Over the next few hours, more girls, no more than four or five at a time got through into Studio 2, until there must have been getting on for a hundred of us waiting for the next round. Suzanne was with the sixth group to appear. She was number 237.

'There was still a long queue outside in the street when I arrived' she said, sitting down next to Alexa and me, 'but the boy with the radio said that everyone is going to get seen.'

'I wonder how many girls turned up altogether,' I said.

A girl sitting nearby had overheard. 'A friend of mine is still in the holding area, and she just texted me to say she's number 482,' she informed us.

Alexa, Suzanne and I exchanged glances. It was going to be an extremely long day.

An hour later, the girl with the radio, Hannah, came into Studio 2. 'Listen up, people,' she said. 'The audition panel are taking a fifteen minute break for lunch. Then we're straight into the next round.'

I thought, just three of us from our year at LAPA are still here. Everyone else has been cut.

'You'll be taught a short routine,' Hannah went on. 'Please wear skirts and heels.'

There was a burst of talk and activity as skirts and heels were retrieved from dance bags, along with the packets of crisps and cereal bars that performers take to auditions to give them a quick energy fix. Suddenly ravenous, I brought out my sandwiches, which turned out to be cold chicken and salad.

'You must've been up early to make those,' Alexa said. She was eating a banana.

I smiled. 'Zac made them for me. He got up when I did this morning. Which was great because he drove me here, so I didn't have to get the tube.'

'He got up at the crack of dawn to make you lunch and drive you to an audition?' Alexa said. 'The man must be besotted.'

'Make the most of it,' Suzanne said. 'A few months down the line and he'll be expecting you to iron his shirts.'

Alexa laughed. 'What's ironing?'

Suzanne didn't seem particularly amused by this remark, but before she could make any comment, the doors of the studio opened, to reveal Hannah, now clutching a clipboard along with her radio. The buzz of chatter coming from the two hundred musical theatre actresses who had got through to the next round of the auditions immediately ceased.

'We're ready to go again,' Hannah said. 'When you hear your number, please go through to Studio 1.' She read out a long list of numbers, including mine and Alexa's. Suzanne mouthed 'good luck' as the two of us sprang to our feet and headed off to face the audition panel for the second time.

As soon as I was inside Studio 1, determined that I wouldn't end up hidden at the back, I lost no time in dumping my bag and sprinting to a space in the middle of the first row of dancers. It was only when I was standing in line, waiting for the audition to begin, that I thought to look at the panel. The three people behind the table had been joined by a fourth. Joe Garcia was sitting directly in front of me.

He had to be in his late forties, but his hair was still mostly dark, with just a touch of grey at the temples. The tight black T-shirt he was wearing showed very clearly that even if he was now in his middle years, he wasn't stinting on visits to the gym. Alexa's right, I thought, he is good-looking – for an older guy. Realising that I was blatantly staring, even though he was probably used to musical theatre actresses gazing at him in awe, I quickly glanced away. Get a grip, I told myself. Don't mess up now.

The younger man seated on Joe Garcia's right stood up. 'Good afternoon,' he said. 'I'm Nathan Nyembe, Choreographer. On behalf of the audition panel – our director, Joe Garcia, and his assistant, Jessica Coleman, Oliver Brady, our MD, and myself – I'd like to say how pleased we are to see you all here today.' He smiled. 'But there are a lot of you, and we do want to see everyone we possibly can, so we're going to go straight into the routine. Thank you, Josh, and Kate.'

This is it, I thought. This is when I get to dance for Joe Garcia.

With Josh and Kate demonstrating, Nathan taught us the routine. It was jazz, but it had a Spanish feel to it, with arm lines reminiscent of flamenco, and much stamping of feet and tossing of heads. As soon as I started dancing, I knew that the style really suited me, and as long as I didn't do anything stupid, I had every chance of making a good impression on the panel. We marked the routine through several times, and then danced it twice with the music. I

167

made myself forget that I was auditioning in front of the most powerful and talented man in musical theatre, and focused on dancing the best I possibly could.

The music stopped.

'Everyone stay where you are, please,' Nathan said. All of us auditionees stood absolutely still, our faces frozen into smiles, while the audition panel conferred amongst themselves.

'Number 24?' Joe Garcia said. 'Could I have your name please?' He was looking straight at me. He'd asked my name. *Joe Garcia* had asked my name.

'Julie Farrell,' I said, hoping I didn't sound as starstruck as I felt. Joe Garcia smiled encouragingly. I noticed that his eyes were very dark – almost black, like Zac's.

'Would you turn and stand sideways for me please, Julie,' he said. 'And the other side, please,' he said. 'And to the front again. Thank you.'

I did as he asked, conscious that everyone in the studio was watching me. Sadly, my moment in the spotlight was soon over, as Joe looked away from me almost immediately and nodded at his assistant.

Pushing back her chair, Jessica Cowen stood up. 'Numbers 16, 24, 25, 36, and 41, please go and wait in Studio 2,' she said. 'The other girls in this group, we've seen all we need for today. Thank you very much.' It was only when she called out Alexa's and my numbers that I realised I'd been holding my breath. Resisting the urge to rush up to my best friend and flatmate and give her a high-five, I collected my bag, and went back to Studio 2.

'Yay, you're through!' Suzanne said, as Alexa and I rejoined her. 'Well done. What was the routine like? Has Joe Garcia arrived yet?'

'He has, 'Alexa said. 'And he spoke to Julie.'

'He spoke to you?' Suzanne said. 'What did he say?'

'It wasn't much of a conversation,' I said. 'He asked my name, and to see my profile.'

Suzanne's eyes widened. 'So now he knows who you are.'

'Which can't hurt your chances of being cast,' Alexa said.

'I'll hold on to that thought,' I said, rummaging in my bag for my phone so I could send Zac a text: *Survived another cut xx*. Before I switched my phone off, I read a text from Laurie: ☺ *Toby* ☺. I smiled. Whatever else happened today, my friend's date had obviously gone well.

The afternoon wore on. Groups of girls vanished into the maw of Studio 1, and considerably fewer of them returned to Studio 2. Suzanne, much to her relief, was among the ones that did. When everyone had been seen, those of us who'd made the cut were summoned back in front of the audition panel to dance the routine again. There was more waiting in line while the panel conferred. Then Joe Garcia stood up, holding a single sheet of A4. A hundred girls crossed their fingers, clutched their lucky charms or simply willed him to call out their numbers. Alexa, standing next to me, was practically hyperventilating.

'First of all,' Joe said. 'I'd like to say how impressed the audition panel have been with the standard of dance we've seen here today. I'd also like to thank you all for your

169

patience, and to assure you that we won't keep you much longer.'

I thought, I'll stay all here all night if it gets me a recall.

'I'm going to read out the numbers of those of you we'd like to come back tomorrow,' Joe said. 'If you hear your number, please remain in the studio, so we can collect in your CVs.'

I heard my number, and Alexa's, and Suzanne's.

'Anyone whose number I've not read out, thank you very much,' Joe said.

Over half the girls stood up and left the studio. Several were in tears. Alexa, Suzanne and I all hugged each other. We were not the only ones. All around us, girls who had survived to the next round of auditions were hugging and congratulating each other. With every appearance of sincerity.

Once Hannah had collected in everyone's CVs, Joe Garcia called for quiet.

'Tomorrow morning,' he said, 'Danspace will be opening at eight-thirty. Please be warmed up and ready to dance by nine. We'll be asking some of you to sing in the afternoon, so please be prepared for another long day.' He looked round the studio and smiled. 'You can go home now.'

I retrieved my phone from my bag and texted Zac: *I danced for Joe Garcia. I got a recall.* He texted back: *And tomorrow you get to do it all again.*

170

CHAPTER 20

'There's Toby,' Zac said, gesturing towards the diminished group of auditionees filtering back into Studio 2 from Studio 1.

'And there's Luke,' Michael said. 'That's all of our lot through to the singing.' Luke weaved his way across the studio and collapsed full-length on the sprung floor next to Alexa.

'W-water,' he croaked. 'Alexa – I need water... What I've suffered for my art...'

'Stop that right now, you idiot,' Alexa said. 'You'll mess up your voice.' Grinning, Luke sat up. Then his face fell.

'Oh, shite,' he said. 'I can't remember if I packed my sheet music.' He began desperately rummaging through his scruffy holdall.

That morning, the day of the recalls, Zac and I had arrived at Danspace just as the doors opened. We'd been instructed to go and warm up straight away in Studio 2, where we were soon joined by Michael and Suzanne, and shortly afterwards by Alexa. Then Luke Harvey had sauntered in and joined us too. Gradually, the room had filled with musical theatre actors. Toby had arrived with a couple of guys I didn't know. He came over and chatted briefly before going off to sit with his friends, but I thought that Zac was probably right about an audition being the wrong occasion to play matchmaker, so I hadn't mentioned Laurie.

171

When the first group of auditionees had been summoned into Studio 1, Zac and I were among them. From behind their table, now covered with CVs, headshots and notes, Joe Garcia and the other members of the audition panel had watched us dance and decided our fate. Once again, the routine had felt good on me, and I thought I'd danced well, but it was with relief as much as elation that I'd heard 'Julie Farrell' named as one of those through to the next round.

Now, I looked around the studio, and counted how many people remained. Of the hundreds who'd danced for Joe Garcia over the last few days, just fifteen girls and fifteen boys would be singing for him in the afternoon.

Luke said, 'Aha! Found it.' He flourished his music, creased, and with what looked like a coffee stain on the front page.

'Oh, for goodness sake,' Alexa said. 'Give it here, and let me try to flatten it.'

Luke handed her the music. Leaning close to her, he whispered in her ear.

'No you can't,' Alexa said, pushing him away. 'Not tonight. I have to be up early in the morning. I'm going to a wedding. In Gloucestershire.'

'Who's getting married?' I said.

'My cousin, Freddie,' Alexa said. 'I'm travelling down with Charles and Hillary. They're picking me up first thing.'

'Did your invitation say "Miss Alexa Hamilton-Jones Plus One"?' Luke said. 'I could be your plus one.'

'You,' Alexa said, 'are far too disreputable to take to a family wedding.'

172

'Mad, bad and dangerous to know, that's me,' Luke said, cheerfully.

After half an hour or so, during which we grabbed a bite to eat and warmed up our voices, Hannah informed us that the audition panel were ready for us.

'Julie Farrell, please,' she said.

Zac, who was sitting next to me, said, 'Good luck, *cariño*. Not that you need it.'

I wouldn't have chosen to be the first to sing that afternoon, but I figured it was better than going last when the audition panel would probably be tired and longing for the day to be over as much as the auditionees were. Clutching my music, I followed Hannah next door, back into Studio 1.

'Hello, Julie,' Joe Garcia said. 'If you could give your music to the pianist, please.' The distance from the doors to the piano suddenly seemed vast, but somehow I walked across it and handed my music to the pianist. She smiled at me reassuringly. I went and stood in front of the audition panel's table. In front of Joe Garcia; I was going to sing for Joe Garcia.

'What are you going to sing for us, Julie?' Joe Garcia said.

'"You Are Mine' from *Warrior Queen*,' I said.

'Whenever you're ready.'

I nodded at the pianist. I heard the opening notes of my audition song. And then I was singing, imagining that it was Zac who was playing for me, putting the thought that I was singing to a man who could make or break an actor's career out of my mind. When I'd sung the last verse I looked back at Joe Garcia.

'Thank you, Julie,' he said. 'We'll only keep you a few more minutes.' For what seemed an eternity, during which my face grew stiff with the effort of maintaining a confident smile, while my insides began to quake, he talked quietly with Oliver Brady, the MD. I couldn't hear what they were saying, but I could see that they were studying my CV. Joe Garcia picked up another CV from those scattered across the table. Still conferring, and with the occasional glance at me, the audition panel passed the two CVs back and forth amongst themselves. I wished I'd stood nearer, so I could see whose it was, and what Jessica Coleman, Joe's assistant, was writing in her notebook.

'Thank you Julie,' Joe said, finally. 'If you would wait next door.'

'Thank you,' I said. I collected my music from the pianist, and made myself walk slowly out of the studio, as if singing for the most important man in twenty-first century musical theatre was something I did every day.

'How did it go?' Zac said to me, as I sank down on the floor beside him.

'Fine… I think,' I said. 'They didn't give much away, but I did get to sing my song all the way through.'

'Always a good sign,' Alexa reminded me.

The afternoon wore on, long hours of waiting, sitting on a hard floor, unable to relax for fear of missing some vital announcement, conversations coming to a sudden halt as an auditonee returned from facing the panel to be cross-questioned by their friends as to how they'd done. Alexa got to sing a verse and chorus of her song before the audition panel told her they'd heard enough, but Luke only got to sing a few bars of his, which convinced him that there was no way he was getting another recall. Michael was stopped almost immediately, which cheered up Luke, although he tried not to show it. Of our group, only Zac and I, and Suzanne, got to sing their audition songs all the way through.

It was Jessica Coleman who came into Studio 2 and read out the names of the people who'd survived to the next round. Zac and I, Alexa, Luke, Michael and Suzanne, and Toby had all got through once again. Hannah handed out slips of paper printed with the date, time and place of the next round of auditions.

'It's at the Aphra Behn Theatre,' Alexa said, her eyes shining with excitement. 'But it's not for another *three weeks*.'

Zac said, 'When Joe was casting *Two Cities,* it took him months.'

'How do you know that?' I said.

'I'm not sure,' he said. 'Somebody must have told me.'

'This show is going to be bigger than *Two Cities*,' Luke said.

***

'Did you notice that Joe Garcia's eyes are really dark like yours?' I said to Zac, as he unlocked his front door. Together with Alexa, Luke, Michael and Suzanne, we'd gone straight from Danspace to the nearest bar, but after one drink we'd left the others to it, and returned to Zac's flat.

'People of Spanish heritage usually have dark brown eyes,' Zac said.

I followed him inside. 'I guess with a surname like Garcia, he must be at least part Spanish.'

'I would think so,' Zac said, taking hold of my hand, and leading me along the hallway. For a moment, I thought we were heading to the bedroom, but instead he drew me into the bathroom.

'I think we need to unwind,' he said. 'We've had a tough day.' He turned on the bath taps, and added a handful of bath salts. When the large corner tub was full, he took off his clothes, and stepped in, lowering himself into the water with a sigh of contentment. Tired as I was, the sight of his naked body still made my stomach flip. I took the time to appreciate his sculpted torso, and his muscular arms resting on the rim of the bath, before stripping off my own clothes and joining him in the scented warmth. The aches in my leg muscles and in my shoulders, the tension and stress of the day, begin to drift away.

'Julie – there's something I think you need to know,' he said.

It came to me that he was about to tell me what it was that he and Laurie never talked about. In an instant, the languor that had overtaken me vanished. I sat up out of the water, sending it sloshing over the side of the tub onto the tiled floor.

'What would that be?' I said.

'I didn't want to mention it in front of your friends – I couldn't think of a way to say it without sounding totally up myself – but I'm almost certain I'm being considered for a main part in *La Pasionaria*. As are you.'

'Me?' I said. 'Seriously?' Whatever he still wasn't telling me couldn't be as big a deal as this.

Zac leant forward and pushed a strand of wet hair back from my face. 'Today, when I went into Studio 1 to sing, the audition panel had half a dozen CVs set out in a row in front of them on the table. Your CV and mine were next to each other. Joe kept glancing at them the whole time I was singing.'

I thought about this. It was definitely what Alexa would describe as a good sign. 'I guess, at this stage of the auditions, he has to start thinking about which actors would look good singing and dancing together on stage?'

Zac nodded. 'I'm not saying he's already decided to put us in his show. Only that he's considering us for parts.'

'Do you think he's looking at us for –' I broke off, not daring to voice the incredible thought that had sprung into my head.

'For the male and female leads?' Zac said. 'I think it's possible. Surely it must have occurred to you?'

'No, not at all,' I said. 'I did think I had a chance of being cast in the ensemble, or maybe a cover, but –'

'You really don't know how talented you are, do you?' Zac said.

'Oh, I have many talents,' I said.

'I'm sure you do.' Zac's mouth curved in a wicked smile. I knew that he was looking at my breasts, and he knew that I knew. Suddenly, dissecting the events of the day, second guessing the casting of *La Pasionaria*, no longer seemed that vital.

'I've always excelled at improvisation,' I said, moving my leg so that my thigh pressed against his. 'I'm also extremely good at taking direction.'

CHAPTER 21

'Thanks for the lift,' I said, as Zac pulled into an empty space a few yards down the road from my and Alexa's flat. He was spending the day with his parents – I'd been a little disappointed that he hadn't asked me to go with him, before telling myself that it was far too soon for *that* – but he'd insisted on driving me, my suitcase and my dance bag back home first.

'You're welcome, *cariño.*' He leant towards me and kissed me, a long deep kiss. When he lifted his mouth from mine, he said, 'There's a Spanish festival on the South Bank tomorrow. We're talking flamenco displays, tapas, wine-tasting. Shall we go and take a look at it? How about we meet up by the London Eye at three?'

'Sounds good,' I said, my heart leaping at his evident eagerness to see me again so soon. I got out of the car and collected my belongings from the back seat. Zac drove off. I shouldered my dance bag and dragged my case along the pavement to my front gate. As I reached it, a man in morning dress got out of a large, expensive-looking car parked outside and stood looking up at our flat.

'Hi, Charles,' I said, recognising Alexa's older brother.

He started. 'Ah! Good morning, Julie,' he said. 'Didn't see you there.' He glanced back at the flat. 'I'm wondering if I should go inside and tell my sister to get a move on, and retrieve my wife and sprogs. We've a wedding to get to.'

'Have you been waiting ages?' I said.

179

'About fifteen minutes,' Charles said, 'and we were already running late. Hilly wasn't ready on time, and then Caspar managed to get chocolate all over himself and India, so that held us up as well. I've called Alexa twice, but she's still not ready. I say, Julie, now that you're home, would you mind asking her to get herself down here sharpish?'

'I will,' I said, 'but why don't you come in and have a coffee while you're waiting.'

'Best not,' Charles said. 'If we start on the beverages, we'll never get going. And the M4's going to be a nightmare.'

'I'll pass on the message.' Smothering the urge to laugh, I let myself in and ran upstairs to the first floor. It was a source of endless amusement to Alexa and myself that Charles and Hillary, who lived in Hampstead, were convinced that if they left their car unattended in a less affluent area of London, they would return to find the tyres slashed and the hubcaps missing.

In the living room, I found Hillary and the children – and Luke Harvey. Hillary, perched gingerly on our sagging sofa, was wearing a silk dress to die for. The children, despite the chocolate incident, looked adorable: eight-year-old Caspar in a miniature version of his father's outfit, and six-year-old India in broderie anglaise. Luke, sprawled in an armchair, wearing the same cut off trackies and T-shirt he'd worn to yesterday's audition and in dire need of a shave, looked as though he had just dragged himself out of bed. Which he probably had. Hillary was laughing uproariously at something he'd just said.

'Julie, dahling,' Hillary said.

'Hi, Hillary,' I said. We exchanged air-kisses. I smiled at the children. 'Hello, you two.'

'Hi, doll,' Luke said.

'Hi, doll,' Caspar repeated.

'Caspar,' Hillary said, 'please say hello to Julie properly.'

'But Luke –' Caspar began.

'Luke is a grown-up,' Hillary said. 'You are eight.'

'Yer ma's right, ya know, mate,' Luke said. Why he was speaking in a Cockney accent when he came from Surrey, I couldn't imagine. I gave him a long look.

'Hello, Julie,' Caspar said.

'Hello, Julie,' India said, shyly.

'Luke was telling me about the auditions for this new musical,' Hillary said. 'It all sounds great fun.'

'Yes, it's very exciting,' I said. 'Hillary, I met Charles outside. He seemed very anxious to get on the road. Shall I go and tell Alexa to get her act together?'

'Oh, would you, dahling?' Hillary said. 'We are a bit behind schedule.' At that moment, Alexa made her entrance, flinging open the door to the living room and posing dramatically just inside.

'Well?' she said. 'How do I look?' She was wearing a strapless, tight-fitting floral print dress that came down to mid-thigh, and she carried a bolero jacket the exact shade of pink as the flowers on the dress. Her very high-heeled stilettos were pink also, as was her matching clutch bag. She'd put her hair up, and on her head was a concoction of pink feathers and lace.

'You look very nice, Alexa,' Hillary said.

'Ya look –' Luke began. He glanced at the children, and obviously thought better of whatever he'd been about to say. 'I like yer hat fing,' he continued in his newly acquired accent.

'It's called a fascinator,' Alexa said. 'Does it make me fascinating, Luke?'

'Ya always fascinate me, darlin',' Luke said.

'Alexa,' Hillary said, 'we really should be on our way. You know what Charles is like when he's got a long drive.'

'Oh, lord,' Alexa said. 'We don't want Charles in a strop all the way to Cirencester.' She turned to me. 'The flat's all yours. We've got rooms for tonight at the hotel where the reception's being held, so I won't be back until tomorrow lunchtime. See you, Luke.'

'See ya, sweet'eart,' Luke said, blowing her a kiss.

'Delighted to have met you, Luke,' Hillary said. 'So nice to see you again, Julie. Say goodbye to Auntie Alexa's friends, children.'

'Goodbye,' the children chorused.

Belatedly, Luke remembered his manners and got to his feet. 'Bye, ladies,' he said. He ruffled Caspar's neatly combed hair. 'Bye mate.'

'Bye, mate,' Caspar said, as his mother ushered him and his sister out of the room.

Hillary's voice carried back from the hall. 'Your friend Luke is such a scream.'

'Yes, he can be very amusing,' Alexa said. The front door closed behind them.

'What's with the Mockney accent?' I said to Luke.

'Oh, Alexa's sister-in-law didn't seem to know quite what to make of my being here when she arrived this morning,' Luke said, in his normal speaking voice. 'So I decided to improvise and play the part of Alexa's bit of rough.'

'I don't quite know what to make of your being here either,' I said.

'Yeah, I'm not sure how it happened,' Luke said. 'But, somehow, here I am.' He stroked his unshaven chin. 'And now, much as I enjoy playing the bad boy, I feel the need to get home and make myself just a little less dishevelled. If I could just remember where I left my shoes –'

'What is it with you and misplacing articles of clothing?' I said.

'Oh, well, you know, in the heat of the moment.'

'Try Alexa's room,' I said. Luke located his trainers – in the kitchen – and left.

I dragged my suitcase into my bedroom, grimacing at the sight of the peeling wallpaper and worn carpet. With a sigh, I unpacked my suitcase, carried most of its contents into the kitchen, and shovelled them into the washing machine.

Yesterday, I'd sung and danced for Joe Garcia. Today, I was doing household chores, and tonight I'd be pounding the pavements, handing out advertising flyers for Club Zone.

CHAPTER 22

When I woke up on Sunday morning, alone in my own bed, the clock on my nightstand showed me it was gone noon. With no pressing need to practise singing 'You Are Mine' or dash off to a jazz class at Limelight, I deliberately hadn't set my alarm when I'd got in from work the night before. I got out of bed and pulled back the curtains to see a cloudless blue sky. Apart from a cat sunning itself on next door's garden wall, the street below me was deserted, a heat haze shimmering above the Tarmac.

I had a leisurely brunch, and took my time choosing an outfit suitable for an outdoor event on what was looking to be the first really hot day of the year: sleeveless top, denim skirt, and flat shoes. Finding I still had an hour or so before I needed to head over to the South Bank to meet Zac, I set up my laptop on the dining table and caught up with friends on social media. The photos on Facebook were all of people taking advantage of the sudden arrival of summer in pub gardens, holding impromptu barbecues or braving the traffic to drive down to the coast. Laurie, who the previous night had talked so much about Toby that he'd handed out less than half his flyers, had posted a picture of the pair of them on Brighton beach.

A welcome breeze drifted into the room, bringing with it the sound of a car's engine, and then Alexa's voice. I went over to the open window in time to see her lifting an overnight bag out of the boot of a white sports car. She bent down and said something to the driver through the passenger window and then stood waving as the car drove off, before heading up our garden path. Moments later, she appeared in the living room.

'That wasn't Charles I saw dropping you off,' I said.

'No, that was a lovely guy called Tim,' Alexa said. 'He was my cousin Freddie's best man.'

I gave her a speculative look. 'Am I right in thinking you had a good time at the wedding?'

'In the end I did,' Alexa said. 'I'll make us some tea, and then I'll tell you all about it.'

Seated on the sofa, mug of tea in hand, Alexa described her cousin's nuptial celebrations. The journey down to Gloucestershire hadn't been as horrendous as she'd feared, as there'd been only one minor hold-up on the motorway. They'd arrived in good time, meeting up with Alexa and Charles' parents and various other relatives outside the church, so Charles had no cause for complaint about the late start.

'The wedding itself was beautiful,' Alexa said. 'Olivia, the bride, looked gorgeous in her white dress, although she's actually quite a plain girl. And the reception was in a stately home that's been turned into a hotel. Fabulous food. Live music. It was perfect – except for the fact that every male over the age of twenty-one was spoken for. So there was I, with no plus one, and no one to flirt with. It was a social disaster.'

'You can't have been the only singleton at the wedding,' I said.

'It seemed like I was,' Alexa said. 'All my female cousins had brought partners – although I suspect that Cousin Vanessa's male escort had been hired for the occasion. Even Cousin Hermione, who's only fourteen, had a gangly youth hanging on her every word.'

'You should have taken Luke,' I said.

'I had actually reached that conclusion,' Alexa said, 'but then Tim saved the day. He's Freddie's best friend, but he was at Cambridge with Charles.'

'Is he a lawyer like Charles?'

'Yes, he is,' Alexa said. 'Anyway, Tim comes over to our table to chat to his old university pal, and Charles says how we have to leave at the crack of dawn in the morning because he's in court on Monday and he has to do whatever lawyers have to do before a court case. So Tim offers me a lift back to London at a much more civilised hour, on condition that I dance with him.'

'He's single?' I said.

'He is,' Alexa said. 'I thought he was with one of the bridesmaids – he'd been dancing with her most of the evening – but that turned out to be best man duty. We stayed on in the bar long after the rest of the wedding guests had taken themselves off to bed – and before you ask, all we did was talk. He didn't make a move.'

'You have my sympathy,' I said. 'Were you very disappointed?'

'Not at all,' Alexa said. 'Tim's thirty-three, which is way too old for me. He's good company though. On the way back to London we stopped off at a country pub, and he bought me a fabulous lunch.'

'Did he ask for your phone number?' I said.

'He did, actually,' Alexa said. 'I didn't want to give it to him, but it seemed rude to refuse when he'd bought me lunch and gone out of his way to drive me home. I doubt he'll call, but if he does I'm not going out with him.'

'You're definitely not interested?'

'I like him,' Alexa said, 'but not in *that* way.' She added, 'Tim's a nice man. If he does call me, I'll make sure I let him down gently.'

CHAPTER 23

'It's Laurie's last shift at Zone tonight,' I said to Alexa, as I rubbed more factor thirty onto my arms, legs and stomach. 'Next week he starts rehearsals for *Iago*.'

'Is he having a leaving do?' Alexa said.

'Well, he's not having a huge party,' I said, 'but a few of us are going to the Troubadour after work. Zac's joining us. What are you up to?'

'I've no plans.' Alexa had been lying on the grass, but now she sat bolt upright. 'I can't stay home alone on a Saturday night. I wonder if Michael's free.'

For more than two weeks now, the warm weather had continued. Today, the Saturday before the next round of *La Pasionaria* auditions, Alexa and I'd decided to make the most of the heatwave by having a picnic lunch. Wearing bikinis under our T-shirts and shorts so we could sunbathe, and having called in at our local supermarket to buy baguettes, olives, tomatoes on the vine, feta cheese, and a bottle of white wine, we took the tube to Hyde Park. Although the park was crowded with other sun-worshippers, tourists, and office workers on their lunch hour, we'd managed to find a quiet spot with a view of the Serpentine.

I passed Alexa the suncream. 'Why don't you come and have a drink with us tonight? Toby'll be there.'

'Will he?' Alexa said. 'I do like Toby. I got to know him quite well when I was dating Jonas.'

'I like Toby too,' I said. 'Laurie's completely smitten with him. It's such a relief when your friends date people that you like.'

'It certainly is,' Alexa said. 'Imagine if Zac and I didn't get on. How awful would that be?'

'It could make for some awkward conversations at the breakfast table when he stays over,' I said. A thought occurred to me. 'I told him he could leave a toothbrush and a razor in our bathroom. I hope you don't mind.'

'Of course not,' Alexa laughed. 'Why would I? Do you keep a toothbrush at his place? You do, don't you? Anyone would think you and Zac were getting serious.' Abruptly, she took off her sunglasses. '*Are* you and Zac getting serious?'

I thought back over the past fortnight. Since our afternoon on the South Bank – sampling Spanish delicacies from the food stalls, Zac chatting to the vendors in their own language, watching the fiery dancers with their clacking castanets, and later in the cool of the evening, eating a meal of paella while a guitar played, the moon rose and lights came on all along the river – Zac and I had seen each other maybe half a dozen times. Sometimes we'd slept at his place, and sometimes at mine. He'd taken me to a matinée performance of *Two Cities* – and even although it was the fifth time I'd seen the show, the last scene still brought tears to my eyes – and we'd climbed a narrow rickety staircase to reach a room over a pub in Southwark, to watch a one-man play. I'd had dinner with him in a luxurious Mayfair restaurant, which made for a fabulous evening, but it was when I was sharing a portion of chips with him as we explored Camden market, singing while he played the piano, laughingly trying to spot him amongst fifty other actors when his advert aired on TV, lying in his arms after we'd made love, that I'd feel a real connection between us and could believe he must feel it too. But if I was honest with myself, I had no real idea where I stood with him. If he thought of me as his girlfriend, he'd neglected to tell me.

I said, 'No, I can't say that Zac and I are serious.' Not yet, at any rate, I thought, but maybe we're heading that way. I drank some wine and lay flat out on the grass. Alexa did the same.

The sound of her mobile made us both start. She checked the screen, but let the phone ring.

'Aren't you going to answer that?' I said.

She shook her head.

'Why not?' I said. The phone stopped ringing.

'It was Tim,' Alexa said.

'And you didn't take his call because…?' I said.

She shrugged.

'You probably should speak to him if he phones again,' I said. 'What with his being your cousin's best man, and a friend of your brother.'

'I guess it wouldn't hurt to speak to him,' Alexa said.

I settled back down on the sun-scorched grass. I heard the drone of insects, and the hum of distant traffic. I shut my eyes.

'I could phone him back,' Alexa said. 'Find out what he wanted.'

I opened my eyes and raised myself on my elbows. 'You should definitely phone him back,' I said. 'It's only polite.'

Alexa pressed 'return call.' 'Oh, hello, Tim,' she said. 'Alexa Hamilton-Jones. I got a missed call from you...'

I ate an olive and poured some wine.

Alexa held out her plastic cup for a refill. 'Well, I was planning on heading over to Covent Garden... No, not the Opera House, just drinks with friends... No, it's a very casual arrangement, nothing I can't get out of...' Her face broke into a smile. 'I'd love to... Oh, don't worry about it being short notice... Yes, I'll see you in the foyer.' She ended the call.

'I take it you're not coming to Laurie's leaving do?' I said.

Alexa shook her head. 'A friend of Tim's has tickets for tonight's performance of *The Time Machine*, but can't use them for some reason, and he's offered them to Tim.'

'Who immediately cancelled all his other plans and asked you to go with him?'

'Well, yes,' Alexa said. 'He remembered my telling him at Freddie and Olivia's wedding how much I loved musical theatre.' Her brows drew together in a frown. 'He's ten years older than me. One of my rules is that I don't date older men – too great an age difference, and it never ends well.'

'Where there are rules,' I said, 'there are always exceptions.'

'I guess,' Alexa said. 'And it's only a night out. It's not like I've agreed to bear his children. It's not even a proper date.'

'A man and a woman going out together on a Saturday night,' I said, 'but it's not a date?'

191

'It doesn't feel like a date,' Alexa said. 'He's a friend of my brother's, for goodness sake.' She put her head on one side. 'I'm sure I heard thunder. Do you think there's going to be a storm?'

I glanced up at the cloudless blue sky. 'No way is it going to rain.' I stretched out again on the grass.

A few minutes later, Alexa said. 'When do you have to go to work?'

'Not for another couple of hours,' I said.

'Right,' Alexa said. 'Two more hours sunbathing. Then I should get home. Find something to wear tonight. Make a bit of an effort.'

'This man Tim that my best friend is not dating,' I said. 'If I ever get to meet him, I do hope I like him.'

***

'Your last night of flyering,' I said to Laurie. 'How does that feel?'

A twenty-something, hand-holding couple walked by, and Laurie gave them a flyer before replying. 'At this moment it mainly feels hot and humid.'

I agreed. 'It was lovely earlier, perfect sunbathing weather, but now it's really close.' I fanned my face with my flyers.

'Was that thunder?' Laurie said.

'It might have been,' I said. Although the sky was now overcast, it was unbearably hot in Leicester Square that evening. At the restaurants, all the outside tables were taken, and the bars were doing a roaring trade in cold white wine and beer. I could feel sweat running down my back. I held out a flyer to a portly young man in a Hawaiian shirt.

'Hi there,' I said. 'Why don't you head over to Club Zone? With this flyer, your first drink's free. The club has air-con.'

Hawaiian Shirt Man took the flyer, but didn't look at it. 'Is this what you do for a living?' he said to me. 'Hand out flyers for a nightclub?'

'Absolutely,' I said. 'This is my vocation. I can't imagine a more rewarding job.'

'So what time do you get off work?' he said.

'Not something you're ever going to need to know,' I said.

'I could meet you when you've finished,' Hawaiian Shirt Man said, with a leer.

'Not going to happen,' I said. 'My boyfriend's meeting me from work.'

'And what does he do for a living?' Hawaiian Shirt Man said. 'I doubt he earns as much as I do.'

'Oh, he doesn't work,' I said. 'He doesn't have time with all his martial arts training. He has a black belt in jiu jitsu.'

Hawaiian Shirt Man shrugged, and turned to Laurie. 'I could meet *you* when you've finished work. I'm in London on business. I have a suite in a really upmarket hotel.'

'When I've finished work,' Laurie said, 'I'm straight back home to my wife and kids.'

'Oh, well,' Hawaiian Shirt Man said, 'maybe some other time.' He ambled off across the square.

'Well, that's a new one,' Laurie said. 'Hitting on both of us.'

'Yeah, gross.' I became aware that while we'd been talking, the light had faded considerably. I said, 'It's getting so dark. It's almost like night.'

Laurie said, 'There's definitely going to be a storm.' Even as he spoke, there was a flash of lightening and a crack of thunder directly overhead. Then the rain came down in a deluge that sent everyone in the square scurrying for cover. Drinkers and diners retreated into bars. Tourists fought with recalcitrant umbrellas. Girls shrieked as their thin summer dresses turned transparent. In seconds, Laurie and I, and our flyers, were soaked through.

'This must be what it's like to be in *Singin' in the Rain,*' I laughed. 'One of the reasons I love musical theatre: there's a show tune for every occasion.'

Laurie laughed too, and then he put his arms around me in a bear-like hug.

'What was that for?' I said.

'That,' he said, 'was to let you know that while I'm very glad this is my last shift for Zone, I'm going to miss you.'

'Oh, don't, Laurie,' I said. 'You'll make me cry.'

'Don't worry,' he said. 'I won't be able to see the tears for the rain.'

'You know what we should do?' I said, tossing wet hair out of my eyes. 'Now that we're not going to be working together, we should meet up once a month for lunch, or whatever. Just us. No one else.'

'You have a deal,' Laurie said. There was another flash of lightning and another roll of thunder. The rain fell harder than ever.

'We may as well go back to the club,' I said. 'No point flyering in this.'

Laurie and I were the first members of the promotions team to get back to Zone, but the others soon followed. Austin was not delighted to find us all gathered in the staffroom, dripping over the furniture, and he was even less delighted when he found out how many flyers had simply disintegrated in the downpour. Still, even he couldn't argue that there was any sense in our going back out on the streets until the rain had stopped.

'We may as well go home,' Harry said. 'Don't you think so, Austin?'

'Not if you want to get paid.' Austin said. 'Once the storm eases up, I want you all back out there. And do try and tidy yourselves up. You look a right state.'

'That's because we're drenched, Austin,' Harry said, as our boss headed out of the staffroom. 'But there's no need for you to be concerned. Who cares if we catch pneumonia, as long as we can hand out flyers?'

Cora fetched everyone a hot drink from the machine. Ben put his earphones in his ears, stretched out on a sofa with an expression of bliss on his face, and promptly fell asleep. For a while, Nadia sat by herself, flicking through a magazine, but then, growing bored, she came and joined me, Laurie, Harry and Cora, who were sitting in a circle of easy chairs, our wet feet up on a coffee table.

'How's your new accommodation working out, Nadia?' Laurie said.

'Oh, it's just fabulous,' Nadia said. 'Now that I'm sharing a house with a famous actress, I'm making so many new contacts.'

'That wasn't quite what I meant,' Laurie said. 'But never mind.'

'And how are you?' Nadia said to Laurie. 'You must be so relieved to be starting an acting job at last. How long is it you've been resting?'

'If you don't count the occasional walk-on, six months,' Laurie said. 'And I'm not relieved, Nadia, I'm ecstatic.'

'Of course you are,' Nadia said. 'Even if your play flops and you have to come back to Zone, at least you'll have had a break from flyering.'

Laurie became very interested in his coffee.

'Laurie,' Cora said. 'If getting the lead in a play as good as *Iago* meant that you'd have to appear naked on stage, would you still have accepted the role?'

'I would if I felt a lack of clothes was integral to the play,' Laurie said. 'I've never been offered a role that's required nudity, so it's not something I've ever had to decide.'

'What about you, Julie?' Cora said.

The thought of standing centre stage naked in front of a packed auditorium made me cringe. 'I don't mind a skimpy costume,' I said, 'but I'd want a costume of some sort, even if it's just strategically placed sequins and feathers.'

'Cora, has someone asked you to get your kit off for the delectation of the theatre-going public?' Harry said.

Cora nodded. 'Last week, I auditioned for a play, a national tour, and the casting director mentioned that the female lead is naked for most of the second act. At the time, I said that would be fine – I honestly thought I was OK with it – but last night, when my agent phoned and told me I'd got the part, I thought about my friends – or my *parents* – coming to see the play, and I turned it down. I

196

keep wondering if I've been stupid. It's not like I'm overwhelmed with offers of work at the moment.'

'It's always hard to turn work down,' Harry said, 'but I think you were right not to accept this particular role, if you weren't comfortable with it.' He grinned. 'I, on the other hand, am quite happy to strip off on stage. If the money's right. There was this play I was in a couple of years ago – let's just say I made sure I kept in shape throughout the run.'

'My boyfriend's pleased I turned down the job,' Cora said. 'Not that he was bothered about the nudity, but he didn't like the thought of me going off on tour.'

'Pursuing an acting career can certainly put a strain on a relationship,' Laurie said.

'Especially if one of you is more famous and successful than the other,' Nadia said. 'Take the guy Julie is… *dating*. When he hooked up with an Oscar-winning actress, their *relationship* didn't last that long.'

'W-what?' I said. 'Are you talking about Zac?'

'Oh, sorry, Julie,' Nadia said. 'Didn't you know about Zac Diaz and Rosalind Adams? The young, up-and-coming actor and the Hollywood A-Lister?'

'No,' I said, quietly. 'I didn't know anything about Zac and Rosalind Adams.' I shot a questioning look at Laurie, who frowned at Nadia, but failed to contradict her.

'Did you not?' Nadia said. 'Well, I wouldn't worry about it. I doubt it meant anything to either of them – rumour has it that Rosalind Adams has slept with half of Hollywood. She may be a very beautiful woman, but I'm sure he hardly ever thinks about her. And there's no way

197

he'd ever get back with her. There's no need for you to feel insecure.' Her mouth curled into a satisfied smile.

I thought, you *bitch*.

'It's strange Zac hasn't told you about her, though,' Nadia said.

There followed a long, agonising silence, during which I became aware that I was clenching my hands so tightly that my nails were digging painfully into my palms. Not that we'd discussed it, but from the first time I'd slept with him, I'd known that Zac must have had plenty of experience with women before he met me. That one of them was a Hollywood leading lady, who'd won two Oscars and had last year come top in *Goss* magazine's readers' poll of the world's most beautiful actresses, shouldn't matter in the slightest. But it did.

Laurie said, 'Something I've been meaning to ask you, Nadia. Did you ever hear from that guy you were... *networking* with at Cora's party while your boyfriend was fetching you a drink?'

Nadia turned her head away from me to glare at him. 'No, I didn't.'

'That must have been so disappointing for you,' Laurie said. 'Although your boyfriend must be relieved.'

'I don't know what you're talking about,' Nadia said.

'Do you not?' Laurie said. 'Sorry. My mistake. I guess none of us should judge others by our own standards.'

Nadia went so red in the face that I feared she might be about to implode. Without another word, she got to her feet and stomped off.

'Goal!' Harry said, crushing a Styrofoam cup in his huge hands and lobbing it into a bin. He then launched into a very funny story about the time he'd done a TIE tour of Italy, having lied about his ability to speak Italian, which soon had Laurie and Cora laughing uncontrollably, and after a while – once I'd remembered that the show must go on – I joined in, although my laughter may have sounded a little forced. Ben woke up, and I fetched everyone another coffee. I told myself that I was an idiot if I let Nadia get to me, and made a conscious effort not to dwell on the images her words had conjured up in my head.

The rain continued to fall. Austin, eventually conceding that wet, torn flyers were not going to entice anyone into Zone, let us go half an hour early. Everyone on the promo team, with the exception of Nadia, went to the Troubadour for Laurie's leaving drinks, where we were joined by Toby and, an hour or so later, by Zac. The Troubadour, being the closest watering hole to several West End theatres, was popular with actors looking to chill out after a show, and our group found ourselves drinking with the cast of the modern dress production of *She Stoops to Conquer*. Harry seemed very taken with their leading lady. Laurie was, of course, the centre of attention, and didn't have to buy a drink all night.

Sometime after midnight, hearing that the rain had finally stopped, Laurie and I fought our way through the mildly inebriated crowd in the bar, and went outside to get some air. Apart from a cluster of smokers by the door, a couple in a clinch, and a woman talking quietly on her phone, the street was empty. The wet pavements reflected the street lamps and the light that was spilling from the open windows of the Troubadour, along with the roar of numerous shouted conversations. It may have been the effect of a sudden cool breeze after the heat and alcoholic fug of the bar, or maybe I'd just had too much wine, but suddenly Nadia's words came rushing back to me.

I said, 'Nadia really wound me up tonight.'

'Yeah, I noticed,' Laurie said. 'I was pretty wound up myself.'

'I don't want to turn into one of those scary girls who obsess about their boyfriends' exes,' I said, 'but I can't seem to stop thinking about Zac and *film star* Rosalind Adams.' My voice caught in my throat. 'In case you were wondering, this is the bit when you tell me that Nadia was lying.'

'Nadia lies all the time,' Laurie said.

'But Zac did have a relationship with Rosalind Adams?' I said.

Laurie nodded. 'They had a fling when he was in the States,' he said. 'For a short time, he was the envy of every straight guy in our year at RoCoDa. The rest of what Nadia said – what she implied – was a figment of her imagination. The woman's a total sociopath.'

'Maybe she is,' I said, 'but I'm still going to have to say something to Zac about… about *knowing* about him and Rosalind Adams. I can't just forget about it. Her photo's in *Goss* and *Innit* every other week.'

A familiar male voice said, 'Whose photo's in *Goss*?'

I started and spun around to find Zac standing directly behind me. I'd no idea that he'd followed Laurie and me out of the bar. I wondered how much of our talk he'd overheard.

'Rosalind Adams,' I said.

'She's an A-List film star,' Zac said. 'Her photo does tend to feature in the tabloids and the celebrity gossip magazines.'

'She's everywhere,' I said. 'Her face is all over the internet.'

'No more than any other celebrity,' Zac said.

'But it was her that you… that you slept with.'

Zac frowned. 'Sounds like somebody's been telling tales out of school.'

'It was Nadia Pincher,' I said. Zac muttered something in Spanish. He didn't translate it for me, but I was fairly sure it wouldn't be heard on TV before the nine o'clock watershed.

Laurie cleared his throat. 'The Troubadour will be closing soon,' he said. 'I'm going back inside. I'm going to remind everyone that it's *my* night and they really need to buy me another drink.' He went back into the bar, leaving me alone with Zac.

I said, 'Rosalind Adams and Zac Diaz. I can't get my head around you and her being together. How did you even meet her?'

'I was in New York,' Zac said. 'I was twenty-three, and I was starring in a play on Broadway. I had the rich and famous coming round to my dressing room every night after the show, telling me how fabulous I was. One night, in the last week of the run, Rosalind knocked on my door. She was very complimentary about my performance, and we ended up going to a bar. After a few drinks, she suggested we went to her hotel –' He ran his hand through his hair. 'Are you sure you want to hear this?'

I nodded. I wasn't at all sure that I wanted to know more about Zac's relationship with film star Rosalind Adams, but not knowing was worse.

'I slept with her,' Zac said. 'The following morning, she suggested that I try my luck in Hollywood, and invited me to stay with her until I found a place of my own. At the time – I was pretty up myself after the success I'd had in New York – it seemed like a good plan, although almost everyone I knew advised me against it. Once the play closed, I flew out to LA, and joined Rosalind at her mansion in Beverley Hills. I stayed for three months.'

He lived with her, I thought. He was her live-in boyfriend. My stomach tightened into a knot.

'It wasn't a grand Hollywood romance with attendant paparazzi,' Zac said, 'and there was no dramatic breakup. We both agreed it wasn't going anywhere and it was time I left. Rosalind wished me all the best and had her maid pack my bag. No hard feelings on either side. We stayed friends.'

'You mean you're still in contact with her?' I blurted. The first thing I'd done when Matt and I broke up was to delete his number from my address book.

Zac raised one eyebrow. 'I saw her now and then when I was in LA,' he said. 'I've had a drink with her a couple of times since she came to London.'

'She's in *London*?' However irrational, I'd much rather Zac's film star ex was in California, with an ocean and a continent between him and her.

'She's over here filming her new movie,' Zac said.

'H-have you seen her since you've been dating me?' I said.

'Only as a friend,' Zac said. 'I didn't have sex with her, if that's what you're thinking.' His dark eyes locked on mine. 'I've not slept with anyone else since I've been with you. When I'm in a relationship, I don't play around.'

My heart started pounding, my voice scarcely above a whisper, I said, 'Are you and I in a relationship, Zac?'

For a moment, he was silent, then he said, 'We do seem to be.' He put his arms around me. I melted against him, resting my head on his chest, acutely aware of the scent of his aftershave, the rough fabric of his shirt against my face, and the heat of his body.

He said, 'You've no need to be jealous of anyone, *cariño*.' Then he kissed me, his tongue deep in my mouth, an arm about my waist, his hand entangled in my hair. I wondered how I could have been so stupid as to listen to a word Nadia had said. When he raised his head from mine, I realised to my surprise, it had started raining again. He took my hand, and we ran to shelter in the doorway of the bar.

'We should go back inside,' he said. 'I should buy Laurie another drink.' He smiled. 'I should probably buy my girlfriend a drink as well. Afterwards, we'll go back to my place.'

I smiled back at him. 'What will we do there?'

'I'm sure we'll think of something,' Zac said.

***

The bedroom was lit by one small lamp. The rain pattered gently against the windows. Zac lay on his back, holding the girl with whom he'd just made love in the circle of his arms. Her head was on his shoulder, her long dark hair

203

fanned out behind her on the pillow. Her eyes were shut, and her gentle breathing told him she was asleep.

What have I done? Zac thought. So much for focusing on work and avoiding emotional entanglements. He slid out of bed and pulled on a pair of jeans and a sleeveless T-shirt. Shutting the bedroom door quietly behind him, he walked barefoot to the main room, and sat down at the piano. It's too soon, he thought, I'm not ready for this sort of commitment.

His hands moved over the piano keys, and without conscious thought, he found himself playing the first few notes of Julie's audition song. A rush of desire – and affection – for the girl asleep in his bed made him catch his breath. The timing was all wrong, and yet... He pictured Julie standing next to Laurie on the staircase at Zone in her red dress. She'd *glowed* in that dress... He thought of all the times he'd played for her, the times they'd sung together... He wanted her. He couldn't stay away from her. He wanted to be with her...

I have to be honest with her, he thought, I have to tell her everything I've kept from her. But if I tell her now, it could affect her performance in the auditions. He played a verse and a chorus of 'You Are Mine'.

He couldn't do or say anything that might throw her, he decided. Not when she was so close to getting cast in *La Pasionaria*.

CHAPTER 24

'Julie, wake up.'

I opened my eyes to see Zac, dressed in a pair of faded denim jeans, standing next to my side of the bed. He set down a mug of tea on the nightstand.

'We need to get our act together,' he said. 'We've overslept. We're supposed to be going to Laurie's place for brunch with him and Toby.'

'What?'

'Don't you remember? Laurie invited us last night, when we were leaving the Troubadour.' Zac opened a wardrobe door and started looking through his clothes. 'Damn. I've left my striped shirt at your place.' I sat up and found that I had a throbbing headache, and my throat felt as though someone had been rubbing it with sandpaper.

'What time is it?' My rasping voice was scarcely audible. I put my hand to my neck.

Zac turned and looked at me. 'Want me to get you some water?' He started towards the door.

'No, I'll get it,' I croaked. I got out of bed, and my legs buckled under me. Somehow, Zac crossed the room and caught me before I hit the floor. I slumped against him, as the bedroom spun around me. He lowered me back onto the bed and pulled the sheet over me.

'I don't feel too good.' I could hardly get the words out. I felt unbearably hot.

'You're very flushed,' Zac said. He sat down beside me and put a cool hand on my forehead. '*Dios*, you're burning up.'

205

'My throat really hurts,' I whispered.

'If you've got a sore throat, don't talk any more than you have to,' Zac said. 'You don't want to strain your voice. And don't whisper, it'll only make it worse.' I looked at him in horror. In four days' time I had to sing again for Joe Garcia. I couldn't have vocal problems right now. I couldn't be ill when I was auditioning for the most important man in musical theatre.

'Zac – my voice – the recall.'

'You'll be fine by then,' Zac said. 'I expect you've just got a chill. Not surprising after you got wet through in the storm last night. I'll get you some aspirin.'

'Laurie –' I tried to sit up, but felt so awful that I had to lie back on the pillow. 'Oh, Zac, I feel ghastly.'

'I'll call Laurie,' Zac said. 'I'll tell him you're not well and we can't make it.'

'You can still go,' I said.

'I don't think so,' Zac said. 'Not while you're feeling rough.'

'I should go home,' I said. 'Whatever I've got, you don't want to catch it from me.'

'That's very thoughtful of you,' Zac said, 'but if what you've got is contagious, I've probably got it already. And you don't want to pass it on to Alexa. I think you should stay here.'

I didn't argue with him. I'd never felt so ill before. It was as though I had the worst ever hangover – and then some. For that day and the next, I lay in Zac's bed feeling totally wretched, drifting in and out of a feverish sleep. I felt even worse at night, waking from nightmares that I couldn't quite remember, my skin hot and clammy with sweat. I tried not to think about the recalls for *La Pasionaria,* because when I did think about them, I felt like crying, which certainly wouldn't help my voice. During the day, Zac didn't spend his every waking moment hovering at my bedside, but whenever I woke up he was either there or he appeared a few minutes later, with aspirin and water, sliding an arm around me and holding me while I drank. Despite his reassurance that I would be fine, I was convinced that my chances of getting into Joe Garcia's new musical were gone for ever.

Then, on Tuesday, I woke up next to Zac feeling a whole lot better. My voice, however, was still very hoarse.

'What am I going to do?' I wailed. 'I have to practise my audition song.'

'Not today you don't,' Zac said.

'I haven't danced in two days,' I said.

'You haven't eaten in two days,' Zac said. 'Today all you need to do is rest and eat. And drink raspberry leaf tea: it's the best remedy for vocal problems.' He yawned, and it occurred to me that my thrashing about in fever induced dreams had meant that he hadn't had any more sleep over the past couple of nights than I had. And I'd stopped him getting to class.

'Zac,' I said, 'thank you for looking after me.'

'You're welcome,' he said. 'You really didn't take a lot of looking after.' He added, 'I let Alexa know you were ill, and I took it upon myself to phone Club Zone and tell them that you wouldn't be able to come in until next week.'

'Thanks again,' I said. All I'd worried about was the recalls. I hadn't given Zone a thought. 'Oh – and you've not gone to work either.'

'A whole week without pulling pints,' Zac said. 'How will I bear it?' He pushed back the duvet and got out of bed, standing with his back to me and stretching. My gaze travelled over the rippling muscles in his back down to his rear and even in my enfeebled state, I felt a twinge of desire – and regret when he put on boxers and a pair of jeans.

'I'll fix us some breakfast,' he said. 'You stay where you are. You're taking it easy today.'

I did take it easy, spending much of the day lounging on Zac's balcony, doing nothing more strenuous than texting Alexa to let her know I was much recovered, and replying to the numerous messages and missed calls that had accumulated on my phone. By Wednesday, I sounded like myself again, but it was not until the afternoon that I summoned up the courage to sing. Zac played some scales on the piano, and I managed those, so I decided to try out my audition song. I sang 'You Are Mine' and waited for Zac's verdict.

'Julie, that was absolutely fine,' he said. 'Your voice sounds as good as it ever did. If you'd been singing on stage, you'd have brought the house down.'

I felt faint with relief. 'I can't tell you how good that makes me feel,' I said, sitting down next to him on the piano stool. 'I was terrified I'd have to withdraw from the audition.'

'I wouldn't have let that happen,' Zac said.

'You'd have forced your way into Garcia Productions,' I said, 'and told the most important man in musical theatre that he had to overlook the fact that I'd temporarily lost my voice, because I'm just *so* talented? And he, of course, would have taken your word for it.'

'Something like that,' Zac said.

CHAPTER 25

'Just so you know,' I said to Alexa, 'Zac and I are now officially a couple.' While Zac had taken himself off for a session at his gym, I was making a flying visit home to pack a bag for the *La Pasionaria* recall, before returning to his flat. I'd discovered Alexa in the living room, doing some stretching exercises.

'Oh, Julie, that's great,' she said, from her prone position on the threadbare carpet. 'From what I've seen of him, Zac's a lovely guy. Of course, it doesn't hurt that he's easy on the eye as well, or that he can get hold of hot theatre tickets. I won't even mention the penthouse.'

I laughed. 'And what about the new man in your life? How was your not-a-date with Tim?' I lowered myself carefully onto the sofa, which creaked alarmingly.

'I had a surprisingly good time.' Alexa sat in box-splits, resting her elbows on the floor, and her head on her hands. 'It turns out that Tim is a regular theatre goer – straight plays, not musicals, but he asked me all these really intelligent questions about musical theatre, and said he could see himself getting into it.'

'So he wasn't too old and decrepit for you?' I said.

'No, not at all,' Alexa said. 'He doesn't seem any older than I am. Apart from the fact he's got a proper job. And a house and a car. Those things that people have when they aren't poverty-stricken, out-of-work actors.'

'When are you seeing him again?' I said.

'I don't know that I will be seeing him again,' Alexa said. 'After the show he drove me home, and by then I'd decided I liked him enough to invite him in. I wasn't planning on dragging him into bed, but I wasn't going to fight him off if he made a move. But all he did was kiss me. And then he leant across me to open the passenger door, and said he'd be in touch. I was so stunned that I just thanked him for a lovely evening, got out of the car and went inside. I guess I'm not his type.'

'Why wouldn't he call you?' I said. 'You say he kissed you.'

'It was a very chaste kiss.'

'Alexa,' I said, 'sleeping with someone on a first date is not compulsory.'

'I know that,' Alexa said. 'I do know that, Julie.'

'Maybe Tim likes to get to know a girl before he sticks his tongue down her throat,' I said.

'Well, we'll see,' Alexa said. 'If he calls, he calls. I'm really not bothered.'

CHAPTER 26

I stood stock still on the crowded pavement half-way along Shaftesbury Avenue, streams of shoppers and tourists flowing around me, and gazed up at the façade of the Aphra Behn, with its theatrical masks, comedy and tragedy, carved in stone above the main entrance to the foyer. I knew there had been a theatre here on this site since the 1890s, and that Joe Garcia had recently had the interior of the building renovated, restoring much of the original Victorian decor. I was about to audition in a place where plays had been performed for more than a century.

'Julie?' Zac said. 'You're very quiet.'

'I'm savouring the moment,' I said. 'This is the first time I've ever walked through the stage door of a West End theatre. I'd take a selfie if it wouldn't make me look totally unprofessional.'

Zac smiled. 'Ready to go inside now?' he said. I thought of all the actors who'd made their debuts in this theatre and had gone on to have long, prestigious careers on the stage. I wanted to be one of those actors very badly.

I said, 'I'm more than ready.'

'I think the stage door is down that alley and round the back of the theatre,' Zac said.

He resumed walking. I hurried after him, fervently hoping that the first time I stepped through the stage door of a West End theatre wouldn't also be the last.

***

Just one hour later – an hour during which I and the other twenty-nine auditionees gathered in the Aphra Behn's light, airy rehearsal studio danced our hearts out for Joe Garcia and his audition panel – there was another cut. I was sitting on the floor with my friends, the seven of us who'd made it this far, when Joe himself called out the names of those he wanted to keep and to hear sing. Zac and I got through, as did Alexa, Toby, Luke, and Michael. Suzanne did not.

Michael, who was sitting next to her, put an arm around her shoulders. 'You've done well to get this far,' he said. 'When you think of the hundreds of talented actors who never got a recall…'

Suzanne didn't say anything. She shrugged off Michael's arm, got to her feet, picked up her bag, and fled the rehearsal room. Michael sighed, and went after her, returning alone in less than a minute.

'Is she OK?' Alexa said.

'No, she's not.' Michael's face was grim. 'She's pretty upset.'

'I'll phone her later,' Alexa said.

'I wouldn't, Alexa,' Michael said. 'I'd leave it a couple of days if I were you.'

'Well, you know her best,' Alexa said, with a shrug.

'We've all been there,' Toby said. 'It never gets any easier.'

'Remind me why I wanted to become an actor,' Luke said.

'What other profession would have you?' Alexa said.

While we were talking, the audition panel had left the studio. Hannah, today without her radio, announced that there would be a ten minute break before they heard us sing in another rehearsal room. As one, the remaining twenty-six auditionees delved into their bags for their sheet music. I went over my song in my head one more time, and drank some water. A boy was called in to sing first, followed by the woman in her thirties who I remembered from the first round of auditions, and then me.

I followed Hannah down one flight of stairs – the studio was on the top floor of the theatre – and into a much smaller rehearsal room. Joe Garcia, Oliver Brady, Nathan Nyembe and Jessica Coleman were again sitting in a row behind a table. An accompanist, who held out his hand for my music, was at a piano.

'As soon as you're ready, please, Julie,' Joe Garcia said. I launched into the first verse of 'You Are Mine', and I knew I was sounding good. I made a point of looking at each member of the audition panel in turn, and all of them were smiling encouragingly. And then, when I tried to belt a high note in the second verse, my voice cracked. My hands flew to my neck. The pianist immediately stopped playing. *No,* I thought, this *cannot* be happening: not to me, not now.

I said, 'I'm so sorry, Mr Garcia. May I start my song again?'

'That may not be wise.' Joe glanced at his MD. 'What do you think, Oliver?'

Oliver Brady leant forward. 'Julie, does your throat hurt?'

'N-no,' I said. 'I did have a sore throat earlier in the week, but it's all right now. I mean, I thought it was all right. Otherwise I wouldn't have sung today. It was fine last night.' I swallowed uneasily. 'It just feels a bit tight.'

Oliver turned to Joe Garcia. 'She shouldn't be singing,' he said.

'Right, Julie, that's enough for today,' Joe said. 'If you'd like to wait in the studio.'

'Thank you,' I said. A leaden ache in my chest, I collected my music from the pianist. That's it, I thought, I won't be walking through a stage door again any time soon.

'Don't look so worried,' Joe said. 'You're not the first singer to have a sore throat. I've leads in two of my shows unable to perform this week because they've got vocal problems. It happens. That's why we have understudies.'

I nodded and tried my best to smile back at him. Moving like an automaton, I walked out of the room, up the stairs, and back into the studio, where my friends all turned expectantly towards me.

'How was it?' Alexa said.

'Awful,' I said, sinking down onto the floor next to Zac. 'My voice cracked.' My friends' faces conveyed both sympathy and horror – all of them knew exactly what this could mean for me.

Zac covered my hand with his. 'Did you tell the audition panel that you've only just got over a sore throat?'

I nodded. 'Oliver Brady said I shouldn't be singing. Joe Garcia agreed with him.'

'It's not like it's the only time they've heard you sing,' Alexa said. 'You could still get another recall.'

'Alexa's right,' Zac said. 'Joe and Oliver know a good voice when they hear it. They're not going to cut you because of one missed note.' He looked up as his name was called. 'You'll be fine, Julie. I promise you.' He got to his feet and went off to sing.

It was a very long day, but by late afternoon everyone had sung for Joe Garcia. Zac, Alexa and Toby were quietly confident that they'd sung well, Michael and Luke would only admit to singing without mishap. Fifteen minutes or so after the last auditionee had returned to the rehearsal studio, the door opened and Jessica Coleman came in, followed by Hannah. Every head in the room turned towards them. All conversation came to an abrupt halt. Suddenly, I was finding it hard to breathe.

'You can relax, people,' Jessica said. 'We've decided we want to see you all again tomorrow.

I gasped, and my body went limp. A couple of people cheered, and then looked rather abashed. All around me, people were congratulating their friends, and strangers too, for all I knew. One girl – there's at least one at every audition – burst into tears, presumably of joy. Luke and Michael exchanged high-fives. I couldn't stop smiling.

'Tomorrow,' Jessica continued, 'we're calling each of you in at different times. All of you will be required to sing, some of you we may ask for a monologue. Please see Hannah before you leave so she can allocate you an individual slot.'

'I can hardly believe they put me through,' I said to Zac, reaching into my bag for my street clothes. 'Not after I so thoroughly messed up.'

'I did tell you it'd be OK,' Zac said.

'You did,' I said, pausing in the act of stepping into my jeans. 'I should have listened to you –' I started as I heard Jessica calling my name. Turning around, I saw her making her way towards me. More than a few of the performers still scattered about the rehearsal room were looking at me with blatant curiosity.

'Just a quick word, Julie,' she said, when she reached me. The thought came to me that she was about to inform me that I alone among the performers who'd sung for Joe Garcia that afternoon, was not getting a recall. I clutched my jeans against my chest.

She said, 'Joe has asked me to tell you that he doesn't want you to come in again tomorrow.'

My breath left me, as though I'd been punched in the stomach.

'He and Oliver think you should be resting your voice for a couple more days,' Jessica went on, 'but they'd like you to attend the final recall. They want you to try out for a named role, not ensemble, so you'll need to learn a few pages of dialogue. I'll email you the material tonight.'

'Oh!' My head was all over the place, but somehow I managed to stammer, 'Th- thank you, Jessica. Thank you! So much.'

'We'll see you back here at the Aphra Behn Theatre next week.' Jessica smiled and turned away. I stood staring dazedly after her, as she retraced her route across the room, and went out the door. Zac put his arms round me.

Luke said, 'Your voice cracks and you're fast-tracked to a final? I'm wondering if I should tell Joe Garcia about my sore throat.'

'You don't have a sore throat,' Alexa said.

'I'll have you know that my performances in the role of Man With Sore Throat have always been very well received.' Luke said, covering his mouth and coughing violently.

Still holding me in the circle of his arms, Zac smiled down at me and said, 'Would it be unprofessional if I kissed you right now?'

'It would be very unprofessional,' I laughed.

He let go of me, and picked up my audition bag as well as his own. 'Then let's get out of here before I start behaving unprofessionally,' he said.

CHAPTER 27

I sat crossed-legged on my bed, a cup of raspberry leaf tea to hand, and picked up the pages of dialogue that Jessica Coleman had sent me the previous night. As soon as her email had arrived in my inbox, I'd printed off a hard copy, and Zac and I'd glanced through it, but I'd been too tired to take it in, certainly too tired even to think about learning it. Besides, all I'd really wanted to do was get into my bed with my boyfriend. Which I had done. Now, alone in my flat – Zac had just left for his fifth recall for *La Pasionaria;* Alexa had gone to hers an hour or so earlier – I read through the scene again.

It was a duologue. Mariana, a sixteen-year-old girl, was trying to dissuade a young man, Javier, from leaving home to fight in the civil war that was ravaging their country. It was only after Javier had exited the stage that Mariana confessed the reason she didn't want him to go was because she secretly loved him. I thought, Joe Garcia is looking at me to play Mariana. Is he looking at Zac to play Javier, the man she loves?

I re-read the scene, speaking Mariana's last line aloud: 'Javier – I love you. Wherever you go, however far away, I will always love you.' It would be one of those moments in a musical when a character is so overcome with emotion that the only way she can express her feelings is through song. I imagined myself standing centre stage, as Mariana, and declaring my love for Zac, as Javier; an orchestra playing, softly at first and then, as I began to sing, soaring to fill the whole auditorium with music; the audience

219

applauding – and rising to give me and Zac a standing ovation when we took our bows. I thought of the way Zac looked at me when we sang together, his smile when he was about to lean in for a kiss, his touch that left me weak with desire, how I longed to be with him whenever we were apart… My mind reeled and the script fell from my hand. My heart started beating very fast.

I loved him. I was in love with Zac Diaz.

Mindful of my voice, I refrained from belting out a show tune, but in my heart I was singing. I thought back to the first time I'd met Zac, at that awful casting when we'd played the role of lovers, and he'd kissed me – a stage kiss – as we lay together on a bare mattress. Acting a love scene under harsh studio lights had in no way prepared me for the way I was feeling now.

A loud rapping brought me back to myself. I floated across the room and opened my door, to find myself face to face with Alexa.

'I've been knocking for ages,' she said. 'Didn't you hear me?'

'No, sorry, I didn't. I…'

I didn't hear you because I was thinking about the man I love, I thought, realising I wasn't about to admit to Alexa how I felt about Zac – it was all too new.

'… I was miles away.' I smiled and stood aside so that she could step into my room. 'How was the recall?'

'It was short, but intense,' Alexa said, flopping down on my bed. 'Only Joe Garcia, Oliver Brady, and a pianist were in the rehearsal room. Oliver took me through some scales, I sang my audition song and did my monologue, and that was it. Joe's assistant, Jessica Coleman, was hovering around outside, and she told me that they'd email me if they needed me to come to the final, and to make sure I checked my inbox.'

'They don't give much away, do they?' I said.

'No,' Alexa sighed, 'but I'm not hopeful. I didn't feel that I sang my best. Can we not talk about it?'

'OK,' I said, 'but I'm sure your singing was better than you think.'

Alexa sighed again. 'I'm not having a great day. On my way home, I got a phone call from Tim. I've agreed to go out with him tomorrow night.'

'But that's good, isn't it?' I said. 'Where's he taking you?'

'A party,' Alexa said. 'Boat on the Thames. A woman he works with is celebrating her birthday in style. Trouble is, I don't know that I want to go. I may phone him back. Tell him I've remembered a previous engagement.'

'Alexa!' I said. 'You can't do that to the guy. He thinks he's got you as his date for his co-worker's party. You can't change your mind and leave him dateless.'

'I should have refused straight away,' Alexa said.

'But why?' I said. 'You like him. And you said that his age wasn't a problem.'

'I'm just worried that he and I aren't compatible,' Alexa said. 'In the sack.'

'Because he didn't jump on you on your first date?' I rolled my eyes. 'Well, if you don't go out with him again, you'll never find out –'

The doorbell rang.

'That'll be Zac,' I said. Leaving Alexa sitting on my bed, I sprang to my feet, ran down the stairs, and flung open the front door. The sight of Zac standing on the doorstep a jacket slung casually over one shoulder, his dark hair falling into his eyes, a smile playing about this mouth, took my breath away.

'Zac,' I said. 'Oh, Zac.'

'*Hola*, Julie,' he said, seemingly oblivious to the effect he was having on my pulse rate. Putting his hands on my waist, he bent his head to kiss me lightly on the mouth. I led him upstairs.

Alexa, who by now had followed me out of my bedroom, said, 'Hi, Zac,' before vanishing into the kitchen.

Zac said, 'I've got a final recall.'

'Well done you,' I said, smiling up at him, this beautiful, talented man who I loved. I'd been sure – as sure as anyone can be, given the unpredictable nature of auditions – that he'd get a final, but it was good to know that Joe Garcia was of the same opinion.

Conscious that Alexa, who didn't yet know if she had another recall, was only yards away and could hear everything we said, I drew Zac into my bedroom and shut the door. He tossed his jacket onto a chair and sat on the bed, leaning back against the headboard, his long legs stretched out in front of him. I sat facing him, aware of a delectable fluttering in my stomach.

I thought, I love you, Zac. I almost spoke the words aloud, but then it came to me with a bitter-sweet clarity that he might not want to hear those words from me. I can't tell him I love him, I thought, not until I know for sure that he feels the same.

'I found out a bit more about *La Pasionaria* today,' Zac said. 'Joe told me that the story is based on a real incident that happened in his Spanish grandfather's village during the Civil War.' He paused, and then he said, 'Joe also told me that he wants me to try out for the male lead, a village boy who goes off to fight, leaving behind a girl named Mariana, who is the main female character.' I heard what he was saying, but it took a moment for it to sink in.

'You were right,' I said, eventually. 'Joe Garcia is looking at you and me for the leads, the roles of Javier and Mariana.'

'Yes, I was right,' Zac said, 'but we can't get over-confident. We won't be the only actors trying out for leads at the final.' He added, 'Jessica Coleman has emailed me the same scene to learn as she gave you. I thought we could work on it together. If you'd like to.'

'Definitely,' I said, with feeling. I glanced at the script I'd been reading earlier, the duologue between Mariana and Javier, which was still lying on the floor beside my bed where I'd dropped it. I wondered what happened in later scenes. Did Javier ever come to love Mariana as much as she loved him? I picked the script up and put it on my nightstand.

Zac said, 'The first thing I'm going to do is teach you how to pronounce Javier.'

'Am I saying it wrong? I said.

He nodded. 'In Spanish, J sounds like an H.'

'Javier,' I said, pronouncing the name the way Zac had, stressing the last syllable.

'*Excelente*,' Zac said. 'Spoken like a native. Maybe I should teach you some Spanish?' His dark eyes glinted. 'I could give you a lesson now. I'll say something to you, and you just have to say "*Sí*" which means "yes".'

'I do know that much,' I laughed.

Zac's mouth lifted in a lazy half-smile. '*Quieres hacer el amor esta noche?*'

'*Si*,' I said.

'*Muy bien*,' Zac said. 'That means very good. You are an A-grade student.'

I gave him a long look. 'What have I just said "yes" to?'

'You'll find out.' He put his hands on my shoulders, drew me towards him, and kissed me, both of us sinking back onto the bed, me lying beneath him, love and desire for him flooding my senses as he kissed my throat and slid his hand under my shirt. '*Me pones cachondo*,' he said.

'What does that mean?' I said, trailing a finger along the waistband of his jeans.

'Roughly translated,' he said, 'it means 'you make me–'

My bedroom door crashed open, causing Zac to roll off me, and me to almost fall off the bed. Alexa – who had apparently forgotten our rule about not bursting in on each other without knocking – was standing framed in the doorway.

'That was quite an entrance, Alexa,' I said.

Alexa took in the sight of the pair of us lying on the bed in disarray 'Oh, sorry! Looks like I need to work on my timing,' she said. Then, unable to contain herself any long, she added, 'I've just had an email from Jessica Coleman. I've got a final recall.'

I sat up. 'That's great Alexa. I'm really pleased for you.'

'Yeah, that's good news,' Zac said.

Alexa beamed. 'I have dialogue to learn. I'm up for the part of Jane, an Englishwoman who's travelled to Spain to

nurse the wounded. I should go and print off the email.'
Still smiling, she backed into the hall, quietly closing the
bedroom door.

'We should get back to your Spanish lesson,' Zac said.

'*Si.*' I lay down beside him, and he reached for me.

'*Hagamos el amor,*' he said.

'*Si,*' I said. I had pretty good idea of what he wanted,
even without consulting a Spanish dictionary. I thought,
what is the Spanish for 'I love you?' And will Zac ever say
it to me?

From behind the door, Alexa said, 'Just one more thing,
Julie, and I'll leave you alone. I've decided I won't cancel
my date with Tim. I'll go with him to this boat party. Can I
borrow your gold shoes?'

CHAPTER 28

'Say that again,' Zac said.

'I love you,' I said.

For a long while Zac regarded me silently. Then, in a stage whisper, he said, 'I love you.'

I said, 'You think I'm saying the line too loud?'

He nodded. 'Javier has just exited the stage. If you raise your voice, it sounds as though you want him to hear you.'

'Maybe I do,' I said. Focus, Julie, I told myself, remember you're *acting*.

Zac picked up his copy of the script, which was lying on the dining table, and skimmed through the scene. 'I think Mariana's talking to herself,' he said.

He and I'd spent most of Saturday working on our dialogue from *La Pasionaria*. Now, on Sunday morning, we'd got up early to rehearse the scene again. Alexa, had wandered in half-way through the rehearsal, and had stayed to watch.

I said, 'Let's try it again.' We performed the duologue one more time, with me pitching my voice more quietly.

'That was really good, Julie,' Zac said.

'You're right,' I said. 'The scene works better if Mariana keeps her feelings to herself.' I smiled. 'Your acting wasn't too shabby either.'

Zac laughed. 'Do you have any notes for us, Alexa?' he said.

Alexa shook her head. 'No, none at all.'

'Would you like us to hear your lines?' Zac said.

'Thanks, Zac,' Alexa said, 'but I haven't learnt them yet. Maybe when I have...'

'Sure,' Zac said. He stroked his chin, which was dark with stubble. 'If we've finished rehearsing, I'm going to go and shave. We need to leave in an hour.'

'That's heaps of time,' I said. 'I've done so many backstage quick-changes, that I can get ready to go out in five minutes if I have to.' Zac smiled and strode off to brave the stained, chipped enamel in our bathroom. I turned to Alexa. 'We're having a pub lunch, but before we go out, I want to hear all about your date with Tim.'

'Well, I enjoyed the boat party,' Alexa said. 'I didn't know a soul, but Tim introduced me to the people he knew.'

'Were they all lawyers like him?' I said, planting myself on the sofa, which twanged in protest.

'Most of them were,' Alexa said. 'A whole lot of them knew my brother Charles. They talked about him as though he's some high-flying, hot-shot. Which was a little strange.'

'Isn't Charles a high-flying hot-shot?'

'Well, yes, he is,' Alexa said. 'But it was still weird to hear people talking about him in tones of awe.'

'I suppose it must have been a bit bizarre,' I said. 'Anyway, that's enough about your brother. What about you and Tim?'

'Oh, we were on the dance floor most of the evening – when we got away from people asking me to mention them to Charles. Tim's a good dancer, considering he's never had a dance lesson in his life.'

'So the date was a success?' I said.

'Depends how you define success,' Alexa said.

'Ah,' I said. 'I'm guessing he hasn't pounced?'

'No, he hasn't,' Alexa sighed. 'He did seem to be heading that way though. There were times on the dance floor when he held me really close. There was also quite a bit of stroking my back and hands on my rear.'

'Did he kiss you?' I said. 'I mean *really kiss* you.'

'Yes, he did. Up on deck. In the moonlight.'

'Oh. My. Gosh.'

'It was pretty good,' Alexa said. 'But he stopped when some other people came out on deck.'

'So he likes his privacy,' I said. 'Nothing wrong with that. He probably didn't want to be the top gossip around the water cooler on Monday morning.'

'Maybe.' Alexa sounded unconvinced. 'Anyway, the boat got back to the Embankment around midnight, and we came back here in a cab. Tim told the driver to wait while he walked me to my door.'

'Was there more mouth to mouth?' I said.

'There was,' Alexa said. 'But he didn't ask if he could spend the night. He waited until I'd opened the front door, and then he got back in the cab and sped off. He did ask me to have dinner with him next weekend, so I guess he must be interested in me on some level. It's just I'd have expected a little more *intimacy* by now.'

'You've known him three weeks!' I said. 'I really don't think that's an inordinate amount of time to not sleep with someone.'

Alexa's eyes widened. 'Isn't it?'

'Perhaps Tim's playing hard to get,' I said.

'Don't be ridiculous,' Alexa said. 'This is a man we're talking about. Playing hard to get is not part of the male mind-set.'

'Well, whether or not he's got the hots for you' I said, 'he's certainly got you interested in him.'

'Yes, he has.' Alexa sounded surprised. 'I'm still not at all sure that he's my type, but I can't seem to get him out of my head. I actually caught myself checking that I hadn't missed any calls from him this morning – which is so not me.'

I said, 'When you think about Tim, do you feel like bursting into song?'

'No, singing is not what comes to mind when I think about a guy,' Alexa said. 'Right now though, I'm thinking I need to hit the shops. I have to get a new dress for my next not-a-date with Tim – low cut, tight-fitting, preferably with a short skirt, but classy, not slutty. The next time that man sets eyes on me, he's going to find me irresistible.'

CHAPTER 29

I pushed open the door of the staffroom and looked around. Cora was standing by the coffee machine, chatting to one of the bar staff. Ben was stretched out full length on a sofa, earphones in place, eyes shut. Nadia was sitting a little way off reading a magazine. At a nearby table, Harry and a couple of waiters were playing poker. In my week's absence, nothing much appeared to have changed. Except that this would be my first night of flyering without Laurie. I reminded myself that handing in my notice was not an option: apart from my usual bills, I needed to buy a new pair of jazz shoes before the *La Pasionaria* final.

I'd just stashed my bag in my locker, when Austin came into the staffroom flanked by a tall, lanky, fair-haired boy.

'Ah, there you are, Julie,' Austin said, scurrying towards me. 'This is Owen Somers, Laurie Fryer's replacement and your new partner. I know you'll show him the ropes.' With that, he turned his back on us and began to walk away.

'Yes, I was off sick, Austin,' I muttered. 'But I'm better now. So kind of you to ask.'

Austin looked back over his shoulder. 'Did you say something, Julie?'

'No, I didn't say a word,' I said.

Austin trotted out of the staffroom. I turned to Owen. He was, I realised, an attractive guy, in a boy-next-door kind of way.

'Sorry about that,' I said to him. 'I sometimes forget that our beloved leader doesn't do small-talk. Good to meet you.'

'Good to meet you, too, Julie,' Owen said, pushing back the hair that had fallen over his forehead, to reveal a pair of very blue eyes. He grinned, and added, 'Austin certainly strikes me as a man who takes his work extremely seriously.'

No one could replace Laurie, I thought, but there's every chance that Owen Somers and I are going to get along.

'Are you an actor by any chance?' I said.

'I'm hoping to become one,' Owen said.

'You're not the only one who has that ambition,' I said. 'Come and meet the rest of the cast.'

I introduced Owen to the rest of the promotions team, and we all trailed out of the club. He and I found ourselves a pitch on the south side of Leicester Square, I gave him a few tips on how to persuade unsuspecting members of the public that all they needed for a great night out was a Zone flyer, and we set to work. It soon became apparent my new partner was going to do a good job. Even on a Monday, the square was swarming with girls who were very happy to take a flyer in exchange for a chance to flirt with a good-looking boy.

'So what were you doing for a living before you signed up for flyering?' I asked Owen when there was a lull in the crowds.

'Oh, all sorts,' Owen said. 'Bar work. Factory work. Mainly, I've been driving a fork-lift truck. I'm on a gap year right now, but I'm starting at the London Academy of Performing Arts in September.'

'That's where I trained,' I said. 'I graduated last year.'

'Did you go to LAPA straight from school?' Owen said.

'I did,' I said. 'All I've ever wanted to do with my life is act in musical theatre.'

Owen sighed. 'I wanted to go into full-time drama training when I was eighteen, but my parents were completely against it. I ended up applying to university.'

A large group of Japanese tourists had stopped nearby to take photographs, so we broke off our conversation to offer them flyers. None of them spoke much English, so we couldn't tell them about the free drinks, but they accepted our hand-outs readily enough and asked us, with gestures and beaming smiles, to pose with them for photos. I didn't mind – they had relieved us of a dozen flyers after all – though it was strange to think we'd feature as examples of the local London fauna in someone's album on the other side of the world.

'So did you go to uni?' I said to Owen, once the last of the smiling, bowing tourists had gone.

'Yeah,' Owen said. 'Worst mistake I've ever made. I lasted a month.'

'Why? What happened?'

'I saw the touring production of *Two Cities*. It was amazing – and I knew that I couldn't go on wasting my life going to lectures and writing essays. I dropped out of uni the next day. I auditioned for LAPA, and got in on a scholarship. In three months, I'll be a drama student.'

'What do your parents think about that?' I said.

'My father,' Owen said, 'who considers that I'm throwing away the very expensive private education that he paid for, is barely speaking to me. My mother takes his side.'

'That must be so hard.' I felt a sudden burst of affection for my own parents, who while they'd worried about my going off to drama school and living in London at the age of eighteen, had never once suggested that I reconsider my choice of career.

Owen shrugged. 'It's their problem, not mine. My scholarship covers my college fees, and I've been working and saving all year. It's not like I'm going to be dependent on my parents for money.'

'I'm sure they'll come round,' I said.

'I hope so.' Owen said. 'But it's my life, and I'm not giving up my dream for them or anyone else.' His very blue eyes locked on mine. 'What about you? Would you ever give up trying to become an actress?'

'Honestly?' I said. 'I don't know. There have been times during the past year when I've thought about it. Ask me again in ten years' time, if I'm still handing out flyers.'

Two girls, both dressed for clubbing, one tall and one petite, approached Owen.

'Could we, like, get one of your flyers?' the tall girl said.

'You, like, certainly can,' Owen said. 'You can have two of my flyers – one each. You hand them to any of the bar staff at Zone, and you each get a free drink.'

The tall girl took the proffered flyer and started reading it. The small girl looked up into Owen's face.

'You have gorgeous eyes,' she said. 'Chanelle, doesn't he have gorgeous eyes?'

Her friend, Chanelle, also stared at Owen. 'Your eyes are *so blue*,' she said. They both giggled.

'Coloured contact lenses,' Owen said.

'Oh. Right,' Chanelle said. She flourished her flyer. 'So, like, where's this club?'

'Like, that way.' Owen pointed across the square. The girls set off, giggling and clinging to each other as they fought for balance in their six-inch stilettos. Their voices drifted back to us.

'No one has eyes that blue,' Chanelle said. '

'That's what I thought,' said the smaller girl, 'but that boy sure was cute.'

'Do you really wear coloured contacts?' I said to Owen.

'No, I don't,' Owen said. 'I just said that to get rid of those idiotic girls.'

'Don't you like it if a girl gazes into your eyes?' I said.

'I like it very much when it's the right girl,' Owen said. 'And when I'm not handing out flyers in the middle of Leicester Square.'

I laughed. 'Being hit on during working hours is a vital part of our job.

The evening wore on. Seven men asked me for my phone number in the first hour, which was a record, but by the time we went back to Zone to eat, nine girls had asked Owen for his, so my record was already broken. I filled him in on some of the things he could expect in his first term at drama school. He told me about a temp job he'd had in a wine merchant's, where the manager was a teetotaller and the rest of the staff were drunk before their twelve o'clock lunch break. I told him that I had a steady boyfriend (I may have talked about Zac more than once), he told me that he was single (what he actually said was that his love life was a disaster). I told him I was through to the final round of auditions for Joe Garcia's new musical, and he was eager to hear about the whole audition process. By the time he'd rushed off at the end of the night to catch a bus to Walthamstow, where he had a room (he described it as a cell) in a shared house, I'd decided that my new flyering partner would do just fine.

CHAPTER 30

On the morning of the *La Pasionaria* final, Zac and I arrived at the station to find that our train was delayed due to a signal failure further up the line. I panicked, convinced that we were going to be late for the audition. Zac calmly hailed a taxi.

'Relax, *cariño*,' he said to me, as I sat on the edge of the seat clutching my bag. 'We'll be there in good time.'

I looked out of the taxi's window. 'Do you think? The traffic's terrible.'

'Julie, stop stressing.' Zap put a finger under my chin and turned my face towards him. 'We'll be fine. Trust me.' I nodded, and concentrated on going over Mariana and Javier's duologue in my head.

We reached the Aphra Behn Theatre only fifteen minutes later than we'd intended. Judging by the number of people who arrived around the same time as ourselves, I had to agree with Zac that there was really no need for us to run up the stairs to the rehearsal room.

In the corridor outside the studio, Zac suddenly pulled me close to him. 'Have you calmed down now?' he said. 'Are you focused?'

'Yes,' I said.

His dark eyes locked on mine. 'I want this very badly. For both of us.'

I thought, I love you, Zac Diaz. Aloud, I said, 'So do I.' He smiled, and gestured for me to precede him through the door.

Inside the rehearsal studio, the audition panel were already seated behind their table, consulting notebooks and looking through CVs. Josh Cavanagh, the Assistant Choreographer, and Kate the Dance Captain were standing off to one side. The pianist was at the piano. Hannah told everyone entering the studio to be ready to dance in ten.

Alexa, Luke and Toby had all arrived before Zac and me. We went and joined them and began warming up. Michael came rushing in a few minutes later, cursing the unreliability of public transport.

'Cutting it a bit fine aren't we?' Alexa said to him.

'Oh, well, it's only the final,' he said. 'I didn't want to look desperate.'

Joe Garcia talked quietly to his choreographer and his MD, and unnervingly drew their attention to one or other of the twelve girls and ten boys in front of him. More than five hundred musical theatre actors had attended the first round of the auditions for *La Pasionaria*. Only twenty-two were left.

Then the most important man in musical theatre stood up and cleared his throat. Everyone in the room froze.

Joe Garcia looked round the studio at the upturned faces. 'Yes, it's getting serious now,' he said, with a smile that belied his words. There was a ripple of nervous laughter.

'We're going to be making some tough decisions today,' Joe went on. 'So I'm asking all of you to really go for it. Show me what you can do. Impress me. Make me believe I can't put on *La Pasionaria* without you.' Again his gaze raked the assembled performers, and everyone sat up just a little straighter. 'We're going to start by seeing the boys dance one more time. OK, guys, find a space to stand in, two lines of five, please. Girls, bear with us, your turn will come. Thank you, Nathan.'

While the girls went and sat amongst the heap of bags at the rear of the studio, the boys ran to bag a space in which to dance. Zac, I saw, had managed to get in the front row.

'The routine you're about to learn is an expression of rage against injustice,' Nathan Nyembe said. 'I want to see anger and defiance, in the way you dance and on your faces.'

With Josh and Kate demonstrating, Nathan taught the boys a jazz routine comprised of angry, violent moves that ended with a jump going into a turn, a crouch, and finally, a triumphant punch to the air. Once he was satisfied that everyone knew what they were doing, he had the boys dance the whole routine through again, while he prowled up and down between the lines, shouting at them to give him more determination, anger, agony, rage – and the more they did, the more he smiled. Joe Garcia stood up and made a circuit of the studio, watching the boys all the while. They were all good dancers – they wouldn't have got to this stage of the auditions if they hadn't been – but some were clearly stronger than others. Zac was definitely one of the best, but even I had to admit that he did have some competition.

Nathan gestured to the pianist to stop playing, and told the boys to go and sit down. A murmur of conversation started up around the room.

'Well done,' I said to Zac, moving my dance bag so that he could sit next to me.

238

'Not that well done.' Zac muttered. 'Not as well as I'd have liked.'

'Zac, you danced brilliantly,' I began, but then Kate called for quiet. The studio immediately fell silent.

'We'd like a few of you to dance on your own,' Joe Garcia said. 'Could we see Ramon Chavez, please.'

Ramon Chavez was tall like Zac, dark-haired and dark-eyed like Zac, but a few years older. All eyes in the room were on him as he walked to a space in centre of the floor and danced the routine by himself.

'Do you know that boy?' Zac whispered to me.

'No,' I whispered back.

'I reckon he's my main rival for Javier.'

'You think?' I watched more closely. He was a good dancer. Very good.

'Thank you, Ramon,' Joe said, as the music stopped and Ramon's right fist hit the air. 'Zac Diaz, please.'

Zac sprang to his feet. He walked confidently to the centre of the studio, then took a couple of paces forward, closer to the audition panel. Joe Garcia nodded at the pianist. Music filled the studio, and Zac began to dance.

By now, I had seen him dance many times, but I had never seen him dance the way he danced that routine in the final recall for *La Pasionaria*. He performed the choreography exactly as Nathan had taught it, and yet somehow his body expressed the emotion of the dance, the rage that Nathan had asked for, more than the other dancers, and made everyone watching feel it as well. Mesmerised by Zac's virtuosity, I forgot that I was in the middle of an audition, and simply watched him dance.

The music reached the last bar. Zac jumped and turned, and seemed to hang in the air before turning again and landing in a crouch, head bowed. He held the position until the music finished, then stood and raised his fist just after the last note died. There was a moment's silence, and then the studio broke into spontaneous applause and cheers. Nathan Nyembe and Oliver Brady, who had surely seen more than one amazing audition in their time, were looking at Zac with an expression that could only be described as awe. Jessica Coleman was clapping her hands – I suspected she had seen fewer auditions than her older colleagues. Joe Garcia leant forward, his elbows on the table, his chin resting on his steepled fingers. His face was expressionless.

'Do you think you could dance like that six nights a week and twice on Thursdays and Saturdays?' he said to Zac, after the applause had died down.

'*Si*,' Zac said. 'Yes.'

Only then did Joe smile. 'Thank you, Zac. *Gracias.*'

'*Gracias*,' Zac said. With every girl and boy in the studio still watching him, their facial expressions a mixture of admiration and envy, he walked slowly back across the sprung floor to where I was sitting. His black vest top clung wetly to his body and his cut-off joggers hung low on his hips, revealing a couple of inches of taut stomach. My own stomach clenched with desire.

'That boy is sex on legs,' a girl sitting a little way behind me said to her friend, presumably more loudly than she had intended. Her friend did not disagree.

Zac sank down onto the floor next to me. Suddenly, I wanted very badly to touch him, to feel his body pressed against mine, and to kiss him on the mouth. And to tell him that I loved him. I contented myself with passing him a bottle of water and a towel.

Three other boys were asked to dance solos, and while they acquitted themselves well enough, they didn't dance anywhere near as well as Ramon, let alone as well as Zac. Then Joe Garcia announced that he would see the girls. I immediately jumped up and hurried to the front of the studio. Oliver Brady put a hand on Joe's arm, and pointed at me. Joe nodded and said something to Oliver too low for me to hear. Oliver stood up and beckoned me out of line.

'How's your throat today?' he said.

'It's fine,' I said. 'Totally recovered.'

'Good,' Oliver said. 'Joe doesn't need to see you dance again, but he does need to hear you sing, and so do I. So I'm going to go through some scales with you while he sees some of the other girls dance, and then he'll join us. If you'd like to fetch your music – two songs, please, 'You Are Mine' and one other – we'll go and find a piano.'

I went with Oliver to the small rehearsal room where I had sung so disastrously at the last audition. He sat down at the piano, and we ran through a vocal warm up and some scales. Then he heard me sing 'You Are Mine', and a second song, 'Another Sunset', from *Scheherazade*.

'Those songs suit you,' he said. 'You sang them really well.'

'Thank you,' I said. I knew that I'd sung well, but it was good to be told so by Joe Garcia's musical director.

Oliver asked me about the shows I'd done in college and the parts I'd played. Then he asked me if I read music.

'A little –' I began, as the door to the rehearsal room swung open and Joe Garcia walked in.

241

'How are you doing?' he said to Oliver.

'It's all good,' Oliver said. 'Do you want to hear both of Julie's songs, Joe?'

'No, if you're happy, I'll just hear 'You Are Mine'.' He smiled at me. 'Sorry, Julie, I know we're talking about you as though you're not here.'

'That's OK,' I said, and thought, you and your MD can talk about me all you want. Joe nodded at Oliver who began to play. I imagined that Zac was in the room and I was looking into his eyes, and sang. When I'd sung the final chorus, I looked at Joe Garcia and saw that he was smiling.

'Remind me how old you are, Julie,' he said.

'I'm twenty-two,' I said. I resisted the urge to tell him that I could play younger. Or older. Or any age he wanted.

'Only twenty-two? I'd certainly like to hear you sing that song again when you're in your thirties.' He leant back in his chair. 'Thank you, Julie. You can go back up to the studio. Then Oliver and I can talk some more about you behind your back.'

I smiled, and took my music from Oliver. Not that he'd really needed it to play 'You Are Mine'. He'd been the MD on *Warrior Queen* after all.

'Thank you,' I said and thought, please, Mr Garcia, don't wait 'til I'm in my thirties to cast me in one of your shows.

Back in the studio, I threaded my way through the sprawl of bodies and dance bags to the place where my friends were sitting, acutely conscious of the speculative glances being cast in my direction, particularly by the other girls.

'We're just hanging around while the most important man in musical theatre hears Julie Farrell sing,' Alexa said, as I stepped over her legs. I grinned at her and sat down next to Zac.

'How'd it go?' he said.

'Good,' I said. 'Joe only wanted to hear 'You Are Mine'. He seemed to like the way I sang it.'

My friends immediately cross-questioned me as to *exactly* what Joe and Oliver had said to me. I was aware that everyone sitting near our group was straining to hear my answers.

'What did I miss?' I said in an effort to deflect attention away from myself.

'Just the girls dancing the same dance we were taught at the first audition,' Alexa said. 'Nathan only went over it once,' she lowered her voice, 'and some of the girls didn't remember it. A few girls really messed up. I was fine though.'

At that moment Joe and Oliver reappeared in the rehearsal studio and re-joined Nathan and Jessica. There was much shuffling of CVs and comparing of notes.

Alexa took a long drink of water. 'It's getting really close in here.'

Luke sniffed the air. 'Ah, the scent of fear. Don't you just love auditions?'

After what seemed an eternity, in reality about ten minutes, Joe Garcia once again stood up.

'If I could have your attention, guys,' he said, as if the attention of every boy and girl in the room wasn't riveted on him already. 'I'm going to read out the names of people we want to see again this afternoon. Those of you whose

243

names I don't read out, I'm sorry, but you've not made it through to the next round, and we're going to need you to leave the audition. Thank you very much.'

He read out his list. Toby's name wasn't on it.

'We'll take a half hour break,' Joe said. 'Then we'll be asking some of you to run through the scenes you were given last week. Everyone to be ready to go again at one o'clock, please.' Immediately, a cacophony of chatter filled the studio, as the successful auditionees and the bitterly disappointed exchanged congratulations and commiserations, and gave their BFFs an update via their mobile phones.

'I'm so sorry, Toby,' I said.

'You win some, you lose some,' Toby said. 'Although, obviously, I'm gutted.'

Alexa gave him a hug.

'Good luck to all of you,' he said. 'I hope you make it into the show. If you do, I'll definitely be asking you for comps.'

We said our goodbyes, and Toby made his towards the exit, along with two girls and one other boy. There was just enough time for the eighteen performers who remained in the studio to grab a bite to eat, before Hannah called for quiet.

'OK, guys, break over,' she said. 'The audition panel are ready for you. If the following people would come with me, please.' She called out my name and Zac's, together with Abigail Dean, Connie Harker and Ramon Chavez. I looked at Abigail and Connie, both of them small and dark-haired like me, and thought, are they my rivals for the part of Mariana?

Hannah escorted the five of us down the stairs to the smaller rehearsal room. She went inside, putting her head around the door a moment later.

'Julie Farrell and Ramon Chavez, please,' she said.

Me and *Ramon*? I thought. Foolishly perhaps, it hadn't occurred to me that I'd be performing Mariana and Javier's scene with anyone other than Zac. I reminded myself that I was supposed to be a professional actress, took a deep breath and followed Ramon into the room, standing next to him in front of the audition panel's table.

'Hi, guys,' Joe said. 'If you'd stand a little further apart –' Ramon and I obediently shuffled a few steps away from each other. 'Take it from the top, please, Julie.'

We played the scene. Ramon proved to be a good actor – which was fortunate, because there's nothing worse than trying to act with someone who doesn't give you anything back – and when Mariana had spoken her final line, I was reasonably satisfied that I'd performed well. The audition panel were all busily scribbling notes: hopefully, a good sign.

Joe laid down his pen. 'Ramon, if you'd like to go back to the studio. Would you ask Zac Diaz to come in, please, Hannah.' Ramon left, and my heart leapt as Zac strode into the room. For an instant, our eyes met, and then his attention was all on Joe Garcia.

'Good afternoon, Zac,' Joe said. 'Julie – from the top again, please.'

I turned to Zac. I was Mariana begging the man she loved not to go to war, and he was Javier, telling her he must join the fight against tyranny. And when he walked away, and I'd admitted that I loved him, it took me a moment to recall that I wasn't Mariana but Julie Farrell, hoping that I'd done enough to convince Joe Garcia that I could play the lead character in his new musical.

'Thank you, Julie,' Joe said. 'You can go back to the studio now. Well done.'

'Thank you,' I said. Well done! Joe Garcia said *well done*. I returned to the large rehearsal studio, but instead of going in, I waited outside for my boyfriend. Abigail came upstairs and went into the studio, and then Connie. Finally, Zac appeared.

'We did good, you and I,' he said. 'That was one acting audition that could not have gone any better.'

'I agree.' I glanced over my shoulder to check there was no one else around. 'What were the other girls like?'

'Connie's a good actress,' Zac said, in a low voice, 'but trying to act with Abigail was like reciting dialogue to a plank of wood. What about Ramon?'

'He was OK,' I said. 'No, that's unfair. He's good, just not as good as you.'

'Not that you're biased,' Zac said.

'As if,' I said. 'What happens now, do you think?'

'Now,' Zac said, 'we wait in the studio until the audition panel decide they've seen enough and tell us we can go home.'

'Do you think we'll find out today if we're cast?' I said. 'I know Joe isn't going to come in and make an announcement, but might he phone later tonight?'

Zac shrugged. 'I would think we're more likely to get a call tomorrow or next week.

Waiting for Joe Garcia to decide my fate proved more draining than dancing, singing or acting. By the time the audition panel had seen everyone who'd been given a script – and some people, including Michael, twice – it was gone seven at night, and I suspected that I wasn't the only performer in the room who was feeling exhausted. Conversation was muted and for once no one was making a call on their phone. Few people were even able to summon the energy to send a text. One boy lay on the floor, closed his eyes and appeared to go to sleep. Alexa and Michael took it in turns to massage the tension from each other's shoulders.

Then the door to the rehearsal studio opened, and Joe Garcia and Jessica Coleman made their entrance.

Joe looked round at the tired faces of the performers seated in front of him. 'No doubt you'll all be glad to hear that the audition panel won't be asking any of you to sing, dance or act for them again today,' he said. There was a collective sigh of relief. Joe's face creased into a sympathetic smile. 'I'm often asked why I bother to hold open auditions when I could easily cast my shows with actors whose work I already know. My reply is that I enjoy discovering new talent. And I have to say that these past few weeks have once again shown me what a wealth of talent is out there. Every single one of you sitting in front of me right now, whether you've been in the business for years or are just beginning your career, is extremely talented. That said, I can't use all of you in *La Pasionaria*. I only wish I could. But if I don't cast you for this show, I do urge you to keep auditioning. If we decide to offer you a contract, my assistant, Jessica, will phone you or your agent. If we're unable to use you at this time, we'll let you know by email. If your availability changes before you hear

247

from us, please email us to let us know. On behalf of Oliver, Nathan, Jessica and myself, thank you very much.'

Joe and Jessica left the studio. Boys exchanged jazz shoes for trainers; girls pulled on jeans over tights. I noticed several people swapping phone numbers and promises to let each other know whether or not they got cast.

'We've done all we can,' Michael said. 'Now it's in the hands of the gods.'

Alexa looked at him quizzically. 'Don't you mean in the hands of the audition panel?'

'Exactly,' Michael said.

Everyone agreed that the final had worn them out, but by the time we had walked down the stairs and gone out through the stage door onto the street, it became apparent that none of us were ready to go home and wait for our phones to ring. After some debate about where we might go to unwind, Alexa, Luke, and Michael ended up coming back with Zac and me to Zac's flat, stopping to buy beer and wine on the way. We put on some music, and raided Zac's well-stocked freezer for pizza. It was only when I was showing a suitably impressed Alexa the view from the balcony that it dawned on me that Zac and I were entertaining my friends. As a couple. *Our* friends. I felt deliriously happy.

'You should give Tim a call,' I said to Alexa in the kitchen. 'Invite him to come over and meet us all.'

Alexa shook her head. 'Not tonight. Negotiations in that area are at a very delicate stage right now. One wrong move and all deals are off. I'll wait to see him on Saturday.'

'Oh. Right. Of course.' I had absolutely no idea what she was talking about. I raised my wine glass to my lips... and found that it was empty.

We went back into the main room where the boys were sprawled on the sofas. I took a step towards Zac, tripped, and fell into his lap. For some reason this seemed incredibly funny and I started laughing. Zac looked a little startled, but then he laughed too and put his arms round me. I smiled benevolently at *our* assembled friends.

'Why don't you phone Suzanne and ask her to join us?' I said to Michael.

'She's working tonight,' Michael said.

'What time does she get off?' I said. 'Ask her to come over when she finishes.'

Michael took a swig from a bottle of beer. 'She won't come. She's always tired after work.'

'Oh. That's a shame.' I felt really sorry for Suzanne working at... at whatever it was she did.

'We were all tired when we came out of the audition,' Alexa said, 'but we're all right now.' She picked up her phone from the coffee table. All of us had our phones within easy reach. As if Joe Garcia – or in Zac or Luke's case, their agent – was going to call us at ten o'clock at night. 'I'll phone her and persuade her to come.'

'I'd prefer it if you didn't interfere, Alexa,' Michael said.

Alexa's eyebrows arched in surprise. 'OK. I won't phone her then.' There was an awkward silence, broken by Zac's enquiring if anyone wanted coffee. Conversation resumed, and the moment passed.

CHAPTER 31

'So what was up with Michael and the not phoning Suzanne?' I said to Alexa the following morning.

'They're going through another rough patch,' Alexa said. 'He told me and Luke after you went to bed.'

Last night, Zac and I'd gone to bed around midnight, leaving our guests to sort out who was sleeping in the spare bedroom and who was going to have to make do with a sofa. In the morning, we'd got up around ten a.m. to find that Michael had already left for work, his father's employees taking a dim view of the Boss's Son failing to be at his desk by eight-thirty. Zac and Luke, who'd had a very satisfying discussion about cars at the audition, had taken themselves off for a further male bonding session at the gym. Alexa and I had gone out onto the balcony to sit in the sun.

I said, 'Did Michael let Suzanne know he wasn't coming home last night?'

'He texted her. Just before he passed out on the sofa. He is such a lightweight. Lord only knows how he managed to drag himself into his office this morning.'

I didn't comment. My memories of the latter part of the evening were a little hazy, but I was fairly sure that Michael wasn't the only one who'd had too much to drink.

After a while, Alexa said, 'I made rather a fool of myself last night. With Luke.'

Oh, surely she hadn't? I thought. 'I don't mean to be judgemental,' I said, choosing my words carefully, 'and I know Luke has his attractions, but I have to say that sleeping with him when you're trying to make a go of it with Tim is not a good choice.'

'I agree,' Alexa said. 'Which is why I made a point of telling Luke that I couldn't sleep with him because I've started seeing someone else. And then I felt totally ridiculous because *he* spent the next ten minutes telling *me* that he's met this really nice girl called Ruby, and asking my advice about where he should take her on their first date. Sex with Alexa Hamilton-Jones was obviously not on his agenda last night. He was just too polite to say.'

I tried unsuccessfully to smother a laugh.

'It's not *that* amusing,' Alexa said, as a familiar ring-tone drifted out onto the terrace through the open glass doors. 'That's my phone!' She leapt to her feet and ran inside.

I thought, is this the Call? I heard the murmur of Alexa's voice – try as I might I couldn't hear what she was saying – and then a piercing shriek. Alarmed, I peered inside the flat, and was reassured to see Alexa still talking on her mobile. I sat watching her, in a frenzy of impatience. After another ten minutes or so, she came back outside, holding her phone in both hands. She was wide-eyed and her face was very white.

I said. 'Was that call, by any chance, from Jessica Coleman?'

'No, it wasn't,' Alexa said. She sank down on a wicker chair. 'Do you remember – weeks ago – I auditioned for a part in *Sherwood*?'

I thought for a moment. 'The TV series?' I said.

'I got it,' Alexa said, her voice oddly calm. 'That was the casting director on the phone. They want me to start filming in August.'

'Oh, Alexa!' Now I was shrieking. 'That's brilliant. Congratulations –' My mind reeled. 'But rehearsals for *La Pasionaria* start in August! Alexa, what about *La Pasionaria*? You can't do both.'

'I know that,' Alexa said. 'I'm going to do the TV series.'

I gaped at her. 'You mean… you're going to turn down *La Pasionaria*?'

'You're forgetting something,' Alexa said. 'I haven't actually been offered *La Pasionaria*.'

'Not yet,' I said. How could she even *think* of turning down Joe Garcia? 'Listen, Alexa, a TV series sounds fabulous, but if you do get into *La Pasionaria*, you have to take your time deciding between the two.'

'There's no decision to make,' Alexa said. 'I've already verbally accepted *Sherwood*. The production team are emailing my contract as we speak.'

'But you don't have to sign it straight away,' I said. How can she choose a TV series over a West End musical? I thought.

'Well, no,' Alexa said. 'I thought I'd get my legal-hot-shot brother to take a look at it first, just to make sure I'm not signing away my soul.'

'And as long as you haven't signed anything, you can still change your mind and do *La Pasionaria* – if you get it,' I said. 'At least wait a few days.'

'I won't change my mind,' Alexa said.

'But... You've always wanted to do musical theatre. You could be in a *Joe Garcia* musical –'

'The thing is,' Alexa said, 'I *want* to do *Sherwood*. I knew I wanted it as soon as I did the first audition. I never thought they'd cast me, but they have.' Her eyes shone. 'It's a once in a lifetime opportunity, and I know I'll regret it for ever if I don't take it.'

I was stunned into silence. I looked at my best friend and thought, she really does want this. It's not what I'd want for myself, but it's what *she* wants. This is the moment when her acting career begins. Suddenly, I too was smiling.

'Your first professional role,' I said. 'This is huge, Alexa. I'm so happy for you. Obviously I think you're insane to give up on *La Pasionaria,* but I'll still text Zac and ask him to buy a bottle of champagne on his way home.'

CHAPTER 32

'I wonder what time Jessica Coleman gets into work when she's not auditioning,' I said to Zac on Sunday evening, as I opened the front door to my and Alexa's flat.

'Let's hope it's early,' Zac said. He and I'd kept our phones within easy reach all day Friday and Saturday, hoping for a call from Joe Garcia's assistant, cutting other phone conversations short. By Sunday, we'd agreed that Jessica didn't work weekends, and neither of us was going to hear from her before Monday morning. We'd spent most of the day with Laurie (the rehearsals for *Iago* were going splendidly) and Toby (whose agent had already lined up several more auditions for him) and both of us had managed not to check for missed calls even once.

'I'll set an alarm for eight,' I said. 'When – *if* – Jessica calls, I don't want to be asleep.'

We trooped up the stairs and had just set foot on the landing, when a man, tall, broad shouldered and with light brown hair came out of the kitchen. He was carrying an open bottle of red wine and two glasses – and he was completely naked. Even if I hadn't had Zac with me, I wouldn't have been particularly alarmed. As a rule, I was inclined to think that a burglar would be unlikely to strip off and pour himself a glass of Chianti. Besides, there was nothing in the flat that anyone would want to steal.

'Er… hello.' The naked man positioned the wine bottle strategically in front of him. 'I'm Tim Devereaux. I'm a friend of Alexa's.'

'Good to meet you,' I said, not allowing my gaze to drop below his handsome face. 'I'm Alexa's flatmate, Julie, and this is Zac.'

Zac automatically held out a hand, then thought better of it and let his arm fall to his side.

'Well, I guess I should…' Tim inclined his head towards Alexa's half-open door.

'Absolutely,' I said. With as much dignity as was humanly possible in the circumstances, Tim turned on his heel and vanished inside Alexa's bedroom. I managed to get into my room and close the door, before bursting into laughter.

'Julie, stop it, they'll hear you.' Zac was also having trouble keeping a straight face.

'I can't stop,' I said. 'You'll have to think of a way to distract me.' He smiled in a way that made my legs turn to jelly, and peeled off his T-shirt.

***

Awake, but still in bed, warmly entwined with Zac, I heard my phone ring. Sitting bolt upright, I grabbed it from the nightstand, only to sink back onto the pillow when I saw that it wasn't Jessica Coleman calling me on this fine summer morning, but my mother. I hit the answer button.

'Hello, Julie,' my mother said. 'It's not too early for you is it?'

'Hi, Mum,' I said. 'No, it's not too early. I've been up for hours. How is everybody?'

'Oh, we're all fine,' my mother said. 'Although I must admit I'll be pleased when Daisy's exams are over – GCSEs are so stressful for parents. How are you?'

'I'm good,' I said. 'I got through to the final for a new musical – *La Pasionaria* – last week.'

'Oh, Julie, that's wonderful news,' my mother said. '*La Pasionaria*. I must write that down.'

'I haven't got the job yet,' I said, before she could ask where to buy tickets. 'I'm waiting to hear. I'm hoping I might get a call today.'

'I have a feeling you will get this job,' my mother said.

Zac got out of bed and pulled on his jeans. 'Do you want tea?' he said.

'Just a sec, Mum,' I said. 'Please, Zac.' He went off to forage in the kitchen.

'Julie?' my mother said. 'Was that a man's voice I heard? Do you have someone there with you?' After a pause, she added, 'Julie, I know you're a grown woman, and I'm sure you have no desire to discuss your love life with your mother, but do you have a new boyfriend?'

'Yes, I'm seeing someone,' I said. 'His name's Zac. He's an actor.'

'You have a *boyfriend*,' my mother said. 'Well, that really is good news. How did you meet him?'

Suppressing a sudden temptation to tell her that Zac had picked me up in a bar, I said, 'A mutual friend, a boy I was working with, introduced us. We've not known each other very long.'

Zac came back into the bedroom, carrying two mugs of tea, handed one to me and sat down on the bed.

I said, 'Mum, I'm sorry, but I'm going to have to go.'

'Of course, no worries. I was only ringing for a chat, and you're expecting an important call.' Having reminded me that my friends were always welcome in the parental abode – a hint, I knew, that she wouldn't object to meeting the new man in my life – and extracted my promise to phone her as soon as I had any definite news about *La Pasionaria*, my mother rang off.

Zac said, 'It occurs to me that my announcing my presence when you were on the phone to your mother may not have been very tactful.'

'Not at all.' I considered asking him if he'd told his parents about me yet, but decided against it: I didn't want him thinking I was edging our relationship to another level before he was ready. I said, 'My mother is delighted to hear that I have a boyfriend. The news that I may be cast in a musical is nothing compared to that.'

'But did you tell her it's a *Joe Garcia* musical?' Zac said.

'I doubt she'd know who he is,' I said.

'Seriously?' Zac said. 'Are there people in the world who don't know the name Joe Garcia?'

'Sometimes I think it's only my family,' I said.

Zac laughed and drained his tea. 'I should get going. I'm meeting a friend, a guy I've not seen since –' He was interrupted by his phone ringing loud and shrill. He snatched it up, but having looked at the screen, dropped it on the bed, and let it go through to voicemail. He didn't tell me who the call was from. Not that he needed to – I'd seen the caller ID. He stood up and put on the rest of his clothes. I found my dressing gown, and went with him to the front door. We agreed that he'd meet me from work that night, and we'd stay at his. Then, having kissed me, he went out. I closed the front door. I was shaken, and it wasn't because of Zac's kiss, but because he'd just had a call from someone named *Ros*, who he apparently didn't want to talk to in front of me.

Ros, I thought. Rosalind Adams. It has to be. The man I love has just received a phone call from his celebrity ex. I reminded myself that Zac had told me he and Rosalind were still in touch, that they were friends and nothing more. There was no reason for me to feel insecure.

I showered, dressed, and went into the living room, setting up my laptop on the dining table, with every intention of checking if anyone had posted about *La Pasionaria* on social media. My fingers hovered over the keyboard, and then, without quite knowing why, I typed the name of Zac's former lover. My screen filled with photo after photo of Rosalind Adams on a red carpet – at the Oscars, at the Baftas, in New York and in California – accompanied by a succession of handsome men, many of them younger than her. They were all A-Listers, film stars, male models or rock gods: none of them could possibly be described as an up-and-coming actor. I typed *Zac Diaz Rosalind Adams* into my browser, but all that came up were more pictures of Rosalind. I thought, why am I wasting time trawling the internet for photos of my boyfriend with his ex, who he broke up with two years ago, when I could be doing something productive – and sane?

I shut my laptop, just as Alexa, wearing a floor-length, ivory silk dressing gown, her hair a tumbling mass of tousled curls, a serene smile on her face, wafted into the living room in a cloud of perfume and settled herself gracefully on the sofa. The sofa ruined the ambience she'd created by twanging very loudly.

'Ow,' Alexa said, rubbing her thigh.

'You and Tim turned out to be compatible then?' I said.

'We so did,' Alexa said. 'We were compatible on Saturday, and we were compatible again last night.'

'So your new dress was a wise investment,' I said.

'It was,' Alexa said, 'although I didn't have it on for very long. On Saturday, when Tim arrived to take me out, I answered the door in my robe –'

'The one you're wearing now?' I said.

'No, the really short red one, so that he got a good look at my legs. I made out that I was running late, and had him wait in the living room while I finished getting ready. I left him for five minutes and then I went in with my dress half-undone at the back and asked him to zip me up. My idea was that he'd spend the whole evening *thinking* about un-zipping the dress and getting me out of it, but he was way ahead of me.'

'You didn't make it to the restaurant?' I said.

'We didn't make it to the bedroom,' Alexa said.

'You mean… in here? On the *sofa?* The sofa with the broken springs. That must have been interesting.'

'It was amazing,' Alexa said. 'Tim was incredible. He went home Sunday morning, but then last night he did take me out – we made it to the restaurant this time – and he stayed here again.'

'I know,' I said. 'Zac and I met him coming out of the kitchen.'

Alexa laughed. 'He was *so* embarrassed about that. I thought you two were going to Zac's, otherwise I'd have warned him to put some trousers on.'

'I do hope our unexpected arrival didn't throw him off his stride, so to speak,' I said.

'Oh, he got over his embarrassment soon enough.' Alexa's smile broadened. 'I've decided I prefer dating an older man. Younger guys just don't have the finesse.'

'I take it you *are* seeing him again?' I said.

'I certainly am,' Alexa said. 'He's flying to New York tomorrow – some frightfully important work thing – but he's back on Friday, and I'm seeing him then.' She stretched languorously. 'He was so delighted for me when I told him about my getting *Sherwood*. I sent back my contract yesterday, by the way, and I emailed Jessica Coleman to let her know I'm no longer available for *La Pasionaria*.'

It's done, I thought. She'll never know if Joe Garcia would have cast her or not. It was hideous to think that I might not get cast in the show, but I couldn't have borne not knowing one way or the other.

'I haven't quite decided how long I'm going to stay working at the call centre,' Alexa went on. 'I definitely want to take a holiday before filming starts, and I'll have to be around for costume fittings. Anyway, it's not for ages. We don't need to talk about it now.'

'Getting your first professional job as an actress is one of the most important things that's ever happened to you,' I said. 'You can talk about it all you like.'

'I don't want you to think I'm up myself,' Alexa said.

'Given that you're going to be in a major international TV series,' I said, 'I think you're entitled to be just a little bit up yourself. I would be.'

'You'd turn into a right diva,' Alexa said.

'My adoring fans expect a certain amount of diva-ish behaviour,' I said.

'Maybe so,' Alexa said, 'but if you keep on refusing to sign autographs you won't have any fans. And as for not turning up for that interview with *Goss* magazine, that was just plain stupid. You know what they say about being nice to people on the way up.'

'*I* don't have to be nice to the little people on the way up,' I said, 'because when *I* reach the top, I'm *never* coming down!' We both started laughing, and were still laughing when Alexa's mobile rang.

Fishing the phone out of the pocket of her robe, she said, 'Hi, Mike. Oh! Oh, well done. Julie, Michael's got ensemble in *La Pasionaria.*'

'Ooh, let me talk to him,' I gasped, holding out my hand for the phone. 'Congratulations, Michael. I'm so pleased for you.'

'I can't quite get my head around it,' Michael said. 'It's not like I'm that great a dancer. Or singer.'

'Don't put yourself down,' I said. I'm a better dancer and singer than he is, I thought. Zac is so much better than he is. Why has Jessica Coleman phoned him and not us? 'You're obviously good enough for Joe Garcia.'

'I guess I must be.'

'So what are you and Suzanne doing to celebrate?'

There was a silence, and then Michael said, 'I don't know. I'm at work. I haven't told her yet.'

261

'Oh. OK. I'd better get off the line' I said. 'Let you call her.'

'Yeah.' Michael said. 'Uh, can you pass me back to Alexa?' I handed Alexa her phone, and she and Michael talked – or rather he talked and she laughed at whatever it was he was saying – for some minutes before he finally rang off. It struck me forcibly that if she'd waited only one more day before withdrawing from *La Pasionaria*, she too might have had the Call. Or not. My gaze slid to my own phone which was sitting on the dining table, taunting me with its silence.

After a moment, Alexa said, 'Julie, I'm sure Jessica Coleman will call you very soon.'

'Well Joe Garcia did say they'd call everyone by the end of the week,' I said. I made myself smile. 'You know you were worried that I'd think you were up yourself?'

Alexa raised one eyebrow. 'Ye-es,' she said.

'You could prove to me that you're still the same loveable down-to-earth girl you always were by doing my share of the washing-up.'

***

Monday passed without Zac or me receiving a call from Jessica Coleman. Neither of us received a call from her on Tuesday or Wednesday. Or Thursday. Or Friday. Which was when Luke Harvey texted to say he'd had an email telling him he was *not* going to be offered a part in *La Pasionaria*. To my shame, I checked my own inbox (oh, the relief when I didn't find an email from Garcia Productions) before texting him back my commiserations.

On Saturday afternoon, reminding myself that Jessica Coleman was unlikely to work at weekends, I left Zac contentedly playing show tunes on the piano, and went to Limelight, where the demands of a ballet class provided a welcome distraction from waiting for my phone to ring. Suzanne was in class, dancing rather badly, I thought, but then everyone has their off-days. Afterwards, we went for coffee in the canteen, finding ourselves an empty table by the window.

As soon as we'd sat down, Suzanne said, 'Do you know yet if you've got *La Pasionaria*?'

I shook my head. 'I haven't heard anything, and neither has Zac.'

'I'm gutted I was cut from the auditions,' Suzanne said, spooning sugar into her Americano, and stirring it so vigorously that it spilled into the saucer. 'Living with someone who's got the job I wanted only makes it worse.'

I was taken aback by this. 'But you're pleased for Michael, right?' I said

'I should be, shouldn't I?' Suzanne gulped down a mouthful of coffee, and then she said, 'Julie, can I ask you something?'

'Of course, hun,' I said. 'What's up?'

'It's… well – I think Mike might be cheating on me.'

'Oh, surely not,' I said. 'I mean, why would you think that?'

'He's been acting strange, shifty. And he's started going out at odd times without telling me where he's going, and… I think… I need to ask you…'

I waited.

Suzanne wouldn't meet my eye. 'Is he cheating on me with Alexa?'

'No,' I said. 'Definitely not. I'd know if Alexa was shagging Michael. She'd tell me.'

'Would she?' Suzanne said.

'Yes, she would,' I said. 'Alexa and Michael are close friends, but that's all they are: friends.' Alexa wouldn't lie to me, I thought.

'Is that why there are eleven texts from her on his phone?' Suzanne said.

'You read Michael's texts?' I said.

'Despicable isn't it?' Suzanne said. 'But I didn't read the messages, only who they were from. I was too worried that he'd come in and catch me to read everything.'

'Listen, Suzanne,' I said. 'Texting someone doesn't mean you're sleeping with them.' A thought struck me. 'Besides, Alexa's seeing someone. And she's really into him. There's no way she'd mess around with another man.'

'You're sure about that?'

'If Michael's cheating on you, it isn't with Alexa,' I said.

'OK.' Suzanne didn't sound convinced, but I was at a loss as to what else I could say to reassure her. Fortunately, a girl from the year above us at LAPA, who was just back from a fabulous corporate gig in Dubai and wanted the whole of the Limelight canteen to know about it, came and joined us at our table, and the uncomfortable subject of Michael's possible cheating was necessarily dropped. After finishing my coffee, I left Suzanne listening to stories of luxury hotels and jeep rides across the desert, and with much more eagerness than usual, went to Zone.

In between handing out flyers in Leicester Square, I told Owen about Laurie and his (hopefully) breakout role in *Iago,* and then we passed the time discussing which other Shakespearean characters deserved their own play. Owen said that he'd always thought Edmund in *King Lear* was hard done by, while I declared that a reworking of Hamlet as *Ophelia: The Musical* would be a runaway West End success.

'In the musical theatre version,' I said, 'Ophelia won't die for love. After the way Hamlet treats her, she breaks up with him, and sings how she's better off without him.'

'So what happens in the final scene?' Owen said. 'Does she marry the heroic Fortinbras?'

'Absolutely,' I said, casting a defiant look at the statue of Shakespeare, just visible through the summer foliage of the trees in the garden area of the square. 'I want her to have a happy ending.'

Owen put his hand on my arm. 'Look. A stag party.'

'I'll take stage left,' I said. 'You take stage right. We high-fived each other, circled around the unsuspecting young men, and moved in for the kill.

The ringing of my phone made me jump, literally, and drop half my flyers. Admittedly, Saturday night was a highly unlikely time for a director's assistant to be calling actors with offers of musical theatre contracts, but I wasn't taking any chances. In a panic I grabbed my phone out of my jeans and pressed the answer icon.

Over the speaker, came a cacophony of shouted conversation and loud music, and then Zac saying, 'Julie?'

'Hey, Zac,' I said, my heart lifting at the sound of his voice.

'I can't speak for long – I'm still at work. I've –' His words were drowned out by the background noise.

'I can't hear you,' I said.

He said, 'Hold on. I'll go into the other bar…' After a moment, the music faded and ceased. 'Can you hear me now?'

'Yes, I can hear you,' I said.

'Julie – I've got the part of Javier in *La Pasionaria*.'

CHAPTER 33

'What a night.' Zac stood by the open window and looked out over the balcony to the city that lay beyond. 'The pub hasn't been that crowded in all the weeks I've been working there. I've never pulled so many pints.'

I picked up a cushion from one of the sofas and threw it at him. 'Yes, what a night. The night you got your dream job. The night you got the lead in Joe Garcia's new musical.'

He turned around to face me, and smiled.

'Are you going tell me everything right now,' I said, 'or wait until I've got the champagne out of the fridge?'

After we'd finished work, we'd met at the entrance to Leicester Square station. I'd had every intention of immediately interrogating him about the Call, but he'd laughingly refused to tell me anything until we were back at his flat, silencing my eager questions with a kiss.

Zac said, 'Champagne is definitely the priority.'

I fetched the bottle and two glasses, and Zac opened it. The cork shot right across the room and the champagne bubbled up out of the bottle, but I had the glasses ready and we managed not to spill any of the fizzing liquid.

I sat down next to him on the sofa, and raised my glass. 'How do I say congratulations in Spanish?'

He said, '*Felicidades*.'

'*Felicidades*, Zac.'

'*Gracias, cariño*,' he said. 'Thank you.' We both drank our champagne.

I said, 'So was it Jessica who called you or Felicity Sanders?'

'Neither,' Zac said. 'Joe phoned me direct to offer me the part.'

'*Joe Garcia* called you?' I gasped. 'He didn't go through your agent? Isn't that what normally happens?'

Zac shrugged. 'He said he wanted to speak to me himself. Someone from his office is going to call Felicity next week to sort out the contract. I doubt she takes work calls on a Saturday night, even from Joe Garcia.'

I smiled. 'I can't tell you how thrilled I am for you, Zac.'

'I'm not going to pretend I'm anything but ecstatic to have got Javier,' Zac said, 'but I very much want to hear that you've got Mariana.'

If Joe was going to cast me as Mariana, I thought, surely I, too, would have got a phone call tonight? Most likely I've not got the part. I nearly said as much to Zac, but caught myself in time. This was his night, and I wasn't going to say or do anything that might spoil it.

'You know how much I want that too,' I said, 'but tonight isn't about me, it's about you.'

'So, it is.' He refilled our champagne glasses. 'Joe wants me to spend some time working with him on Javier's scenes before the rest of the cast start rehearsals.'

'One-to-one drama coaching from Joe Garcia. Amazing.'

'Yeah,' Zac said. 'He's asked me to go and stay at his place in Gloucestershire. Just for a couple of weeks.'

I gaped at him. 'You'll be his house guest? That's unreal.'

'It certainly wasn't something I expected,' Zac said. 'I'm going to drive down to his country pile tomorrow.'

So soon, I thought. I was deliriously happy for him, this beautiful, talented man who I loved, knowing what an extraordinary opportunity it was for any actor to work with Joe Garcia, but at the same time, I knew I'd miss him horribly while he was away.

Zac drained his champagne and set the glass down on the floor. He reached out touched my face, tracing the line of my mouth with his thumb.

He said, 'Julie...' He leant forward and kissed me. 'Julie. I —' His dark eyes fastened on mine.

And suddenly my heart started hammering as the thought came to me that the night he'd learnt he'd got the part of Javier, was also the night he was going to tell me he loved me. He kissed me again, and orchestral music soared around us, fountains rising from an extravagant set, aerialists flying on wires above our heads, cymbals crashing, dancers high-kicking, the two of us standing together, hands clasped, in a single spotlight.

Zac said, 'Have you ever had sex with the male lead in a Joe Garcia musical?' The music screeched to a discordant halt, violin strings broke, fountains dried, pyrotechnics failed to ignite.

'I can't say I have,' I said. I located my glass and swallowed a large mouthful of champagne.

'Well you're going to tonight,' he said.

I reminded myself this night was all about Zac getting into *La Pasionaria*; it was *not* about me. Drawing on all my acting skills, I managed to smile. Very soon, in Zac's bedroom, I was smiling for real.

CHAPTER 34

'Tell him many, many congrats,' Alexa said. 'Of course, as his girlfriend's best friend, I expect comps for his opening night.'

'I'll tell him,' I laughed. 'I'm so happy for him, Alexa.' From where I was sitting on the balcony, I could see Zac through the glass doors that led into the main room of his flat. My stomach lurched pleasantly as I watched him lounging on the sofa, talking on his phone, as he had been all morning, calling Laurie and other friends to let them know he'd got the role of the male lead in Joe Garcia's new musical. I'd rung Alexa as soon as I thought it was late enough for her to be awake.

Alexa said, 'Michael was telling me that Suzanne's been really off with him since he got into *La Pasionaria*.'

'Have you seen Michael recently?' I said.

'Not since that night at Zac's,' Alexa said. 'But we talk on the phone a lot, mainly about Suzanne. He says it's like she can't bear to see him doing better than she is.'

'I don't think it's that,' I said. 'Well, not just that. I had a coffee with her after class yesterday, and she was in a bit of a state. She thinks Michael's cheating on her.'

'No!' Alexa said. 'Who with? He's not doing the dirty with one of the girls in his father's office, is he? The Boss's Son would be quite a catch.'

'Suzanne's not sure.' I debated telling Alexa that she was Suzanne's prime suspect, but given Alexa's touchiness about her and Michael's friendship, decided it wasn't a conversation we needed to have.

'She's probably imagining the whole thing,' Alexa said, dismissively. 'Oh. I have to go. Tim's car just pulled up outside. We're off to Cambridge to visit some frightfully clever friend of his who teaches at the university. I'll be home tonight.'

'I'll see you then,' I said, and ended the call.

Zac came out onto the balcony, still on his phone, but now speaking in Spanish. I let his voice wash over me, enjoying the sound of the language, even although I couldn't understand a word. He carried on talking for a good fifteen minutes before saying '*adios*', which even I knew meant 'goodbye'.

'That was my parents,' he said.

'They must be so proud of you,' I said. I thought, did he say anything about me? Do his parents know I exist? It was, I supposed, perfectly reasonable that a twenty-six year old man could have a fifteen minute conversation with his parents and not mention that he had a steady girlfriend.

'Naturally they are,' Zac said. 'My mother is overjoyed that I'm back on stage where, according to her, I belong. I may even be forgiven for going to California now that I'm in the West End.' He smiled, but I wasn't at all sure that he was joking.

I said, 'So is there anyone else you need to ring? What about your uncle?'

'My uncle?' Zac said.

'Oh, I guess your mother will want to phone him herself,' I said.

'You're right about that,' Zac said. 'I'm sure she's phoned him already.' He added, 'I should go and pack. I'll drive you home before I go to Joe's.'

271

I said, 'I wish I was coming with you. Not that I'm going to miss you, but I wouldn't mind a bit of drama coaching from Joe Garcia.'

'I might miss you if I was going anywhere else,' Zac said, 'but as I'm going to be working with Joe, I doubt I'll have the time.'

We smiled at each other.

I said, 'If Joe should say anything to you about who might be playing Mariana to your Javier, will you let me know?' I'll probably get an email tomorrow telling me I've not been cast, I thought.

Zac nodded. 'I'll put in a good word for you with Joe, if I get the chance. Now, come here.'

I stood up and went to him, and he folded me in his arms and kissed me. It was, I thought, going to be a very long two of weeks.

***

Zac pulled off the motorway into a service station and filled his car with petrol, before going to the dining area and buying himself a coffee. He sat down at a table, grimacing at the canned music provided for the entertainment of hungry motorists, and scrolled through the messages on his phone. It was only a couple of hours since he'd dropped her back at her flat, but his mind drifted to Julie, last night in his bed, her smile as he covered her body with his, and her gasp as he entered her, this afternoon when they'd kissed on the balcony, the warmth of the sun, the taste of her in his mouth... The ringing of his phone jerked him abruptly back to the present. He accepted the call.

'Did you tell her?' Laurie said, by way of greeting.

'No,' Zac said. 'I decided it was better not to tell her just before I left her on her own for two weeks.'

'So where does she think you're going?' Laurie said.

'Obviously, I told her I was staying at Joe's so he could work with me on the part of Javier,' Zac said.

'Didn't she think it rather odd that a theatre director would invite an actor into his home for weeks at a time?'

Guilt made Zac defensive. 'If she did, she didn't say.'

'That girl is way too trusting,' Laurie said. 'You can't expect me to keep covering for you. If you don't tell her soon, I will.'

'No, you won't,' Zac said.

Laurie sighed. 'No, you're right, I won't, but you're putting me in an incredibly awkward position.'

'I know,' Zac said. 'I'm sorry. I'll sort it – as soon as I get back to London.'

'Just tell her, Zac,' Laurie said, and ended the call.

Zac drummed his fingers on the table. I should have told her, he thought. Nothing he could do about it now. He drained his coffee and left the dining area. Walking across the car park, he sent Julie a text. Then he got in his car and continued on his journey.

CHAPTER 35

I sat cross-legged on my bed and studied the text Zac had sent me, warmth spreading slowly through my body: *I was wrong. I am going to miss you. Z* followed by *xx*. It might not be a declaration of love – everyone I knew routinely signed texts with xx – but it did at least mean he was thinking of me, that he cared about me. I texted back: *I'll miss you too. J xx*. I heard the front door open and shut.

Alexa called out, 'Julie? Are you there? I've got chips. Do you want some?' I went out into the hall to find her alone, clutching a parcel of chips wrapped in newspaper. We fetched plates and tomato ketchup from the kitchen and sat down opposite each other at our rickety dining table.

Alexa said, 'Tim and I broke up.'

'*What*? Oh, Alexa –'

'I broke us up,' Alexa said.

I stared at her. 'I don't understand.'

'It's very simple,' Alexa said. 'I told him I didn't want to be with him.' I searched her face, certain that she could not be as calm as she appeared, but her blue eyes looked unwaveringly back at me.

'But why?' I said. 'I thought it was all going so well. What happened?'

Alexa dipped a chip in ketchup and ate it before answering. 'We were on our way back from Cambridge, and we'd stopped to have dinner at this rather fabulous restaurant, when Tim announced that his firm is sending him to the States for six months to work in their New York office. I told him I wasn't into long distance relationships, and that he and I were finished –' Her voice faltered, but she took a deep breath and continued talking. 'He came up with all sorts of arguments about how we could make it work. He's a lawyer, he's good at arguing.'

'You had a row in the restaurant?' I said.

'No,' Alexa said. 'Tim isn't the sort of man who would cause a scene in public. He just tried to talk me round. He said I could come out to New York before I start filming, and... Oh, it doesn't matter.' Alexa looked down at her hands. Her blonde hair fell forward, concealing her face.

'Alexa?' I said. 'Are you all right, hun? Can I get you anything? Water? Tea? Wine?'

'I'm fine,' Alexa said, sitting up straight and tucking her hair behind her ears. 'When Tim realised I meant what I said, he told me he'd drive me home. The waitress had already brought our first course, but Tim said he wasn't hungry. He got out his wallet, threw a handful of notes onto the table, and marched out of the restaurant. I went after him and we got in his car. He didn't speak to me the whole way back to London. When he stopped the car at the end of our road, I tried to tell him that once he was living in New York he'd see that he's better off without me, but he told me to get out. So I did. And he drove off. And then I noticed that I was starving, so I went and bought chips.' She added, 'I hurt him, and I feel bad about that, but he'll get over it.'

I thought, it sounds like the poor guy was devastated. Aloud, I said, 'Are you sure you're not making a huge mistake? It's only six months. Couldn't you at least give the LDR thing a chance?'

'There's no point,' Alexa said. 'LDRs never last. They drag on with tearful phone calls and self-indulgent emails, until one of you shags someone else. I'd much rather Tim and I have a clean break.'

'But you've been so happy with him these last few weeks,' I said. 'It seems awful to throw it all away.'

'It was fun while it lasted,' Alexa said, 'but now it's over. Oh – Damn! I've just realised I've left my suitcase in the boot of Tim's car.'

'I'm sure he'll drive it here if you ask him,' I said, envisaging a scene where Alexa opened the door to Tim, fell into his arms, and the audience left the theatre smiling.

'Like I can do that,' Alexa said. 'I'll have to live without it.'

Alexa picked up our empty plates and carried them out to the kitchen. She didn't seem to realise that I'd seen the single tear that was running slowly down her face.

CHAPTER 36

'So that's what I've been up to,' I said. 'Not quite as exciting as rehearsing Joe Garcia's new musical.'

For five days, I'd heard nothing from Zac other than a couple of texts – *Rehearsals going great. Z xx* – and having no idea as to his schedule, I hadn't called him, much as I wanted to. Now, on Friday morning while I was still lying in bed, I'd picked up my ringing phone and seen his name on the screen, and my heart had flown up into the stratosphere. He'd told me how he and Joe were working on developing Javier's character through improvisation, and that Oliver Brady had driven down from London with the sole purpose of coaching him on Javier's songs. I'd told him about the classes I'd attended at Limelight, the friends I'd met for coffee, and my sister Daisy's visit to London. I'd met her at Victoria Station and seen her safely back onto her return train, much to my mother's relief. I hadn't told him that I was lying wake each night into the early hours, my body aching for his touch. I hadn't told him I was still jumping out of my skin every time my phone rang in case it was the Call. I hadn't told him that I loved him.

Zac said, 'It's been an incredible few days. Joe is the most inspiring theatre practitioner I've ever worked with.'

'I can imagine,' I said. I wish I didn't have to imagine it, I thought; I wish I was there with you.

Zac said, 'Julie, I'm going to have to go. Joe's expecting me in the studio. Did I tell you his house has a rehearsal studio?'

'No, you didn't mention that,' I said. 'Zac. Before you ring off, has Joe said anything about casting Mariana? Has he said anything about me?'

'No, he hasn't,' Zac said.

'Even if he tells you he's given the part to someone else, you will let me know?'

'I will,' Zac said. 'But now I need to end this call. I can't be late for my director.'

'Zac – wait –' I hadn't had a chance to ask him if he'd read the entire script of *La Pasionaria*, if he'd discovered what happened in the later scenes, if Mariana and Javier got to be together.

He said, '*Adios, cariño.*'

'Bye, Zac,' I said, and he was gone. I lay in bed a while longer, picturing him in a mirror-walled studio, speaking Javier's lines while Joe Garcia gave him direction, and felt such a longing for him that it was a physical pain inside me. Enough, Julie, I told myself.

I heard our front door slam shut – that'd be Alexa going to work at the call centre – and decided it was time I got up. I dressed, made my habitual breakfast of tea and toast, and took it into the living room – where I discovered Michael McCabe asleep on the sofa, wrapped up in an old duvet. Even as I stood there wondering if I should wake him, he opened his eyes and sat up, yawning and stretching, revealing that he'd slept in his clothes.

'Uh… Hi, Julie' he said. 'Alexa and I went out for a drink last night, and she reckoned you wouldn't mind if I crashed here.'

'Of course not,' I said, 'although I don't know how you managed to get any sleep on that sofa.'

'It wasn't the best night's sleep I've ever had,' Michael said, 'but I couldn't face going home.'

I raised my eyebrows.

'I quit working for my father,' Michael said, 'and Suzanne's giving me a hard time about it. She thinks I should have stuck it out, kept bringing in a wage, until I start rehearsals for *La Pasionaria*.'

If his and Suzanne's finances are anything like mine, I thought, she does have a point. And she could do without money worries on top of everything else she's got on her mind right now.

Aloud, I said, 'Listen, Michael, I know it's none of my business, but if you and Suzanne are having problems, maybe staying out all night isn't the best way to solve them.'

'Yeah, you're probably right,' Michael said.

'But since you're here,' I said, 'would you like some breakfast?' He shook his head. I sat down at the dining table and took a bite of my toast.

Michael said, 'Alexa told me Zac's already rehearsing with the great man himself.'

'He is.' I smiled. 'I've just been talking to him on the phone, and he told me rehearsals are going brilliantly.'

'I wish Suzanne was as happy for me to have got into *La Pasionaria* as you are for Zac,' Michael said.

'She's still upset that she got cut?' I said, noticing that Michael had bracketed me and Suzanne together as *not* having got into *La Pasionaria,* while he and Zac had. I reminded myself that as far as I knew, the role of Mariana hadn't yet been cast.

'She's upset about a lot of things at the moment,' Michael said. 'I can't seem to do anything right.' He sighed. 'I guess I should get home and face the music. Can I use your shower first? She'll go mad if I turn up reeking of beer.'

'Sure,' I said, thinking that Suzanne was going to be mad at him – with good reason, in my opinion – whether he smelt of alcohol or the exorbitantly priced, flower-scented shower gel that Alexa insisted on buying for our bathroom.

A few minutes after I'd let Michael out of the flat and gone back upstairs, the doorbell rang. I dashed downstairs again, half-expecting Michael had forgotten something, and was taken aback when I opened the door to find myself face to face with Tim. He was dressed in a sharply tailored, dark grey business suit with a subtle pinstripe, a white shirt, and a plain tie. Beside him on the doorstep was a large suitcase.

'Hello, Julie,' he said. 'Is Alexa in?'

'No, I'm sorry,' I said. 'She's at work.' This is hideously awkward, I thought. The first time I meet the guy he's stark naked, the second time I meet him, he's just been dumped by my best friend.

'She left her suitcase in my car,' Tim said. 'I wanted to give it back to her.'

'I'll take it.' I reached for the suitcase, but found myself quite unable to lift it.

Tim observed me in silence for a moment, and then he said, 'Would you like me to carry it up?'

'Please,' I said. 'If you wouldn't mind.'

'Not at all,' he said. I led him up the stairs. Instinctively, he opened Alexa's bedroom door. And then he closed it again, and put her suitcase down on the landing.

He cleared his throat. 'Did Alexa tell you she broke up with me?' he said. 'Did she tell you why?'

'Er, yes, she did,' I said, reluctantly. Discussing my best friend with a man who was virtually a stranger wasn't exactly high on my day's agenda.

'She... she's not answering my calls,' he said. 'I have to see her, to talk to her. Would you tell her that for me? Would you ask her to call me?'

'I will,' I said, 'but I'm sorry, Tim, I can't promise that she'll listen to me.'

'She knows her own mind,' Tim said, 'but I have to try to win her back –' He broke off, and his shoulders slumped. I resisted a sudden impulse to hug him: actors are tactile creatures, lawyers possibly not so much.

'Tim,' I said, 'would you like a coffee?'

He hesitated, but then he said, 'Could I have tea? No milk or sugar?' I pointed him towards the living room and went and made us both a drink.

'So did you skive off work to try and see Alexa?' I said to him, once I'd handed him his mug of tea.

'Skive off?'

'Well, you're wearing a suit.'

'Oh, I'm not due in the office until this afternoon,' Tim said. 'This morning I had to go to the American Embassy to sort out my visa. For my secondment to New York.'

'This secondment,' I said, 'it sounds like an amazing opportunity.'

281

'It is,' Tim said. 'To turn it down would be professional suicide.' He raked a hand through his hair. 'I thought Alexa would understand that. Don't you actors have to go off on location or whatever?'

'Sometimes,' I said.

'It's not like it's a permanent move,' Tim continued. 'I'll be back by Christmas. I may even be able to manage a few days holiday in England before then.'

'Did you tell Alexa that?' I said.

'Many times,' Tim said. 'I didn't realise she could be so –'

'Unreasonable?' I suggested. 'Stubborn?'

He almost smiled. 'I was going to say determined. She's also vivacious, funny and smart. And she has great legs.'

'I'll pass that on to her,' I said.

'If you think it'll help my case,' he said.

I didn't think there was anything I could say that was going to change Alexa's mind, but I didn't have the heart to tell him that. We talked a while longer, or rather he talked – 'I can't *not* go to New York. It's my career, my livelihood. It's only for six months. We can Skype...' – while I listened and nodded. Eventually he checked the expensive watch on his left wrist, and decided he had to get to his office.

'Thanks for the tea and sympathy,' he said, as stepped out into the street.

'You're welcome,' I said. 'I hope you and Alexa can work things out, I really do.'

'So do I, because I feel –' For a moment Tim's self-control deserted him, and he broke off. 'I felt we could have a future together.'

I thought, is he in love with her?

'I need to see her just one more time,' Tim said, 'and then, if she still doesn't want to be with me, she'll never hear from me again.' Without another word, he walked hurriedly down the street, got into his car, and drove away.

***

I was seated at my dressing table, painting my nails, when Alexa, back from the call centre, came into my bedroom without knocking, and sat down on my bed.

'Michael was feeling very sorry for himself last night,' she said.

'And this morning,' I said. 'Much of it's his own fault.'

'That's a bit harsh,' Alexa said. 'Suzanne's being very unsupportive.'

I thought, Michael's woes aren't upmost in my mind right now. 'Tim brought your suitcase back,' I said.

'Yeah, I saw it.' Alexa picked up a book that I'd left on my nightstand, studied the cover, and put it down again. 'How was he?'

'Hurting,' I said.

'I'm sorry to hear that,' Alexa said.

'He wants to see you,' I said.

She bit her bottom lip. 'It's better if we don't meet – for him as well as me.'

'You could at least answer his calls,' I said. 'You owe him that much.'

'I don't *owe* him anything,' Alexa said.

'Bad choice of word,' I said. 'But I still think you should speak to him.'

'There's no point,' Alexa said. 'I can't be in a relationship with someone who's living on another continent. I can't make that sort of commitment.'

'The boy isn't going to get the girl?' I said.

'Tim and I aren't characters in a musical,' Alexa said, tossing her hair over her shoulder. 'Besides, contemporary musicals don't necessarily have the traditional happy ending. Talking of musicals, I hope I haven't been demoted from my position of best friend *ever* for not asking if you've heard from Jessica Coleman today.'

'No worries,' I said. 'When – *if* – I get the Call, I'll text you.'

'I'm sure you'll hear very soon,' Alexa said. 'I've got this feeling about it.'

'You do realise you sound exactly like my mother?' I said.

'If your mother and I think the same thing,' Alexa said, 'we must be right.' She got to her feet. 'I need to pack an overnight bag: I'm staying at Charles and Hillary's. They're going to a charity fundraiser, and couldn't find a babysitter, so I volunteered.'

'That's noble of you,' I said. 'Although, I imagine Caspar and India aren't much trouble.'

'I bribe them to behave with ice cream,' Alexa said, 'but don't tell Hillary. Anyway, I'll see you tomorrow. Maybe we could go to Covent Garden in the afternoon? Do a bit of shopping before you go to Zone?'

'Sure,' I said. Handing out flyers in the Covent Garden piazza was a regular part of my job, but an expedition to the daytime market was still an enticing proposition. I didn't have to buy anything, I could just look, after all.

Alexa went off to pack her bag. A short while later, I heard her singing along to *The Howling*.

For Tim, the show had closed far too early, but I honestly couldn't see any chance of a revival and a longer run.

CHAPTER 37

Meandering through the arts and crafts stalls in Covent Garden, selling anything from jewellery and ceramics to paintings and handmade soap, proved an extremely pleasurable way to spend a Saturday afternoon. Alexa treated herself to some scented candles, while I, despite the meagre amount of spare cash in my purse, was seduced by a pair of silver earrings. We watched acrobats perform an impressive tumbling routine in front of the Actors' Church on the west side of the piazza, and listened to the opera singers who busk in one of the market halls. We were still in the market, Alexa trying to persuade herself that she needed rather than wanted a hand-embroidered shirt, when I saw with some surprise that it was already twenty past five, and if I didn't leave her to it and run all the way to Leicester Square, I was going to be late for work.

'I'm sure you won't be handing out flyers much longer,' Alexa called after me as I trotted off. 'You'll be in *La Pasionaria* with Zac.'

Owen, Harry and Cora had said much the same when I'd told them of Zac's success. Ben had smiled and nodded in agreement. I could only hope they were right.

By the time I reached the club, it was almost half past five. I hurried down the alleyway to the staff entrance, and along the corridor past the kitchen. As I drew near the staffroom, I was surprised to hear raised voices coming from within. I pushed open the door and slipped inside.

In front of me, Harry and Nadia were glaring at each other across a table, on which there was an open magazine.

Cora and Owen were standing on one side of Harry, a little way behind him, while Ben, minus his earphones, stood on the other. Several waiters and bar staff who had yet to start their shifts were still in the staffroom, drinking coffee or in the midst of a card game. All of them were fixated on whatever was going on between the members of the promo team.

Harry said, 'I can't believe even you would do this, Nadia.'

'*Innit* is on every news stand in London.' Nadia's voice came out as a screech. 'She's going to see it whether I show it to her or not. She's going to *know*.'

'Yes, she is,' Harry said, 'but you didn't have to bring the frickin' magazine in here to rub it in her face.'

Cora put her hand on Harry's arm. 'Harry – Julie's here…'

Suddenly everyone in the room was looking at me. I took a step forward.

Nadia turned to face me. 'Julie.'

'Nadia,' I said.

'Have you seen the today's edition of *Innit?*'

'No,' I said, 'I haven't.'

'Well, you should,' Nadia said, 'you should see the centre pages.' She stepped to one side so that I could see the magazine spread out on the table.

'I am so sorry, Julie,' Nadia said, her smile pure saccharine. 'I did try to warn you.'

My heart beating uncomfortably fast, I walked up to the table and bent over the magazine. In front of me was a page of photographs of A-List film star Rosalind Adams. In the first photo, she was seen from a distance going up the front steps of a large, white stucco house, arm in arm with a dark-haired man. In the next photo, presumably taken with an extremely powerful zoom lens, because it was a very clear image, she was seen looking out of a window on the first floor. The dark-haired man stood next to her. She was wearing a yellow dress and he was wearing jeans and a striped shirt. In the third photo, which took up half the page, they were locked together in an embrace. The man in the photos was Zac.

From somewhere far away, I heard Nadia say, '"Hollywood actress Rosalind Adams, on location in London, auditions a co-star."' It took me a moment to understand that she was reading the caption under one of the photos.

'Shut up, Nadia,' Harry said.

'I warned you, Julie,' Nadia said again, her eyes alight with triumph. 'I told you what Zac is like.'

'He – he's not –' I stuttered. 'He wouldn't… There has to be some mistake.' I lifted my gaze from the photos. My eyes met Harry's, then Cora's and then Owen's, and the look of sympathy they gave me was a knife in my heart. Ben shuffled uneasily from foot to foot. I stepped away from the table, pivoted around, and walked stiffly out of the staffroom, shutting the door behind me. Once I was out in the corridor, I started to run, sprinting towards the female restroom, only just making it into one of the cubicles before I threw up.

When I came out of the cubicle, Cora was standing by the row of sinks.

'I brought your bag,' she said.

'Oh, thanks.' I must have dropped my bag at some point. I hadn't noticed. I turned on a tap, rinsed out my mouth, and surveyed myself in a mirror. My lipstick was smeared, so I wiped it off with a tissue, and with a shaking hand, reapplied it. Then I found my mobile and speed-dialled Zac's number. There was no reply. The phone went to voicemail.

'Hi, Zac, it's me,' I said, deliberately keeping my voice light. 'Phone me when you get this.' I ended the call. My mobile showed the time as ten to six. 'We need to get out flyering. Austin's going to go crazy.'

'Julie,' Cora said, 'why don't you go home? I'll tell Austin you're not well.'

'No. I –' *Rosalind Adams and Zac Diaz.* I couldn't think straight. 'I – We have to hand out flyers.'

Cora looked at me doubtfully. 'OK.'

I hoisted my bag onto my shoulder, and Cora and I went back to the staffroom, which was empty now except for Owen and Harry, who were sitting on a sofa talking, and Ben, who was sitting opposite them listening to what they said. My suspicions that they were talking about me were confirmed by the way they fell silent and drew apart from each other as soon as Cora and I came into the room. *Innit* magazine with its photos of Zac with another woman, holding her, caressing her, was no longer on the table.

'Where's the magazine?' I said.

'I think Nadia put it in her locker,' Owen said.

'You've seen it,' Harry said. 'You don't need to see it again.' He added, 'There's nothing on the *Innit* website – I checked.'

My stomach churned. This could *not* be happening.

'The photos...' I said. 'There has to be an explanation, right? Zac wouldn't cheat –' My voice caught in my throat.

With an apologetic glance towards Owen, Harry and Ben, Cora said, 'He's a man – he would.'

'If he's cheating on a girl like you, he's an idiot,' Owen said. 'And that's not me coming on to you, by the way. I wouldn't, obviously, because I don't think of you like that. Well, not obviously, because you're gorgeous. But I don't. And I'm going to shut up now.'

Ignoring Owen's outburst, Harry said, 'Is Zac working tonight?'

'I don't know,' I said. 'He's away from home. He's been away all week –' I broke off, aware of how damning that sounded. I thought, how do I know where he is? Or who he's with?

'Why don't you give him a call?' Harry said.

'I tried,' I said. 'I got his voicemail. I'll try again later. Right now I have to hand out flyers.' I went to my locker, and shoved my bag inside. I closed the locker door, and for a moment stood motionless, with my face pressed against the cold metal.

Harry said, 'Are you sure you're up to flyering tonight?'

I turned around. 'Yes, I –'

'Why are you five still here?' Unnoticed by any of us, Austin had come into the staffroom. 'It's gone six. Unless there's a really good reason why you're not out working, I'll have to dock your pay.'

'It's my fault, Austin,' I said. 'I – I threw up. The others were making sure that I was all right.'

'And are you all right?' Austin said.

'Y-yes,' I said. My boyfriend is cheating on me with a Hollywood film star, I thought. No, I'm not all right. Tears pricked my eyes.

'Then you all need to get out on the streets right away' Austin said. 'And you're only to take a half hour meal break.'

Owen muttered something under his breath, but picked up a handful of flyers and held them out to me. I stepped towards him, my hand held out to take them, and suddenly the room and the faces of my friends blurred and swam around me. The next thing I knew, I was sitting on a chair, with my head between my knees, Owen's hand resting lightly on the back of my neck. I sat up. Cora perched on the arm of the chair, and pushed my hair back from my face.

Harry crouched down in front of me. 'Julie? You fainted. Do you want some water?' He handed me a Styrofoam cup.

'So you vomited,' Austin said, 'and now you've fainted. Are you pregnant? Because if you are, I can't let you work until you've completed a Risk Assessment Form. Health and Safety Regulations are very clear on that point.'

'No, Austin,' I said, wearily, 'I'm not pregnant.' I swallowed a mouthful of water and made myself get to my feet. 'I'm perfectly capable of handing out flyers. Or do you want me to take a pregnancy test before I hit the streets?'

'That will not be necessary.' Austin studied my face. 'You do appear to have recovered from your fainting fit, but you are a rather strange colour. You'd better take your full hour's break.'

'OK.' I must look dreadful, I thought. My friends and I picked up our handfuls of flyers, and headed for the door.

Once outside, I found myself totally at a loss as to where Owen and I should be going, but he steered me across Leicester Square to Piccadilly Circus. I stood where he told me to, and held out a flyer. It was Saturday evening, and central London was heaving, but none of the people looking for a good night out spared me a second glance. I knew I had to talk to these strangers, to persuade them that Club Zone was where they wanted to be, but it all seemed like too much of an effort.

'Have a flyer,' I said. 'Have a flyer. Have a flyer.' I repeated the same words over and over again, until Owen put his hands on my shoulders and told me to stop. He took my flyers, and I stood and watched him hand them out along with his own. Then, holding my arm, he led me back to the club. Before we went inside, I tried phoning Zac, but there was still no reply.

The thought of eating just made me feel nauseous again, but I followed Owen to the staffroom trying not to flinch when Ben, who was already half way through his meal, smiled at me sympathetically, or when I overheard someone say 'Rosalind Adams' in what could only be described as a tone of awe. Owen sat me down at a table in the corner – I knew he'd chosen it because it was the furthest away from where Nadia was sitting, for which I was grateful – and he fetched our meals from the kitchen. After a while Harry and Cora came in and joined us. I watched Owen devour his fajitas and then passed him my plate.

'You should try to eat something,' he said.

'I can't.' I realised I had spoken too loudly when a barmaid and a waitress on a break, who were sitting nearby, turned to look at me, and then quickly looked away. I thought, why hasn't Zac called me back? Is he with Joe right now – or is he with *her*? I willed myself not to cry. I said, 'I'm going to try calling Zac again. Owen, I'll meet you outside.'

Walking out of the staffroom, knowing that the rest of the promotions team were watching me and pitying me – or, in Nadia's case, gloating no doubt – I held my head high, even though inside I was falling apart. I tried Zac's number twice, and twice the phone went to voicemail, so I left him a message and sent him a text asking him to call me, however late that night. Owen appeared and looked at me questioningly.

I shook my head. 'I can't talk about this any more.' To my relief he took me at my word, and led me to Shaftesbury Avenue without attempting to make conversation of any sort. For the rest of the evening, I just stood next to him, a miserable, silent shadow, while he handed out enough flyers for two.

Back in the staffroom at the end of our shift, everyone was more concerned with catching their buses and trains than discussing Julie Farrell's private life, and I only had to endure a few covert glances while I retrieved my bag. Owen walked outside with me, and stood a little way off while I tried yet again to call Zac. When I still got no answer, he linked his arm through mine.

'I'll see you home,' he said. 'I'd like to know you're all right.'

'Oh, that's so kind of you,' I said, 'but you don't need to. I'm not about to throw myself off Waterloo Bridge.'

'Of course you're not,' Owen said. 'But you fainted earlier, and you walked off a couple of kerbs without looking, so being entirely selfish, I would really appreciate it if you allowed me to escort you home. Just so that I can sleep tonight.'

'Th-thank you, Owen.' Once again tears stung my eyes.

By now we'd reached the station. We went through the ticket barrier, and down the escalator, reaching the Northern Line platform just as a train arrived in a blast of warm wind. Owen put his hand under my elbow, and we stepped through the sliding doors into an almost empty carriage. I slumped into the nearest seat, and Owen sat next to me. On the seat across the aisle was an abandoned copy of *Innit*. I stood up and reached for it.

'Don't, Julie,' Owen said. I hesitated. Did I really want to look at those photos again? Then I put the magazine in my bag.

Owen didn't say much for the rest of the journey, but I was glad of his comforting presence, and when I stumbled getting off the train at my stop, he caught me and set me back on my feet. If I'd fallen at that moment and I'd been on my own, I don't think I would have been able to stand up again. On the walk from the station I clung to his arm, and when we arrived outside my flat, I realised that I was reluctant to let go.

Owen said, 'Is your flatmate home?'

'I don't think so. Alexa makes it a point of honour never to be home on a Saturday night.' I vaguely remembered her talking that afternoon about going to a house party with a bunch of people from the call centre.

'Would you like me to come in and stay with you 'til she gets back?' Owen said. I knew that I should let him head off home, but at that moment I couldn't face being alone.

'Please, Owen,' I said. We went inside and he volunteered to make tea. Having pointed him in the direction of the kitchen, I sat on the sofa and tried once again to call Zac. There was still no answer. I took the copy of *Innit* out of my bag, and turned to the centre pages, forcing myself to look closely at each photo in turn. I thought, West End lead Zac Diaz and Hollywood movie star Rosaline Adams. Zac and Ros. He smiles at her the way he smiled at me. He has sex with her. In the morning, hers is the first face he sees. That was when I started crying.

Owen came in and put two mugs on the floor beside the sofa. He sat down next to me, and put his arm around my shoulders while I sobbed.

Eventually I got myself under control. 'S-sorry,' I said. 'I-I didn't mean to make a show of myself.'

'Don't worry about it,' Owen said, removing his arm and shifting along the sofa. 'I'm used to crying women.'

'I'm sure you've never made a woman cry,' I said.

'Not that I know of,' Owen said, 'but my sister cries fairly often. Usually over a man. She has terrible taste in men.'

The front door slammed, footsteps clattered up the stairs, and a moment later Alexa came into the living room.

'Well that was a waste of four hours of my life,' she said. 'What a tedious –' Her gaze alighted on Owen and then on me. 'Julie? Have you been crying? What on earth's wrong?'

'Zac –' My throat constricted. 'Zac's cheated on me.'

Alexa stared at me wide-eyed. 'No,' she said. '*No.*'

'He's cheated on me with Rosalind Adams,' I said.

'With *who?*' Alexa said.

I passed her the copy of *Innit*. Her mouth tightened as she took in the photos. She sat down heavily in a chair.

'What the hell does he think he's doing?' she said.

'I think those pictures make it fairly obvious what he's doing,' I said.

'But – *Rosalind Adams?* How?' she said. 'How would he get with *her?*'

'They have a history,' I said. 'They lived together when he was in the States. He told me they were over.'

My phone rang. Zac's name was on the screen. I snatched it up, almost dropping it in my haste to hit the answer key.

'Hey, Julie,' Zac said. Hearing his voice was enough to make my eyes again fill with tears.

'Zac –' This, I thought, is not a scene I want to play in front of an audience. 'Wait –' I stood up and leaving Alexa and Owen in the living room, went to my bedroom and shut the door.

'I've seven missed calls from you,' Zac said. 'Are you OK?'

'What do you think?' I said. 'Zac, I know. I *know.* I've seen the photos.'

'What photos?' Zac said. 'I've no idea what you're talking about'

'Don't give me that,' I said. Surely he'd seen them, or someone he knew had seen them and told him about them. 'There are photos of you in *Innit* – you and Rosalind Adams.'

There was a long silence, and then Zac said, 'I'm not aware of any photos of me – with or without Rosalind – in any magazine.'

'Then I'll describe them to you,' I said. 'You and Rosalind Adams, arm in arm, going into a large white house. You and Rosalind Adams inside the house, in a clinch right by a window. It's a very sharp image, considering it must have been taken with a telephoto lens from the street.'

Another silence. 'I've been to the house Rosalind's renting while she's in England,' Zac said, eventually, 'but-'

'So you admit it.' I thought of how often Zac had failed to call me, how he'd never introduced me to any of his friends or his family, *that thing we never talk about.* Suddenly it all fell into place. All those times I'd had no idea where he was or what he was doing, he'd been with her. I said, 'Were you at her house tonight? Is that why you didn't answer my calls? So much for not playing around.'

'I am at Joe's,' Zac said. 'I've been here all week–'

'So the photos were taken before you left London.' I'd been pacing around the room, but now my legs started shaking and I sank onto my bed.

'Julie, listen to me,' Zac said. 'There's nothing going on between me and Rosalind Adams. I went to her house when she first arrived in England –'

'Don't lie to me,' I said. 'I'm not stupid, although you seem to think I am.'

'I've never lied to you,' Zac said.

I don't believe him, I thought. And I can't be the girlfriend of a man who has sex with other women.

As if from a long way off, I heard myself say, 'I can't do this, Zac. You and I are finished.'

'What?' Zac said. 'This is crazy! Let me explain about me and Rosalind –'

'You slept with her,' I said. 'I'm breaking up with you. We're over.' Before he could say any more, I pressed 'end call'. Immediately, he rang me back. I rejected the call, and turned off my phone.

Tears were running down my face. My body wracked with misery, I sat on my bed and wept.

CHAPTER 38

I opened my eyes. I was lying in my bed. For some reason, I'd slept in the jeans and T-shirt I'd worn the day before. I sat up, and my reflection in the mirror on my dressing table showed me that my face was streaked with mascara and my eyes were puffy and red. Then it all came flooding back to me: Zac and Rosalind Adams – Zac and I no longer in a relationship. Pain lanced through me, leaving a leaden weight of misery in its wake.

My memories of the rest of the night, after Zac's call, were vague and disjointed. I remembered crying, and not being able to stop, Alexa and Owen's voices in the hall outside my bedroom, Alexa sitting on my bed and stroking my hair until, too exhausted to cry any longer, I'd fallen asleep. Alexa must have taken off my shoes and covered me with my duvet, I realised. She'd stayed with me for the rest of the night it seemed, for she was now lying across the end of my bed, wrapped up in a blanket, asleep.

I sat up and saw that my phone was lying on my nightstand – presumably Alexa had put it there. I reached for it and turned it on. There were four missed calls from Zac, two from last night and two this morning, and a text.

At the end of the bed, Alexa stirred, opened her eyes and raised her head. She watched me scrolling through my messages.

'Has he called you?' Alexa said.

I nodded.

'Are you going to call him back?' Alexa said.

299

'There's no point,' I said. 'We're done.' I pressed 'delete all' and returned my phone to my nightstand.

After a short silence, Alexa said, 'Your friend Owen missed his train home last night. I didn't want to leave you on your own when you were so upset, so I slept in here, and he crashed in my room.' She arched her eyebrows. 'There's a cute guy in my bed, and I'm sleeping elsewhere. That has to be a first.'

I made a feeble attempt at a smile. 'Alexa, last night – thank you for being there for me.'

'No thanks required,' Alexa said. 'Providing a shoulder to cry on when a man does a girl wrong is part of the best friends package –' She broke off talking to yawn.

'I must have kept you up half the night,' I said. 'Why don't you try and go back to sleep.'

'I might just do that,' Alexa said. 'What are you going to do?'

Good question, I thought. The man I love is shagging his celebrity ex. What am I going to do? If I was in a musical I'd be sitting alone on a dimly lit stage, singing about heartbreak, and there wouldn't be a dry eye left in the house. But I wasn't in a musical. And I'd never felt less like singing.

'Right now,' I said, conscious that I'd been wearing the same T-shirt for twenty-four hours, 'I'm going to take a shower.'

I pushed back the duvet and stood up. My head ached, my eyes were sore, and my limbs felt heavy, so that walking from my bedroom to the bathroom was a huge effort. A fresh wave of misery hit me when I saw Zac's toothbrush and razor by the sink. I stood under the shower until the hot water ran cold – not that it took very long for our flat's hot water to run out – but, even after I'd towelled myself dry, I still felt sluggish and barely able to think. I slipped back into my room, careful not to disturb Alexa who had managed to drift off again, and pulled on the first clothes that came to hand, before going to the kitchen and making myself a cup of strong black coffee. Armed with caffeine, I went into the living room, where my gaze was immediately drawn to the copy of *Innit* that was lying on the sofa. I sat and, unable to stop myself, picked up the magazine and started to turn the pages. When I came to the photos of Zac and Rosalind Adams, I found that I couldn't bear to look at them. I ripped the magazine in two, and threw it against the wall.

Zac. I thought of the night before he went to Joe Garcia's, and how he'd made love to me, murmuring softly in a mixture of English and Spanish. Had it all been an act, no more meaningful to him than the stage kiss we'd shared at that awful commercial casting where we'd first met? It didn't seem possible that the man I'd fallen in love with could turn out to be a liar and a cheat. And yet there were the photographs, evidence of his cheating that he couldn't explain away. He'd been with Rosalind, and he hadn't even tried to deny it.

'Julie – Julie, where are you?' The living room door crashed open. Alexa ran into the room, holding my ringing phone. 'You need to take this –' The phone stopped ringing. 'Too late –'

'Give it to me,' I said. 'I'll turn it off.'

'No, don't turn it off,' Alexa said. 'Check your messages.'

'I'm not interested in anything Zac has to say to me,' I said.

'That wasn't Zac,' Alexa said. 'It was a call from an unknown number.'

'Oh!' My heart started thumping. 'D-do you think it was Jessica Coleman?'

'Find out.' Alexa handed me the phone. I went into my voicemail, putting the phone on speaker.

A disembodied voice said: 'Good morning, Julie. This is Jessica Coleman from Garcia Productions. Please can you call me back on this number as soon as possible. I look forward to hearing from you.' A land-line number followed.

'You've got it!' Alexa said. 'You've got into *La Pasionaria*.'

'We don't know that,' I said.

'Why else would Joe Garcia's assistant be phoning you?' Alexa said.

La Pasionaria, I thought. A new musical by Joe Garcia. Starring Julie Farrell as Mariana… and Zac Diaz as Javier. My throat constricted. The idea of walking out onto the stage of the Aphra Behn and acting with Zac, six nights a week, and twice on Thursdays and Saturdays, made my stomach churn. With a shaking hand, I put my phone down beside me on the sofa.

'*If* I've got the part of Mariana,' I said, 'I'm turning it down. I couldn't play a love scene with Zac. Not now.' As I spoke, it felt as though a part of me had died.

Alexa gaped at me. 'I don't believe I'm hearing this.'

'I should call Jessica back straight away and get it over with,' I said. I made to pick up my phone, but Alexa was there before me, snatching it up out of my reach.

'Julie Farrell,' she said, her eyes fierce, 'you are not going to let some guy who can't keep his flies done up destroy your dream and everything you've worked so hard for.'

I stood up and held out my hand. 'Give me my phone, Alexa.'

'Not until I'm sure you're going to tell Jessica that you accept the part of Mariana,' Alexa said, backing away from me.

'Oh, for goodness sake. Just give me my frickin' phone –' At the sound of footsteps on the landing, we both fell silent. Owen, his hair still tousled from sleep, came into the living room. His gaze went from me to Alexa and back again.

'Is everything all right,' he said. 'I mean, I know that everything's not all right, but –'

'Julie missed a call from Joe Garcia's assistant,' Alexa said. 'We think she's going to be offered the female lead in *La Pasionaria*. I'm trying to persuade her not to wreck her chances of seeing her name in lights by turning it down.'

I slumped onto the sofa. 'I can't play Mariana to Zac's Javier. I know you mean well, Alexa, but I can't.'

Owen's blue eyes fixed on mine. 'I understand why you'd never want to see or speak to Zac again,' he said, 'but the show must go on.'

'Not for me,' I said.

'OK,' Owen said. 'Let's set the scene.' He took up a position in the centre of the living room.

'Owen, what are you doing?' I said.

He ignored me. 'Take a seat in the stalls, Alexa.'

Alexa shot him a quizzical look, but sat down next to me.

'It's a cold winter's night ten years from now,' Owen said, 'and you, Julie, are walking along Shaftesbury Avenue, handing out flyers.' He hunched his back, wrapped his arms around himself, and took a few shuffling steps. 'It's snowing, by the way.' He shivered. 'You offer a flyer to a couple of lads out on the pull, but they won't take it unless you write your phone number on it.' He sighed. 'You come to the Langtry Theatre, where your former Club Zone co-worker, Owen Somers, is the male lead in –? Help me out here, Alexa.'

'A new musical by Joe Garcia,' Alexa said.

'Y-you c-carry on,' Owen said, his teeth chattering, 'until you find yourself outside the Aphra Behn. *La Pasionaria* is still playing – although the original cast have long gone on to other shows. A girl comes towards you and you hold out a flyer, but she walks straight past you, and goes in the stage door. And you think, that could have been me once…' He hung his head. His shoulders shook.

Beside me, Alexa clapped and said, 'Bravo.'

'You are so going to do well at drama school,' I said. Owen bowed.

'And if Joe Garcia offers you a contract,' he said, 'you are so going to ask him where you sign.'

Alexa pressed my phone into my hand. 'Don't make a mistake that you'll regret for the rest of your life.'

They're right, I thought. I can't give up the dream. If Joe Garcia wants me in his show, I can't turn him down. I got to my feet, and went and stood by the window, with my back to Alexa and Owen. My heart racing, I took several deep breaths, and called Jessica Coleman. She answered immediately.

'Hi, Jessica,' I said. 'It's Julie Farrell returning your call.'

'Hello, Julie,' she said. 'Thanks for getting back to me so quickly. I know this is very short notice, but the casting of *La Pasionaria* is still not finalised, and we're wondering if you'd be able to come in and see us again tomorrow? We've asked the actor who's playing Javier to come in as well, as Joe thinks it would be helpful to see you work together.'

My head spun. I clutched at the windowsill to stop myself sinking to the floor. She wasn't offering me the role of Mariana. She was inviting me to yet another recall. And Zac would be there.

Pulling myself together, I said, 'Yes, tomorrow's fine. What time?' I can do this. If I want the role of Mariana, I have to do this.

'Not too early, you'll be glad to hear,' Jessica said. 'Ten o'clock at the Aphra Behn Theatre.'

'I'll be there,' I said.

'Great,' Jessica said. 'It's an acting call – no singing or dancing – but wear something you can move in. Come to the stage door, and I'll come down and meet you.'

'Thank you,' I said. 'See you tomorrow morning.' She rang off. I stared out of the window, without seeing anything, until my legs stopped trembling, and then I turned back to Alexa and Owen.

'Again?' Alexa said. 'Joe wants to see you *again*?'

305

'It'll be a walkover,' I said. 'All I've got to do is convince the most important director working in musical theatre to cast me, an unknown twenty-two-year-old with no professional stage experience – actually, make that no performing experience at all since I left drama school – as the female lead in his new West End musical. That would be the musical that everyone's saying is going to be even bigger than the show that made his name. And I get to do all this while showing him how well I work with my two-timing ex-boyfriend. How hard can it be?'

CHAPTER 39

I opened the stage door of the Aphra Behn Theatre and went into the lobby. The doorkeeper, seated behind a desk, looked up from the sports pages of his newspaper.

'Hi, I'm Julie Farrell,' I said. 'Joe Garcia is expecting me.'

The doorkeeper picked up a phone and muttered, 'Julie Farrell to see Joe... Yeah, I'll tell her.' Replacing the phone on his desk, he said, 'They're sending someone down for you. Sign in, please.' He held out a clipboard with a list of names and a pen, and I placed a tick against 'Julie Farrell'. If I'm cast in *La Pasionaria*, I thought, I'll be signing in and out of the Aphra Behn every day except Sundays. *If* Joe Garcia casts me.

'Thank you,' I said, handing back the clipboard. The doorkeeper grunted and went back to the football scores. I helped myself to a seat on a wooden chair in the corner of the lobby, shifting it slightly so that I had a good view of the door that led backstage. My mouth felt dry, so I drank some of the bottled water that was in my bag. I checked my make-up in my mirror, and smoothed down my hair.

The door that led backstage creaked open. I sprang to my feet, a smile on my face, ready to greet Jessica Coleman, but the person who appeared in the doorway was Zac.

'Julie,' he said.

My chest tightened, and I fought a rising panic. The show must go on, I told myself, the show must go on. I can do this. Tilting up my chin, I made myself look directly into his dark eyes.

'Hello, Zac,' I said.

'If you'd like to come with me,' he said.

I followed him through the door, and he closed it.

He said, 'We need to talk.'

'Not now, we don't,' I said. '*I* need to concentrate on doing a good audition.'

'And I'll help you with that in any way that I can,' Zac said. 'Whatever's happened between us, we leave it at the stage door, agreed?' Without waiting for my answer, he turned his back on me, and led me up a flight of stairs and along a couple of corridors to a rehearsal room that I'd not seen before. Joe and Jessica were sitting on two of the half-dozen metal chairs that had been placed in a circle at one end of the room, drinking coffee.

'Good morning, Julie,' Joe said. 'Have a seat.'

I sat, trying to appear more relaxed than I felt. I was acutely conscious of Zac sitting down next to me.

'Julie, I know that we've not told you directly,' Joe said, 'but you've probably realised that we're considering you for the part of Mariana?'

'Oh, I was so hoping you were,' I said.

A smiled flickered across Joe's face. 'What I want to do today is focus on your acting. I'd like you to improvise a scene with our Javier, Zac Diaz. Are you comfortable with that?'

'Oh, yes, that's fine,' I said. I can act with the man who broke my heart if it gets me into *La Pasionaria*, I thought. Suddenly, it seemed incredible to me that only the day before I'd considered turning down a role in the show.

Now that I was here in the audition room, I'd walk barefoot over broken glass to get cast as Mariana.

'OK, Julie,' Joe said. 'Your character is a woman who arrives home after work to find someone in her house who she doesn't expect. Zac, you're that person, whoever he might be. It's entirely up to each of you how you play the scene.'

Zac stood up and pushed back his chair, so I did the same. He placed the chairs at an angle a few feet away from one another in the centre of the room.

'Shall I start on stage?' he said.

'Sure,' I said, thankful that my three years' training at LAPA had included a weekly improv class. 'I'll enter stage right.'

Zac sat in a chair, leaning back, his legs sprawled wide in front of him. Raising a hand to his face, he mimed smoking a cigarette. I walked into the performance space. I was a young woman who had just arrived home after a hideous day's work handing out flyers, and this man was the last person I wanted to see.

'What are you doing here?' I said. 'How did you get in? And put out that cigarette.' I coughed and waved my hand to get rid of the cigarette smoke. Zac mimed stubbing out the cigarette. I sat down in the other chair, and glared at him.

'We may be separated,' Zac said, 'but this is still my house, and I still have a key.'

'You can't just barge in here whenever you feel like it,' I said. 'Anyway, it won't be your house much longer. I'm filing for divorce.'

309

'You think you'll get to keep this place?' Zac said. 'I have a lawyer too, you know.'

'I'm taking everything after what you did to me.' I stood up, and pointed stage right. Raising my voice, I said, 'You need to leave.'

Zac strode across the stage and thrust his face into mine. 'Make me,' he said.

I yelled at him, 'Get out.'

He jerked away from me, as though I'd hit him. In a quiet voice, he said, 'Julie, don't do this. Don't throw away what we have together.'

'I can't be with you,' I said. 'I saw you with – with that woman.'

'What you saw,' Zac said, 'was me saying goodbye to a friend. We'd had lunch together at a restaurant, coffee back at her house, and then I left.'

'You slept with her,' I said.

Zac sighed. 'You saw my arms around her and you made the assumption that I'd slept with her.'

'You didn't even try to deny it,' I said.

'You didn't give me a chance,' Zac said.

In the silence that followed, the image of him holding Rosalind Adams reared up my mind. When I'd first seen the photo, I'd been convinced that it was proof of his cheating, but now my certainty faded.

Zac said, 'There was a time in my life when I slept around, but since I've been with you, I've desired no other woman.'

A man and a woman hugging by a window, I thought, that's all the photo showed. The rest, that he'd cheated on me with his ex, I'd constructed out of malicious gossip and innuendo. It was all in my head. I saw that now, with a terrifying clarity.

'I didn't sleep with her,' Zac said. 'She and I are friends, nothing more. You have to believe me.'

There was another, longer, moment of silence. Zac's dark eyes searched my face.

'I – I do believe you,' I said at last, my voice scarcely above a whisper.

Zac took a step towards me. I stepped closer to him, and then I was in his arms, he was holding me against his chest, and I could feel his heart beating next to mine. I wanted him never to let me go.

'I love you, Julie' he said.

'Oh – *Oh* –' Whenever I'd pictured this scene, the moment when Zac said those words to me, it hadn't been in a rehearsal studio with the most important man in musical theatre and his assistant looking on. The soaring violins, the showers of golden ticker tape, the pyrotechnics of my imagination were conspicuous by their absence. This wasn't a musical, and Zac wasn't speaking lines written by someone else. I gazed up into the face of the man I loved, and I smiled.

Joe Garcia said, 'And on that dramatic note, we'll finish for today. Come and have a seat, guys.'

Zac released his hold on me, which was when I became aware that my whole body was shaking. While he replaced the chairs we'd used in the improvisation back in their original positions, I took a couple of calming breaths, and got myself together. Zac held out a chair for me, and I sat.

Joe said, 'Thanks, for coming in today, Julie. You did a great job.'

'Thank you,' I said. Given the way my stomach was fluttering, I was somewhat surprised to find myself able to talk in a level voice. 'That's good to know.' I glanced sideways at Zac, but he was looking at Joe Garcia.

'We still have some difficult decisions to make,' Joe said, 'but I'm determined that *La Pasionaria* will be fully cast in the next few days. Whether or not we can use you this time, in this show, we'll be in touch with you. For now you can go home and relax.'

I doubted that I'd be doing much relaxing while I waited for my phone to ring, but I nodded and smiled.

'Zac, you may as well go home now too,' Joe said. 'I'll expect you at eleven o'clock tomorrow. Perhaps you'd show Julie the way to the stage door?'

'My pleasure,' Zac said. We got to our feet and chorused our goodbyes. Together, we walked out of the rehearsal room, the door swung shut, and the two of us were alone.

Zac's gaze immediately fastened on mine. 'Julie, what I said to you in there, the last thing I said to you, I wasn't acting.'

'I know,' I said. 'Neither was I.' He was in love with me. My heart brimmed over. 'I love you, Zac.' For a long while, all he did was stare at me. Then he put his hands on either side of my face. My body sang at his touch.

'*Te amo, cariño.*' He bent his head and kissed me softly on my mouth. 'There's so much I want to say to you, but first I'd like to show you something, if that's OK with you?'

I nodded. He took my hand and led me along the corridor in the opposite direction from the way we'd entered the theatre, down one flight of stairs and up another, coming to a halt outside a heavy black door. He opened it, and I saw that it led to the wings at the side of the stage. Directly in front of me, were the steel ropes that raised and lowered the backdrops during a performance, a prop table, and the monitor that the stage manager would use to watch and cue a show.

'We can't go in there,' I said.

'Why ever not?' Zac said. 'Jessica showed me the stage this morning before you arrived. I want you to see it too.' His fingers laced through mine, he led me through the wings, and onto the stage itself.

'*Ooh!*' I stood very still, looking out into the auditorium, my gaze sweeping over the tiers of red velvet seats in the stalls, up to the dress circle and then up higher still to the upper circle and the gods. With the theatre's Victorian décor restored to its original gilded splendour, the sight was breathtaking. This, I thought, is the place I'm meant to be.

'It's impressive, isn't it?' Zac said.

'It's wonderful.' I thought of all the great actors, the stars of musical theatre, who had performed in the Aphra Behn Theatre. 'Oh, Zac, if only I could sing on this stage.'

'That's easily arranged,' Zac said. He walked further downstage, and started to sing Darnay and Lucie's duet from *Two Cities,* the song we'd sung at his flat the day after we'd first slept together. I listened to him for a couple of lines, and then I couldn't resist joining in. When we'd sung the last verse, Zac took hold of my hand again, and together we bowed to the rows of empty seats. To my astonishment, I heard the sound of clapping from the back of the auditorium. I froze. Zac let go of my hand and peered out into the stalls.

Joe Garcia was walking along a side aisle towards us. When he reached the front of the auditorium, he climbed the treads and joined us on stage.

'Hey, Joe,' Zac said. 'I've been giving Julie a backstage tour.' To my relief, far from being annoyed that we'd been wandering round his theatre uninvited, Joe was smiling. He, too, looked out over the auditorium.

'It's years since I performed professionally,' he said, 'and what I do now, creating my own shows, is what I love, but I still get a thrill standing here in this space.'

I remembered that he had started out as an actor before he'd turned to directing. 'Don't you miss acting?' I blurted out.

'No, not at all.' Joe smiled again. 'Although I suspect that right now you find that hard to understand.'

'All I've ever wanted to do is perform in musical theatre,' I said. 'I can't imagine ever not wanting it.' Shut up, Julie, I thought, as if Joe Garcia's interested.

'What about when you're older?' Joe said. 'When you're too ancient to shoulder your leg and your voice has gone?'

'Oh, then I'll become an old character actress,' I said.

Joe laughed. 'Well, you've a good few years of dancing and singing ahead of you before that happens.'

A door at the back of the auditorium opened. A man called out, 'Joe? Are you ready for me?'

'My set designer.' Joe raised his voice. 'Yes, Brian, come on up.' To us, he said, 'Sorry, guys, we're going to need an empty stage.'

Zac and I repeated our goodbyes, and exited stage right.

We were outside the theatre when he said, 'Shall we go to my flat?' I nodded. He slid an arm around my waist, and we started walking along Shaftesbury Avenue towards Piccadilly Circus and the tube. I glanced back over my shoulder for one last look at the Aphra Behn.

I may not get into *La Pasionaria*, I thought, I may never get cast in a West End musical, but I can always say that I've sung a musical theatre song on a West End stage with a West End star. And Joe Garcia was in the audience.

CHAPTER 40

As soon as we were inside Zac's flat, he took me in his arms and kissed me, a gentle, tender kiss.

'Why don't you go out onto the balcony?' he said. 'I'll make coffee.'

I wouldn't have objected if he'd taken me straight to his bed, but I was happy to take some time to just be with him, to sit in the sun and talk, to erase the memory of my shouting down the phone at him, telling him I never wanted to see him again.

While he went to the kitchen, I went to the balcony, taking my mobile with me – no way was I going to miss the Call, if it ever came – and sat on a wicker chair. I knew that Alexa would be at work – it was her last week – but I'd promised to let her know how I got on at the audition, so I sent her a text: *Audition good, as far as I can tell. Am with Zac at his place ☺ xx.* Which told her everything she needed to know, I felt. To Owen, who'd sent me a good luck message that morning, I texted: *Zac and I good. Photos not what they seemed. Audition good.* After a moment's thought, I added: *Am not working tonight. See you tomorrow xx.* Then I texted Austin to inform him I wouldn't be handing out flyers that evening.

Zac came out of the flat carrying two mugs of coffee which he put on the table. He sat in the chair next to mine, his body turned towards me.

'I bought a copy of *Innit*,' he said. 'That night. After I'd spoken to you. Joe's house is in the middle of nowhere, but I found one at the local garage. Rosalind and I really are

316

just friends, but when I saw those photos, I did understand why you were so upset.'

'I over-reacted,' I said. 'I got myself in a state.'

Zac reached out and put his hand over mine. 'I didn't sleep much that night. In the morning, I was planning to drive back to London, to make you listen to me –'

'You'd have walked out on Joe Garcia?' I said.

'Not without telling him,' Zac said. 'I'd have made some excuse that didn't involve you, of course. But before I could say anything, he told me he'd decided to call you in again and that he wanted me there at your audition. I was desperate to see you, but with you so angry with me, and with the audition the next day, I thought it better to give you some space.' He added, 'Despite everything, you did good today. Joe said so himself.'

'I just hope I did enough to convince him to cast me,' I said. The thought that I'd almost not gone to the audition sent a cold shiver down my spine. I got off my chair, and sat on Zac's lap. He put his arms around me, and I settled against him, resting my head on his chest.

He said, 'Julie, there's something I need to say to you – about my last few months in LA. I'd rather you heard it from me than from anyone else.' I raised my head, and when I saw the serious expression on his face, I sat up.

Zac said, 'I've told you that when I first went to California I lived with Rosalind. After we split up, I moved into a cheap apartment, and hung out with other unemployed actors, still convinced that I was going to be Hollywood's next big star. As you know, it didn't happen, and I became increasingly disillusioned. I stopped going to class, and I partied way too hard. When I woke up in a

317

strange house with a raging hangover and a girl whose name I didn't know, and no idea how I'd got there, I finally admitted to myself that I was out of control. And that going to LA to be with Rosalind had been the worst decision I'd ever made.'

That thing we never talk about. I'd not thought about it in weeks, but now the scene came back to me: Zac and Laurie sitting on the balcony; the conversation I'd overheard, and before that, Laurie telling me that Zac hadn't always made the right choices. I looked at the man I loved, and knew that none of it mattered.

Zac said, 'I came back to London determined to focus solely on getting back the successful career I'd thrown away, and with no intention of getting into another relationship. Then I met you and… I couldn't help myself. I fell in love.' He reached out and touched my face. 'It was only when I thought I could lose you that I realised how much I loved you, and that success doesn't mean very much unless you have someone to share it with.'

I slid my arms around his neck, and drew down his head so that I could kiss him.

He said, 'I want very much to go to bed with you right now.'

I smiled, and we stood up and went inside. Stopping every few steps to kiss, we walked slowly to his bedroom and sank down on the bed, holding each other close. It felt so good to be lying at his side, his strong arms about me, so right. I slid my hands under his T-shirt and stroked the smooth, sculpted muscles of his back. He sat up, and took his T-shirt off. With his dark eyes on me, I did the same, and then I took off my jeans. That morning, as I was going to the audition, I'd dressed in underwear I could move in rather than the wisps of silk and lace I'd wear for a date, but from the expression on his face as he looked at me, Zac didn't seem to mind. Even so, I quickly peeled off my sturdy Lycra, and stretched out languidly on the bed, one arm above my head. Zac sat unmoving.

'Aren't you going to take off the rest of your clothes?' I said.

'*Si*,' he said. 'I will. Just let me look at you for a moment. You are so very beautiful, *mi amor*.' He placed a hand under my chin and traced the line of my mouth with his thumb. Then, in one sinuous movement, he swung his legs over the side of the bed, stood up, tugged his jeans and boxers off over his hips, and kicked them aside.

'*Te deseo*,' he said. He lay down beside me, a hand on my shoulder urging me onto my back, his naked body above me. His mouth sought mine, his tongue probing, a hand cupping my breast. A delicious heat grew within me, as his other hand slid between my thighs.

'*Te amo*,' I said.

'Oh – Julie –' He was breathing hard now. '*Te adoro. Tú eres mi vida*. You are my life.' He rolled away from me, I heard the drawer of the nightstand open and shut, and then he was lying on top of me, gliding into me, the two of us moving as one, *adagio, accelerando, crescendo, fortissimo,* a duet in perfect time and harmony…

Our bodies still joined, Zac kissed me, a long deep kiss. I felt him slide out of me. He lifted his mouth from mine, and raised himself off me and onto his back. I lay beside him, my head on his shoulder, my eyes shut, the taste of his kiss in my mouth.

'*Te amo*,' Zac said. '*Te amaré siempre*. I will always love you.'

'I love you,' I said. 'There's nowhere I'd rather be than here with you.'

'Even centre stage at the Aphra Behn?'

'Not at this precise moment,' I said.

He laughed softly, and held me a little tighter. We were both quiet for a while, and I'd almost drifted off to sleep, when he said, 'Julie. *Vivirás conmigo?* Will you live with me?'

I opened my eyes and sat up. Zac sat up as well. I was so taken aback that all I could do was stare at him.

He said, 'I love you. I would like very much for us to live together. You could move in with me, or we could find a new place, if you didn't want to do that.' His gaze searched my face. 'Julie? Please say something. Anything. Even if it's "No".'

No songwriter, I thought, has ever written a lyric that describes how happy I feel right now.

'Yes, Zac,' I said. 'I'll live with you.'

His face broke into a smile. 'I think I should probably kiss you again,' he said.

CHAPTER 41

Zac drew into a parking space a few yards down the road from my flat. I undid my seatbelt and reached for the handle of the passenger door. He put his hand on my arm.

He said, 'Julie, I swear this is the last time I'm going to mention those photos, but if you should happen to get a phone call from an unknown number, and the caller asks if you'd like to comment on the pictures of Rosalind Adams and Zac Diaz in this week's *Innit*, it's best if you hit the end call button, unless you want to be quoted in the tabloids.' It took me a moment to understand what he was talking about.

'Do you seriously think the press might contact me with questions about my boyfriend and his film-star ex?' I said.

'It's unlikely,' Zac said, 'but it could happen. Readers of celebrity magazines and showbiz blogs have an insatiable appetite for gossip about their idols, and Rosalind has a huge fan base. It's possible that a journalist might wonder if there's a story behind a picture of her with a younger guy, and decide to do a bit of digging. If it's a slow week.'

'I'll screen my calls for the next couple of days,' I said. Given the number of photos on the internet of Rosalind Adams enjoying the attentions of younger men, it seemed to me that it wasn't remotely likely any journalist would bother to use their investigative skills to discover Zac's name or his relationship status. There again, he'd had some experience of dealing with the media, while I'd had none. Zac smiled, and leaned in for a kiss.

321

'What time is Joe expecting you?' I said, after some minutes.

Zac shrugged. 'Joe can wait.' He kissed me again.

'Zac!' I said. 'You have to go. You can't be late for Joe Garcia.'

'No, I really can't.' With a sigh, Zac settled back in the driver's seat. 'I'll see you Monday morning. I love you, Julie.'

I smiled. 'I love you.' Deciding that persuading him to stay in London with me rather than returning to Gloucestershire and Joe Garcia's rehearsals wouldn't be advantageous to his career in musical theatre – or mine for that matter – I got out of the car. I waited on the pavement until he'd turned the corner, and let myself into the flat. Only a few more days, I thought, and he'll be back. And by the end of next week, by the weekend, I'll be living with him. I will be his live-in girlfriend. I felt dizzy at the thought.

'Hey, Julie,' Alexa's voice floated down to me from the landing, where she was leaning over the bannisters. 'As you didn't come home last night, I take it things are all good with you and Zac?'

I walked up the stairs. 'More than good,' I said. It was only then that it came to me that the start of my new life with Zac would be the end of my old life sharing a flat with Alexa. I headed to the living room, and sat on the sofa, narrowly avoiding a spring, which was poking through the fabric. Alexa came after me and sat on a chair, tucking her legs up under her.

'I have to ask,' she said. 'The photos?'

322

'Pictures of a guy saying goodbye after having lunch with an ex-girlfriend with whom he's remained on good terms,' I said.

'Did Zac tell you this before or after you had sex?' Alexa said.

I rolled my eyes. 'All you need to know is that Zac didn't cheat on me. Rosalind Adams and he are still friends – nothing more.'

Alexa drew in her breath and put her hand on her chest. 'I'm so relieved,' she said, 'because if he'd cheated on you – my best friend – even if *you'd* forgiven him, I'd have found it very hard to be around him, even if he is the star of Joe Garcia's new musical.'

'You are most definitely the best friend ever.' I have to tell her I'm moving out, I thought, and I have to tell her today. It's only fair. 'And it's very important to me that you get along with Zac.'

'I do like him,' Alexa said. With a grin, she added, 'As long as he treats you right.'

I said, 'I'm in love with him, Alexa.'

'I knew it!' Alexa said. 'I knew you were.'

'No, you didn't,' I laughed.

'I suspected it,' Alexa said. 'Ever since I saw the two of you rehearsing *La Pasionaria* together. "I love you, Javier, I will always love you." The way you were looking at him. You're a good actress, Julie, but you're not that good.' We both smiled.

I said, 'I love Zac Diaz, he loves me and... he's asked me to live with him. And I've said I will.' I waited apprehensively for Alexa's reaction.

Her eyes widened. 'Moving in with a boyfriend – it's a big step. Are you sure it's what you want?'

'I've never been more certain of anything in my life,' I said. 'I love him, and I want to share my life with him.'

Alexa leapt up from her chair and hugged me. 'Then I'm very happy for you, both of you.'

She's my best friend, I thought. Of course she's going to be pleased for me, even though my moving out is going to leave her without a flatmate. My mind drifted back to the previous night, Zac and I talking for hours, the plans we'd made.

I said, 'I'm going to move into his place next week. Obviously I'll pay my share of the rent here until our tenancy agreement runs out. Or until you find someone else to share with.'

'You don't have to do that,' Alexa said.

'I want to,' I said.

'Don't even think about it.' Alexa glanced round the room. 'It'll be weird, you not living here.'

'It'll be strange for me too,' I said. 'We've had some good times in this flat.'

'We have, haven't we?' Alexa said. 'Do you remember that party we gave when we were in our second year at LAPA? When Luke got stupidly drunk and fell asleep in the bath?'

'And we didn't know he was there 'til the morning when you turned on the shower,' I said. 'I think that was the night Michael pulled Suzanne.

'It was,' Alexa said. 'I'd forgotten that.'

324

'I'm so happy that I'm going to be living with Zac,' I said, 'but that doesn't mean I'm not going to miss living here. I'll miss you.'

'I'll miss you,' Alexa said. 'But this flat isn't the sort of place that people live in for ever.' She gestured at the wall. 'Can you imagine being thirty and still coming home to that ghastly wallpaper?'

'I guess not,' I said.

'Neither can I,' Alexa said. 'The flat was the right place for us when we were at drama school, and this last year while we were still living like students, but things are different now. I have a job. You're in a serious relationship, and I'm sure you'll have a job soon. It's time for a scene change.'

'Do you think you might move to a new place as well?' I said.

'Not right away,' Alexa said. 'Not until my wages for *Sherwood* start hitting my bank account. But it's something I'm going to be thinking about.'

'Act I is over,' I said. 'Act II is about to start.'

'Whatever happens in the rest of the play,' Alexa said, 'you and I will always be friends.'

I smiled, and then started at the sound of the front door bell.

'Expecting anyone?' Alexa said.

'No,' I said. Then an alarming thought came to me. 'Oh, no. Zac warned me this could happen – the press have got hold of the name of the guy with Rosalind Adams in the *Innit* photos.'

'And they're outside our place because…?' Alexa said.

'Zac isn't at his flat, they think he's here,' I said. 'They've found out he's my boyfriend.'

Alexa raised her eyebrows. 'I hate to spoil your delusions of celebrity,' she said, 'but it's much more likely to be the postman. Still, just in case, I'll go to the door and stall them while you change into your red dress – it'll look good in the photographs – and for goodness sake put on some lipstick.' Laughing, she went out of the living room, and soon afterwards I heard the front door open.

Not entirely convinced that I wasn't about to face a crowd of mic-wielding journalists and flashing cameras, I crept out onto the landing and peered over the bannister in time to see Alexa coming back into the flat carrying a huge bunch of red roses.

'Sorry, Julie,' she said, 'you're not famous after all. You do, however, rate a Loveflowers.com special delivery.' She ran up the stairs two at a time and handed me the cellophane-wrapped flowers. I took them into the living room and put them on the dining table.

'There's a card,' I said. I opened the small envelope with my name on it and a Loveflowers.com logo in the top right hand corner. On the card inside were the words '*Te amo, cariño. Z xx*'.

'They're from Zac,' I said, somewhat unnecessarily.

'Two dozen red roses,' Alexa said. 'Oh, my days, that boy *adores* you.'

I buried my face in the roses, inhaling their glorious scent. 'I rather think he does,' I said.

***

Zac sat at Joe's piano and after a couple of false starts, played the melody that had been in his head the whole time he'd been on the motorway. It still needed work, he thought, but it was almost there. He flexed his fingers and played the tune again, adding the vocals as they came to him, stopping occasionally to jot them down on the back of a page of script from *La Pasionaria*, which was the only paper he had to hand.

His mobile, which he'd placed on top of the piano, vibrated with the arrival of a text: *Thank you so much for the flowers. They're beautiful. J xx*

Zac smiled, and texted back: *You're beautiful. Z xx*

I love her, he thought, and I could have lost her because of a photo of me with a female friend that was made out to be something it wasn't. The thought made his blood run cold.

The door to the rehearsal studio swung open and Joe came in. Knowing how much he disliked interruptions during rehearsals, Zac switched off his phone.

'I heard you playing,' Joe said, 'but I didn't recognise the tune.'

'It's a song I'm writing,' Zac said. 'It's not finished.'

'Let's hear what you've got so far,' Joe said.

Zac played and sang a verse and a chorus.

'It's good,' Joe said. 'I didn't know you'd started writing your own material.'

'I've not being dong it very long,' Zac said.

'Let's hear it one more time,' Joe said.

Zac turned back to the piano, accompanying himself as he sang the love song he'd written for a dark-haired girl who loved to dance and sing.

CHAPTER 42

'I wasn't looking forward to going into work last night,' I said.

'Unlike every other night when you do?' Laurie said.

My former flyering partner had called me that morning, suggesting that, as he wasn't needed in rehearsal until mid-afternoon, we have lunch together. I'd met him in a café opposite the Ellen Terry Theatre, where *Iago* was due to open in a fortnight's time. The theatre already had its advertising billboards in place, and I'd had the surreal experience of eating brochette and drinking coffee with an actor whose larger-than-life-size photo was visible from across the street. Laurie was eager to hear my news – 'I'm such a rubbish friend, Julie, I've no idea what's going on in your life...' – and I'd given him an edited version of the events of the last few days – Nadia showing me the photos, Zac and I breaking up and getting back together again – leaving out the parts where Zac told me he loved me in the middle of my *final* final audition for *La Pasionaria*, and what happened after we got back to his flat, which was too much information, even for Laurie. He hadn't seen the *Innit* photographs, but he swore he'd never buy the iniquitous magazine ever again.

'You know how much I enjoy handing out flyers,' I said. 'Anyway, I thought I'd have to run a gauntlet of sympathy from anyone at Zone who was still convinced that my boyfriend was shagging a celebrity, but Owen had made a point of telling a couple of the waiters who unfailingly pass on gossip that all was well with me and

Zac. He told them in strictest confidence, of course, so by last night everyone knew, and no one cared. Apart from Harry saying he was pleased to hear that Zac wasn't a two-timing love rat, Ben agreeing with him, and Cora shedding a few happy tears. Even Nadia seems to have lost interest in my love life. Now I come to think about it, she didn't speak to me at all last night. Which suits me just fine.'

'The public are so fickle,' Laurie said. 'One day they're fighting for your autograph, the next you're forgotten.'

'Have you had any requests for autographs yet?' I said. 'Now that you're a West End star?'

'Sadly, no,' Laurie said. 'But Toby has already bought a scrapbook in which he intends to paste all the good reviews I'll get on press night.'

'Only the good ones?' I said.

'There won't be any bad reviews,' Laurie said. 'Toby knows this for a fact.' He looked at his watch. 'I have to be at the theatre in ten minutes, so if you have any more scandal for me, you need to start talking.'

I smiled as I thought of the packed suitcases in my room, the spare set of keys to Zac's flat that he'd left with me to get copied while he was away.

'In other news,' I said, 'Zac and I are going to live together. I'm moving into his flat on Saturday.'

Laurie's eyes widened, but he made no comment.

'You seem shocked,' I said. 'Aren't you pleased for us?'

'Of course, I'm pleased,' Laurie said. 'I'm delighted. It's just that you've not been together very long. Living with someone, sharing *everything*, it's a whole new level.'

That thing we never speak about. The words echoed around my head. *So few people know.* This, I told myself is the moment to ask Laurie what that strange conversation was about, or decide never to mention it or think about it again.

Laurie,' I said, 'is there some reason why you think Zac and I shouldn't move in together? Something he doesn't like to talk about? He's told me that he went off the rails in LA, and as far as I'm concerned that's all in the past. But if there's anything else that you think I need to know, however bad it is, I'd rather you told me now.'

'There's nothing bad to tell,' Laurie said. 'Nothing bad at all. There's no reason why you shouldn't live with Zac. I was surprised, but only because it's so sudden.'

'It was a surprise for my parents when I rang them this morning,' I said, 'but once they'd got over the shock that their daughter was going to be sharing a postcode with a man they hadn't met, they were pleased, if somewhat over-eager to accept my and Zac's invitation to visit us once he's back in London.' I smiled. My mother had told me she had a really good feeling about Zac Diaz.

'Have you met any of Zac's family?' Laurie said.

'Not yet,' I said. 'His parents are on holiday right now, but Zac called them and told them about me – about us – and we're going to their place for a meal as soon as they're back. His mother's going to cook a paella.'

'You'll like Zac's parents,' Laurie said. 'They're lovely.'

'What about his uncle?' I said.

'Oh, I'm sure you'll like his uncle,' Laurie said, 'when you get to meet him properly.'

'I just hope he likes me,' I said. 'I know they had that awful falling out in the past, but Zac seems very fond of him.'

'They do seem to have got over their differences,' Laurie said. Again, he looked at his watch. 'Sorry, but I'm going to have to shoot across the road or I'll be late for rehearsal.'

I walked with him as far as the stage door.

'I guess the next time we see each other will be at the *Iago* after-party,' he said.

I gaped at him.

'I've six guest tickets for *Iago's* first night and after-party,' Laurie said. 'I'm hoping you and Zac might like two of them. If you've nothing better to do, of course.'

'A West End opening night,' I said. 'I'll check my diary, but I should be able to fit it into my extremely busy schedule.' I flung my arms around Laurie and gave him a hug.

He went into the Ellen Terry to rehearse for his West End debut. I checked my phone for missed calls – it had been noisy in the café, and it was just about conceivable that I might not have heard if Jessica Coleman had called me – before going to a tap class at Limelight and then heading to Leicester Square and Club Zone.

Jessica Coleman *not* calling me, I reflected, was becoming a regular occurrence in my life.

CHAPTER 43

I surveyed myself in my full-length mirror. My hair and make-up looked good, I thought, and my sundress – strappy, white with a scattering of red flowers – fitted perfectly, showing just the right amount of cleavage. I tried on my flat sandals, followed in quick succession by my black pumps, and several pairs of high heels, but none of my shoes looked exactly right with the dress. What I needed, I decided, was Alexa's tan wedges. She'd been out when I'd got back from Zone around midnight, but I'd heard her come in some time in the early hours. I went and knocked on her bedroom door. After a moment or two there was a reply of 'Hey, Julie,' which I took as an invitation to enter.

I said, 'Zac's going to be here in less than an hour, and I don't have a pair of shoes that go with my dress – Alexa?'

My friend was awake, but lying in bed. Her hair was a tangled mess, and she obviously hadn't bothered to remove the previous night's make-up. Under streaks of mascara, and smudges of dark eyeshadow, her face was deathly pale.

'You want to borrow some shoes?' she said, sitting up and swinging her feet off the bed and onto the floor. I saw that she was wearing a shift dress, presumably the dress she'd worn to go out the night before, although it was now creased, and smeared with make-up.

'Forget the shoes,' I said. 'What's wrong?'

Alexa put her face in her hands. It was a hot day – with the windows closed, her bedroom was stifling – but she was shivering. Spotting her dressing gown on the end of

332

the bed, I draped it over her shoulders, before sitting down next to her.

'What's happened?' I said. 'Please tell me what's wrong, hun. You're worrying me.'

Her voice scarcely above a whisper, Alexa said, 'I've done something terrible.'

I sat down next to her. 'What is it you've done? I'm sure it can't be anything all that bad.'

Alexa said, 'I slept with Michael.'

'Oh! Alexa!' I was completely unable to keep the shock out of my voice.

'I've had sex with another girl's boyfriend,' Alexa said.

'Yes, I get that,' I said.

'I've broken my own rules,' Alexa said.

'After all you said about you and Michael.' And after all I'd said to Suzanne, I thought.

'I'm a horrible person,' Alexa said.

'No, you're not,' I said, 'but – sorry, this is me being judgemental – but what were you *thinking*?'

'I never meant for it to happen,' Alexa said. 'Michael rang me last night and told me that he and Suzanne'd had this huge fight. She'd stormed out of their flat, and gone to her sister's, and he wasn't sure if she was ever coming back. He sounded really cut up on the phone, like he needed a friend, so I suggested we meet for a drink. We shared a bottle of wine, and then we went back to his. We had some more wine. And he kissed me. Or maybe I kissed him first. I don't remember. I should have left then, but I didn't. I went with Michael into his and Suzanne's bedroom, and I had sex with him in their bed.' Alexa raised stricken eyes to mine. 'It was awful. Michael was banging

333

away on top of me, and over his shoulder I could see this photo of him and Suzanne, and they looked so *happy*. And afterwards Michael just lay there. He put his arm over his face, and I knew he was thinking about Suzanne. I cried.'

'You *cried*?' I repeated.

Alexa nodded miserably. 'Michael thought he'd done something wrong. Well, we both knew we'd done something *wrong*, but he thought he'd been too rough, and he really hadn't. And even when we got over that, he kept saying he was sorry, and I kept telling him it was all my fault. And then I had to borrow some money from him for a cab home. What I've done... I'm so ashamed.'

I couldn't remember Alexa ever being so upset before, certainly not when a guy was involved, not in the four years I'd known her.

I said, 'Listen, Alexa, you made a bad choice, but Michael's not exactly blameless. He's had the hots for you since we were students.'

'I know,' Alexa said. 'I always knew. And however much I liked him as a friend, I shouldn't have hung out with him so often. Well, he's over me now.' Her voice caught in her throat. 'I just hope that he and Suzanne can work things out. It's what he wants.'

'That's between the two of them,' I said, 'but you need to keep your distance from Michael for a while, and give them the space to do it.'

'You're right there,' Alexa said with feeling. She added, 'I've really messed up. I slept with the wrong man.'

'You're not the first girl to do that, hun,' I said, 'And you can't keep beating yourself up about it.'

'You don't understand,' Alexa said. 'When I was with Michael, all I wanted was to be with Tim.'

I gasped. 'You wanted Tim?'

'I think… I think I love him,' Alexa said. 'I miss him dreadfully. I was such a fool to break up with him.'

My head reeled, my gaze coming to rest on Alexa's mobile, which was lying on her nightstand. I pictured Tim in his sober business suit, the day he'd returned Alexa's suitcase, his smile when he talked about her having great legs, the pain in his face when he'd told me he needed to see her just one more time. I picked up the phone and held it out to her.

'Call him,' I said.

'What?' she said.

'Call Tim and tell him what you've just told me,' I said.

'I-I can't,' Alexa said.

'Do you want him to go off to New York without knowing how you feel about him?' I said.

Alexa's eyes glistened with what looked suspiciously like tears. 'I treated him very badly. He's stopped calling me. He doesn't even text me now. He may not want me any more.'

'Well if you don't call him, you'll never know,' I said. 'Listen, Alexa, you've made one mistake, don't make another.' I pressed the phone into her hand. 'I didn't want to go to the *La Pasionaria* recall, but you told me that if I didn't, I'd regret it for the rest of my life. I'm saying the same thing to you now.'

'I *rejected* him,' Alexa said. 'I can't just call him and tell him I love him.'

'Ask him if he'll meet up with you and take it from there,' I said.

'I guess I could do that,' Alexa said.

'I'll give you some privacy.' I stood up, but she caught hold of my arm.

'No, stay,' she said. I sat back down on the bed. Alexa accessed her address book for Tim's number and put her phone on speaker.

His phone rang several times before he answered, 'Tim Devereaux.'

Alexa was trembling. 'Tim. It's Alexa. How are you?'

There was an interminably long silence before Tim said, 'Why are you phoning me?'

'I – I need to talk to you,' she said.

'I'm listening,' he said.

'No, not on the phone,' Alexa said. 'I... I hoped – Could we meet up, maybe? Please, Tim?'

There was another silence, longer than the first, and then Tim said, 'All right. Are you free this evening?'

'Y-yes. I –'

'Do you know the Oasis Bar in Fulham?'

'Yes, I do,' Alexa said.

'I'll see you there at seven.'

'Thank you, Tim –' Alexa began, but he had already rung off. 'How did I do?' she said to me.

'You did fine,' I said.

'You reckon?' she said. 'Tim didn't exactly sound thrilled to hear from me.'

'You hurt him, Alexa,' I said. 'He's bound to be wary.'

'At least he's agreed to meet me,' Alexa said. After a moment, she added, 'You know what, Julie, my tan wedges would go really well with your dress.'

'That's what I was thinking,' I said. She fetched her tan shoes out of her wardrobe, and I slid them on to my feet.

'Perfect,' Alexa said. Her mouth half-lifted in a smile. 'Although once Zac gets back, I doubt you'll keep that outfit on for very long.'

***

'I was intending to take you out to lunch,' Zac said, several hours later, when we were lying in my bed, our limbs entwined, 'but once I saw you, I changed my plans.' My gaze travelled to my dress which was still lying on the floor where it had fallen when Zac had unzipped it and slid the straps off my shoulders.

'So, basically, you only have to set eyes on me to be overcome by lust,' I said.

'That sounds about right,' he said.

'I can live with that,' I said. 'If you're hungry, I'll cook you something. I've stocked up on frozen pizza.'

'I'd rather take you out to dinner,' Zac said, 'Only it'll have to be soon. I've got us tickets for *Midsummer Night's Dream* in Regent Park.'

'Oh, Zac, that sounds wonderful.' I kissed him. 'We should probably get up now. I'm guessing I need to re-do my make-up.' I started to get out of bed, but Zac caught hold of my arm.

'Wait a sec,' Zac said. 'You asked me to tell you if Joe said anything about casting Mariana…'

'Has he said anything?' I was sure that if Joe Garcia had told Zac he'd cast me, he have told me straight away. I prepared myself for disappointment.

Zac said, 'Last night, Joe and I were sitting on his terrace, drinking a rather good Rioja –'

'You mean you were chilling out with him? With *Joe Garcia*?'

'I was staying in the man's house,' Zac said. 'We didn't work 24/7.'

'No, of course not,' I said. 'Sorry. Just having a major starstruck moment.'

'So Joe and I were *chilling*,' Zac said, 'and he told me that at the first female audition for *La Pasionaria* he'd only just sat down with the rest of the panel when he looked up and saw Mariana standing right in front of him.'

'Me?' I said.

Zac nodded. 'All through the recalls he was willing you to do well, and you didn't disappoint him. He thinks you're very talented, and that you have a great career in musical theatre ahead of you.'

I should have been overjoyed at Zac's words, but something in his voice told me that he had more to say, and I wasn't going to like it.

I said, 'But he hasn't cast me?'

'Not yet,' Zac said. 'He's concerned that you don't have any professional experience, and that you might not be ready to carry a West End musical.'

'There's not much I can do about my lack of credits,' I said, 'but I know I can play Mariana.'

'I know that too,' Zac said. 'I told Joe that I thought you were a terrific actress and you were exactly how I imagined

338

Mariana too. I almost told him that we're together, but I decided not to say anything without checking with you first.'

'Wouldn't it be odd – unprofessional – to tell him?' I said. 'There's no reason he should know.'

'OK. I won't tell him about my love-life unless he tells me about his.' Zac got out of bed, located his clothes, which – like mine – were scattered around the floor, and pulled on his boxers and his jeans. 'Joe can't take much longer to make up his mind about Mariana. In ten days, rehearsals start for the whole company.'

By the middle of next week, at the very latest, I'd have heard if I was cast in *La Pasionaria*. I was so tired of waiting for my phone to ring, I just wanted to know one way or the other.

CHAPTER 44

'Are you sure I can't persuade you to come back to bed?' I said to Zac the following morning, letting the plaid shirt I was using as a dressing gown fall open.

'You could,' Zac said, 'if I wasn't going to a costume fitting.'

I did up the buttons on the shirt, and found my keys. We went out of my bedroom – Alexa's door was ajar and I noted that her bed hadn't been slept in, which was a good sign, I thought – and down the stairs so that I could let Zac out of the flat.

'I'll meet you outside Zone after your shift,' he said. '*Te amo, cariño.*'

'*Te amo,*' I said. 'I'll see you later. *Hasta la vista.*' My knowledge of Spanish was still limited, but Zac's smile whenever I spoke to him in that language made me want to learn more. He turned to go. Then he turned back.

He said, 'Julie, why don't you just give up your job at Zone? Hand in your notice tonight.'

'That's a tempting proposition,' I said, 'but what if I don't get Mariana?'

'Even if Joe does decide he needs a more experienced actress,' Zac said, 'I can still pay all our bills, and it'd be my pleasure to pay for you to go to class. If you don't work until you get an acting job, that's fine by me.'

I thought about this – for roughly two seconds. 'That's so lovely of you, Zac, and I don't want you to think I'm ungrateful, but it wouldn't feel right for me not to work. It's like what you said about bartending so that you weren't living entirely off your uncle's money. I hope you understand.'

Zac put his arms around me. 'I do understand. You'll tell me if you change your mind?'

'I will,' I said. He kissed me, and headed off.

I went back to my bedroom, determined to make an inroad on the amount of packing I still had left to do. I'd emptied the wardrobe, but my chest of drawers was still overflowing. There were books lined up along the windowsill, shoes under my bed, and sheet music on the dressing table. It was, I thought, going to take more than one car journey to transport all my possessions to Zac's – soon to be our – flat.

I heard the front door open. Footsteps coming up the stairs were followed by a knock on my bedroom door.

Alexa called out, 'Julie? Are you on your own in there?'

I opened the door. 'So how did it go with Tim last night?' I said, although Alexa's dreamy smile had already told me the answer. I transferred a heap of leotards and dance tights to the floor, so that there was room for both of us to sit on the bed.

Alexa said, 'I arrived at the bar early – the last thing I wanted was to be late and for Tim to think I wasn't going to show – but he was already there, sitting at a table outside. I felt really awkward, but I sat down, and he got us a drink, and then I just started talking. I told him that I regretted breaking up with him, that I missed him… and that I was in love with him. He didn't say a word at first. I was terrified I'd blown it, but then he took hold of my hands, and – Oh, Julie – he told me he was in love with me too.'

I smiled. 'A pavement café, hands clasped across a table for two. It's a classic love scene from a musical.'

'Tim and I didn't do much singing,' Alexa said, 'but when we got back to his place, it was lights, camera, action.' She fanned her face theatrically with her hand. 'We talked for hours about how we can make a long distance relationship work. Tim's planning to spend most of his salary on trans-Atlantic air fares.'

'Without wanting to sound like my mother,' I said, 'I have a really good feeling about you and Tim.'

'He is lovely, isn't he?' Alexa said. 'Although, there is one bad thing about dating him.'

'What would that be?' I said.

'My parents are so going to approve of him,' Alexa said.

***

The staffroom was empty except for a group of waiters playing a rowdy game of cards, and Ben, who was lying on a sofa, his hands conducting the music playing on his phone. He paused to wave at me. I stowed my bag in my locker, got myself a coffee, and sat down to await the arrival of the rest of the promo team.

I don't have to be here, I thought. If don't get into *La Pasionaria* or anything else by the autumn, I should at least try to find a job that lets me work inside. Harry came in and joined me, and was soon followed by Cora, who announced that she'd got a whole two weeks of extra work on a feature film.

Maybe, I thought, I should look into signing up with an extras agency. It wouldn't be a regular income, and it wouldn't be something I could put on my CV to impress a casting director, but it would get me off the streets and onto a film set.

Owen came into the staffroom and hurried over. 'I've just seen our beloved leader heading downstairs from his lair,' he said.

Ben sat up and took off his earphones. 'Ah – I need to talk to Austin.'

I drained my coffee and picked up a bunch of flyers.

At the same instant, Austin scuttled through the doorway. 'Time is money, people,' he said.

'Evening, Austin,' Harry said. 'As you can see, we're on our way out. Once more unto the breach.'

Austin frowned. 'Why are there only five of you?' he said. 'Where's Nadia? Have any of you see her?'

Ben said, 'Nadia's not working at Zone.'

'She's not coming in tonight?' Austin said. 'I've not had any notification.'

'She rang me and asked me to tell you,' Ben said.

'She phoned *you*?' Austin tutted and shook his head. 'This is most irregular. You all know that you have to phone *me* if you need time off.'

'Yeah, Nadia said she tried to call you but couldn't get through,' Ben said. 'She'll phone you tomorrow.'

'What do you mean she'll phone me tomorrow?' Austin said. 'Is she not coming in to work tomorrow either?'

'Nah,' Ben said. 'She's not coming back to Zone. I'm going to need a new flyering partner.' The rest of us were already moving towards the door of the staffroom, but as

343

one, like a well-drilled chorus line, we all turned back to Ben and Austin.

'Nadia is leaving Club Zone?' Austin said. 'She's resigning? Without going through the proper procedure?'

'She has another job.' Ben was grinning now, clearly enjoying the scene he was creating. I'd ever seen him so animated. 'She's going to be Cassie Clarke's Personal Assistant.'

'That doesn't sound like a day job,' Harry said. 'A celebrity's PA isn't going to get much time off for her own auditions.'

Cora's eyes grew wide. 'You don't think Nadia's given up acting? I know she's not had an audition in months.'

'Acting's given her up more like,' Harry said. 'I reckon she's upset so many people in the industry, that she can't get seen for anything.'

I said, 'Be nice to people on your way up…'

'Wise advice,' Harry said. 'Like so many things we say in the theatre.'

Owen said, 'I could never give up acting.'

'Me neither,' Ben said.

'Nor me,' Cora said. 'Even if I never get to perform Shakespeare at the National, I won't stop auditioning.'

'I may never star in an action movie,' Harry said. 'But when I'm in front of a camera, even if I've only got one line, I know I'm in the right profession.'

Suddenly, they were all looking at me. I was centre stage in the spotlight.

I said, 'I can't remember when I didn't want to perform. When I walk out on stage, something happens. The years of training, dancing 'til my body aches and my feet bleed, the

344

hours of singing scales again and again, none of that matters. The only thing that exists is the performance – the music, the dance, the songs and the character I'm playing. I feel this *connection* between me and the other actors. And then, afterwards, when the audience applauds, I know they felt it too. I've created something special, even if it's only for a few hours. There's nothing else like it. I may never be a successful actress, I may never get into the West End, I may never get cast in a professional show, but I have to keep trying.'

It seemed so obvious to me now. I would *never* give up my dream. I smiled at Owen, Harry, Cora and Ben, who smiled back at me. I even smiled at Austin, who looked confused.

'Acting is what I do,' I said. 'I am an actor.'

CHAPTER 45

'My last night in this flat,' I said to Zac. 'One more sleep and we'll be living together.'

'I'm so looking forward to waking up next to you every morning,' Zac said. He reached for the wine bottle and topped up my glass. 'I've cleared out another drawer for you, by the way.'

'Thanks,' I said. 'Which reminds me – I've still got one last bit of packing to do.'

'Do you want some help?' Zac said.

'No, it's OK.' I got up off the broken sofa. 'It won't take long.'

It was, I thought, as I surveyed the last few stray items of clothing strewn about my bedroom, a good decision of mine to have taken the night off work. I wouldn't have wanted to stagger in at midnight and start folding jumpers. I wondered if I actually needed six black T-shirts – maybe I should leave a couple of them for Alexa. I heard the distant ringing of my phone. For an instant, I froze. Then I leapt towards my bedroom door, caught my foot in the strap of my dance bag, and fell. Luckily, I landed on the bed.

'Zac,' I shouted, 'can you get that?' The phone ceased ringing. Get a grip, I told myself, you're not going to get the Call at nine-thirty on a Friday night.

I heard Zac say, 'Julie Farrell's phone.' Then I heard him say, 'Hey, Joe... Yes, it's Zac.'

I ran to the living room. My heart was thudding in my chest.

346

Zac laughed. 'Yes, Joe, I know you lose track of time when you're working... Yes, Julie's right here. I'll pass her the phone.' He held out my mobile. 'Joe Garcia would like to speak with you.'

My hands were shaking, but somehow, I managed to take my phone.

'H-hello, Mr Garcia,' I said. My heart was beating so hard now that I felt sure that Joe could hear it.

'Hello, Julie,' Joe said. 'It's late, and I think I've kept you waiting long enough for this telephone conversation, so I'll come straight to the point. I've reached my final decision on the casting of *La Pasionaria,* and I'd like to offer you the part of Mariana.'

I screamed.

'I take it that you accept?' Joe Garcia, the most important man in musical theatre, was laughing.

'Yes, oh, yes,' I said. 'Yes, please. Thank you. Oh, thank you so much.'

'You don't have an agent do you, Julie?' Joe said.

'No, I don't,' I said.

'Well, Jessica will phone you on Monday, and arrange a time for you to come into the office. She'll go over your contract with you, and I want to have a talk with you about my plans for the show. I'm very much looking forward to working with you.'

'Oh, thank you so, *so,* much,' I said again. 'I can't tell you how much I wanted this.'

'I've a fair idea,' Joe said. 'Now you go off and celebrate, and I'll see you next week. Would you put Zac back on the phone, please?' I passed my phone to Zac and sat down next to him on the sofa.

'*Felicidades, cariño.*' He planted a kiss on my mouth and put his arm around me, before turning his attention to what Joe Garcia was saying to him. 'Yes... Yes, we are a couple... No, of course I didn't hit on her at your audition! I'd been dating her for weeks before the first round...' He smiled at me. 'I agree, she'll be wonderful as Mariana... *Si... Si... Buenas noches*. Goodnight, Uncle Joe.' He ended the call.

I sat up straight and stared at him. 'Uncle Joe?' I said. 'Goodnight *Uncle* Joe?'

'Ah,' Zac said. 'Julie, there's something I've been meaning to tell you...'

CHAPTER 46

'You're Joe Garcia's *nephew*?' Half an hour after Joe Garcia had me told I'd got the female lead in his new musical, I was still trying to get my head around the fact that he and Zac were family.

'He's my uncle,' Zac said. 'That makes me his nephew.'

'But your surname isn't Garcia,' I said. 'It's Diaz.'

'My mother is Joe's sister,' Zac said. 'She was born Teresa Garcia.'

'You are Joe Garcia's nephew...' Maybe if I said it often enough, it wouldn't sound so unbelievable. A thought struck me. 'When we first met, the morning after we first slept together, you told me you'd fallen out with your uncle.'

'At the time, Joe and I weren't speaking,' Zac said. 'For him, theatre is everything, and he'd assumed that for me it would be the same. He was extremely proud of my success in *Film Noir,* but when I decided to try my luck in Hollywood, he phoned me and told me that I was squandering my talent. We had the most godawful row. I told him to stop interfering in my life. Which he did: I heard nothing more from him the entire time I was in America – and I was too angry to care.' He drank some wine. 'My parents didn't exactly take Joe's side, but they, too, were bitterly disappointed I'd stayed out in the States. When I did come back to London, it was a while before my relationship with them was as close as it had been, and even longer before I swallowed my pride and called my uncle.'

'You visited him in the country,' I said. 'I remember you saying you'd made things right with him.'

Zac nodded. 'We talked. We drank wine and played guitar. We forgave each other.' His gaze anxiously searched my face. 'Julie – are you angry with me?'

'No, of course not,' I said. 'Why should I be? It's not like you have a mad wife locked up in your attic. You don't have a mad wife locked up in your attic do you, Zac?'

'I didn't the last time I looked,' Zac said.

'I'm not angry,' I said. 'Although, considering the number of times we've talked about Joe Garcia, I do think it's strange that you never thought to mention that you and he are blood related.'

'Laurie said you'd think it was strange,' Zac said.

'Laurie knows?' I said. He's Zac's best mate, I thought, of course he knows. *That thing we never talk about.*

'He is one of the very few people who do,' Zac said. 'And he's hated keeping it from you. He's been on at me to tell you.'

'So why didn't you?' I said.

'I rarely tell anyone,' Zac said.

'But *why*?' I said.

'It's complicated,' Zac said. 'Mainly it's because I want to make my own way as an actor, which is partly why I trained in straight acting rather than musical theatre. I don't want to get work, or have people say I've got work, just because I'm Joe Garcia's nephew.'

'No one would think that once they'd seen you dance or heard you sing,' I said.

'You reckon?' Zac said. 'If you'd known I was Joe's nephew when I told you I'd been in the West End production of *Two Cities* as a child, wouldn't you have assumed my uncle had something to do with it?'

'No, I honestly don't think I would,' I said. 'Besides, you know you're talented. What does it matter what other people think?'

'In some ways it doesn't, but it can be extremely irritating.' Zac drained his wine and poured himself another glass. 'It isn't just about my acting. You'd be surprised how many people with theatrical aspirations suddenly want to be your friend when they think you can introduce them to the most important man in musical theatre.'

I thought, are there people in our profession who are really that shallow? Sadly, I knew the answer. I said, 'Have other actors actually asked you if you can get Joe to give them work?'

Zac nodded. 'When I was doing youth theatre it happened all the time. By the time I got to drama school I'd learnt not to mention my famous uncle, but I suspect that adult actors wouldn't be any different. The irony is that Joe would never cast me or anyone else in one of his shows unless he was sure we were right for the part. He wouldn't cast my mother, his sister, in the original production of *Two Cities*. Not even in the ensemble. He told her that her dancing wasn't strong enough.'

'Was she very upset?' I said.

'She wasn't overjoyed,' Zac said, 'but she knew Joe was right. She was in her thirties by then and she'd worked constantly as a dancer, but without ever getting into the West End. When her own brother wouldn't cast her, she decided it was never going to happen. She gave up dancing professionally. And had me.'

I smiled at that. 'Then I may be being selfish, but I'm glad Joe didn't put her in his show.'

'So am I,' Zac said, 'and so are my parents. Most of the time.'

'Who does know about your dynastic connections?' I said. 'Apart from Laurie.'

'In the theatre world, far fewer people than you might think. My mother's dancer friends from back in the day know that she's Joe's sister, but most of them are no longer working in showbusiness. Oliver Brady has always known, but he's a family friend. I used to play with his son when we were kids. Of my friends who are actors, very few.'

'Does your uncle go along with all this secrecy?' I said.

'Joe's been dealing with the downside of fame for years,' Zac said. 'He only told Jessica Coleman and Nathan Nyembe who I was after I'd been cast as Javier. He understands how I feel. I hope you do too.'

'I totally get why you don't want to tell other people,' I said. 'Truly, I do. But I still don't understand why you didn't tell *me*?'

Zac hesitated, but then he said, 'When I first met you, when we first started seeing each other, I'd no intention of getting into a long-term relationship, so I had no reason to tell you. Later, I never seemed to be able to find the right moment. And the longer I left it, the harder it got. When you were doing so well at the *La Pasionaria* auditions, I didn't want to say anything that might throw you. I thought I'd have to tell you when you got ill, because if you'd had to pull out of the recall, I'd have been phoning Joe and begging him to see you some other time.'

'You'd have done that for me?' I said.

'Of course,' Zac said. 'But you were fine, so I didn't have to. You were so pleased for me when I got Javier that I almost told you then, but I was straight off to Joe's country pile. I decided to wait until you knew if you'd got Mariana. Or until we visited my parents. They'd have been bound to mention Joe, with you being a musical theatre actress.'

'So your parents don't know that I don't – didn't – know that…' My head was spinning.

'I should have listened to Laurie and told you a whole lot sooner,' Zac said. 'I certainly should have told you before I asked you to live with me.'

'Maybe you should,' I said, 'but I know now.'

'And are you cool with it?' Zac said. 'Are we OK?'

'Zac,' I said, 'I love you. I couldn't care less who you're related to.'

'I am so sorry, *cariño*,' he said. 'I've been such an idiot.'

'I'm not arguing with you,' I said.

'*Te amo*.' Zac put his arms around me, and I tilted up my face for his kiss. And Alexa made her entrance.

'Oh, good, you two are still up,' Alexa said.

I said, 'Alexa, I –'

'Now, don't worry,' Alexa said. 'I'm not about to interrupt any plans you might have for your last night in the flat. I just want to let you know that Tim and I have decided to stay here tonight, so that we can see you off in the morning.'

I said, 'I'm so glad you're here, I –'

'I wasn't going to let you leave without saying a proper goodbye,' Alexa said. 'Tomorrow morning, we can all have breakfast together. Tim can help Zac load the rest of your stuff into his car and –'

'Alexa,' I said, 'I've got the part of Mariana.'

If anything, Alexa's scream was louder than my own had been. In seconds, an alarmed Tim, wearing only his boxers, appeared in the doorway.

'Alexa, are you all right?' he said.

'I most certainly am,' Alexa said. 'I'm so happy for Julie! She's got the female lead in *La Pasionaria*.'

'That's wonderful news,' Tim said. 'Many, many congratulations, Julie.'

Alexa said, '*La Pasionaria:* A new musical by Joe Garcia, starring Zac Diaz and Julie Farrell.'

'Joe Garcia?' Tim said. 'I'm not sure I know that name?'

'You do, Tim,' Alexa said, 'We've talked about this. Joe Garcia is the most important director and producer working in contemporary musical theatre. He's a genius. And he's *hot*... for an older guy.'

And he's my boyfriend's uncle, I thought. I shifted uncomfortably, and the broken sofa twanged.

Tim was grinning. 'Alexa, I may not know much about musicals, but I have heard of Joe Garcia. Since I've been dating you, I find his name crops up in conversation fairly frequently.'

'Oh, Tim, you were *kidding.*' Alexa laughed, as though Tim had just made the most amusing remark she'd ever heard.

Zac put his hand over mine. 'Julie, that thing we used to never talk about, now might be the right moment to tell Alexa. If you want.'

'Tell me what?' Alexa said.

I looked questioningly at Zac. 'You don't mind?'

'It's fine, *cariño*.'

I said, 'Zac is Joe Garcia's nephew.'

Alexa staggered, and clutched Tim's arm. 'You are Joe Garcia's *nephew?*' she said,

staring wide-eyed at Zac '*Joe Garcia* is your *uncle.*'

'Yes, I am,' Zac said, 'and he is.'

'You and Joe Garcia are *family*?' Alexa said. 'How long have you known about this, Julie?'

'Zac only told me tonight,' I said. 'Just before you came in.'

'Tim,' Alexa said, 'if you have any relatives who direct West End musicals, feature films or award winning TV shows, please feel free to tell me immediately.'

'The nearest my lot get to the stage or screen is in the audience, I'm afraid,' Tim said. 'Although we do sometimes play charades. Alexa, I've suddenly realised that I'm standing here in my underwear. If we're going to stay up talking, I'll go and put some clothes on.'

'No, don't do that,' Alexa said. 'It's late. We should get to bed. But, Julie, I am so going to hear every detail about Zac's double life before you move out tomorrow.'

Tim said, 'Congratulations once again, Julie,' and he and Alexa went off to her bedroom. A few seconds later Alexa was back.

'Zac,' she said, 'you won't tell Joe Garcia what I said about him being hot for an older guy, will you?'

'Strangely enough,' Zac said, 'that's not a conversation I can ever imagine having with my uncle.'

'No, of course not,' Alexa said. 'Oh, my days. My best friend's boyfriend is Joe Garcia's *nephew*. Sorry. Just a bit starstruck right now.' She went out closing the door quietly behind her.

'She'll get over it,' I said. 'Thanks for letting me tell her.'

'That's OK,' Zac said. 'I could tell you felt bad when she started rhapsodising about Joe. Besides, she's your best friend. I'd never have expected you to keep it from her.'

'Shall I ask her not to tell anyone else?' I said.

'That wouldn't be fair on her,' Zac said. 'And trying to hide the fact that Joe's my uncle when I'm going to be working with him, would be a little absurd. Not that I'm planning to go in on the first day of rehearsal and announce it, but it's bound to come out. I want to work with Joe – if I want a career in musical theatre, working with Joe Garcia is a given. I'm going to have to get over myself and deal with it. As are you.'

'Me?' I said.

'You know what the theatre is like for gossip,' Zac said. 'Unless you're planning not to speak to me outside the rehearsal studio and never go out for a drink with the rest of the cast, it's soon going to be common knowledge that we're a couple. And there'll be plenty of people thinking Zac Diaz was only cast as Javier because he's Joe Garcia's nephew, and Julie Farrell was only cast as Mariana because she's shagging Zac Diaz.'

I shrugged. 'We both know that's not true. We were cast on talent alone.'

'You're right about that,' Zac said. 'We're both very talented.'

'But not at all up ourselves,' I laughed. 'Whatever you say, I'm sure it's not all bad being Joe Garcia's nephew.'

'If I'm honest,' Zac said, 'there are some advantages. If I want tickets for a West End show, I can always get them through his office. If I want to book a table at a fashionable restaurant, I only have to mention his name. Joe is generous to a fault. And not just with his money. He's always willing to share his knowledge and experience of the theatre –' He broke off. 'And we are so going to stop talking about my uncle. This is *your* night, Julie. You've got the female lead in *La Pasionaria*.'

'Yes, I have.' Suddenly, I couldn't stop smiling. 'I'm a West End leading lady.'

Zac said, 'So how do you feel about playing a love scene with me six nights a week and twice on Thursdays and Saturdays?'

'It's always hard to make a love scene convincing,' I said. 'We're going to need a lot of rehearsal.'

'I'm thinking we should start rehearsing straight away.' Zac raised his glass. 'To you, *cariño*.'

'And to you,' I said. 'To us.'

'To us,' he said. And then he kissed me.

ACKNOWLEDGEMENTS

Many, many thanks to Hazel and Katrin at Accent Press, and to my editor, Penny.

And to my writer friends, who are always ready to talk about writing and books.

And to Guy, Joanne, Sara, David, Iain, Laura and Marc for the beta-reading, book-trailer making, website designing, and the all-round, general cheerleading. And for so patiently answering my questions about the theatre and film industry – muchly appreciated!

ABOUT THE AUTHOR

Lynne Shelby writes contemporary women's fiction and romance.

Her debut novel, *French Kissing* won the Accent Press and Woman magazine Writing Competition. When not writing or reading, Lynne can usually be found at the theatre or exploring a foreign city, writer's notebook, camera and sketchbook in hand. She lives in London with her husband, and has three adult children who live nearby.

THE ONE THAT I WANT
Lynne Shelby

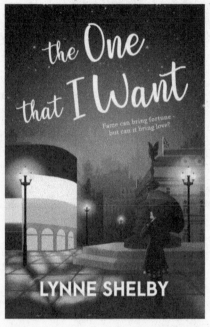

When Lucy Ashford lands a top job at a leading theatrical agency in London, work mixes with pleasure, as she literally falls into the arms of Hollywood heartthrob Daniel Miller. Can she tame the A-list bad boy or is she just one more girl in Daniel's long line of conquests?

Then there's Owen Somers, fiercely talented but as yet uncast in a starring role. After she takes him onto the agency's books, Owen and Lucy's friendship slowly grows.

Lucy's leading man might be right before her very eyes...

Proudly published by Accent Press

www.accentpress.co.uk